The Madrid Connection

Tim Parfitt

MARAVILLA
PRESS

Published by Maravilla Press 2025

ISBN: 978-1-7393326-5-5

Ebook ISBN: 978-1-7393326-4-8

Cover design, Llorenç Perello. Main image: *David and Goliath*, by Caravaggio, Museo Nacional del Prado, Madrid, Spain. File version: Wikimedia Commons.

The Madrid Connection is a work of fiction. All names, characters, businesses, organisations, companies, places, events and incidents are either products of the author's imagination or are used fictitiously. Any resemblance to actual persons, living or dead, or actual businesses, companies, events or organisations is purely coincidental.

Praise for Tim Parfitt's *A Load of Bull – An Englishman's Adventures in Madrid.*

'Parfitt is no ordinary Englishman … his light touch and neat line in self-deprecating humour perfectly suits this entertaining urban spin on the old tale of Brits having fun under the Spanish sun.'

— The Sunday Times

'Hugely entertaining memoir … frequently laugh-out-loud funny.'

— The Daily Express

'A love letter to Madrid … brilliantly captures a truly eccentric and hedonistic place.'

— The Daily Mirror

'A Load of Bull chronicles his Spanish experiences in often hilarious detail.'

— BBC

'Magnificent … brilliant and moving, hilarious and truthful.'

— La Vanguardia

Praise for Tim Parfitt's *The Barcelona Connection.*

'Not just breathlessly rapid and action-packed, but over-flows with humour and satire … The excellent plotting, the local knowledge, the surreal humour, the political satire and the speed of events … it's an admirable and very readable crime novel.'

— Catalonia Today

'A fast-moving page-turner with a helter-skelter plot.'

— La Revista

'Two plot lines interweave, with some highly ironic as well as suspenseful results … this book has a lot to offer the reader, from pure entertainment to possibly a fuller understanding of the complexities of Spain and Catalonia in particular.'

— Spain in English

'A thrilling page-turner' - 'Great characters, a plot that interweaves fantastic insight into the work of Dalí - clever and gripping' - 'A brilliant, breathless thriller that captures the magic of Dalí and a depiction of Barcelona you can almost smell. Wonderful novel' - 'A thriller that kept me hooked, with laugh-out-loud black comedy, too'.

— From Amazon and Goodreads

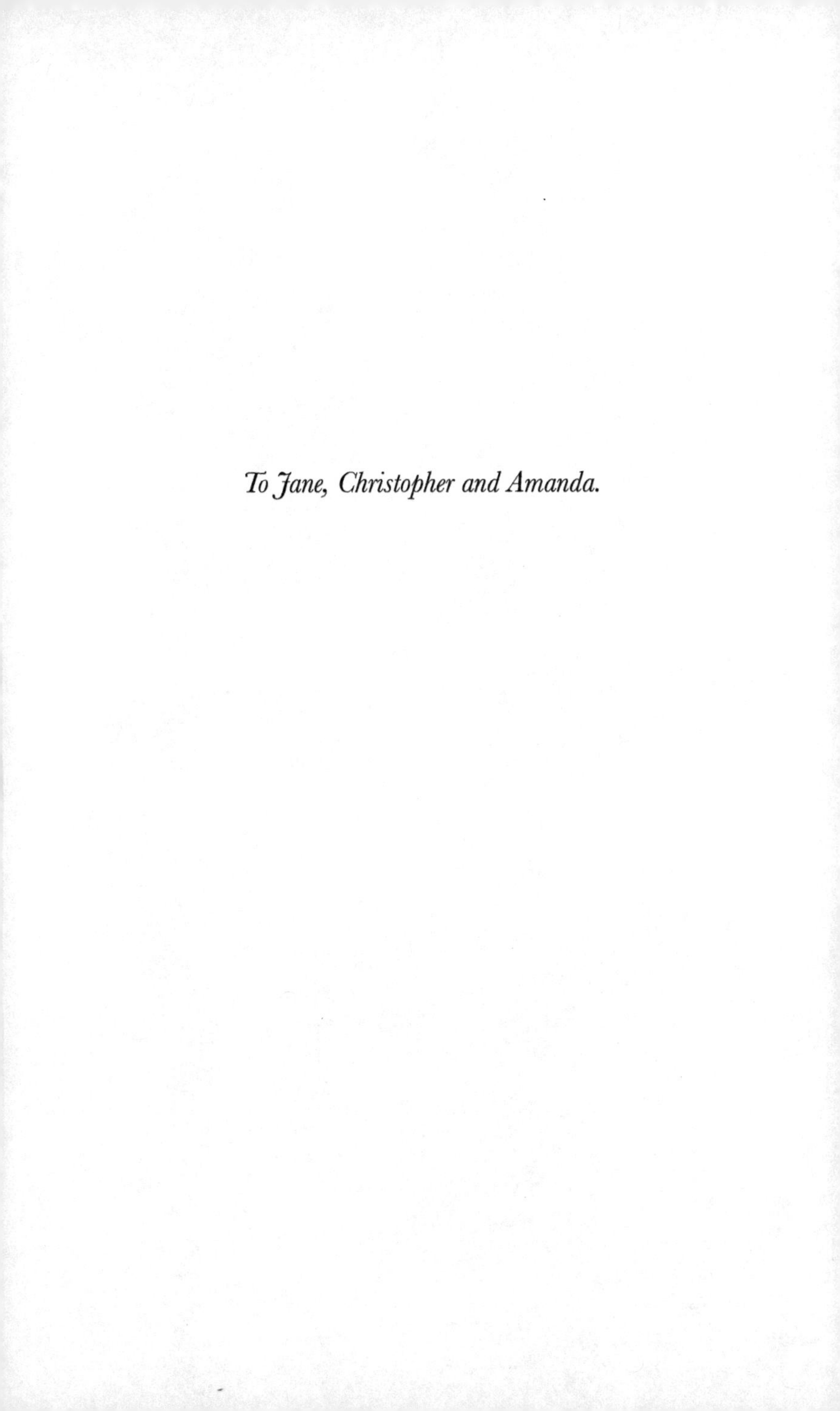

To Jane, Christopher and Amanda.

Prologue

At night, the Prado Museum in Madrid belongs to the paintings. Once the public has gone, the museum sinks into a heavier stillness; the galleries feel older, and they seem to watch each other in a private, unbroken vigil.

On this night, however, that hush was fractured by the soft chatter of a reception in the Goya rotunda – a sound that thinned as a young man stepped away from the main crowd, a silent authority pacing one step behind to keep him on the path already chosen for him.

They had fought to be here – not tonight, but *here*. Winning the contract had taken months – pitch decks polished to a shine, charm deployed like a weapon – but in the end, it was theirs. The profit margin was laughable; the prestige was not. And prestige meant proximity.

This season's first invitation-only 'Prado by Night' event was a modest affair – a scattering of patrons, sponsors, suppliers and *Amigos del Museo* mingling in one of the main galleries – but it was enough. It was meant to strengthen relationships, mark another year of working together. For most guests, it was about the wine and the canapés – with the occasional selfie, angled carefully to avoid the paintings, as museum rules required. For them, it meant the opposite – slipping clear of the small talk, away from the glassy smiles. It meant space to walk, to look, to move without questions.

They eased away from the laughter and the clink of glasses, drifting into the quieter wings, through the half-empty galleries that had been opened for the night. Italian Renaissance portraits glowed under the warm lights, Flemish paintings hung in sombre rows, the Spanish masters held court with their saints and kings.

He walked ahead, jacket unbuttoned, discreetly scanning the positions of security cameras. He caught sight of a guard at the far end of one gallery, leaning casually against the doorway. The man's posture said bored, not alert.

Behind him, the shadow of authority followed. Sometimes the figure paused to consider a canvas, lips tightening in a private evaluation. Sometimes the young man glanced at the plaques, pretending to care about the centuries and names.

By the time they came to the rooms displaying Italian Baroque, the air felt cooler, as if the museum had closed itself around them. They turned a corner into another gallery. The figure behind him slowed, giving the faintest nod towards the wall ahead.

He followed the cue and stopped before the painting, studying it in silence. A moment later, the figure stepped beside him, voice lowered to a whisper meant only for him.

'This is the one I mentioned. The story, the message – everything we want to send. And its value will open the right doors when the time comes.'

He didn't answer. But in his head, he was already mapping it out – one floor up, the painting so close to the tall French doors, their pale, canvas-like screens filtering the streetlights and the night beyond into a ghostly blur. No shutters. No grill. Glass not too thick.

Somewhere behind them, the museum guests' laughter swelled and then faded again, followed by the sound of polite applause. His companion turned to go.

'Come. They'll wonder where we are.'

He followed, noting how the guard in the adjacent gallery still hadn't moved.

As they rejoined the main reception, a staffer's gaze locked on his for a beat too long, then broke away.

Part One

1

The Severed Heads

Sunday 8 December – Casa de Campo, Madrid.

Alicia's feet pounded a frost-dusted path in Madrid's vast Casa de Campo park, each breath forming a misty cloud that vanished into the crisp morning. Her slender frame sliced through the chill accompanied by the dawn chorus of birdsong and the hum of distant traffic west of the city. She loved this time of the day, with the stillness and the solitude. The sun was slowly climbing; the clean light setting the sky a glorious winter blue.

The fabric of her jacket rustled softly with each stride, a faint whisper beneath the sound of her steady breathing. Her dark ponytail bobbed as she veered onto a wider track shadowed by ancient trees ... which is when her eyes locked onto the horror that would unfold before her.

There was a white Seat car, wedged in a snarl of

bare branches and a mass of dark evergreen. She could hear the engine running, and the vehicle's tyres squealing as they spun against the ground, unable to gain traction. It was an eerie sound in the otherwise tranquil, sprawling parkland.

Alicia slowed and approached the vehicle, her runner's high replaced by a prickling sense of something sinister. As she reached the car door, she jumped back, horrified to see a headless corpse sitting in the driver's seat. The severed stump of a neck gaped with a gruesome, jagged mess of sinew and muscle protruding like the frayed ends of a cut rope. A wide arc of blood, still wet and sticky, had squirted across the dashboard and the inside of the windscreen, soaking the driver's seat and clothing.

Then she saw the severed head on the front passenger seat. It was facing upwards, its wide-open eyes and mouth hung ajar in a frozen expression of shock and terror, as if caught mid-scream in the final moments of life.

Overcome with nausea, Alicia threw up against the side of the car. Reeling and turning away, she caught sight of a long cable wire, about thirty metres away, with one end tied ominously to the bark of a nearby tree. Forcing herself to look into the vehicle again, she could see the decapitated figure had its seatbelt fastened, with its blood-streaked hands still clasping the steering wheel. The car was in gear, and a foot – it looked contorted or crushed – was pressed down on the accelerator pedal. The doors of the vehicle were closed, but the left rear window behind the driver's seat was shattered.

She heard a noise – the low growl of another engine. With a sigh of relief, she saw a park ranger's vehicle rolling into view between the bare trees. She stepped into its path, waving it down.

Fifteen minutes later, Inspector Jefe Félix Barroso stepped out of an unmarked police car, his eyes immediately scanning the scene. His arrival brought a sense of foreboding to three municipal police officers who'd arrived first, his very presence casting a shadow over the already macabre setting. The inspector was Madrid's senior homicide detective in the judicial police's UDEV unit. Someone had either dispatched him to the scene, or he happened to be in the vicinity and had heard about it over the radio.

Middle-aged with short, greying hair, Barroso's stocky build gave him an imposing presence – an image he cultivated as carefully as his grudges. He had a gruff, unapproachable demeanour, and little patience for those who dared to question his methods or his authority. He had sly, appraising eyes that judged people against his own narrow standards, quick to dismiss them for the colour of their skin, where they came from, their gender or sexuality. People said he was dangerous to cross. The truth was much worse – he knew how to make someone's life very difficult, very fast, and very painful.

He neared the vehicle with slow, deliberate steps. He wasn't looking for evidence; he was measuring. Weighing. Somewhere behind his eyes, a calculation was already being made. As two of the municipal cops stepped back, he paused and turned towards them, his gaze holding each in turn.

'Have you touched anything?' he asked, to whoever dared to reply, and after noting that the vehicle's engine was still running.

'Nothing, sir,' said one of the agents.

Barroso took in the cop's accent and cut of his uniform. 'Whose is that?' he said, sneering and pointing at the splatter of vomit on the driver's door.

'The lady who found the car,' said the agent, nodding towards Alicia standing with the park ranger about fifty metres away. She was talking to the third police officer who was making notes.

Barroso glared in her direction. 'I want her full details,' he said, ice in his tone. 'Then get rid of her.'

He pulled on latex gloves, opened the vehicle's door and then reached over the headless corpse to turn off the engine, as if calmly selecting a ripe fruit at a market stall.

His eyes lingered momentarily on the severed head, curiously placid on the passenger seat. It looked almost comical; a dark joke set against the gore. Yet Barroso's face remained an impassive mask, betraying none of the sardonic amusement that tickled the back of his mind. He'd seen this treatment before; it was another message – but he had to appear unfazed in front of the municipal agents.

He stooped as he reached into the car again, using his stocky frame to block his actions from the agent still hovering nearby. His hands moved with the practised touch of someone who already knew what he'd find, or what he'd arrange for others to find.

He unfastened the seatbelt, placed what he needed to place in a side pocket of the corpse's jacket, then extracted its wallet and checked the ID. He adjusted the dead driver's shoe against the accelerator pedal, then finally tilted the rearview mirror as if to afford the decapitated head a better view of its former perch. The gesture seemed at odds with the grisly scene, yet it was deliberate – a small act in Barroso's theatre of investigation.

This wasn't the first time he'd repackaged a murder as something else, and it wouldn't be the last. As before, it chipped at something in him. Every staged suicide was a rehearsal, keeping his hand steady for the day he could return the favour for the one real death he'd never been allowed to avenge.

When he straightened, the faintest curl of satisfaction touched his mouth – gone before anyone could read it. He stared at the agent, then sighed on hearing the radio chatter and the sirens in the distance, slowly getting louder as other vehicles approached.

'Who else have you called?' he asked.

'Forensics and –'

'Why am *I* even here?' he said, lip curling. 'This isn't a homicide.'

'Sir, we didn't –'

'Look at the angle,' Barroso said, his voice low. He pointed to the broken side window behind the driver's seat, then to the wire rope that hung from the tree like a morbid snake. 'The way the wire is looped, the position of the body … it's consistent with someone determined to end their own life in a rather repulsive manner. It's vehicle-assisted ligature decapitation.' His voice stayed steady, but behind his eyes was a flash of another scene – a younger face, neck twisted wrong, police tape shivering in the wind. He forced it away.

The agent simply stared at him.

'Look … the driver wrapped the wire noose around his neck, left the rear side window half-open for it to reach the tree to which it is attached. Putting the car in gear and then accelerating, the wire sliced his head off, which bounced off the headrest and against the rearview mirror before landing on the passenger seat. The noose, meanwhile, shattered the back window as it sprung back against the tree. You'll find body tissue and blood on it, for sure. Have you checked yet?'

'The vehicle's registered to –' started the agent.

'I *know* who the vehicle's registered to,' snapped Barroso, passing the agent the dead driver's wallet and ID card. 'Fabrizio Negrini. An Italian resident in Madrid. Forty-three years old. I'd say he was around ninety-eight kilos and one metre seventy-five, at least with his head intact. Would you agree?'

Barroso spoke with an assuredness that left no room for debate, his tone clipped and commanding.

'This isn't a homicide. It's a case of self-inflicted tragedy – a miserable suicide, nothing more,' he said. 'Consider the personal turmoil behind such an act. You'll no doubt find that Negrini had a troubled past, some history of mental illness. Maybe his wife left him, maybe he was facing bankruptcy, taking antidepressants –' He reeled off the script, but his mind was elsewhere – replaying old evidence files, old faces, and the one truth he still carried like a knife.

'With all due respect, sir, surely we should –?'

'You think I don't know a suicide when I see one?' cut in Barroso. His words hit deeper than the rookie could know, but his eyes held a flicker of warning. It was the kind of look that made people glance away, unsure what they'd just been accused of.

'No, sir.'

'*Suicide*,' he repeated, like a verdict. No hesitation, no doubt – and no invitation for argument. The word tasted bitter, as it always did, dragging up the case file he could never close. One day, he always told himself, the right corpse would end up on his desk, and then the verdict would be his for real.

The agent cleared his throat to speak again but thought better of it.

'You're wasting the time of a forensic team,' said Barroso, not waiting for a reply. 'Just inform the next of kin. Now – get me the details of that woman over there, then get her the fuck out of here.'

As the agent turned away, Barroso permitted himself the ghost of a smirk.

Back in his car, he didn't start the engine straight away. He sat with the heater ticking, eyes fixed on the windscreen, fingers drumming the wheel in a slow, deliberate rhythm. The boy's face came uninvited, same as always – and the promise he still hadn't kept.

From a distance, still in a haze of shock and wrapped in a police space blanket, Alicia witnessed the detached air of indifference of the plainclothes detective, simply from his body language. It was as if he'd seen it all before. Then when he'd glared in her direction and locked his eyes upon her, a shiver had run down her spine and her heart skipped a beat.

~

One month later.
Friday 10 January – Calle de Lagasca, Madrid.

The Italian Embassy in the prestigious Salamanca district of Madrid occupies an entire block between the streets of Lagasca, Juan Bravo, Velázquez and Padilla. The three-storey palace overlooks a garden of some seven hundred square metres, sealed off from the street by an ornate, wrought-iron gate and spiked railings.

It was from one of these spiked posts on Calle de

Lagasca that a plastic bag was discovered hanging on that Friday morning – a hard Madrid dawn, cold enough to bite, the air stripped clean and colourless.

It was Miguel Hernández who found it.

In his late fifties with an impressive beer belly, Hernández was a street cleaner working for Madrid City Council. Dressed in a bright, reflective jacket, he also wore headphones to protect his ears from the noise of a leaf blower slung over his shoulder. He was using it to blow litter off the sidewalks and from underneath vehicles into the path of a road-sweeping truck moving slowly behind him. Occasionally he'd use a broom that he carried in his other gloved hand to tackle stubborn debris that the blower missed.

Halfway along Lagasca, he spotted the plastic bag hanging from the railings outside the embassy. The white bag, smudged with red stains, sagged heavily, its shape bulbous – as if it held a football or basketball. He reached up to unhook it with his broomstick, which is when a severed head, its eyes bulging, dropped onto his shoulder. The grotesque ball of skull, brains and soggy flesh then slid down his chest and rolled off his huge beer gut before it slapped onto the ground with a squelch of jellied blood.

Hernández staggered back and retched. Frantically waving his colleague to stop the vehicle sweeping the kerbside, he gazed down at the horrific mess, its bloodied eyes staring back at him from the sidewalk. Even in the faint light of dawn, he could still make out a swollen mass of facial bruising and a wide gash in the middle of the dead man's forehead.

Four hours later, Inspector Jefe Barroso sat alone in his car outside the embassy, watching forensic officers pack away their equipment after searching the gardens and the surrounding streets.

He'd been unable to oversee the initial investigation procedures alone. Earlier, five different police vehicles had come and gone from the scene, and even an ambulance had arrived – but for what precise reason, it was unclear. Worse, the press had shown up. The traumatised street cleaner had been ordered not to divulge any details of what he'd found, and the media had to suffice with a 'discovery of a body part' official quote. But the fact that it had taken place outside the Italian Embassy meant they already had their headlines.

Facial recognition technology had so far failed to detect the identity of the severed head. According to initial estimations from a forensic pathologist, the victim had not been dead long – possibly killed just five or six hours prior to the gruesome discovery.

All twelve CCTV cameras on the embassy's railings that covered the four sidewalks had been checked. An obscure figure covered in a dark hood could be seen hooking the bag onto the railings at around three in the morning, and then fleeing on a bike or scooter. It wasn't much to go on; Barroso doubted any officer would be able to extract and use anything from it.

The embassy's night security guard had been inter-viewed, and eventually most of the embassy staff. The Italian ambassador and his wife had retired to their private quarters at around ten-thirty last night, after a function. They, including other personnel, had since been presented with images of the severed head, but no one had shown a flicker of recognition. No members of staff had been reported missing, nor was anyone under suspicion.

Barroso already knew that much. But a cold knot of fear twisted in his gut – an unfamiliar feeling. This wasn't just another message or threat; it was a calcu-lated taunt, twisting the knife that had been buried in his side since well before the Casa de Campo incident – a phantom wound now raw and festering.

Checking that no one was approaching his car, he picked up his cell phone and made a call.

'Why the hell didn't I hear about this first?' he said, his voice low and, he hoped, threatening.

Static. Then a voice – calm, almost bored. 'Not everything needs your approval.'

'That's not how we agreed to work.'

'Maybe we don't need to work with you again.'

Barroso forced a dry laugh. 'Don't get clever. You still need me.'

'Perhaps. Perhaps not.'

The line went dead. Barroso stayed where he was, catching his own eyes in the rear-view mirror. There was something in them he didn't recognise – a flicker of doubt, almost fear.

Part Two
Six months later - Saturday

2

Benjamin

Saturday 7 June – Atocha to Plaza del Ángel, Madrid.

Benjamin Blake, forty-one, art detective – mid-divorce, patience wearing thin, living out of a suitcase while work kept him in Spain – had to admit things weren't going quite as he'd hoped.

Events at Atocha station when he arrived in Madrid didn't exactly help matters.

He wasn't a huge football fan, although he liked the big games, the Euros and the World Cup. He knew it was the Champions League final in Madrid that evening – even Elena had told him that – but he hadn't expected the city to be so alive with it.

Stepping off the train was like walking into a madhouse. The arrivals concourse was overrun with fans – hundreds, possibly thousands of them – a seething mass of red, white, black and sweat. French and Italian supporters, all draped in the colours of Juventus and Monaco, spilling into each other like a riot waiting to happen, with security guards scarcely able to keep them apart. The noise was a wall, an assault. Chants, drums – and some nutter blowing a vuvuzela like his life depended on it.

'Shit,' he muttered, tightening his grip on the handle of his wheelie bag as he felt the tension in the air. His meeting near the British Embassy was in just under an hour and he'd hoped to grab a coffee or something before taking a taxi. But first, he had to barge his way through the mess.

He tried to zigzag through the mob to reach the escalator up to the taxi rank, dodging sloshing cups of beer. Someone shoved past him, elbow connecting with his ribs, hard.

'Hey, watch it,' snapped Benjamin, but the oaf, a broad-shouldered Italian draped in a Juventus flag, didn't even turn around. Someone bellowed a chant to his left, a deep, throaty roar that was quickly taken up by others … and then it happened.

A beer.

One second, he was moving and dry; the next, he was blocked and drenched. A plastic pint full of beer, flung or spilt, exploded against his shoulder, soaking the front of his shirt and splattering his face. His hair – which had a life of its own – also took its fair swill. His first instinct was to pretend it hadn't happened; it usually worked. But then the beer trickled into his eyes.

'For fuck's sake,' he said, wiping his face with the

back of his hand. Nobody was listening. Nobody cared. His shirt clung to him, already sticky and yeasty. He finally made it up the escalator to reach the taxi rank outside. It was a sea of human chaos.

With the late-afternoon sun still blazing, two taxi queues had formed – two chanting snakes of red and white for Monaco, black and white for Juventus. Fans swayed, yelled, faces flushed with booze and adrenaline. The taxis nosed in and out, drivers frazzled, refusing to take most of those waiting in line anywhere … Benjamin included.

He thought he was in luck at first. He didn't look like a football fan – wheelie bag, a light jacket pulled over the beer-stained shirt. He abandoned the arrivals rank and went to the drop-off lane, only to find hundreds with the same idea. So, he crossed the main thoroughfare, edged away from the worst of it, then managed to flag down a cab by practically throwing himself in front of it.

'Paseo de la Castellana, two-five-nine,' he said, sliding into the back with his bag and showing the driver the address on his phone.

The *taxista*, a middle-aged Madrileño with a weary face, took one look at the details and shook his head, waving his finger in the air.

'Paseo de la Castellana, two-five-nine,' said Benjamin again. 'Or as near as possible. There's a place I have to go to near the British Embassy which is in the Emperador tower –'

'*No puedo,*' came the reply. 'Not now.'

'What do you mean, *not now*?'

'Is after stadium. *Fútbol*. Traffic not *posible*. *No voy*.'

'You're joking, right?' said Benjamin, checking the map on his phone. He could see that the address in the Paseo de la Castellana was further up than the Santiago Bernabéu stadium, where the final was being held. He could imagine it might be gridlocked, but that wasn't really his problem. 'There must be a way. You *are* joking, right?'

The driver was still shaking his head and waving his finger. He wasn't joking.

'Jesus Christ,' said Benjamin. He briefly wondered whether he could take the metro, quickly abandoning the idea on seeing the mosh pit of fans still converging around Atocha station.

The driver jerked his thumb at the door.

'Wait,' said Benjamin, pivoting to Plan B, which should have been Plan A: pick up the Airbnb key, wash, call his contact and say he'd be late. He angled his phone so the driver could see the address.

'*Cerca*,' the driver said, shooing him with both hands. '*Dos o tres calles. Taxi, no.*' Then, in patient English: 'Walk. Out.'

'I'm sorry?'

'Walk. *Go out of my cab.*'

Things didn't go much better on foot, and it was more than a few blocks away.

Dragging his wheelie bag, shirt still soggy with beer,

he called the office number for his embassy contact – Duncan someone – the only number he had. The switchboard led him through a maze of options he didn't need – lost passports, births, deaths, emergencies, other services – then rang into nothing. *Saturday.*

This Duncan someone had asked Benjamin for help on a restitution case – to recover a painting of sentimental value confiscated during the Spanish Civil War. But why insist on meeting near the sodding embassy? In the end, Benjamin stopped walking and found his email address, then sent him a brief note to apologise:

'Traffic impossible due to the match. Can we meet nearer the city centre or at any time tomorrow instead?'

He then checked the WhatsApp exchange he'd had with the owner of the Airbnb. From earlier emails and messages, the instructions had been weirdly vague – to meet in front of a kebab shop a few blocks from the apartment. Why a kebab shop? It had felt bizarre, but back in Barcelona he hadn't had the time or patience to question it. He'd messaged from the train to say he'd be there after his meeting, but now messaged to say he'd be there in around half-an-hour. Finally, there was a response: 'OK.'

Checking the map on his phone, he headed up Calle de Atocha, skirting the Museo Reina Sofía. He earmarked a return for Picasso's *Guernica*, hopefully with Elena, if and when she turned up.

For a moment he thought he'd escaped the crowds, with the only sounds being his wheelie bag on the flagstones and the chirping of the pedestrian crossing lights. Despite the sticky feeling of the drying beer making him itch, the sky was deep blue, the late afternoon light crystalline, and life felt good.

Very soon, however, he was wading through a river of bodies flowing in the opposite direction. Football fans spilling out of bars, raising their voices, arms or middle fingers, all trying to work out how to get to the stadium. At least that's what he assumed, with the kick-off now just a few hours away.

'Move,' he said, clenching the handle of his bag as he tried to edge past a group of men blocking the crossing at Calle del León. A car horn blared. A shirtless bulldozer of a man turned, bellowing in French at the driver, beer spilling down his arm. His mates roared as he flung his plastic cup at the car – most of it splattering over Benjamin again as he was trapped in the middle. Patience now shredded, he barged through, spouting a string of profanities that got lost in the noise. More jeers, a shove or two, then he was free.

Benjamin thought back over the past two weeks. It hadn't been easy. He'd come to Madrid for some quiet, but the city clearly had other ideas.

Back in Barcelona, the Spanish police had iced any chance of him ever working undercover with a false identity again, after some idiotic boy-scout law-enforcement agent released his image as a *terror suspect* – all while he was simply trying to authenticate a possible Dalí painting. The press mocked the police – not him – but once his real name, photo and art-recovery work were exposed, he'd become a target for underworld heavies, especially those nursing grudges from past stings. He'd considered suing the police in Spain; pointless. Elena's own reports hadn't helped – his new journalist friend had a knack for stirring things up – but they'd already clashed over that, and he didn't want a rematch.

Ten minutes later, still dodging hordes of fans, he reached the busy Plaza de Jacinto Benavente and found the kebab shop – the *Edessa Doner Kebab* – open 24/7.

At the front of this take-out joint, a guy in a dark jacket and baseball cap loitered, acting as if he'd rather be anywhere else. Pale, thin, jittery on his toes – the sort who looked like he could vanish into the crowds at any moment, and very soon did.

'You Ben?' he asked, eyes cutting between the football fans, tourists and the plaza.

'Benjamin,' he said. 'Where's the key or code? You got my transfer, right? The address – it's near, isn't it?'

The man fumbled in his jacket, fished out a small envelope and pressed it into Benjamin's hand. 'No trouble, right?' he said.

Benjamin couldn't place the accent – Australian, maybe. 'No trouble?' he said, tearing the flap and sliding out a key and a folded note before glancing up. 'Why would there be any trouble?'

The man's smile was short-lived; he was already backing away, melting into the crowds in the plaza.

'Why would there be any trouble?' Benjamin called after him.

Alone, he stared at the envelope, then stuffed it into his pocket. He knew something wasn't right, but he was too rattled and beer-sticky to deal with it now. He'd opted for an Airbnb in the first place because most of the city's hotels were fully booked due to the football. It was one of the only apartments still available. It was also listed as having two bedrooms, which was perfect if Elena finally joined him; he'd been wary of misjudging any hotel arrangements. Paying by bank transfer outside the Airbnb platform was a bit of a risk, but Benjamin had never been risk-averse.

He found the building on Plaza del Ángel – cream stucco, bottle-green shutters – two minutes from the kebab shop. It was an area he remembered from a previous visit several years ago, with a nearby jazz club. It matched the photos, which was a relief.

The key slid into the lock smoothly. Things were looking up. Stepping into the cool, quiet lobby area with his wheelie bag and leaving the madness of the streets behind, he then took the elevator up to the fourth floor, where he entered the code from the instructions he'd been given. The front door to his apartment buzzed open.

Inside also matched the photos: compact but elegant – high ceilings, exposed beams, big windows throwing light across everything. Two bedrooms in soft neutrals, slick lighting, hotel bedding. A decent bath-room; an open-plan kitchen that looked showroom-new. The whole place felt staged, not lived in.

And no Wi-Fi.

He realised it quickly – somewhere between unpacking his MacBook to send a longer email to his embassy contact and thinking about a shower.

He opened the Airbnb thread on his phone with the 'host' – the kebab-shop middleman, Mr No-Trouble-Right. The listing promised WiFi; the flat didn't. No details in the email, nothing on a card by the door, on the counter, or pinned to the fridge. No router box in sight. He didn't need it immediately, but it annoyed him; there was only so much he could do on a phone.

He called No-Trouble-Right; straight to voicemail. He fired off a WhatsApp message, fingers jabbing at the screen: *Urgent. I need WiFi details.*

He waited for the blue ticks – nothing. Then his phone rang.

'What's the WiFi code?' he snapped, the stench of beer still clinging to him.

'Hello, Benjamin, it's Walter Postlethwaite.'

Walter bloody Postlethwaite – his divorce lawyer.

'Not now, Walter, sorry,' Benjamin said, cutting him off. Which is when the doorbell started buzzing incessantly.

He'd assumed the buzzing meant something good. As the persistent, piercing sound echoed through the apartment, he'd hoped it was someone arriving to give him the WiFi details.

It wasn't.

The old man in the doorway, bald and leathery, was all bone, angles and fury. His wiry frame trembled with barely contained violence.

'*Ruido – ilegal,*' he spat, pointing a bony finger up towards the ceiling as if it were a loaded gun.

'Hi,' Benjamin said, raising a hand in what he hoped was a calming gesture. '*Hola.*'

The old boy's face twisted in disgust. He leaned in closer, yelling now, the words coming faster and angrier. '*Airbnb – turista – ilegal.*'

Benjamin caught the gist of it, but it didn't help. 'I'm not a tourist,' he said, trying to keep his voice steady. 'I'm here for work. I'm not here to party or whatever it is you're worried about.'

The man's eyes narrowed, his expression hardening. '*Turista,*' he sneered, spitting the word out as if it was poison. '*No queremos turistas aquí.*'

'Yes, well, I'm not a tourist,' Benjamin said. '*Trabajo. No fiesta.*'

The man just stared at him, a muscle twitching in his jaw. '*Mentiroso,*' he snapped, starting to shout again.

Before Benjamin could react, two other neighbours appeared behind the man, like reinforcements to finish the job. An old woman with a face like a weathered rock, her eyes practically buried in crinkles, and a middle-aged woman with a tumbling, copper mane.

'Marvellous,' Benjamin muttered. 'A welcoming

party.' He lifted his voice and raised a hand. 'Hi, everyone.'

For a beat they stood silently in what felt like an uneasy, static truce. But then the middle-aged woman with the copper hair moved to the front and took over in English with a lofty, imperative tone – heavily accented, but she clearly wanted to show Benjamin that she could speak it. She did away with any pleasantries and simply said, 'This Airbnb is illegal.'

'I'm sorry?'

'This Airbnb is illegal. You should not be here. You must leave.'

Benjamin raked a hand through the bramble of his hair and didn't say anything for a while because he didn't know what to say. He knew it was his turn to say something, but all appropriate comment had eluded him. He finally offered a smile that looked like a smirk.

'You must leave,' she said again.

Her gaze dropped to his stained shirt; she sniffed. He knew he reeked of beer, but not from drinking – not yet. Now he craved a glass of something, *anything*.

She was wearing a black trouser-suit and white-frilled blouse. Benjamin saw a flash of gems on the second and third fingers of her left hand. She projected a superiority-complex that he instantly loathed. The type of woman who any second now was going to mention that her husband or son was a lawyer, before crossing her arms tightly over her chest, her lips pressing into a thin, threatening line as she eyed him with disdain. She didn't let him down.

'My husband's a lawyer.'

Bingo, he thought.

'You foreigners,' she continued. 'You come here, make noise, leave rubbish, but this is not a hotel … and the owner of this flat does not have a tourist licence …'

Benjamin sighed.

He'd come to Madrid not just for a low-profile job on a modest fee while he was still in Spain, but for a break – a few days to clear his head: work, the divorce, the Barcelona bedlam. A lecture from this sour, red-headed dragon was the last thing he needed.

'I repeat,' she said. 'This Airbnb is illegal. You should not be here. You must leave.'

Sweat prickled the back of Benjamin's neck. This had the shape of an Airbnb scam: kebab-shop courier, off-platform transfer, neighbours on a war footing. No-Trouble-Right wasn't the owner – more likely a former tenant, or a mate, sub-letting behind the landlord's back. He'd seen headlines about locals in Spain squirting tourists with water pistols – fed up with mass tourism. The crackdown on unlicensed rentals was probably real. But Benjamin didn't care. He wasn't here to squat, throw wild orgies or trash the place. All he wanted was a shower, a drink and some peace.

'You realise we'll have to call the police,' the copper mane was now saying.

Benjamin had heard enough. 'Look, stop,' he said, palm up.

The haughty woman tilted her head, eyeing him as if he was a puzzle she couldn't quite figure out.

'I have no idea if this Airbnb is illegal,' he said, 'but *I'm* here legally – in good faith.'

The trio in the hallway exchanged glances, with some kind of silent conversation passing between them.

'But don't worry,' continued Benjamin. 'I'll probably move out tomorrow if I can't get the WiFi to work. As for you calling the Spanish police, go ahead. They previously issued a terrorist manhunt to find me but that was a total cock-up. So, who knows? They might appreciate the tip-off. Now, I hope you all have a lovely evening. *Adiós*. No trouble, right?'

And with that, he slammed the door.

A little later, he discovered there was no hot water and no towels. After a fast, cold shower, he dried himself with a dishcloth and T-shirt. Then he decided to do what half of Madrid was probably doing: go out and watch the football. And drink a lot.

3

The Intruder

Saturday – Prado Museum.

Just before midnight on Saturday, the cleaning squad signed out and the Prado Museum sealed itself for the night.

Nearly three hours later, Eduardo 'Edu' Moreno, head of night surveillance, sat at his workstation in the control room, his piercing green eyes fixed on the rows of monitors in front of him. Beside him, Diego Padilla, his younger deputy, was reviewing the system logs, tracking the usual nightly activity reports. The room was quiet, save for the steady hum of the equipment, punctuated by occasional clicks of the keyboard and the soft hiss of static from the radios.

Every gallery door was locked, every camera feed active. The motion sensors scattered across the hall-ways and corridors hadn't registered any movement since the last surveillance patrol – Edu's own team of guards who sauntered around the museum, each one clocking up to seven or eight kilometres a night.

On nights like this, it was easy to fall into a routine – to let the silence become your lullaby. But Edu never did; the stakes were too high. The Prado wasn't just any museum. It held Spain's history, its national treasures, its priceless works of art. With his neatly trimmed white beard hinting at the depth of his experience, Edu stayed constantly on alert – fiercely protective of the art and his staff. Ever since the Louvre heist, he'd been uneasy about the Prado's defences – reliable, but ageing; too many cameras and sensors overdue for upgrades.

A soft blip echoed through the control room.

It wasn't loud or urgent. Not the blaring alarm they were trained to respond to in case of a major security breach. This was more subtle, a single *ping* from one of the cameras on the first floor. It was enough to make Edu frown, his instincts kicking in. Something had triggered it, and every blip mattered.

'Did you hear that?' Edu asked, his voice tense.

Diego turned in his chair, his brow furrowing as he glanced towards the bank of screens. 'Where was it?'

'Not sure …'

Edu's fingers flew across the keyboard, pulling up the live feed of multiple rooms. The circular hallway, also known as Room One, directly adjoined to the Goya entrance of the museum on the first floor, was dimly lit, the cloakrooms for leaving bags were both closed, the audio guide and information desks empty, and the twin X-ray machines and body scanners looming idle either side of the entrance.

Nothing.

'No, there,' Diego said, pointing at the corner of another screen. 'Room Four.'

Edu leaned in, his pulse quickening. The feed flickered briefly, and then it was clear: *movement*.

A small, dark shape, low to the ground, almost gliding across the marble floor. It had been just at the edge of the camera's view, easy to miss if you weren't paying attention.

'Got it,' Edu muttered, switching to the playback. He rewound the feed and played it back in slow motion. The figure came into focus – small, slight, almost child-sized, dressed head to toe in black, emerging in the corner of Room Four like a shadow coming to life.

Diego straightened, uneasy. 'Where the hell did he come from?'

Edu rewound the footage further, scanning each frame. The gallery had been completely empty. No alarms had tripped. The figure had simply appeared, as if it had been part of the darkness itself.

'This is weird,' Edu said, his eyes glued to the screen. The intruder was calm, his movements smooth, almost too smooth, there was something almost inhuman about him. He tried to track him, but the camera angles made it difficult. Could he have been hiding? Where? *Impossible.*

He leaned forward, tapping the screen, then switched to live feed, following the intruder's path as he moved silently towards Room Seven. The figure walked with a purpose, no hesitation, no panic; it looked like he knew exactly where he was going. Room Seven led to the larger galleries on the first floor. One of the crown jewels, *Las Meninas* by Velázquez, was in Room Twelve.

'We have to stop him,' Edu said. He grabbed the radio, his voice low and controlled, but there was an edge of urgency. 'Control to all units, we've got movement on the first floor. Unknown intruder, black-clad, masked, small build. Currently moving through Rooms Five and Six. All units respond immediately.'

He knew they wouldn't be fast enough. The Prado was a fortress, but it was also vast. Even with his guards on red alert, the response time would never be instantaneous. And this intruder? He'd clearly planned this with meticulous detail, and Edu now had a sick feeling in his gut.

Diego was already pulling up the other cameras, tracking the figure's movements from different angles.

For now, no alarms blared, no sounds echoed through the museum's marble halls. Edu had held back on a full-scale lockdown because he believed he now had the intruder trapped. But he appeared to stop as he reached Room Seven … and then they lost him.

'What the hell are we dealing with here?' Diego asked, his voice tight, his eyes also scanning the monitors in search of the intruder – before two camera angles finally aligned perfectly.

The intruder was standing still near one of the tall window shutters, not far from Room Seven, his head cocked slightly as though listening or waiting for a signal. Edu's gut twisted tighter as he caught sight of objects gleaming faintly from his waist under the low emergency lights – a gun, knives, cable cutters?

He was armed.

Of course … he was armed.

As the intruder turned towards the camera for the briefest of moments, Edu thought he glimpsed the faint lift of his mouth – not a smile, something colder, barely perceptible beneath the ski-mask. *The bastard knew.* He knew he was being watched, and he didn't care. He was there, real and dangerous, and Edu realised something was about to go very, very wrong …

'*Vicente Rojas,*' Diego said.

'What?'

'Vicente Rojas is almost there – he's approaching Room Seven –'

'No, wait –' Edu said.

A crackle came over the radio. '*Control, this is Vicente, I'm on the first floor heading towards the location.*'

Vicente Rojas, a gentle soul with a quiet presence, had spent a couple of decades as one of the museum's night surveillance guards. His slow, deliberate movements and kind, weathered smile reflected years of calm observation. As his retirement neared, he remained ever vigilant, watching over the silent exhibits with the same steady care he'd always given to everything in his life.

But now he was in danger.

'Vicente, wait,' Edu said, leaning close to the mic, his voice low but intense. 'Do not approach alone. I repeat: *do not approach alone.* You must wait for back-up.'

The radio remained silent.

No reply.

'Vicente, copy?'

Nothing.

'*Vicente —?*'

'There's no way he's heard us,' Diego said, his voice edged with desperation.

Edu's eyes shot to the screen as Vicente came into view. He was moving calmly through the galleries towards Room Seven, his flashlight sweeping over the dark paintings that lined the walls. He had no idea what was coming, only a few steps away now, just beyond the shadows.

'*Vicente, do not enter Room Seven — I repeat, do not enter Room Seven — do not —*'

It was too late.

The intruder lunged, slipping behind the guard like a shadow coming to life, with a gleaming wire suddenly unfurling from his gloved hands.

'*Christ, no — no —*' Edu cried, eyes wide with horror. His hand shot to the Prado's main alarm button, slamming it with enough force to bruise his palm. A piercing klaxon erupted through the museum, reverberating off the ancient walls, echoing through the dark, hollow corridors. The shrill sound was like a relentless, chilling scream, drowning out Vicente's hideous, wet gurgling.

~

'*Shh,*' the intruder hissed, drawing the wire tight. The alarm screamed through the corridors, but here, in this locked instant, silence was the point – a harrowing communion between predator and prey.

Vicente clawed desperately at his neck, trying to get underneath the wire, but blood spurted between his fingers. His eyes bulged as he fought for air, his legs kicking out wildly.

The intruder twisted the wire and pulled harder. The self-tightening loop held. He guided the guard's body to the floor. It convulsed and twitched as life ebbed away.

He stood over him, pausing to take in his handiwork – a brief flicker of satisfaction crossing his otherwise impassive face. To him, it was simply another masterpiece.

The alarm, however, forced him into action. Every second counted now. No time to unwind the cable; it stayed where it was.

The canvas was already free, cut from its frame earlier, in silence. His breath stayed steady as he rolled it into a tube and slipped back through the broken French window – gone before the guards or police reached the rear perimeter.

Part Three
Sunday

4

Elena

Sunday 8 June – Girona, northeast of Barcelona.

Elena Carmona had woken to the sound of her phone bleeping on the bedside table. Thirty-one, Seville-born and Girona-based, a rising journalist with a knack for stumbling into trouble while chasing a story, she blinked at the ceiling. She didn't remember setting an alarm. Then again, there was a lot she didn't remember about last night. The final of the Champions League had been a wild ride – just like everything else in her life recently.

She rubbed her eyes. Her head was pounding, and she realised that the last beer at the bar had been a terrible idea. The last three were probably all mistakes. Maybe she should have stopped after the first half of the game. The *normal* game, before it all went mad.

Juventus versus Monaco had been the kind of

match that made you wonder if football wasn't just a metaphor for life – brilliant moments buried under endless stretches of confusion and chaos. She supported neither club, but it was a match not to be missed. Her team was Real Betis – Andalusia in her blood, home of her Romany roots. Here in Catalonia, she sometimes followed the Girona Femení team, or any club that wasn't Barça.

Last night's final played in Madrid had been brutal – neck-and-neck, vicious tackles, yellow cards tossed like confetti. By the time it was one-all and extra-time loomed, the bar in central Girona where she'd watched it with friends was crackling with tension. There wasn't an inch of space left, people standing shoulder-to-shoulder, craning their necks to get a glimpse of the screen. Her father had been there, too, sitting with his injured foot propped up on a stool, clutching his beer like a lifeline. He didn't care much for football, but he liked the drama of a crowd.

And the night sure delivered drama.

As the match dragged into penalties, Elena could barely hear herself think over the roar of the bar. When a penalty from Juventus was disallowed and Monaco clinched the title, the room exploded in a mix of cheers and groans. Elena had thrown back another drink without even thinking about it, trying to process the sheer insanity of what she'd just witnessed. It was one of those matches that you knew would be talked about for years, but in that moment, all she could think about was getting some air. And maybe something to eat.

Now, groaning, she fumbled for her phone. It was 6.15am and she was supposed to catch the train to Madrid in – *joder* – an hour.

She sat up, swung her legs over the edge of the bed, and stared at the half-packed bag on the floor. In her post-match haze last night, she thought she'd been more organised. Clearly not. She glanced back at the phone. A message from Benjamin, sent late last night:

Did you watch the game? Crazy. Madrid's buzzing. See you soon?

Benjamin. Ten years older. English. The art guy. She'd only met him a couple of weeks ago, yet already he was edging into her life in ways she hadn't invited – ever since her kidnapping scoop in Barcelona, the one that landed her reports on the front-page and him almost in handcuffs.

Her English was very good; she'd learned it – *earned it* – the hard way: night shifts, cheap language academies, and a lot of stubbornness.

Benjamin, who hardly spoke a word of Spanish, had bought her a train ticket to Madrid, but she planned to refund him since buying her own ticket for this morning. He'd told her that he had an assignment in Madrid and had invited her along to stay at some Airbnb. 'There's plenty of space, two, maybe three bedrooms,' he'd said, like it was no big deal. 'It'll be fun.'

Fun?

Right. Because sharing an apartment with some *tío* she'd only just met and hadn't initially trusted – in fact, she'd wanted to turn him into the police or *kill* him in self-defence – couldn't possibly end awkwardly, could it? A laugh escaped her throat – dry, sharp, sarcastic. The kind of laugh that comes from too much beer and too little sleep.

She didn't care how many rooms his Airbnb had – there was no way she was staying there. She didn't want to give him the wrong idea. She was curious, that was all. Seriously. *Honestly.* Okay, yes, he was attractive, in that offbeat, probably-trouble kind of way. And, fine, there was something in the way he looked at her, like he could see things she hadn't shown yet. But he wasn't her type. Not really. Besides, he was knee-deep in a divorce and had a twenty-two-year-old daughter – so, yeah, he'd started early. She didn't need that kind of chaos in her life right now.

She wasn't sure if he'd understood, but she'd told him that, yes, she would be going to Madrid, but not to be *with* him, although she might see him there. She'd been commissioned to write a long piece for *El País* newspaper, something that combined sport, her speciality, but also investigation. Since suddenly gaining credibility for her role in the kidnapping story, editors were finally taking her seriously – and *El País* was even paying for her trip.

It had started as a passion project and something she'd pitched to them. A deep dive into the ugly under-current of racism in Spanish football and what the different clubs and governing bodies were really doing about it, if anything at all. It was a topic close to her heart and one that she was determined to get to the bottom of.

The media group had also come up with a very small expense budget, but it was better than nothing. They'd even told her that the racism investigation had the potential to become part of their podcast or video series, but that she had to get the groundwork done.

She'd booked an early train on Sunday – not just because it was cheap, but she had meetings lined up in Madrid for when she arrived. They'd reserved a room for her at a small hotel for two nights – easier to find now that the Champions League final was over.

She pushed herself off the bed and stumbled towards her tiny bathroom. The cold water splashing on her face was a shock, but it did the trick. She stared at herself in the mirror. Her olive-skin currently looked pale, and with her messy, jet-black bob of hair and dark circles under her eyes, she thought she looked vaguely like a panda. *Fantástico.*

After a quick shower, she tossed some clothes into her bag – skinny jeans, T-shirts, a light jacket, a blouse, one skirt, a pair of heels. Nothing fancy; she didn't own anything fancy. *Screw it*, she thought. *It's who I am.*

The train wasn't going to wait and there was work to be done. Racism in football was a hot topic, a huge issue right now, and the public wanted answers. She had some important interviews lined up that could make her career, if she didn't blow it.

Twenty minutes later, she was out the door with her bag and laptop and heading down the narrow stairs of her apartment building. The streets of Girona were quiet, the city sleeping off its collective hangover. She walked towards the train station, her father's words from last night ringing in her ears.

'Careful in Madrid,' he'd said, his foot propped up on the barstool, looking slightly ridiculous with his walking boot. 'Too much excitement for one girl.'

He had that overprotective fatherly tone, like she was still sixteen and taking her first trip alone.

At the station, she grabbed a coffee – black, no sugar – and sat in the waiting area. She checked her phone again. No new messages from Benjamin. She wasn't sure whether that was a good sign or not.

Eventually, she joined the slow shuffle of passengers boarding the train, found her seat near the window and threw her bag into the overhead compartment. It wasn't long before she'd closed her eyes, letting the rhythmic clatter of the tracks lull her into a state of half-sleep. Madrid was only a few hours away, and her brain was already running through everything she had to do once she got there. The meetings, the story, the interviews – and the people who had so far refused to respond to her written requests for information. But the thought of Benjamin hung there – quiet, insistent, yet not entirely unwelcome. Why was she even thinking about him when she had a major report to write?

5

Benjamin

Sunday – Plaza del Ángel, Madrid.

'*Can you hear me?*'

'Yes – and I'm fine,' Benjamin lied. 'What's up?'

He pressed the phone to his throbbing head. He was a wreck. His hangover was horrendous, and the last thing he needed was a call from his estranged wife.

'*Benjamin, are you okay?*'

'I just said I'm fine. I can hear you. What is it?'

'You don't sound fine –'

'It's early for a Sunday, Claire.'

'You sound terrible.'

'I was still asleep. What is it?'

There was a pause.

'Do you have company?'

'Claire – *no* – I am alone. What is it? What's happened? Is everything okay?'

'Nothing's happened. I just need to talk to you.'

'First thing on a Sunday morning?' Benjamin said.

'I'm in Madrid – I'm sure you were informed.'

'*Informed?* You mean via lawyers? You could have just spoken to me –'

'Jesus Christ, Claire, this was the way you insisted things had to be from now on, remember?'

'Okay, I *know* you're in Madrid. How much longer are you going to be in Spain? Sophie said she's planning to go over. Did everything get sorted out with the police? The *Daily Mail* did a thing on it, you know, and *BBC*, *Sky* … even *Fox News* and *CNN*, I'm told –'

'Shit,' Benjamin groaned.

'But look, your lawyer hasn't responded to my lawyer about certain –'

'Claire,' Benjamin cut in, rolling onto his back. 'It's hardly the time to –'

'It's the *only* time,' Claire said. 'I called you now because it's the only way to get hold of you. Otherwise, you're always travelling, or busy, or in meetings, or – *I don't know* – in police custody, trying to clear your name. You still haven't told me everything that happened over there.'

'Didn't the *Daily Mail* tell you?'

'*We* need to talk about things, Benjamin. *You and I.* And about your other life and that other passport.'

Benjamin squeezed his eyes. He felt hideous.

'Claire – it wasn't *another life*. It's all quite simple, really –'

'*You* think it's simple, Benjamin, but my lawyer

wants to know whether you've got hidden assets or offshore accounts to go with your secret passport.'

'Your lawyer wants to know, or you want to know? There's nothing. It wasn't a secret passport – it was an administrative cock-up. And, no, I don't have hidden assets. I was trying to uncover someone else's stolen assets. I've explained all this, for Christ's sake.'

'Are we in danger, Benjamin?' Claire asked, after a pause.

Benjamin sat up.

'What?' he said, now wide awake.

'Are we in danger?'

'No – why? Why ask that? What's happened?'

'Something that Sophie said. It's probably nothing, but she thought someone was following her.'

Half an hour later and Benjamin was fully dressed, having had another cold shower in the absence of hot water, and having dried himself with a pillowcase in the absence of any towels. He still felt like death. He desperately needed some coffee, but now he couldn't shake the creeping anxiety in his gut, the unease spurred by the words from Claire that were pounding his head. His daughter Sophie *thought someone was following her ...*

She didn't seem frightened, Claire had said. *She just found it weird.*

He muttered it under his breath as he paced the apartment, although saying it aloud didn't make it any less troubling. Sophie wasn't the type to overreact. If she'd said something, it meant she felt uneasy – and that made it impossible to dismiss. He'd called her twice and left a voice message, asking her to get in touch as soon as she woke up. No response yet.

It's still early, he told himself.

He grabbed his phone again, typing out a message that he hoped would spur her to reply:

Sophie, I'm now in Madrid, like I told you. If you're feeling uncomfortable or if something strange has happened, let me know. Are you still coming to Spain? Come to Madrid! I'll text you the address below. If you haven't booked a flight, I'll do it – just let me know. Call me the moment you can. Xx.

He hit send and placed the phone on a counter in the kitchen area, then rubbed his face with his hands. The air felt thick, and his eyes burned – not just from the hangover, but from the worry that now clung to him. If Sophie was in danger, nothing else mattered. And if it was because his undercover work had been compromised, he'd never forgive himself.

The apartment was too quiet. The muffled hum of the empty refrigerator and the occasional creak of floorboards above only heightened his awareness of how alone he was. He glanced at his phone for the tenth time, but the screen remained blank. No message from Elena, either. He'd invited her along and booked her a train ticket, but she'd changed it to arrive today … if he'd understood her correctly. He wasn't entirely convinced she'd turn up.

Nor was there any email response from Duncan at

the British Embassy. As for No-Trouble-Right, Benjamin had lost hope of getting any WiFi in the Airbnb … the *illegal* Airbnb, according to his cantankerous neighbours.

He tried to think of other things, but replaying the chaos of last night didn't exactly help matters. After the hassle of being accused of staying in an unlicensed tourist apartment, he'd hoped for a good meal and decent Rioja, tucked-away in a tavern somewhere in old Madrid, but any chance of finding a quiet table was wiped out by the football madness engulfing the city.

He'd eventually stumbled into an Irish pub that was showing the match on several screens, the only place that still had some space, and where he managed to snag a stool at the far end of the bar. It had felt like a small victory – the first of the day – and he'd stayed put, mainly because he had no choice. Very soon, he was hemmed in by the growing crowd as the pub became a riot of voices, spilled drinks and fiery tempers.

Ravenous, he'd ordered the pub's so-called 'signature dish', a Shepherd's Pie served with peas and a dollop of English mustard. It was far removed from the Madrileño cuisine he'd craved, but it did the job. The wine was another story, dodgy enough to explain the constant drumming in his head right now. At the time, however, he didn't complain, and a tall Irish barmaid with tattoos and multiple piercings kindly ensured that his glass was regularly refilled. He'd briefly wondered if the oafs who'd doused him with beer earlier that evening were in the bar, too, as everyone else seemed to be. He'd raised his glass, boozily, to forgive them.

The match itself had been chaotic, a blur of noise and protests against the referee's decisions more than anything else. He recalled there being a dog in the bar, and it had started barking as the game stretched into extra time. When it eventually went to penalties, fire-crackers started exploding outside, the sharp cracks adding to the havoc.

He had too much to drink, but he still popped into another bar for a nightcap on his way back to the apartment, his head spinning from the noise, the wine and the magical madness of Madrid at night.

He picked up his phone again and stared at the still blank screen. It was no good. He needed air. He needed coffee. He needed to sort out his hangover.

The day ahead loomed large: he had to somehow get in touch with Duncan from the embassy, find out if Elena was coming to Madrid or not, and re-think the whole Airbnb mess.

Above all, he needed to speak to Sophie.

6

Detective Pilar Castro

Sunday – Prado Museum.

As the harsh buzz of alarms reverberated through the Prado Museum's galleries, Edu Moreno, head of night surveillance, had stood paralysed in the control room, his assistant frozen beside him. On the CCTV screens, they'd watched helplessly as the masked, black-clad intruder callously slaughtered the patrol guard Vicente Rojas, before fading into the shadows again.

Believing that the killer was still inside the museum, Edu had activated a full lockdown, the piercing sound of the alarm shrieking through the corridors as other night guards raced towards Room Seven. But they were too late. The intruder had vanished, leaving behind only death, a shattered French window door – and an empty frame that hung like a taunt in his wake.

By 3.15am, the Policía Nacional had received the

frantic call from Edu, his strained voice relaying the grim details: '*An intruder has murdered a guard – a painting's been stolen – the killer has escaped.*' Edu had also contacted his chief, the overall head of security for the Prado, as well as the museum's director.

Just five minutes later, the first patrol car screeched to a halt outside the Prado's Goya entrance, its flashing lights slicing through the quiet streets of pre-dawn Madrid. A faint chill hung in the air and the city remained eerily still, save for a few drunken stragglers stumbling home under flickering streetlamps. It was a stark contrast to the simmering tension within the museum, where the galleries had transformed into a battleground of flashing red lights and echoing sirens.

The first officers exited their vehicle swiftly, scanning their surroundings as they radioed their arrival and ran towards the main Jerónimos entrance. Moments later, two more patrol cars arrived, taking positions outside the Murillo entrance to the south, and along the main boulevard of Paseo del Prado. It was there, at 3.45am, that an elite response team from the UDEV also arrived – the violent crime and homicide unit of the Judicial Police Brigade – followed shortly by a forensic team and, finally, Pilar Castro, a seasoned investigator with the judicial police.

Detective Castro made her way towards the Jerónimos entrance, her substantial silhouette framed by the harsh glow of portable floodlights that were already being set up below a broken window on the first floor of the museum. Her bulky brown anorak – functional, not fashionable – hung awkwardly on her broad shoulders, doing little to disguise her overweight frame.

Castro was used to long hours, over-snacking and irregular sleep, and her body bore the marks of her lifestyle: a slight stoop, dark circles beneath her eyes, and the occasional wince when she had to bend too far. She wasn't vain; she had long ago stopped worrying about her looks or weight. Her unremarkable grey hair was pulled back into two limp ponytails that hung just below her ears. Loose strands curled at her temples, framing her round face in a way that emphasised its fullness. Yet the face itself betrayed nothing – years of interrogations and crime scenes had schooled it into a mask of steady impassivity.

She approached the museum's head of night surveillance who looked pale and shaken, talking to UDEV officers at the entrance. The building was now still and sombre, save for the echo of hurried footsteps or the crackle of a distant police radio. The outside perimeter had been secured, and the forensic team with a medical examiner had already moved inside. Castro was impatient to join them.

'Where's the body?' she said. 'Take me there.'

The corpse of Vicente Rojas lay twisted on the cold, marble floor of the gallery known as Room Seven, like a sculpted exhibit gleaming under the moonlight that seeped through from a shattered window in the adjacent room. The victim's head lolled to one side at a grotesque angle. A dark, viscous pool of blood encircled the body, but there were also gleaming puddles further away, where blood had spurted from the guard's neck, spraying the floor in a series of arcs. Now just a gruesome, contorted carcass, the man had clearly been attacked by surprise, dropping his flashlight during it all. It was still on the floor, its beam spotlighting the horror.

Forensic officers kitted out in protective clothing were setting up lamps and taking photographs. A medical examiner crouched over the body, murmuring into a recorder.

Castro pulled on a coverall and peered closer at the victim. His face was a blotched, livid purple, eyes bulging, tongue slack between his teeth. She studied it without flinching, as if cataloguing another entry in a long, grim ledger.

A thin wire, taut and glistening with crimson, had been looped around the guard's neck. It remained embedded in the surrounding flesh – in the part of the neck still connected to the body. The fingers on the victim's hands were curled, as if he'd been desperately trying to claw at the wire tightening around his throat. He wouldn't have stood a chance. It had dug in like a blade; the incision was meticulous, deep, efficient. It was a killing of horrifying precision, almost surgical.

Castro's immediate thought was that the method was *too* professional, too cold and calculated to be a one-off. It had the chilling hallmark of being carried out by someone who'd done it before. But when and where – she had to find out.

She scanned the adjacent open-plan gallery comprised of Rooms Two through to Six, turning her attention to the smashed glass on one of the five double French window doors, where the killer had likely made both his entry and escape. The double doors were still closed, sealed by a steel bar across the bottom wooden frame – but that hadn't stopped the intruder breaking through the full-length glass of one of them. There were shards glittering like ice under the forensic lights. One officer was waving a UV light over them, while another methodically dusted the wooden shutters for prints.

Castro moved closer to the broken window. A thin strand of black thread clung to a corner of the jagged glass – a remnant of the intruder's clothing, perhaps. She plucked it carefully with gloved fingers, handing it to a forensic officer who then bagged it.

She stepped even nearer to the window and leant out. Gazing down at the patio below, she could see more agents searching under floodlights. The drop wasn't far – three or four metres, maximum.

'What's down there?' she asked a UDEV agent standing beside her.

'An enclosed courtyard with an outdoor cafeteria,' came the reply. 'It's open to the public during the museum's opening hours but locked at night.'

She could see the railings encompassing the courtyard would have been easy enough to climb and vault over, virtually unseen in the dead of night. To get from the courtyard up to the windowsill without a ladder was another matter – but they'd be searching for any evidence of that below. In the gallery, each of the five sets of double French doors had steel bars fixed across the base, though the wooden shutters were all open. By the time guards reached the smashed window after any alarm rigged to it had gone off – if any alarm *had* gone off – the killer could have been in and out of the museum. But that took planning. Familiarity.

She would look at what they'd caught on CCTV when she made it to the security squad's control room. For now, she turned to face Room Seven again, standing motionless for a moment, taking in the coppery tang of blood, her imposing frame casting a shadow in the moonlit passageway.

The body of the guard was now partially obscured by a couple of forensic technicians meticulously swabbing its head, neck, hands and blood-soaked uniform, while a third tech swept a UV lamp across the floor, searching for any other trace evidence. Another team member was dusting for fingerprints along the gilded edges of an empty frame on the far wall of the gallery.

The painting.

Castro strode towards the frame. The sides were ornate, gilded in gold leaf, dulled by time. Where a painting once hung, it was now hollow, except for a wooden stretcher support with four diagonal corner strips. Behind, there was just a half-torn silk fabric, through which the gallery's wall could be seen. The painting had been cut from its stretcher pinned to the frame, leaving tiny stitches of canvas in the corners.

Castro spun round to study the room, where six other paintings were on display – all undamaged. She knew little about art, but it was clear that this wasn't some impulsive heist. The theft had been as precise, deliberate and as calculated as the killing. Why just take one painting with what the Prado had to offer?

Her eyes shifted back to the empty frame. The plaque beside it read: *David vencedor de Goliat – David with the Head of Goliath* – Caravaggio (1571-1610).

'Can you pull up the painting?' she asked the room.

An officer stepped forward with a tablet. She studied the image, then she stared at the corpse again – for a long, long time.

Several minutes later, she became aware of someone muttering in her ear. Something about the director of the museum and head of security having finally arrived and being upstairs. She could also hear the distinct clatter of high heels approaching on the marble floor of the adjoining gallery, the same pattern of clickety-clacking she'd heard several times before, and a sound that she'd come to both loathe and mistrust. Her stomach tightened as she turned to see the *juez de instrucción*, Adriana Varela. Castro had hoped the judge wouldn't personally show up at this time of the morning. It was the last thing she needed.

Judge Varela exuded an air of aloof superiority that grated on most people she interacted with – especially Castro. Accustomed to commanding a room, her presence carried as much force as her words – usually laced with icy criticism and condescension. She was ruthless with anyone she deemed incompetent, though Castro suspected her cold demeanour masked something darker. There'd been whispers, unproven yet persistent, about her connections to powerful figures in Madrid's underbelly. Castro didn't trust Varela one bit, but here, at the crime scene, she held all the authority.

The judge was tall, slim, with a sharp, angular face and pale complexion that gave her an almost ghostly appearance in the light of the gallery. Her jet-black hair was pulled back into a taut bun, emphasising her stony, penetrating gaze. Her figure clad in a tailored skirt, jacket and tight blouse stood in sharp contrast to the detective's dowdy, triple-extra-large attire. Castro was used to Varela's put-downs, the barely concealed smirks. But what mattered was solving the case, even if meant enduring the judge's disdain.

'Detective Castro,' Varela said, her tone clipped as she approached. 'Why wasn't I informed sooner?'

'The call went out as soon as we –'

'Where's Inspector Jefe Barroso?' she cut in. 'I was expecting *him*.'

Castro bristled, biting back a retort. Félix Barroso was a figure who many people trod lightly around. His reputation preceded him, not for any brilliance but for methods whispered about in backrooms and bars. He bulldozed through cases with a mix of intimidation and dodgy deals – evidence that appeared from nowhere or was conveniently overlooked, confessions wrung under dubious circumstances. He was a brute who bent the rules until they snapped, yet no judge ever seemed to care.

Barroso was her boss, head of Madrid's violent crime and homicide unit – untouchable. Castro knew that once this case drew attention, he'd swoop in and take it over, maybe within hours, unless he was still asleep or holed up in some shady bar or brothel. She knew she wouldn't be left on the case alone. But if anyone tried to push her out, she wouldn't go quietly.

'It looks like a professional hit,' she said, ignoring any mention of Barroso. 'It looks as if –'

'*I'll* decide what it looks like, thank you.'

Castro took a step back, folding her meaty arms across her chest. She hated this part, waiting for permission to do her job – but she knew how the game was played.

As if reading her mind, Varela continued, her voice sharp and unyielding, no doubt recalling how the French authorities had been publicly humiliated after the Louvre heist – a humiliation Spain could not afford right now.

'Detective Castro, let's be clear: this is far bigger than your remit. So, let's not waste time pretending you're equipped to run it alone. A murder and the theft of a masterpiece from Spain's most sacred institution is not a routine homicide. It's a national emergency. The

Ministry of Culture is already involved, and the cultural heritage brigade will be working alongside you. That's non-negotiable. You'll have the press and half the government on you, and every step you take examined under a microscope. Have you grasped that yet?'

Castro remained silent.

'Inspector Jefe Barroso will be leading this investigation, someone who understands the weight of it all. I only want to hear the details from him, and you will follow his lead. Fail to adapt, or worse, resist, and you'll be swept away – by him, or the ministry, by the media, and by me. Is that understood?'

Holding Varela's glare, Castro gave a slight nod, but she'd caught a flicker of apprehension beneath her forewarning tone. Did the judge already know something? Was she out of her *own* depth? She suddenly felt it – something bigger was at play here.

'We should meet with the museum director and head of security, who have just arrived,' Castro said.

'*I* am going to meet with them right now,' the judge replied. 'You will remain here and wait for Barroso. Whatever you have, I'm sure he will add it in. But please … spare us any of your theories.' She paused, fixing Castro with one last look. 'And suffice to say, there will be no noise on this. No more sirens, no flashing lights. Nobody talks to the press until we know exactly what we're dealing with. Understood?'

Without waiting for a reply, she turned and walked away, the clack of her stilettos fading as her silhouette slipped into the adjoining gallery.

7

Lorenzo Martelli

Sunday – Hotel Ritz.

Lorenzo Martelli's opulent suite at the Ritz was bathed in a sharp dawn light, gold seeping through the drapes that framed the master bedroom's turret windows. The only sound was the rhythmic ticking of an antique clock. Rare art adorned the walls, the scent of polished wood mingling with his cologne, while gilded, hand-crafted furniture sat as though carved for a monarch.

The suite was strewn with the usual 'welcome back' gifts he received in Madrid – unopened champagne left to warm in buckets of melted ice, baskets of exotic fruit, lilies thick with scent. Gilt-edged invitations and embossed cards from sponsors and well-wishers cluttered the tables beside glossy, ribboned packages.

None of it mattered.

The city outside was slowly waking, but inside,

billionaire Martelli had managed only three fitful hours of sleep, tossing and turning as his mind replayed the chaos of last night. The humiliation on the pitch, the whispers in the presidential box, and a vague rumour in the VIP lounge that one of Juventus's most powerful shareholders might be losing his grip. His phone had kept buzzing through the night. Not condolences – complaints. Warnings. Old allies sniffing weakness.

No, he would *never* lose any power.

At seventy-two, Martelli's body was still a temple of disciplined vanity, his shoulders broad, his frame powerful. Tall, with a Roman nose, chiselled jaw and slicked-back silver hair, it was his eyes that truly unnerved. They were unforgiving, unblinking, hard, cold – the coldest eyes in any room.

He stood motionless by the window, his custom Italian suit faintly creased from wear. A half-empty glass of Spain's finest wine sat on a side table from last night, its deep crimson hue a reflection of his simmering rage. His knuckles whitened around a tumbler of water that he now held, the crystal almost cracking under the pressure. Violence brewed inside him, but he wasn't a man to lose control. He saved his fury for those who earned it.

And someone *had* earned it.

Somewhere in Madrid, the rat who had dared to humiliate him was hiding – or plotting an escape – fooling themselves they were safe. Martelli knew exactly who. Football wasn't just a game; it was power, prestige, money. And Juventus – the club he'd bankrolled and bent to his will – had been beaten by a team unworthy to be on the same pitch. Not a defeat. Sabotage.

A message. He should have seen it coming. Three of his men in Madrid erased in the past six months – two of them neatly decapitated – and the Spanish police, once in his pocket, had barely lifted a finger. Now this. No coincidence. Someone was carving chunks out of his network.

The soft creak of leather caught his ear, and his head turned slightly towards the open door leading to the suite's private quarters. One of his bodyguards, a hulking man with close-cropped hair, shifted uncomfortably in a chair that he occupied in the lounge area. Another guard in a dark suit lingered near the dining table, thumbing through his phone in search of updates.

'Anything?' barked Martelli, his voice ripping through the silence.

'No sign of him yet,' the dark suited guard said. 'But they'll find him.'

Martelli's lips curled into something that might have been a smile if it weren't so cold.

'*No sign*,' he echoed softly.

He set his tumbler of water down, adjusted his gold cufflinks, and walked closer to the guard, his polished shoes silent on the thick carpet of the lounge.

'You've been in my employ for how long, Dario?'

'Ten years, sir.' He straightened, a bead of sweat sliding from his temple.

'And in those ten years, have I ever tolerated incompetence?'

'No, sir.'

Martelli's voice dropped, venom dripping from every syllable. 'Then why are you still standing here? *Go*. Help Enzo find him – and bring him to me.'

Dario swallowed hard and nodded, backing towards the door, past the burly thug of a bodyguard, who had now also straightened his posture.

Martelli gave him a curt nod and turned back towards the master bedroom. In addition to Enzo's men on his payroll in Spain, he'd flown in from Turin without his current wife, his mistress, or any of his dolled-up Lolitas, but with an entourage of seven armed guards. One of them doubled up as a chauffeur and air-steward on the Gulfstream jet still idling at Barajas Airport. The pilot, also on his payroll, had remained at the airport. The jet's engines had been warmed and ready for hours, but Martelli wasn't going anywhere – not yet.

One of the bodyguards, the hulk-like figure named Matteo, always remained in Martelli's presence. Another was hovering in the corridor outside his suite, while two others were stationed in the hotel foyer. Martelli's security was always airtight – necessary, given the enemies he'd made – but right now it felt like a cage.

For decades, Martelli had built his empire on

power, wealth and fear. He'd taken over his father's failing real estate business in Naples, transforming it into one of Europe's most powerful conglomerates. His wealth was now boundless, his holdings sprawling. A majority stake in Juventus. A Formula One team. Dozens of high-rises in Milan, Rome, Turin and Naples. He owned a vineyard in Tuscany, an island in the Bahamas, two superyachts, as well as the jet. His palatial estate on the shores of Lake Como boasted an impressive collection of art, from Renaissance paintings to contemporary sculptures – and he'd donated just enough money to various museums and arts foundations over the years to give him kudos among the cultural elite. But ever since the early years in Naples, with the alleged 'assistance' that he'd received from certain powerful families, every business deal had carried the faint stain of violence, or controversy at the very least.

The construction deals, the shipping routes out of Genoa, the casinos across the Adriatic and now also in Western Europe – they were more than business ventures. They were monuments to his ruthlessness. Bribes to politicians, judges and senior police officers over the years had paved the way for permits, while threats had ensured silence.

Investigators had circled him like vultures for years, sniffing around accusations of money laundering, embezzlement and racketeering. Nothing had ever stuck. Witnesses disappeared, evidence vanished, prosecutors retired suddenly – or their careers were often cut short by mysterious tragedies.

The rumours stretched into football – match-fixing, player transfers and sponsorship deals said to be vehicles to wash vast sums of dirty cash. But those whispers about his finances were tame compared to those about his sex life.

His penchant for sexual asphyxiation had always been the subject of hushed gossip, but his much darker, depraved appetites had never been proven. The endless procession of beautiful, wide-eyed girls on his yachts and island. Some were of age, yes, but most not. Young girls who'd been flown in from poor villages in Eastern Europe and Southeast Asia. The younger the better. It reminded him of a time when he'd held all the vitality of youth himself. They were trophies, playthings, tools to assert dominance.

The rumours, however, were unrelenting: the missing Ukrainian girl who'd been seen on his yacht just days before her family reported her disappearance. Then there was the Singapore journalist planning an exposé on Martelli's alleged role in sex trafficking of underage girls. Officially, she died in a freak accident with a hotel glass door that sliced her neck like a guillotine. Unofficially, everyone knew Martelli had arranged it. Just as with the Italian prosecutor bold enough to suggest charges: his body was found hanging from a bridge with piano wire. The choice of wire wasn't accidental – it was strong enough to hold, and cruel enough to send a message. Another 'tragic accident.' Another warning.

Now someone else had dared to challenge him, to spit in the face of the empire he'd spent a lifetime building. Martelli had always dealt with disloyalty swiftly and mercilessly. When the rat was found, there would be no mercy, no forgiveness. They would suffer. They would beg for death before the end, and Martelli would savour every second of that suffering.

He raised the tumbler of water to his lips. His hand was steady, but he needed air, or at least the illusion of it.

Pushing the drapes aside, he gazed out the window and down at the police vehicles outside the Prado Museum, adjacent to the hotel. Their presence irked him. He'd never trusted the Spanish authorities, but they had no jurisdiction over him … no power that his money couldn't neutralise.

The Prado.

His art … his fetish …

His mind filled with violent imagery again.

When he found the rat, their death would become yet another masterpiece.

8

The Prado

Sunday – Prado Museum.

The first reporters who'd taken an interest in the police activity outside the Prado Museum at around 4am on that Sunday weren't exactly seasoned professionals. One was a wide-eyed rookie still scrambling for a byline; the other, his ambulance-chasing *amigo*, a paparazzo-in-the-making who'd shove a lens in a dying man's face if it meant selling a shot.

Drawn like vultures to the flashing blue lights, they'd hoped to sniff out whatever scandal or disaster had unfolded inside the museum's sacred walls. They were looking for a scoop, any scoop, but were ignored by the officers securing the perimeter. They weren't allowed within fifty metres of the museum, but instead had to make do with loitering behind a police cordon on the Paseo del Prado.

The city wasn't asleep, not entirely. A few stragglers from last night were still making their way home – some staggering, some arm in arm, heels in hand, eyes glassy with alcohol. A couple of passing taxi drivers rubbernecked as they rolled by. Two clubbers paused on the pavement, giggling as they took a selfie with the police lights in the background. One of them uploaded it with the hashtag *#PradoPolicía*. The first ripples of social media speculation had begun.

Soon, the trainee and his paparazzo sidekick weren't alone anymore. A few other early vultures had shown up – bloggers, freelancers and just bystanders – also loitering behind the police tape, angling for a shot and throwing out questions that got them nothing but blank stares from the officers on duty.

By 6am, a few professional hacks had arrived, and the police presence had also thickened. A radio journalist with a mic in hand asked questions sharp enough not to be waved off entirely. Meanwhile, officers drew a more structured perimeter, their body language shifting from mild annoyance to something harder. Whatever was happening inside, it was serious.

The streetlights dimmed as dawn crept in. More reporters had appeared, pressing up against the cordon. A TV crew rolled up, the presenter – flawless in her navy-blue blazer – rehearsing her lines under the glare of a camera lamp. The rookies were now just background noise, edged out by those who knew how to handle cops and tease out morsels of information without getting shut down.

Social media was in overdrive by 7.45am. The EFE news agency had issued a breaking news report with images of flashing lights outside the Prado, quickly echoed by the RTVE state broadcaster citing 'unverified reports' of a break-in and fatality. Satellite vans parked up along the Paseo del Prado; a helicopter whirred overhead. Spain's biggest media outlets had staked their ground – logos and microphones thrust forward. Madrid was wide awake, and the media circus was already in full swing.

9

Benjamin

Sunday – Plaza del Ángel.

Dishevelled and head still pounding, Benjamin slid onto a wobbly stool at the café bar, angling himself to avoid the sunlight streaming through the window. The stool lurched sharply to the left; he caught the edge of the counter just in time, his palm slapping a few packets of sugar onto the floor, his other hand flailing before he finally managed to steady himself.

A barmaid approached; one eyebrow arched. No greeting – just the blank hostility of someone who didn't want to be there any more than perhaps he did.

'Shit, sorry. Er, *café solo*, please. *Por favor.*' His voice came out croaky. He pointed across the counter. 'And one of those croissants. Make it two. *Dos. Gracias.*'

She nodded, and then moved away without a word.

Claire's voice still rattled in his head: *Sophie thought*

someone was following her. Who? A student from her uni, some idiot with too much time on their hands – or someone far worse, someone with a grudge against Benjamin and his family?

Paris came back to him, uninvited, like the hangover gnawing behind his eyes. The Joussets – Cécile and Claude. The sibling duo from hell. Money laundering through auction houses, intimidation, dismembered remains left floating in the Seine.

They'd believed Benjamin was 'Brandon Bartholomew' – with the passport that Scotland Yard had supplied. He'd played the slimy art dealer, slipped inside their circle and helped Europol bring Claude down. He could still see Claude's shark eyes as the cops dragged him off, spitting two words: *Tu verras. You'll see.*

The French gangster had served his time, but Cécile had never been touched. Too clever, too careful – she'd rebuilt the operation into something darker. And now thanks to Barcelona and the Dalí mess, Brandon Bartholomew had been exposed in the press and Cécile would know Benjamin's real name.

He'd always told himself he could handle the fallout from Paris. But Sophie hadn't been part of the equation. Now it wasn't fear, but irritation – at how the Joussets still clung to him like a bad smell. Dangerous? Yes. Callous? Absolutely. But he'd dealt with worse. People who thought they could rattle him into submission, who mistook stubbornness for weakness. He'd been a step ahead of them once. He could be again.

Of course, this was assuming it *was* the Joussets.

Sophie's shadow back in England could just be some lovelorn student, or – God forbid – a sick, stalking pervert. But if it *was* them? He'd deal with it.

Sophie had to get to Madrid, or at least tell him she was fine. He'd made three unanswered calls and sent three more texts, as well as sending her the details of where he was staying – her silence wasn't helping matters. But she was smart. If there was a real threat, she'd let him know. If there wasn't, he'd still sleep easier once she was in Madrid and under his roof – the roof of whatever illegal tourist trap he was in.

Still no news from Elena, either. He'd also messaged her twice and tried calling. He couldn't keep doing so, otherwise she'd label *him* a stalker.

His coffee arrived and he downed it fast. Leaning gingerly on the bar, praying the stool wouldn't implode, he beckoned the barmaid for another – plus some water – then tore into the croissants.

The café was quiet – just the clink of spoons, the clatter of cups and saucers, the hiss of the espresso machine. In the corner, a group of old men argued, hands flying. A couple of tourists. A few locals nursing Sunday hangovers. No one stood out. No one looked at him for long.

His phone suddenly buzzed on the counter of the bar. He snatched it to answer, and the stool started to sway again.

'Hello,' he said, once he'd caught his balance.

'Benjamin, it's Duncan Carter-James from the embassy.'

'Duncan,' said Benjamin, thinking that *of course* Duncan was double-barrelled. 'Good morning.'

'Good? Depends on who you ask,' came the reply. 'I got your email about yesterday – no probs – half the city was chock-a-block – anyway, we've finally got one another's number – should've done that earlier, but better late than never, no? So, all's well that ends well and we can certainly meet today – the sooner the better for me, in fact. I had a padel match planned, but it's been cancelled – how are you set?'

Duncan had a very fast, very annoying and extremely jolly voice. Benjamin could barely keep up.

'*Hang on, I'm on the phone* –' Duncan was now shouting to someone else.

In the background, chaos erupted – kids started screaming at full volume, something crashed, a woman began yelling in Spanish. Then what sounded like a toy piano was being smashed repeatedly against a surface.

'You okay there?' Benjamin asked.

Duncan didn't immediately reply, but the yelling and screaming continued. Not wanting to keep talking in the café, Benjamin waved the barmaid over, slid her a ten euro note, then left the change.

'Duncan?' he said, stepping out to the street. 'You still there?'

'I'm still here,' came the reply, followed by another shriek and the crash of ceramic. 'Where shall we meet? Right now's good – I can get to wherever you are.'

Benjamin figured Duncan was just desperate to escape the domestic pandemonium; probably the same reason he'd pushed for a meeting yesterday evening. But unless the restitution case was urgent, Benjamin wanted to keep his options open – at least until he'd heard back from his daughter. And from Elena.

'Yes, well, the thing is –' Benjamin started.

'There's a great place for brunch in the Plaza del Rey, for example, or anywhere central that's best for you –' Duncan was saying, cheerfully oblivious to the kids' screaming in the background.

'I'll have to come back to you, Duncan. I'm waiting on another call –'

'From Ignacio?'

'What?'

'The other call. Ignacio. Did he get in touch?'

'Who's Ignacio?'

'Culture ministry,' Duncan chirped, amid more background shrieking. 'Lovely chap. We used to play more padel together before the terrible twins came along. Thought it might help if you met – his English is perfect. I gave him your contact details only half-an-hour ago, just in case he could do with some help –'

'I wish you hadn't –'

'We were meant to play padel this morning, but he had to cancel on account of the Prado incident –'

'What Prado incident?'

'Haven't you heard?'

'Heard *what*, Duncan?'

10

Elena

Sunday – Girona to Madrid.

Elena hadn't slept on the train. She'd tried – head against the window as the northeastern tapestry of Spain blurred by. Alternating shades of green, gold and reddish-brown under a hard blue sky. Rolling plains one minute, rocky terrain the next; the monotony broken by the occasional cluster of olive groves, crumbling ruins or the neat rows of a vineyard. The train's rhythm should have been soothing, but her mind refused to switch off, buzzing with caffeine, hang-over haze, the assignment ahead … and the memory of a sexual assault she would always link to Madrid.

She'd been to Madrid a few times, but the city had never felt like hers – never wrapped her up in the way Barcelona or Girona did. Nothing bad had happened there – not directly – but she felt a small shiver of tension as the memory resurfaced.

It had been two years ago, at a corporate soirée in a Barcelona hotel. He was a cop, off duty and stinking of alcohol, cornering her while she worked catering shifts to pay for her studies. She'd either walked past him too quickly with a tray of drinks, or smiled too politely, or done nothing at all. She could still hear his words: *'You're lucky I'm being nice.'* As if the badge he pulled from his jacket gave him every right.

He was from Madrid. He'd made that clear, flaunting it like a mark of superiority, bragging about his city, about how the Madrid police outshone Catalonia's Mossos. She'd focused on trying to avoid him as she continued to serve drinks.

He lingered after the event was winding down, one of the last to leave, even as the other guests drifted into the warm Barcelona night. Elena was alone, clearing glasses, when she noticed him leaning against the bar. His tie hung loose, his jacket slung over one shoulder, his smirk heavy with drink and entitlement.

'I've got a room here,' he said, voice thick with sleazy insinuation.

She tried to step around him, but his hand shot out, gripping her arm just above the elbow, fingers pressing hard into her skin.

'Let me go,' she said, her voice steady despite the knot of anger in her chest.

He didn't. Instead, he leaned closer, his breath sour

with whisky, his free hand reaching for her waist, then creeping higher with the aim of fondling her breasts.

'*Venga, chica* … you know you want it,' the scumbag whispered, starting to rub his body against her.

That's when the adrenaline kicked in. She twisted out of his grip, knocking over a tray of glasses in the process, the sound of shattering crystal splitting the air.

'*Get away from me,*' she yelled, loud enough to carry across the emptying room, as other staff looked over.

For a moment, he froze, squinting – weighing up whether to push ahead and grope her again. Then, with a scoff, he stepped back, smoothing his tie as if she'd overreacted, as if *she* was the problem.

'You should learn to take a compliment,' he said.

She stood her ground, her chest heaving, until he turned and walked away.

The next day – a day too late – she reported the assault at a police station back in Girona. She filed every detail she could remember: his appearance, part of the badge number that she'd glanced, the smug smile that had never reached his eyes. Then … *nothing*. No follow-up. It was as if her complaint had been nothing more than an inconvenience to the system.

The train jolted slightly, pulling her back to the present. It didn't matter what ghosts Madrid held; she'd dealt with worse. She needed to focus. She had a job to do, people to interview, a report to write.

The subject was all-consuming. Racism in football was a deep-rooted pocket of evil; it was also a mine-field. Spanish football had been wrestling with it for years, clubs and officials spinning out the same hollow promises while the abuse festered on the terraces. She planned to follow the money – as the money never lied. At the start of the season, La Liga had unveiled a multimillion-euro fund to tackle racism. Now, at the season's end, she wanted to know where the money had gone and what, if anything, it had achieved. The public wanted answers. Her editor wanted a thorough report. The league just wanted good **PR**. And here she was, trying to balance it all on a few hours' sleep.

She spent the rest of the train ride scrolling through social media, catching up on the madness from last night's Champions League final. The referee's decisions – some of the worst she'd ever seen – were trending everywhere, with clips of the disallowed penalty looping endlessly on her feed. She watched the Juventus coach screaming at the fourth official, then swiped to grainy shots of fans clambering onto the roof of a bus outside the stadium.

Then came the fights. Brawls in every corner of Madrid. Videos of fans punching, kicking and screaming obscenities were plastered across every site. One clip showed a Monaco supporter tackled to the ground by a mob of Juventus fans before she put her phone down. Exhausting. *Football madness at its finest.*

When her phone buzzed again, a breaking news alert flashed: an incident at the Prado Museum, maybe a theft. She didn't have the bandwidth to focus. It just looked like another headline in a city addicted to uproar.

11

Benjamin

Sunday – Calle de las Huertas.

Benjamin had been relieved to end the call with double-barrelled Duncan, not least for the shrieking backing vocals of his terrible twins. They'd agreed to meet later in the day – at Duncan's insistence – a man itching to do a runner from the family madness.

They had to meet so Duncan could hand over the restitution file. It was the British Embassy, via Scotland Yard's Art & Antiques Unit, who'd asked Benjamin to hop to Madrid from Barcelona. They wanted him to investigate a painting that originally belonged to a British volunteer in the International Brigades – but it had been seized during Franco's regime, then presumed lost, and had now resurfaced in a well-connected private collection with murky papers.

For now, squinting into the sharp morning light

outside the café, Benjamin breathed out, long and slow, thinking instead about the Prado – and the scant details Duncan had said about an incident there.

A break-in. An 'alleged' theft. A 'possible' fatality. Any of those, let alone all three, made it a major incident. Apart from a small Flemish oil on copper that vanished in 1971, the Prado's security was solid.

Maybe it was vandalism by climate activists again. They'd managed to glue themselves to the frames of Goya's *Las Majas* earlier in the year – although from Duncan's tone, this sounded much more serious. With thieves snatching Napoleon's jewels from the Louvre using a furniture lift and power tools in broad daylight, anything felt possible.

He checked his phone again. Nothing from Sophie, nothing from Elena. He had nowhere else to be while waiting for any response, and his curiosity got the better of him. He found his feet moving before his brain had fully decided. The Prado was no more than a kilometre and a half from the plaza where he'd just had coffee, and it was a straight enough shot down the Calle de las Huertas from his illegal Airbnb. Madrid was a city best handled on foot. So, he'd set off, hands in his pockets, head down against the morning glare.

He'd met the Prado's director once before – brisk, formal at first, but calm and reliable. If there really had been a break-in at the museum, it wasn't Benjamin's problem, anyway. The Spanish police would see to that. No love lost since the chaos in Barcelona, which suited him just fine.

At the bottom of Huertas street, adjoining the Paseo del Prado, the Retiro district's Comisaría de Policía was swarming with squad cars, lights flashing, sirens off. Officers rushed in and out of the doors, barking into radios. The place had the hum of something escalating. The kind of tension that suggested things weren't totally under control.

He crossed the road towards the Prado. An organised scramble. Blue lights strobed against the museum's façade; a barrier held back a swelling mix of onlookers and reporters. A news crew had set up just beyond the cordon, their anchor already mid-broadcast. Benjamin worked the fringe, reading faces, clocking the flow of uniforms and suits as the scene took shape.

The main action was clustered at the northern Goya entrance and, more intensely, behind it, at the Jerónimos door, where white-suited forensics huddled. Benjamin edged towards Plaza de Cánovas del Castillo, planning to slip up the parallel street for a sightline over the back of the museum – if he could clear the barriers and cross the road for a glimpse of –

'*Señor – atrás, por favor.*'

A policeman cut him a glare, hand hovering near his belt. Benjamin eased back, just enough to avoid any follow-up – when his phone vibrated in his pocket. Unknown number. He answered.

'Sophie?' he said.

'*Soy Ignacio Lázaro, del Ministerio de Cultura,*' the caller said. Then, in careful English: 'Duncan Carter-James gave me your number.'

12

Inspector Jefe Félix Barroso

Sunday – Prado Museum.

It was in the middle of the media scrum that Inspector Jefe Félix Barroso finally arrived at the Prado, just after 9.15am, later than he'd wanted, and much later than he should have. His team, some of whom had been there since dawn alongside Detective Castro, had beaten him to it, and he hated playing catch-up.

He stepped out of the unmarked car, slamming the door harder than he needed to. Shirt crumpled, tie slack, eyes burning – his face carved with lines that spoke of more than just exhaustion. Not a hangover – he was long past those. Too little sleep, too much whisky, and a knot in his gut that never eased.

The pressure had been building for months. Threats dressed up as favours. He'd bent rules, lost files, looked the other way. He'd allowed himself to be dragged in too deep. He'd done too much for men who didn't send warnings. They sent bodies.

And for nearly four months now, they'd gone quiet. No calls, no cash. He needed the money to clear more gambling debts. But it was the silence that ate at him. With men like that, silence was the sharpest threat of all.

As he strode towards the museum, the old fear twisted again – the same cold bite he'd felt when that line went dead months ago. He told himself it was just another crime scene. But the thought kept needling: what if it wasn't? What if the game had already moved on – without him? And what if he was a marked man?

He pushed through the throng of reporters like a shark in shallow water – silent, slow, radiating a quiet threat. One journalist shoved a recorder towards him.

'Inspector, is this a robbery? A murder? What can you tell us?'

Barroso didn't break stride. His lip curled; he sneered. He hated reporters. Parasites, the lot of them.

More voices, more questions. Someone called his name; another shoved a microphone too close. He ignored them all, pushing ahead with the dead-eyed patience of a man used to getting what he wanted, by any means possible.

At the museum's Goya entrance, Castro and two UDEV officers were waiting. Before following them inside, he glanced back at the sea of cameras. He smiled, briefly. It wasn't a pleasant smile.

13

La familia Falcó

Ramón Falcó.

Sunday – La Moraleja.

The Falcó family's residence stood behind high gates and discreet security in La Moraleja, one of Madrid's most exclusive and prestigious neighbourhoods, just northeast of the city centre. For the status-obsessed Ramón Falcó, the property offered the kind of silence and privacy that only money could buy.

The sun had risen, the swimming pool was now glittering, but the house was dark. Outside, a gardener had already arrived to clip the hedges and sweep the long drive. Inside, everything was silent, but Ramón couldn't keep still.

His aides had left hours ago, but he hadn't slept. Thick-necked and bloated, he was still in his suit – tie discarded, shirt reeking of cigars and sweat – as he paced his study. His face, once sharp enough to charm newspaper editors and ministers alike, had softened with years of good wine, rich food, and the certainty that no one ever said no to him twice.

Last night, he'd left the VIP box at the Bernabéu stadium the moment the last penalty hit the net, as the reality settled like acid. No handshakes. No explanation. Just a quick nod to his chauffeur-bodyguard and a silent, urgent walk to the Mercedes. He hadn't looked for Lorenzo Martelli in the crowd. He hadn't needed to. He already felt the weight of his gaze.

Juventus should not have lost. Not with the officials Ramón normally had locked down. Not after everything he'd arranged.

His son Borja's seat in the VIP box had been empty all night. Second row, two in from the aisle. It was the first thing Ramón had noticed, even before the kick-off. No call – no apology – just absence, yet again.

He walked to his liquor tray, poured a splash of something pale and expensive, but let it sit untouched.

Christ, get a grip, man – *it's only eight in the morning.*

He'd built all this from nothing. Not just the house, but the network, the wealth, his *status*. He'd started as a provincial councillor in Valladolid, just another young lawyer with a family name no one remembered, but with a talent for making things happen quietly. It wasn't long before he understood where the real power lay – not in speeches or votes, but in signatures.

Zoning permissions, public housing grants, stadium construction projects. Decisions that generated enormous loyalty and even larger kickbacks. By the time he arrived in Madrid, he already had stakes in two construction firms, a logistics company used for moving sports equipment, and a consultancy that 'advised' local governments on infrastructure planning.

The presidency of Spain's higher council for sports – the Consejo Superior de Deportes – came later. Once a quiet part of the Culture Ministry, it was now within Education and Sport. It didn't pay much, but it didn't need to. It gave him what he needed: visibility, protection and unfiltered access. Through it, he could reach every layer of influence in Spanish and European sport – not just the domestic football club owners or La Liga and Spanish federation presidents, but UEFA delegates, FIFA middlemen, global sponsors, the power players who controlled broadcast and streaming rights, as well as the agents who whispered into players' ears. It wasn't just a seat at the top table. It was control of the guest list. And as long as the contracts looked legitimate, no one followed the trail of payments too closely.

The role enabled him to steer investigations away from the wrong bank accounts. He didn't consider himself corrupt – *no*, he was a realist. A 'manager of interests'. He understood that money needed channels, it needed to flow through 'alternative structures', often offshore – structures that didn't leave fingerprints. He simply helped to legitimise illegal commissions for national and international clients ... and especially the Italians.

His wife, Cayetana, was perfectly suited to the life he'd built. Tall, elegant, composed, thin to the point of fragility, with long legs and aristocratic cheekbones − 'well-bred', they said − but if she ever smiled, which was rare, the skin around her eyes no longer moved. She ran a cultural foundation and navigated fundraiser seating plans like a military strategist. Their marriage was a pact, not a relationship. They hadn't shared a bedroom in over a decade, but their public appearances were flawless. That was the agreement.

Status was also Cayetana's oxygen. She had no idea where their money came from but knew how to spend it − and how to convert it into power. It was why she tolerated Ramón's silences, his late nights, the whispers that always followed their son's name. What mattered most was remaining untouchable on the society circuit: flawless in photographs, lethal across a gala table. Nothing else mattered. Not even their son, *Borja* ...

Borja had been a disaster from the start. Cocaine at sixteen. Rehab at seventeen. Ibiza by eighteen − all-night raves, orgies and overdoses. In the early days, the paparazzi had loved him − shirtless on yachts, drunk in beach clubs, once snapped in a compromising pose with a minor royal.

Then there'd been that other boy, barely twenty years of age. The one who fell from the roof of a villa after a forty-hour binge. Borja had been at the same rave, hazy in the background of the grainy tabloid photo, eyes bloodshot, smiling at something no one else remembered. Drugs everywhere – the press asking too many questions.

It was an accident, though … *allegedly*. At least that's what Ramón managed to negotiate. No charges. Just a pay-off. But it was a line crossed.

It's when he finally brought Borja back from Ibiza and created Innovation Sports – a 'sports marketing consultancy' in appearance, but nothing more than a glossy shell neatly registered in his son's name. He ordered Borja to wear a suit and tie and look busy, rented him a slick office with some decent art on the wall and an Italian designer sofa, from where he would oversee a list of staff who rarely turned up for work. Innovation Sports soon won a few legit, minor clients – but nothing that would attract real scrutiny.

Borja didn't know the mechanics. Didn't need to. He still partied, attended all the star-studded sporting events, nodded through contracts and occasionally appeared in the press when told to. Meanwhile, the real money moved in other rooms. Sponsorship consulting, player image rights, the laundering, the negotiations with FIFA, with UEFA, with their Italian partners – that had always stayed in Ramón's own hands. Anti-corruption investigators had circled once or twice – searching for twenty million euros in uncollected fees for TV rights – but nothing had ever stuck.

Not yet.

Ramón's phone illuminated from the polished leather console beside him.

'*Buenos días, señor presidente,*' his PA said, as she did every morning at eight – weekend or not – to confirm his schedule for the day.

'*Buenos días*, Cristina.'

'I'm just confirming your luncheon today with –'

'Cancel it,' cut in Ramón. 'Clear the schedule.'

'Of course,' came the reply.

'Have you heard from Borja, by any chance?'

'No, sir.'

Ramón closed his eyes.

'Regarding tomorrow's schedule,' his PA continued, 'there's a press interview with *El País*, if you recall. I've allocated fifteen minutes for it after the meeting with –'

'Cancel it,' said Ramón. 'Cancel it all. Just do it.'

'Understood, sir.'

He ended the call, staring at his phone. Martelli hadn't called him – the silence was ominous. It meant he was moving other pieces. If the machinery was in motion, he wouldn't be able to stop it.

There were no new messages. He'd called Borja three times. No answer. He called again now. Voice-mail. He didn't leave a message.

His son's absence at last night's match couldn't be

explained away by drugs or a hangover. Something was off. Borja had done something – or *failed* to. If he'd flipped, even without realising it, he'd opened a door that couldn't be closed. Martelli didn't just punish betrayal. He erased bloodlines. And he had enough on Ramón to bury him without a trace.

He walked back to the study window and stared out at the perfect lawn. It had always felt it would last forever – the house, the role, the invitations to sit beside royalty in stadiums and gala boxes.

But if the media now got hold of any of it – the fake contracts, the shadow accounts, the trail of missing rights revenue – it wouldn't stop at Borja. *He* would be the scandal. Every favour he'd ever traded would come crawling into daylight. The house, the foundation, the photographs on the walls, his *status* – all of it would be ash.

He caught his reflection in the glass. He finally took a swig of the drink he'd poured, then stared down at his trembling hand.

~

Borja Falcó.
Sunday – Malasaña district.

Borja woke with a jolt in a flat he didn't recognise, the shutters half-drawn, the air sour with last night's heat and someone else's perfume. His mouth was dry, his heartbeat erratic, and there was a dull, persistent thud somewhere in the back of his skull. He sat up slowly, eyes scanning the room for clothes, for a drink, pills, anything that could settle the chaos in his brain.

Outside, the street noise drifted up – vendors shouting, a dog barking, scooter engines whining, shutters rattling open – Madrid coming to life on a Sunday morning. Where the hell was he? Not where he was supposed to be. Too central, too loud, too *cheap*. The kind of area he'd normally sneer at. But maybe that was the upside: no one would think to follow him here.

He blinked into the half-light of the room. It was spinning at first, but then it steadied, and he could see that it was small, high-ceilinged, with old floor tiles. A leather jacket that wasn't his was draped over the arm of a faded chair. There was lipstick smeared on a wine glass. Smudged white lines on a low glass table. A door was open to a kitchen, another door to a bathroom. Someone's phone charger was plugged into the wall. But no one else was there.

The memory of last night flickered back in a blurred loop – a rooftop bar, someone laughing, an accent he couldn't place. Asian, maybe. South American? All the same to him. One person or two? He remembered a hand on his chest, nails digging into his shoulder. Whoever she was – he hoped it was a she – he couldn't even remember if they'd had sex. Or if he'd paid for it.

He recalled a flash of conversation: one of the Chinos – he never bothered with their names –

nudging him, grinning, dropping the word *UEFA* like it was a private joke. Borja had nodded, pretended to get it, too wired to care. There'd been a girl on his lap, head thrown back, laughing, while the other karaoke boys watched – like they were taking notes.

He grabbed his phone. Ten missed calls. Several from papá. Two voicemails from a number he didn't recognise.

He sat on the edge of the bed, hunched over, eyes fixed on the floor. His head still pulsed, but beneath the hangover lay something worse. Not nausea. Not shame. Not drug-induced paranoia. Fear.

Something had gone wrong – very wrong.

He'd fucked up.

Big time.

He should have been at the stadium last night. Looking happy. Networking. Sitting near the old man, smiling for the cameras, shaking hands with UEFA's top dogs. That was the script. But the quiet ones with sharp suits and powder-laced promises – the Chinos he'd first met in Marbella – had got to him weeks ago. They hadn't needed much – just a name here, an introduction there, a door opened at the right hotel, in exchange for more of the usual 'good times'. They were always more fun to be around, so he hadn't thought twice. He'd told himself it was harmless. Just favours traded for favours. That's how things worked. He hadn't told papá – because papá had no interest in any of his new business ideas.

Last night wasn't about setting anything up. It was the party after – champagne, powder, girls, more envelopes pressed into his hand, the karaoke boys laughing like they owned him. He'd enjoyed it, of course. Too much. But this morning, it felt different. It didn't feel like business anymore.

He hadn't meant to betray anyone. But what scared him now was the match result: Juventus had lost.

That wasn't supposed to happen.

No one said anything about the Italians losing.

The Italians could *never* lose.

Borja swallowed hard, stomach twisting. He'd seen what the Italians did to people who owed them. But maybe this would blow over. Maybe the result was just football. One upset in a game full of them. Lorenzo Martelli – papá's associate – would be furious, yes, but not irrational. Not petty. He had bigger enemies, surely. And if not – well, Borja wasn't important. He wasn't the story. He never had been.

He rubbed his face with both hands, then hauled himself upright and shuffled unsteadily towards the tiny kitchen. He opened the fridge. There was a single bottle of water and two takeaway boxes. He didn't recognise anything. Whoever lived here, or brought him here, was gone – at least temporarily. He wasn't going to wait for them to come back.

Moving from the kitchen to the bathroom, he stared into the mirror. He'd always looked like someone who'd overstayed their welcome at every party, but now he looked gaunt, draggled, used up. Once, he'd hovered at the edge of Madrid's jet-set, but they wanted nothing to do with him anymore. He wasn't 'In'. Despite all his efforts to stay trendy, the schoolboy prettiness he'd once coasted on had thinned and soured – substance abuse had seen to that.

He knew what he was, and he hated it: an addict, a washed-up socialite, a fucked-up daddy's boy. A has-been. Maybe a never-was. Yet for all that, he'd never thought of himself as corrupt. Not really. Not until now. He turned away from the mirror.

Fuck, everything felt so raw right now.

His phone buzzed on the bed. Another number he didn't recognise. The noise outside swelled – closer, sharper.

He had to move. *Now.* Before they came for him.

Ibiza? Too obvious. They'd look there first. He needed somewhere quiet, somewhere neither papá's contacts nor the Italians would trace.

South America? Morocco?

He needed cash. A lot of it.

Go, Borja. Just fucking *go.*

14

Benjamin - Ignacio Lázaro

Sunday – Hotel Ritz.

'It's a Caravaggio.'

'You're kidding?'

'No.'

'*Fuck.*'

They were sitting at a quiet table in the lounge area of the Ritz hotel, just across from the Prado. Ignacio was leaning in, his voice low. Despite his fluent English, he had a strong, deep Spanish accent – and Benjamin had to keep edging closer to fully understand what he was saying.

The call had come less than fifteen minutes earlier. He'd said he was from Spain's Culture Ministry – the body responsible for the museum. He said he'd called Duncan to cancel their Sunday padel match because of 'what's happening at the Prado', and then Duncan had mentioned that Benjamin was in Madrid.

'Yeah, well, I'm near the museum right now,' Benjamin had said, while still watching the scene outside.

'Where, exactly?'

'By the Ritz, trying to get a better view of whatever the hell is going on.'

'Okay, perfect. Meet me in the Ritz itself, then. Ten minutes.'

'Wait – what?'

'Ritz reception. *Diez minutos.*'

Click. That was it.

Ignacio hadn't explained why he wanted to meet, and Benjamin was initially irritated by the assumption that he would drop everything to do so, as if he had nothing better to do on a Sunday morning in Madrid. But the reality was that he didn't have anything better to do, other than wait to hear back from his daughter or Elena.

A few bellhops and officials in dark suits clustered near the entrance of the hotel. Inside, chauffeurs loitered by the marble pillars, checking their phones while keeping a watchful eye on the lounge area. A pair of heavyset men – bodyguards, by the look of them – stood near the lifts, scanning everyone who walked in. Near the reception desk, a small pack of journalists hovered with cameras slung over their shoulders – like an overspill from the media frenzy outside the adjacent museum.

Ignacio arrived in a navy suit, white shirt and silk tie – polished, but not flamboyant – although too formal for Benjamin's liking. Either he dressed like that all the time, or he'd come from a meeting far more official than this one. He clocked the raised eyebrow at his own dishevelled state – wrinkled shirt, wild hair, the usual disrepair. Benjamin was used to it by now, though lately, part of him wished he wasn't.

Wire-rimmed spectacles sat neatly on Ignacio's nose, yet he moved with the sharp impatience of someone already running late, or with an urgency to get something resolved. Studying him closer, Benjamin could see that his tie was slightly askew and loose, and his face looked tight with worry. He also had little time for pleasantries.

'So, you're Duncan's friend,' Benjamin said, not sure what else to offer.

'Yes. Poor Duncan,' came the reply. Nothing more.

Poor Duncan because he couldn't stand being at home with his wife and screaming twins, Benjamin assumed.

'I don't have long,' Ignacio said, checking his watch before nodding to the lounge area. 'Let's go over there.' He led the way to a quiet corner table. 'Duncan said you were here on other business. But I'd already heard about you.'

'What had you already heard about me?'

'Even before the madness in Barcelona with the Dalí –'

'Let's not go there.'

'I'd heard about you via the BPH.' A pause. 'Our brigade of —'

'Yes, I know who they are,' Benjamin cut in. Spain's police unit for crimes of cultural heritage. 'I've worked with them before.'

'Exactly,' Ignacio nodded. 'I'd heard you recover stolen art and uncover forgeries.'

'Among other things,' Benjamin muttered. He glanced around, half-hoping someone might offer to bring them decent coffee — anything better than the stuff at the café with the treacherous bar stools. But Ignacio had other things on his mind.

'This conversation is strictly confidential,' he said, his voice low, yet urgent.

Benjamin didn't say a word.

'It has to be,' pressed Ignacio, 'as we haven't released a statement yet. I'm due for a debrief in the museum shortly …'

Benjamin nodded, watching him check his watch again.

'A guard was murdered last night, and a painting was taken,' murmured Ignacio.

Which is when he told Benjamin it was Caravaggio's *David and Goliath*.

15

Kai Leroux

Sunday – San Andrés.

While Sunday morning in central Madrid was buzzing, the southern industrial zone of San Andrés lay almost deserted. Cranes stood frozen above empty construction sites, warehouses and shuttered units sat in silence, the stillness broken only by the bark of a chained dog. It was the kind of emptiness that suited Kai Leroux.

He swung off his motorbike and clipped his helmet to the front wheel. Short, compact, built tight as wire, he would celebrate his thirtieth birthday the next day, but had the controlled stillness of someone long acquainted with danger. There was always a faint coiled tension in him, the kind that came from a lifetime of being underestimated – for his height, his looks, whatever people thought they saw. He dressed for invisibility – black T-shirt, dark jeans, no shine, no flash. The skin was pale, hair cropped hard against the skull. Eyes sharp and predatory. You could miss him in a crowd – until you couldn't. Until he moved.

He unlocked one of the units they used, a squat rectangle with corrugated shutters that could have been used for anything. This one was his: stripped bare, mats taped to the floor, a punch bag swinging from a steel hook, and a frame bolted into the concrete for pull-ups. In one corner a row of kettlebells sat scuffed and mismatched, their handles worn smooth. A climbing rope hung from a ceiling beam, frayed near the knot where his hands always gripped.

Kai moved straight into stretches, with the loose precision of someone who'd trained his body to be elastic. His routines were hybrids: movements stolen from Tai Chi, kicks sharpened from kickboxing, balances from gymnastics. He barely needed sleep, and last night had given him none. But fatigue was a concept for others. He knew how to burn it out.

The cut had gone clean. The blade had slipped between canvas and frame with barely a whisper.

The guard – well, that was something else. Stupid man, wrong place. But Kai knew he'd lingered longer than he should have, letting the moment stretch, telling himself it was necessary. But it wasn't. He'd wanted the grip, the tightening, the final slack. He'd waited for it. Savoured it. The darkness had worked on him in ways he couldn't control.

The Principal would not like it. He'd been told not

to kill again. The Prado job was meant to be spotless. Clean, quick, bloodless.

The previous killings hadn't shifted the balance the way they'd hoped; this was meant to be different. The Principal had been explicit about that, and he'd promised. He could already hear the voice when news of the guard reached them: disappointment first, then the cold edge. But forgiveness would come. It always did. After all, the asset was already delivered – secure in the locked safe, exactly as agreed. Enough to make the Spanish government dance when the time came. Enough to prove he wasn't just the protégé the Principal had shaped. He was the successor.

At least twenty-five million dollars' worth of leverage, rolled carefully and sealed inside a courier tube – a thing so ordinary it could have carried blueprints or posters. Now, it held a Caravaggio. A guard had died for it, and here it was disguised as nothing more than a delivery item, the kind that riders in Madrid wheeled around every day. The absurdity made Kai grin.

He checked his phone between stretches. Nothing yet on the news, no official statement. Just social media rumours of an 'incident' at the Prado. Bureaucrats always moved slower than blades.

He pictured Martelli waking up in his hotel suite, still drunk on rage from last night's match. The flowers and gifts all arrived during yesterday – he always got them. The rider had slipped the postcard in with them, as instructed. Once the news broke, Martelli would fully understand. They weren't just bleeding his team. They were taking him down. And Kai liked the symmetry of it – a man undone by something he never saw coming.

He bent low, palms flat to the floor, and chuckled.

The Falcós, too – they'd be scrambling by now, searching for escape routes before the Italians caught their scent. He almost wished he could watch them.

But the numbers mattered more. He paused, flicked open the accounts on his phone, watched the figures glow. Transfers moving, money cleaned. They hadn't just laundered last night's profits under everyone's noses. They were taking over the fixers and runners across Europe, using Kai's new encrypted code to broadcast the shift through every syndicate.

At least the Principal would be proud of that. The instructions had been simple enough: *Prove you're ready. Bring down the beast.* Well, he had. The old order had cracked, and the change in allegiance was already spreading – beyond Madrid, unstoppable.

He rolled his shoulders. The guard's face returned – the wet gurgle. He brushed it aside. He dropped into a one-armed plank, held it steady, body straight as a bar. Then the other side. Sweat beading. Muscles tight.

A low laugh slipped out, not at himself but at the thought of who'd be watching the news first – the ones who counted. By tonight, they'd understand.

He placed both his palms flat on the mat, body rising into a handstand, legs scissoring in silence. He held there, breath shallow. He smiled, his skull thudding with blood.

16

Elena

Sunday – from Atocha to Chamartín district.

Elena's train pulled into Atocha just before 11am. The concourse was littered with stragglers from last night's match, some still chanting, others slumped against the walls with their heads in their hands. She tossed her bag into the back of a taxi and told the driver she wanted the Hotel Eurobuilding, near the Bernabéu. Two police cars screamed past, sirens splitting the air. The driver muttered about the mayhem left over from last night, but Elena wasn't in the mood for small talk.

She gazed out the window, tracing the skyline – glass towers shoulder to shoulder with elegant old façades. The sun climbed higher, casting shadows across pavements already alive with Sunday noise.

The taxi eventually jerked to a halt just shy of some police barricades, caught up in the snarl of traffic choking the Chamartín district. The driver swore under his breath, gesturing at the chaos ahead – municipal trucks rumbling through to collect trash, a line of police vehicles still idling near the Bernabéu.

'*Lo siento*,' he said, his tone resigned. 'This is as far as I can get you.'

'No problem,' Elena said, fumbling for cash to pay the fare. She knew the Hotel Eurobuilding wasn't far – just two blocks away. 'I'll walk from here.'

As she stepped out of the cab with her bag, the noise and stench of the clean-up hit her. Stale beer and scorched firecrackers still hung in the air. Workers swept broken glass into piles; the scrape of their brooms cut through by the shrill blasts of a traffic cop's whistle. Chamartín, usually neat and businesslike, looked like the aftermath of a battlefield. Pavements strewn with beer cans and plastic cups, flags and scarves trampled into the gutter – most of them soaked in God knows what.

The colossal stadium loomed ahead, its iconic shell glinting in the sun while tourists posed for selfies outside. Elena hitched her bag higher on her shoulder and kept moving. Further on, the smell of churros and coffee drifted from a cafeteria's doorway, but she strode past and up towards the four-star hotel.

She'd arranged a meeting with Jaime Zamora, the Spanish football league's Director of Public Affairs and Institutional Relations. His remit included the league's anti-racism initiatives, so if anyone knew where the money had gone, it was him.

She'd emailed him twice – first with soft questions about the league's strategy against racism, then with sharper ones about budgets and results. Zamora hadn't replied to either. Instead, his PA offered her this Sunday noon slot, a placatory gesture at a hotel near the stadium, where Zamora had some corporate engagement that morning.

Elena had read that the Eurobuilding was always bustling on match weekends – a haunt for VIPs, sponsors' guests and visiting UEFA or FIFA delegates for international games played at the Bernabéu. Sleek cars with tinted windows lined the kerb, chauffeurs waiting just inside the lobby. Even after the chaos of last night, the hotel retained its air of exclusivity. Guests in suits with branded lanyards wheeled expensive luggage across the floor, while others slouched near the bar, nursing espressos or scrolling on their phones.

She knew vaguely what Zamora looked like but couldn't see any sign of him in the lobby. After a few minutes of aimless standing, she decided to find somewhere to sit in the lounge area, tucked to the side but still within sight of the lobby and the lifts. Flicking briefly through a glossy brochure, she learned that the hotel offered a state-of-the-art gym and spa, massage services, and even a padel tennis court. Its culinary options included a Michelin-starred restaurant and a 'renowned sushi bar'.

Perhaps Zamora was stuffing his face with maki or having a massage – maybe *both* – blissfully unconcerned about missing their appointment. She forced herself to wait, eyes flicking between the lift doors, the lobby, the bar. As the minutes dragged, her irritation deepened. Something wasn't right. The cynic in her – the part shaped by years of Spanish sexism – was already bracing for a no-show. She couldn't shake the sense she was wasting her time.

She took out her phone and fired off a terse email to both Zamora and his PA: *I'm here. Hotel lobby. I hope the meeting is still on.*

She then decided to call, but it clicked to voicemail. Ending it without leaving a message, she grabbed her bag and strode towards the reception desk.

'I'm waiting for someone,' she said, leaning against the counter. 'Jaime Zamora. He was supposed to meet me here this morning. Has he left a message?'

The receptionist, a young man in a crisp navy suit with a practised smile, tapped at his keyboard. 'Zamora,' he said, dragging out the name as though it might spark recognition. 'No, I don't see anything left under that name.' He glanced up, apologetically.

'Is he staying here?' Elena asked.

The receptionist's eyebrows lifted slightly. 'I'm sorry, but for privacy reasons we cannot provide information about our guests.'

Elena kept quiet.

'If you're waiting for someone, you're welcome to wait in the lobby, or if you'd like to leave a message, I can keep it at the desk in case they come by,' said the receptionist, offering the same neutral, polite smile that seemed glued to his face.

Elena stepped back from the desk. She checked her phone for any email response. There was nothing, other than a missed call from Benjamin – and that could certainly wait. She felt the heat rising in her cheeks from sheer frustration.

Zamora leaving her in the lurch was just typical – exactly the kind of indifference that seemed ingrained in the league's attitude towards racism. It was like being fobbed off again with that pre-season press release they'd issued about zero tolerance, when they'd promised a new 'task force', a major anti-discrimination campaign labelled *SOS Racismo,* and the multimillion-euro fund supposedly earmarked to eradicate hate from football. But where had that money gone?

She felt bitter just thinking about it. Whenever a player reported racist abuse from the terraces, verbal and even *monkey gestures* – *unbelievable* – the league's response was a shrug dressed up as PR. A statement. Oh, it was an 'isolated incident'. They did nothing that changed anything. Matches should have been stopped, clubs docked points, bans issued, arrests made. Instead, the 'isolated incidents' kept echoing through the stands, shrugged off as part of the game. And worse, as part of Spanish society. That was the real obscenity.

It burned deeper for her because she knew that indifference all too well. Taunts like 'gypsy bitch' were always waiting for her – whispered, spat or worse. She'd brushed them off, but they were always a reminder that no matter how good she was, she didn't belong in some people's eyes.

La Liga didn't get it. Maybe they didn't want to. It wasn't about slogans or task forces – it was about shutting down hatred in the moment, no matter how inconvenient. That kind of action took guts. And she was starting to think there wasn't a pair of *cojones* in the whole damn league. If Zamora thought he could stand her up to dodge the hard questions, he had no idea who he was dealing with. She wasn't giving up – on this story, or on him.

As she turned to leave, a flicker of movement caught her eye. A delivery rider stepped from the lift; a slight figure dwarfed by the oversized yellow box on his back. His face was half-hidden – scarf, dark glasses, cap pulled low. Early June in Madrid wasn't scarf weather, and in the bright sunlight slanting across the lobby, he looked out of place. Wrong. Menacing.

He moved with sharp, purposeful strides, crossing the lobby as if he belonged, gliding past the reception desk like a shadow. No one stopped him, no one questioned him, and that also felt strange. The hotel didn't scream 'takeout'. It had Michelin stars, a sushi bar, VIP lounges. Who the hell ordered delivery here? And why had they let him up to a room?

The rider slipped through the revolving doors. On impulse, Elena followed. Outside, he crouched by the kerb, beside his bike. She thought he was securing the box. Instead, he reached into it, his movements precise.

He pulled something out. Small, rectangular,

wrapped in plain brown paper. Nothing that looked like food. He held it for a beat, gloved hands weighing it, testing it, too deliberate to be casual. Then he slipped the package into his jacket, straightened, and carefully secured the yellow box to the bike.

Elena watched, uneasy. Maybe it was the way he moved – methodical, controlled, almost mechanical.

He climbed onto the bike but didn't ride off. He paused at the kerb, head tilting like he was listening. A faint blink of blue light at his ear – Bluetooth, maybe, or something else. Then, slowly, he turned, scanning the hotel entrance.

Their eyes met.

Most of his face was hidden, but not his gaze. Dark, piercing, expressionless. It wasn't the fleeting glance of someone checking their surroundings – it was a stare. Cold, deliberate, like he was memorising her face.

Her instincts screamed to look away, but she couldn't. Her heart thudded until he finally broke the connection, turned his head and pedalled off into the sluggish stream of traffic.

She glanced back at the revolving doors, half-expecting someone – a guest, an employee – to come out in search of him. No one did.

She told herself to move on, to focus on her next meetings, the calls, the report. But the stare stayed with her: masked, hard, calculating. Burned into memory.

17

Benjamin - Ignacio Lázaro

Sunday – Hotel Ritz.

'Did you just say it was cut from its frame?' Benjamin asked, leaning forward to try and catch everything Ignacio was saying.

'I did.'

Benjamin's immediate thought, therefore, was that in addition to killing an innocent guard, the scumbag thief – the *murderer* – had no respect for art. Cutting a painting was immoral, and a savvy trafficker or extortionist would have never ordered it to be cut from its frame – although he kept that to himself.

'I can only imagine it would have been too difficult to remove the frame from the wall,' Ignacio added.

'Too difficult to remove a frame from the wall, but not difficult to break into the museum and murder someone.' Benjamin left the comment hanging there.

'Yes, well … they're obviously looking at how he got in,' Ignacio muttered. 'It was directly above the courtyard cafeteria, and I was told that the poor guard had this throat slit.'

Benjamin kept quiet. Best not to picture the guard's throat – blood had always been his undoing, the one thing that could drop him cold, and it wasn't a good look. A ridiculous flaw, one he despised, but no bravado could hide it if it happened. Better to shove it aside and stick to safer ground: the painting. Someone had cut a Caravaggio out of its frame. That, at least, he could be angry about. *That* made his own blood boil.

Cut from its frame …

He could picture a scalpel tearing along the edge of the masterpiece, paint flakes spraying, canvas threads popping, ripping it from its stretcher and frame. Precious paintwork cracking and chipping as it was rolled up. Damaged. Scarred. The *bastards*. And *murderers*, too. It could have been personal, of course. Someone with a vendetta against the museum, or the guard, or against that particular painting.

'Did the guard have any issues with other staff?' he asked Ignacio.

'None whatsoever. According to –'

'Have you contacted the Vienna and Rome museums?'

'What for?'

'Well, you know,' Benjamin said, although he

wondered if Ignacio *did* know. 'Caravaggio painted two other versions of *David and Goliath* –'

'Yes, I know –'

'So, they should be made aware of what's happened here. As they could be targeted, too, by some wacko, copycat extremist with – *God knows, I don't know* – militant views about Middle Eastern geopolitics, perhaps – you know, some fanatic desecrating a biblical vision of divine intervention in battle because it –'

'What are you saying?'

'What?' Benjamin said.

'What are you saying?'

'What am I saying?'

'Yes, what are you saying?'

'What I'm *saying*,' Benjamin said, 'is that you should at least let the Vienna and Rome museums know, in order to be wary of a similar attack.'

'Yes, we should, but it's not an *attack*. This painting has been stolen.'

Benjamin stared at him in silence. He didn't want to patronise Ignacio, but paintings were never stolen out of sheer greed, as if in some Hollywood heist by an eccentric billionaire, or to hang in a Bond villain's bunker in the Bavarian Alps – and let alone damaged in the process. There was always another connection: drugs, weapons, ransom collateral, prostitution, money laundering, human trafficking or whatever else crawled through the cracks of the racketeers' gangland.

But sliced from its frame, the painting was never going to be easily bartered back to the Prado or the

Spanish state. He knew they wouldn't cough up any ransom cash … not officially, anyway. There were always other envelopes for that.

He thought again about it being an attack. Pure vandalism was the vogue these days, but why wait until the dead of night to rip the canvas from the wall? A public spectacle would have made a far stronger state-ment – like the cretins who glued themselves to Goya's *Las Majas*, as if that ever saved the planet. But if someone had wanted one of Caravaggio's three versions of *David and Goliath*, then surely the museums in Vienna or Rome would have been easier targets. But maybe not. Or rather, *no – clearly not.*

'Benjamin?' Ignacio was saying.

Benjamin's mind was still wandering. When he'd heard about the Prado incident, curiosity had dragged him here, but getting involved? That was another thing entirely. Helping Ignacio would mean taking on yet another problem, and unless there was something in it for him, he wasn't exactly eager to sign up for more unpaid trouble. He already had a full circus going on – the divorce-from-hell with lawyers bleeding him dry, someone stalking his daughter, his line of work dangerously exposed … and now he was holed up in an illegal Airbnb with no hot water, towels or WiFi, hoping to hook up with a reluctant Elena, as if she held the last piece of whatever the hell he used to be.

Besides, he already had an assignment: a restitution case for the double-barrelled jolly Duncan at the

British Embassy. But it wasn't well paid, and he certainly needed an injection of cash …

'I'm not sure what you want from me,' Benjamin said finally, while also checking his phone.

'Your help,' Ignacio said, bluntly.

'With what, exactly?'

'Finding the painting. Your reputation is –'

'Slightly in tatters,' Benjamin cut in, 'after the Barcelona mess.'

'Not at all.'

There was a pause.

'Your police won't want me involved,' Benjamin said, checking his phone again.

'They won't, no,' Ignacio agreed. 'Not homicide, anyway. But on behalf of the culture ministry, you could liaise with the heritage brigade. You said you've worked with them before. This has caught us off guard. The **BPH** chief is on his way back from an archaeological site in Extremadura right now, and they're stretched thin with looting cases.'

Benjamin knew exactly what Ignacio meant by *liaise.*

Despite his undercover work being blown in Barcelona, he still had contacts in the international underworld of stolen and forged art that Spain's heritage unit couldn't begin to imagine – informants who never returned calls from ministries or spoke directly to cops. His job had always been to step in where the official channels couldn't, or *wouldn't,* go. Doing the things that institutions weren't built for.

Whatever happened at the Prado still struck him as a straightforward attack, but whether the canvas was still in the country or halfway to Dubai or Mexico, he could probably get a line on it. Maybe even negotiate its return. And unlike the Spanish police, he didn't have to worry about warrants, red tape, or a judge's signature to go looking. No protocols … or any ethics at all, strictly speaking.

They wouldn't call it a ransom. They never did. It would be a *reward for information leading to recovery*, or some other term to make everyone feel less dirty. He needed the money. That part wasn't in question. But he also needed fewer enemies, quieter nights, and some proof that whoever was watching his daughter had nothing to do with the people he'd crossed before. Still, Ignacio's request felt clean. Low risk. At least compared to the rest of his life.

'Listen,' Ignacio said, more urgently. 'We don't have much time. They'll be tightening the circle around this thing. I want you to help, but if *you* want to help, we'll need to move fast. I'd like to put you together with Alfonso García at the BPH, as soon as he's back in Madrid. There has to be an international angle to this – no Spaniard would target the Prado without help.' He checked his watch, exhaled sharply, and then he finally said it. 'We can agree a fee, in addition to a finder's commission if your own work leads us to recovering the painting.'

A moment passed.

'What figure are you proposing?' Benjamin asked.

18

Borja Falcó

Sunday – El Viso neighbourhood.

Earlier, a cab that Borja had rushed to grab in Malasaña dropped him off near the dolphin fountains in the Plaza de la República, a few streets down from the office. He didn't want the driver remembering his face or destination. As he got out, he caught his own reflection in the vehicle's windows – shirt untucked beneath last night's crumpled suit, hair a mess, eyes bloodshot. A dark smear of something – maybe wine, maybe blood – had dried at the cuff of his shirt. Pouring with sweat, he looked like someone who'd just ruined his life. Maybe he had.

Get to the office first and grab all the cash.

Then the apartment for the passport. Then go.

He moved quickly, head down, his collar still

holding a trace of someone else's perfume – someone he still couldn't remember.

The sun was already warming the elegant façades in the neighbourhood of El Viso. Leafy and deceptively calm, its privilege was so entrenched it didn't need to be seen. Residential, not flashy, this enclave of Madrid breathed money – old, institutional, inherited, and some of it newer, dirtier, laundered just enough to pass. Papá's money, for example.

Aside from the soft tread of a dog-walker in tennis whites, the streets were hushed, buttoned-up – as if the whole neighbourhood was still sleeping off some private dinner behind high gates, tucked between embassies and private schools. A dinner Borja would never be invited to again; it was a world he had only ever borrowed. Every house looked ready to close ranks against him, and he couldn't shake the sense that eyes were on him from every window. *Judging him.*

Some of El Viso's villas had been converted into premium offices – all frosted glass and brushed steel, pretending to be low-key. Like the one he occupied with Innovation Sports, SL. Offices built for people like him – or at least people he was supposed to be.

Papá had chosen the location for its discretion.

'The right kind of neighbours,' he'd said. 'Close to the Bernabéu, near enough to the Castellana to matter, but tucked far enough away not to attract attention.'

He'd been right. It was a short walk to Chamartín's business belt, and not far from the Castellana's midpoint, where the banks, law firms and polished boardrooms began. Borja's office had been positioned just so – a place to play at legitimacy. But now it felt like a showroom for a life he'd never really owned.

By the time he'd reached the building, his shirt and suit jacket stuck to his back. The keypad flickered in the morning sunlight. For a second, he'd hesitated. Would the code still work? Had someone already moved against him? He wiped his palm against his trousers and pressed the numbers. The front door clicked open.

He hurried past the unstaffed concierge desk and down the hallway that led to his office suites.

Then he saw her.

A cleaner. Latin American maybe, small-framed, rubber gloves, plastic bucket and a trolley blocking the corridor. She glanced up from a mop and gave him a nod. No smile, no warmth, just a quick scan of his face, weighing him up.

Borja paused. He'd never seen cleaners here before. But then he'd never been here at the weekend. Normally, at this hour on a Sunday, he'd be crawling into bed – or someone's bed – not fleeing his own life.

'Perdona,' he muttered, brushing past her.

Further down the corridor and out of view, he had to jiggle the key twice before the door opened.

Inside, the lights flickered on automatically as he locked the door behind him. The plants were fake; the Italian sofa still looked showroom-new; the art on the walls still striving to give the pretence of legitimacy. The place hadn't changed, but everything else had.

He'd moved fast through the outer office, the one meant for staff – though no one ever stayed long – and into his private corner suite. He went to each window and quickly twisted the Venetian blinds shut.

He knew where the stash was. In the cabinet under the tax files no one ever checked – not even the accountant papá paid to keep up appearances. He'd placed all the bundles there himself, weeks ago, with sweaty hands and a sense of pride. His hands shook again – but for different reasons.

It was all there.

Bricks of cash. Some still stacked in bank-branded packs, others messily tied with rubber-bands, grubby at the corners. Five-hundred-euro notes, mostly. Not twenty grand. Not fifty. He hadn't counted it, but it had to be over two hundred grand. Probably closer to three. Enough for now.

He'd dropped to his knees and yanked out an old Adidas gym bag from under the desk. Never used. Still had the tag. He unzipped it and began jamming the bundles of cash inside.

It was *his* money, not papá's. It was money they'd given him – but it hadn't come from any uptight, po-faced Italians. Borja had told himself it was a way of expanding the business – opening new doors with new associates. *His* kind of people; people who knew how to party. This new venture would take Innovation Sports global, he believed. Asia. The Gulf. Maybe even Saudi. It was the future.

The first envelope had come after a party in Marbella – a party that wasn't really a party. More like a trap. Borja hadn't needed to set it up – he'd just needed to bring the UEFA contact there. Drunk, high, horny, whatever. The fixers did the rest.

Borja never knew what they'd filmed the UEFA guy doing – or who with. A trans sex worker, maybe. Someone underage. Maybe both. He hadn't asked. He didn't need to know. He'd just been told it was enough to get the ball rolling.

They'd said that wire transfers would be coming next. Millions, in due course, if he continued to help them. They would come directly to his private account, not to the account that his father still controlled, the one shown to their auditors, or the ministry officials who signed off on the commissions and tax exemptions. Borja would receive the transfers from Dubai, Hong Kong, the Caymans or wherever, they'd said. No more bundles in fat brown Jiffy bags. All he had to do was occasionally help, then wait. And stay quiet.

The Adidas bag full of cash wouldn't close. He'd sat on it, forcing the zip shut, cursing under his breath. One step done. Next: to grab the passport from his apartment. If he was fast, he could be out of Spain within a couple of hours. He could run the new venture from anywhere.

He stood, shouldered the bag, and stepped out into

the corridor. It was empty. No cleaner. No mop. No plastic bucket.

Outside, he spotted a taxi cruising slowly towards the junction and raised a hand. It didn't stop. He cursed, wiped his forehead with a sleeve. Another cab appeared, this one empty, and pulled over without hesitation. Borja slid inside without looking back.

Across the street, the woman with the bucket was already tapping her phone. Her message was simple, pre-agreed, no need for extras.

He's just left. Bag in hand.

In a black SUV further down the street, Enzo — a man with pocked skin and a silver chain around his fat neck — locked eyes with the driver. No words. He started the engine.

'Rats are easier to follow when they think they've got space,' Martelli had told them.

They'd let the pig-ignorant Borja scoop up whatever scraps from his office he thought might save him — papers, files, whatever — but they knew where he'd have to show up eventually.

The flat. The passport. That's where others would be waiting. It's where the real fun would begin.

Martelli's instructions had been very clear. Find the son first. Later, let the father watch.

19

The Prado

Sunday – Prado Museum.

The polished boardroom table gleamed under the soft light. Inspector Jefe Félix Barroso sat with his hands clasped, eyes fixed somewhere between the museum director's furrowed brow and the judge's neatly ordered notes. At the far end sat the head of security, beside some culture ministry bureaucrat who'd slipped in late. Barroso had two of his senior UDEV homicide agents at his side.

The museum director was speaking about 'cultural heritage' and 'a crime against all of Spain', but Barroso could only muster a nod, the words barely landing. His mind kept pulling him back towards the scene he'd just left in the gallery below.

The body. The head almost severed. Brutal, deliberate – a style he recognised too well. Except he hadn't known it was coming.

That's what sent the real chill down his spine. The fact that he hadn't known.

Every other time he'd been warned, paid, kept in the loop. In parks, hotel rooms, garages – he'd known in advance. The only exception was months ago, when a severed head turned up in a plastic bag outside the Italian Embassy. That had rattled him, but he'd told himself it was a one-off, a message not meant for him.

Italians, always Italians. Part of the game, even though it had all gone too far. But this? This was different. A Spanish national. A museum guard, a *grandfather* on the verge of retirement.

This time there'd been nothing. No call. No envelope. Just the scene waiting for him like everyone else.

If it *was* them, they'd moved without him. After months of silence, it had widened into something colder – he wasn't part of the game anymore. And after all the promises whispered in exchange for his help. A cut of the spoils once the Italians were squeezed out. Instead, here he was, left in the dark – being ignored.

Right now, he had to ensure there was nothing that could connect his past cooperation to whatever had happened here. Everything – every detail of the investigation, every scrap of evidence – had to go through him first. He had to steer this in the right direction, bury what needed burying, and redirect attention elsewhere.

No one could start asking the wrong questions.

No one could get in his way.

The voice in the boardroom droned on, but Barroso's thoughts snagged elsewhere – another night, another room thick with smoke. A hand sliding an envelope across the table. A voice promising revenge for his son. He shoved the memory down before it could take root. Not now.

'Inspector Jefe?'

The voice yanked Barroso back to the present. He shifted in his chair, noticing the expectant glances directed at him.

'I'm sorry?'

'Have you read the draft of the press statement?' asked Virginia Guzmán, the museum director.

Barroso rubbed his thumb against the faint ridge of scar tissue on his palm – a nervous habit that had settled in over the years. He then picked up the sheet of paper that had been placed in front of him and scanned the short text. It was the same bland phrasing he'd seen a hundred times before.

'… regrets to confirm the death of a night surveillance guard during an incident in the early hours of this morning … the police are treating it as a homicide … our thoughts and prayers are with the family at this very difficult time …'

'As we have agreed,' Guzmán was now saying, 'this will be issued immediately by the ministry. A second statement should be issued later today regarding the break-in and theft of the painting, but that is a subject that now requires much further discussion ...'

Barroso's eyes drifted back across the table before settling on her.

He didn't think she would cause him any problems. She was an academic, though. A left-wing academic. The worst kind. Only in her forties, he guessed, but with cropped grey hair worn like a badge of intellectual superiority. No effort to dye it. As if letting yourself go naturally grey somehow made you a philosopher. The designer spectacles didn't help. They were black, thick-rimmed monstrosities that she probably thought made her look even more, what ... *progressive?* He'd glimpsed her flat, hefty boots when they'd all entered the meeting room. Some women had a way of making flat shoes look elegant. This one made them look like orthopaedic equipment. Lesbian? Probably. Or simply one of those feminists who thought femininity was beneath them. The ones who wrote opinion pieces about the male gaze while sipping vermouth with their equally miserable friends in Chueca bars, mostly wearing purple.

If she *did* cause him any problems, he'd dig deep into her lefty lifestyle and pin something on the bitch. Besides, the break-in and butchery had happened on *her* watch. The media could rip her to shreds, if necessary – and that would save him a job.

'We must start with the information we already have from your initial investigation ...' she was saying.

Her voice had that dry, brittle texture of someone

used to delivering lectures to half-empty auditoriums, pondered Barroso. How was she even appointed to her role? Years in the arts sector, moving from committee to committee with the same dreary certainty as a guided museum tour, then handpicked by the minister of culture at the time, probably because they went to the same university. The type who believed art could fix society. Now here she was, sitting across from him, earnestly discussing how best to explain a murder. She had no idea who or what she was dealing with.

'We?' he said.

There was a silence.

'You said *we*,' he repeated, making his resentment very clear. 'What do you mean by *we*?'

His eyes shifted briefly from the museum director to the judge, Adriana Varela, sitting beside her. The difference between them was almost comical.

He'd worked on previous cases that Varela had been assigned to in the past, and he'd had no problems with her. The lace trim of her blouse stretched taut across her cleavage as she now moved in her chair. Her heels – sharp, patent stilettos – clicked against the marble floor as she adjusted her posture. Deliberate? It certainly drew his attention to them for a second too long. His eyes then flicked upwards to find her holding his gaze. Another second. Two. Then there was the faintest tilt of her head. *Does she know something?* he wondered. *Stop being paranoid.*

'What I mean is that we are all in this together,' Guzmán was saying. 'This has to be a team effort –'

'This is a police investigation,' Barroso said, cutting her off, and as his gaze fell away from the judge.

'Of course, of course,' Guzmán said, 'but there are things we need to discuss.'

'This is a police investigation,' Barroso repeated.

The director's cheeks flushed pink. She adjusted her oversized designer glasses, scribbled a note with brisk irritation, then looked up. 'I understand this is a tragic homicide,' she said, 'but it is also a theft – and of one of the museum's most valuable works of art.'

Barroso remained silent, hoping that he was giving her enough rope to hang herself. Meanwhile, the bureaucrat from the culture ministry at the far end of the table had started to pass an image of the painting around to each person in attendance.

'The early 17th century Italian masterpiece that was cut from its frame and stolen from the museum –' Guzmán started.

Italian, clocked Barroso.

'– is Caravaggio's *David and Goliath*.'

Italian.

A UDEV agent had mentioned the missing painting in the gallery just moments earlier, but for the inspector – who had no interest in art whatsoever – the Italian connection hadn't registered at all.

'This *Caravaggio* painting,' he said. 'Who owns it?'

He caught Guzmán flicking her eyes towards the man from the culture ministry, a faint smirk tugging at the corner of her mouth, as if suppressing either amusement or mild disbelief at what she'd just been asked. There was a shared look between them, almost mocking. Heat crawled up Barroso's neck. His fingers curled slightly against the table. Whatever patience he had left was wearing thin.

'It is, of course, part of the royal collection, first listed in an inventory of the Buen Retiro Palace in Madrid in 1794,' Guzmán said. 'It is oil on canvas measuring a hundred and ten centimetres in height and ninety-one in width —'

'What's it worth?' Barroso asked.

'There are two other similar and later versions of the same theme by Caravaggio,' she continued, ignoring him. 'One is in the Kunsthistorisches Museum in Vienna, and the other is in the Galleria Borghese in Rome. Both were painted around 1605, certainly not before. *Our* painting, however, was finished during 1600, and probably started in 1599 —'

'What is it worth?' Barroso asked again.

'Inspector —' started the judge.

'I need to know,' Barroso cut in, turning briefly towards her, before adding: 'Your honour.'

The culture ministry bureaucrat then joined the conversation without invitation, adjusting his wire-framed glasses. His suit was crisp but unremarkable — department-store standard, the kind chosen more for durability than style.

Barroso hadn't missed the way he'd slipped in late with no apology, as if the meeting could wait for him. That alone had riled him. Since then, the man had kept glancing at his phone, tapping out a message before the meeting began, and then checking it at least twice more, brow creased. Waiting on something, Barroso guessed. Something he thought mattered more than the inspector's presence in the room.

'Well,' the bureaucrat said, his voice measured, 'when we talk about the painting's value, we're dealing with abstract figures. In a legitimate market, a Caravaggio like this might command a hundred and fifty million euros or more. But this painting could never be sold on legitimately –'

'*Legitimately*,' Barroso scoffed, under his breath. His sneer was automatic, but the figure – a hundred and fifty million or more – lingered. If that kind of money was in play, then maybe there was a new opportunity for him to take some kind of a cut.

'So, if the ability to sell the stolen work is restricted,' the bureaucrat continued, 'it might be that it will be held as collateral or as a commodity for bartering something else, *or*, of course, to ransom back to us …'

He hesitated before meeting Barroso's gaze.

'In other words,' he said finally, 'it's only *worth* something if someone else is able and willing to ignore all the alarms and trade it in for something else.'

He spoke with the assured, almost rehearsed clarity of someone accustomed to explaining such concepts to people who didn't quite grasp them. Risk assessors, lawyers, accountants. Barroso felt the slight burn of being patronised. It wasn't just the words – it was the delivery. The feeling of being talked down to. That trace of superiority and condescension that came so easily to men like this: privileged, comfortable back-grounds, good schools, family weekends with tennis courts and swimming pools. The kind of man who'd never had to scrape through life or make ugly choices to survive. He disliked him already. *Intensely.*

'Sorry, I didn't catch your name earlier,' Barroso said, with a thin smile.

'Ignacio,' came the reply. 'Ignacio Lázaro. I'm the culture ministry's deputy head of state acquisitions and guarantee service.'

'Guarantee service …' Barroso said. 'What is that, exactly?'

'The state's guarantee service, Inspector,' Ignacio said, 'is when Spain provides a public insurance to works of art lent *to*, or being lent *from*, other institutions to be exhibited in venues owned by the Spanish state – although it's just one element in the overall insurance of those works –'

'*Wait*,' Barroso cut in. 'This Caravaggio is part of the royal collection, we've just been told. And so it is *owned* by the state, that *owns* the Prado. It wasn't on loan, was it?'

'Correct.'

'So, are you also saying it's not insured?'

'It's slightly more complicated than that –'

'Why don't you just keep it simple and answer me?'

Ignacio took a deep breath.

'It is not covered by the state's guarantee service, no,' he said. 'But when we're talking about its value, it's an abstract figure, as I explained earlier –'

'I know what you explained earlier,' Barroso snapped. He started to scratch the ridge of scar tissue on his palm again.

What the hell had they done? Why were they now targeting priceless art owned by the Spanish state? Because it was Italian?

Judge Adriana Varela finally broke the awkward silence, which was probably just as well. Barroso had had enough of the Ignacio creep, who he'd just watched check his phone again. Whatever message he was waiting for, it wasn't boredom. It was something else. Something Barroso would need to stay on top of.

'To continue this meeting,' Varela said, 'we are dealing with a brutal homicide and the theft of cultural property of incalculable value. And make no mistake – one can't be separated from the other ...'

Barroso could sense what was coming next, but he wasn't about to let it happen. Crimes of cultural heritage were primarily investigated by the BPH – the Brigada de Patrimonio Histórico – a much smaller team of the judicial police, working alongside his UDEV unit.

The BPH had already been called – of course they had. Procedure. The museum, the culture ministry, maybe even Ignacio himself, the little shit, had seen to that before the blood was dry. Barroso had been told that the unit's head, Alfonso García, was already on his way back from some archaeological site in Extremadura to 'assist with the Prado case'.

He almost snorted. The BPH – a slow-moving, paper-shuffling relic of a division. Let them write their reports and follow protocols. He wasn't about to let a squad of detective librarians tell him how to run a case – or risk them sniffing too close to the wrong things. He straightened, cutting off the next inevitable question.

'Yes, BPH is involved,' he said, his tone deliberately measured. 'I've already spoken to them.' It wasn't true, but it would be. On his terms. 'They've begun their process. And we're coordinating, of course.'

He let that hang for a second, letting his ownership of the case settle in the room. Then, with just enough weight, just enough control, he added: 'But this is first and foremost a murder inquiry. That puts the UDEV in control of the operation.'

A statement, not a debate. No room for argument. No room for interference.

He was pleased to see judge Varela nodding. She clearly wanted things to be kept as simple as possible, as in previous cases. Ignacio Lázaro and Virginia Guzmán, however, had exchanged another wary glance.

'I agree that the BPH has limited resources ...' Ignacio started. 'That's why we feel that we also need outside help.'

'Outside help?' Barroso said, with a sneer. He glanced at the two senior UDEV agents sitting beside him, who both raised their eyebrows. 'Are you suggesting my men are incapable?'

'We're not suggesting that at all,' Guzmán said.

'Obviously, recovering the painting is crucial,' Ignacio said, adjusting his cuffs. 'Our concern is that it might already be on its way out of the country. So, given the circumstances, any outside help –'

'*Outside help?*' Barroso snapped. 'You said it again.' He leaned back, arms folded, eyes cold. 'What do you think happens next?'

Silence. Ignacio shifted, glancing at the director.

'This case is already on the police wires,' Barroso said. 'On the *system*. Every cop from here to fucking Helsinki will know your precious painting has been snatched. And guess what? If it pops up somewhere on the radars of Europol or Interpol, then they'll flag it. *If* they care …'

He caught it again – that *look* – the one Ignacio just flicked at the museum director. A slight lift of the brow. A shared moment of quiet amusement. A *smirk*.

The museum director cleared her throat. 'Inspector Jefe, you must understand –' she started, but that was as far as she got.

Barroso slammed his palm flat against the table – hard. The sound echoed through the room, silencing them instantly. He leaned forward, his voice lowering to something far more dangerous.

'Don't *ever* tell me what I must do or must understand,' he said.

Guzmán looked towards the judge for some support, but it wasn't forthcoming.

'I'll tell *you* what I understand,' Barroso continued, 'and it's that someone let a killer enter the Prado like they owned the place. There was clearly *inside help*. Which means that right now, every single employee of this museum is a possible suspect … as is anyone with close links to the museum.' His eyes shifted briefly towards Ignacio, and then back to the director.

'That includes your management team, curators, admin, IT, your cleaners, your tour guides, retail staff, visitor services and *especially* those overseeing the café and restaurant operations.' He paused, eyeing the notes that his **UDEV** agents had shared with him. 'As we already know, the killer entered and left the museum via a glass door above the cafeteria in the courtyard alongside the Jerónimos entrance. We're already examining the **HR** records of all your catering staff, but that's just the start …'

He now turned, his gaze drilling into the museum's head of security, who sat beside Ignacio at the end of the table. He had remained silent in the meeting until now.

The man looked like he belonged on a different side of the law – thick neck, close-cropped hair, and a face that had encountered some violence. Barroso had pegged him as ex-police or ex-army. Somewhere in all his training, he'd clearly learnt to speak only when spoken to, which the inspector might normally have admired.

'And you?' Barroso said. 'You've got nothing to say? Not a word? Maybe because you're still trying to figure out how your security amounted to absolute shit?'

The man didn't flinch.

'You'll stay in this room with my men,' continued

Barroso. 'They've got plenty of questions. Another team is upstairs, working through your night staff.'

The head of security gave a slight nod, but still said nothing. There was something about the way the man held himself that unsettled Barroso. He might become a problem – not someone to be brushed aside easily – but he let it rest for now.

A knock at the door cut through the tense silence. One of Barroso's agents moved to open it without waiting for his signal.

The large, dishevelled frame of Detective Pilar Castro filled the doorway – as stone-faced as ever in her bulky brown anorak. She was flanked by two other detectives, both young, with the hard-edged look of men who'd seen too much, too soon. Behind them, a forensic officer stood with a slim black case in hand. None of them spoke. They just stood there, lined up in silence, waiting.

Barroso glanced at his watch. 'Yes, I'll now join you for the debrief,' he said, gazing up at them, his voice clipped. 'Let me just finish here.'

The newcomers now lingered inside the meeting room, spreading along the wall like an extension of Barroso's authority. Watching and listening – their silent presence only adding to the pressure bearing down on the room. The mood had shifted, and the inspector could feel it. The message was clear – his grip on the investigation was absolute. The museum's director, the security chief and ministry bureaucrat were now sitting a little straighter, as if the sheer number of police pressing in around them made the gravity of the situation harder to ignore.

'This investigation is under a *secreto de sumario*, by order of the judge,' he said, his eyes flicking to Varela — part formality, part courtesy. She nodded. 'If you don't understand what that means, it's a gag order to prevent the public or media from accessing or publishing crucial information related to the case.'

He let that sit.

'We're doing it to avoid tipping off any suspects, and to prevent the spread of misinformation that could interfere with the investigation,' he continued. 'We'll release details when *we* think it is necessary, and it will remain in place for as long as the judge believes it necessary to protect the investigation … am I right?'

Judge Varela nodded again.

'We won't authorise any statement about the painting for at least twenty-four hours,' Barroso went on. 'We don't want to give the thieves and killers any kudos, or confirm they've taken something of value.'

Ignacio looked as if he was about to protest, but Barroso didn't give him the chance.

'As for any statement after twenty-four hours,' he said, 'I want to see it first. Every word.' His voice lowered, thick with loathing. 'But let me give you some advice. The less said, the better. No numbers. No talk of value. No promises of any reward. We don't want every parasite with a fake tip wasting our resources.'

Silence again.

'I'd brace yourselves,' Barroso said, his gaze drifting pointedly between the museum director and the ministry bureaucrat. 'When this goes public, the outrage won't just be aimed at the bastard who slit your guard's throat. Or the thief who walked out with a national treasure.'

Guzmán shifted uneasily. Even Ignacio, for all his polished arrogance, seemed a little paler.

Barroso leaned back, enjoying the moment. 'Remind me,' he said, 'how long did it take for the Louvre director to offer her resignation after their heist? And the French culture minister? Two days?' He paused. 'And theirs didn't even include a homicide.'

Guzmán and Ignacio stared at the table.

'The outrage is going to fall on you,' Barroso went on, his voice colder. 'For your failures. For your incompetence. For letting it happen on your watch.' He gave another thin, mirthless smile. 'People love someone to blame.'

He tilted his head towards the newcomers standing along the wall, then back to the table. 'From this point on, we'll need full access to the museum's telecoms – internal and external,' he said. His tone was matter of fact, but the implication wasn't lost on anyone in the room. 'If there's any contact at all from the people who have your painting, we'll be the first to know.'

He turned slightly towards the judge. A brief, wordless moment passed between them. He knew she'd authorise it – she'd have no choice.

The tension had curdled, but no one dared speak. Barroso shoved back his chair and rose to his feet.

'This museum is a crime scene and will remain closed until we give the order that it can re-open,' he said, looking directly at Guzmán. 'You and your staff must cooperate with all police requests.'

As he joined the others now waiting for him at the doorway, he gazed back across the room, at the museum director, the judge, the head of security still holding his ground, and finally Ignacio, who was checking his phone again. Barroso beckoned over one of his UDEV agents for a quiet word.

'Get someone to keep tabs on the creep from the ministry,' he murmured. 'I don't trust him.'

The agent gave a subtle nod.

'We have a killer to find,' Barroso said, striding out the door, the newcomers falling into step behind him.

Beneath the surface, Barroso's mind churned. If whatever had happened here tied back to the people he'd previously covered for, the ones who had him by the throat – he needed to get ahead of it. And if someone out there was getting ideas about talking, he had to find them and shut them up. Fast.

On top of that, he needed to know where he stood. They'd promised him a share once the Italians were cut out. If they thought they could edge him aside, they were wrong. One way or another, he'd collect what was owed.

20

Elena

Sunday – Chamartín district.

Elena pressed her phone to her ear with one hand and shaded her eyes with the other. The Madrid sun was already stabbing down, sharp and relentless. Her feet ached. All she wanted was some straight answers.

The call rang twice.

'*Sí?*' said the football agent. Background noise – traffic, clinking glasses – suggested he was having brunch or whatever on some terrace.

'*Hola*, Carlos,' she said. 'You were supposed to confirm a venue for the meeting with your client – at noon, remember?'

A short silence, then a laugh. Dry, dismissive.

Her stomach turned. 'Is there a problem?'

'He's not doing it. Not today. Not tomorrow. Not next week.'

'What are you talking about? This was confirmed. You said he was willing to meet. I came all the way from Girona for this –'

'He changed his mind.'

Elena paced in a tight circle on the pavement, fighting the rising heat in her face. *Carlos*. She'd known him a couple of years. Nobody ever quite knew where his money came from: transfer commissions, sponsorship side deals, a few favours traded in back rooms. Connections in the upper tiers of Spanish football, yes – but everything around him felt a shade too slick, too murky. Good contacts, zero trust. She should have seen it coming.

'*No*,' she snapped. 'You changed it for him. You're afraid he'll say something that actually matters. Something you can't spin. What's the real reason – did the club tell you to shut it down?'

Another chuckle, this time lower, more calculated. 'You know what your problem is, Elena? You think anyone still cares about this story.'

Her fingers tightened around the phone.

Carlos continued, his voice full of professional arrogance. 'He said what he had to say back then. Made his little statement, got his headlines, ticked the boxes. You think dragging it back up now is going to change anything? No one's listening.'

'I'm listening,' she fired back. 'I'm writing. I *care*. And if he actually spoke honestly – really spoke – it could make a difference. To kids. To clubs. To players too scared to open their mouths.'

'That's sweet. It really is.' A beat. 'But let me explain how the world works. People don't want truth. They want distraction. They want goals, gossip – and the racism tucked out of view so everyone can clap and move on. That's the machine you're kicking at.'

'I'm not kicking – I'm reporting.'

'Elena, it's a crowded subject. The real rot tends to hide beneath the headlines.'

She kept quiet.

'I've said it before,' Carlos continued, 'you're shouting into a hurricane with this story. You want to be useful? Dig into the rot that actually runs the game – UEFA, FIFA, the CSD, envelopes stuffed with cash. I mean, *real* shit. Not just chants from the stands. Not these woke panic pieces that get two likes and a pull-quote from Amnesty.'

Her voice went low. 'Did you just call racism a woke issue?' He didn't answer. 'I'm meeting with the CSD tomorrow,' she said.

'Good.'

'And don't you dare lecture me about what's real, when your client – your friend – was the one who'd said he feared for his life after that match. When they threw banana skins at him. When he got death threats.'

'That was two years ago, Elena. He's moved on. He has a life. A business. A wife who doesn't want him dragged back into the press cycle. And frankly, I don't want to deal with it either. So – enough.'

She stopped walking. 'I need this story,' she said, barely above a whisper.

'Write something else,' Carlos said. 'Seriously, Elena, take my advice. There are some major stories out there. Someone should dig into them. Sex trafficking in women's football, for example …'

'What do you mean?'

A silence. Then the agent's tone shifted. Smoother, oiled. 'Yeah …' His voice trailed off, momentarily. 'But wait, look – I've got something for you. There's a thing happening today – *Fútbol Sin Fronteras*. Rooftop event. Grassroots, empowerment through sport, diversity campaign … all that fluff.'

Elena frowned. 'Who for?'

'Girls, mostly. Youth academies. Women's football. Backed by La Liga and one of the telcos. Not what you're looking for exactly, but maybe you'll get a quote you can twist into relevance. You'll meet people, Elena. You might even get a free canapé.'

She didn't reply.

'Look, I'll text you the address. You might already be on the media list. Or just tell them you're freelancing for *El País*. No one at these things checks credentials. Try not to shout at anyone in the first five minutes, though, okay?'

Elena opened her mouth.

'Good luck,' he added, and hung up.

Two interviews. Two cancellations. More men who thought she wasn't worth their time. Another reminder that she never quite fit.

A moment later, her phone pinged. A location pin. *'Fútbol Sin Fronteras. Hotel Plaza de España, 18h.'*

The agent's words rang in her head: *You'll meet people, Elena.*

The city moved around her: traffic noise, the clang of café chairs being set out. A bus hissed past, and the gust of air it left behind felt like a slap.

She checked her phone again: more alerts about a break-in and possible homicide at the Prado. A high-profile crime, unfolding in real time. What the hell. She was already in Madrid; might as well follow the scent.

The problem? It wasn't her story. She was just a freelancer, meant to be chasing racism in football. *El País* would have crime reporters at the museum already. But maybe she could say hello, remind someone she existed. Maybe pick up a scrap of information they didn't have. Try stopping her.

She turned towards the Metro and walked.

Thirty minutes later, she was outside the museum, lingering near the edge of the police cordon, eyes flicking between the growing crowd and the screen on her phone. She initially caught snippets of conversation from the public around her – a mix of tourist curiosity, local irritation and wild theories that ranged from vandalism to a major terrorist plot.

Whatever had happened at the museum, it was pulling in Spain's broadcast media the way blood draws sharks. Elena recognised a few of them, radiating that familiar scent of self-importance – polished, camera-friendly faces, the ones who delivered breathless updates with perfect hair and practised concern. It reminded her of that lech of a lecturer who'd once told her she had the looks to be a TV sports presenter, as if journalism was a beauty contest. Ken and Barbie, live from the crime scene. No, thanks.

As for some of the other reporters, she'd already tried chatting to a few of them. Stonewalled. They'd looked at her like she didn't belong, that she shouldn't be there, and it had riled her. Amateur sleuth. Bystander. Not part of their club. A freelancer *and* female? Or maybe their problem was her olive skin.

Elena had never been good at walking away. Never been good at leaving things to the so-called experts. Journalism required patience, she'd been told, but patience was a virtue she rarely embraced. Her thumb hovered over her phone's screen.

Art. Madrid. Trouble. It had Benjamin written all over it – the art expert. *Alleged* art expert. She'd seen his messages and missed calls. She just hadn't decided what to do about them. Yet.

But now? Now she had a reason. A professional excuse, at least. Maybe he could give her some insight about what was going on, possibly even a quote or two, something to send her editor. That was all. Just work. Nothing else. Obviously.

Well, maybe – if she was honest – she also wouldn't mind the company. Especially after two no-shows in the same morning.

Standing outside the Prado, watching the unfolding chaos, she tapped the call button.

21

Benjamin - Ignacio Lázaro

Sunday – Hotel Ritz.

Benjamin had stayed put, because that's what he'd been told to do. Ignacio had muttered something about being late for a police briefing at the Prado across the road, promised it wouldn't take long, told Benjamin to 'help himself to a coffee or whatever', and then vanished in a flurry of bureaucratic self-importance.

Half an hour, Ignacio had said. Fifty-five minutes later, Benjamin was still in the air-con of the Ritz Palm Court lounge, nursing a coffee that at least tasted better than what he'd endured on the dodgy barstool near his illegal Airbnb. He'd even considered a sandwich, maybe even brunch, until the menu made him blink twice. He wasn't stingy, but highway robbery was highway robbery, even when dressed up as haute cuisine.

So, he'd remained at the table, thinking of Caravaggio's *David and Goliath*, sliced from its frame. He'd tried calling his daughter again, no answer. And then he'd turned over Ignacio's offer, weighing up the invitation to meet with the **BPH**. He met the heritage brigade's Alfonso García before – diligent, by-the-book, not the sort who would ever invite Benjamin in unless someone leaned on him. Which meant Ignacio had been serious. Which meant Benjamin would have to take it seriously, though the whole thing felt less like an opportunity and more like being dragged into a slow-motion train wreck.

Just as he was checking his watch for the tenth time, Ignacio reappeared. Flushed, tie askew, he hurried into the lounge and dropped into the chair opposite, phone clutched like it might offer absolution. His smile was tight, his nerves written all over him.

'Thank you for waiting,' he said quickly. 'I can't stay long. I've exchanged messages with Alfonso. He's on his way back from Extremadura and will contact you directly, and *strictly confidentially*, before the end of the day. In the meantime, the ministry is grateful. Your cooperation will mean a great deal.'

Benjamin gave a polite nod, though what he really wanted was for Ignacio to glance at the bill sitting on the silver tray and pick it up. After all, it had been his idea to meet at the Ritz, his idea that Benjamin stay put. But the tight-fisted little functionary didn't so much as flick an eye at it. Benjamin stifled a sigh. Not even an offer of croissants – just as well, since he'd probably have had to pay for those, too. If Ignacio was this slippery over a *café con leche*, what chance was there of trusting him with a finder's fee for the Caravaggio?

It made Benjamin realise he'd need something in writing. He was about to let it slide when he caught the bureaucrat looking even twitchier than before. Eyes darting, fingers fussing with his phone, checking his watch twice in a minute. Jumpy, cagey – a flicker of wariness he hadn't shown earlier. Benjamin couldn't shake the sense there was something bigger he wasn't telling him.

He leaned forward. 'Listen, Ignacio. I'm going to need something on paper –'

Then his phone buzzed on the table, abrupt, cutting through the moment.

It was Elena.

A plainclothes UDEV agent had trailed Ignacio from the Prado Museum to the hotel and now sat in the reception area, blending in with the morning bustle while pretending to scroll on his phone. But his focus was clear – watching Ignacio as he angled closer to speak with the bushy-haired man in the lounge, across from the lobby. He didn't interrupt or approach, just observed, his posture relaxed but his eyes sharp.

Something about Ignacio's companion tugged at a memory, however. The feeling was faint but persistent – he'd seen him before. Somewhere. Not just a passing

face. No, it was more than that. His mannerism, too –
it seemed familiar. A case file, maybe. Or a briefing.
But which one?

The man didn't look Spanish, that was for sure –
but foreigners drifted through Madrid all the time.
What was he? Late thirties, maybe forty? The agent
considered trying to take a shot of him on his phone to
send to his superior, but something held him back. No
point raising flags until he was sure. For now, it was
better to wait – to watch.

Ignacio, meanwhile, seemed to be doing most of
the talking, his gestures tight and clipped. Whatever
they were discussing wasn't casual, that much was
clear. He leaned back, pretending to check his
messages while he studied the man again. He knew
that face. He just couldn't remember why.

22

Kai Leroux

Sunday – Glorieta de Embajadores.

Guidebooks always described the Embajadores neighbourhood of Madrid as 'eclectic' or a 'melting pot' – some kind of 'bohemian kaleidoscope of cultures, flavours, murals and street art'.

From Kai's balcony, it was none of that. Just the Glorieta de Embajadores grinding with traffic. Even on a Sunday, horns spitting angry blasts, scooters weaving through gaps, buses that were meant to be electric or hybrid but still coughed out a dirty haze. He noticed it every time – the sting in his throat, the sour taste at the back of his tongue. He hated breathing it in.

He pulled the blinds shut and turned back inside. His open-plan loft was stripped to function: steel table, a few chairs, a double mattress on the floor. There was a pull-up bar bolted above a doorway, free weights stacked in a corner, resistance bands coiled like snakes across the floor. No pictures. No books. One cabinet held clothes folded with military tidiness; the other contained burner phones and SIM cards in labelled bags.

A workstation dominated the far wall: three monitors, cables tied cleanly, a compact computer unit tucked beneath. Across the screens were frozen fragments of his world: a betting dashboard mid-refresh, a block of code half-written, a paused CCTV camera view of some depot, and a dark-web marketplace left open in another window.

Under the desk, half-hidden, sat a hi-vis vest and a delivery rider's yellow thermal box – one of several disguises he rotated when he needed to disappear. As ordinary or as dangerous as he needed it to be.

Kai opened the fridge. Bottles of water. Greens in plastic. Protein tubs. He unwrapped a slab of salmon, sliced it into precise rectangles, laid them on a plate with leaves and kimchi, then poured mineral water into a glass. Healthy food for a man who had killed someone around nine hours ago.

He kicked off his shoes, went barefoot across the concrete, and sat at the steel table. His tablet lay there in the dim light, screen already awake. He ate while scrolling the headlines with his free hand. An official statement, just released:

The Prado Museum regrets to confirm the death of a night surveillance guard during an incident in the early hours …

He read it out loud, mouth half full. '*Our thoughts and prayers …*' he said to the empty flat.

No mention of the painting. Impatience gnawed at him; they were holding back.

His phone vibrated on the tabletop. He didn't need to check the screen. He answered.

A voice – cool, exact.

'Why was it necessary to kill a guard?'

'He got in the way,' Kai said, picking a shred of salmon from his teeth. He didn't mention how long he'd waited in the dark for a guard to appear, or the wire biting into flesh, or how long he'd held on.

'You assured me it would be clean.'

'It was. The asset's clean. The guard won't matter.'

'We wanted symbolism, not slaughter. You've complicated everything.'

'He saw me,' Kai said. 'He would have talked.'

Silence – sharper than any accusation.

'You lingered,' the Principal said at last. 'You waited for someone to appear.'

He didn't answer.

'You enjoyed it.'

The line went dead.

Kai set the phone on the table. The voice stayed, as it always did – the only approval he'd ever wanted, the only judgement that mattered.

He drained the mineral water, wiped his mouth with the back of his hand. He leaned forward, elbows on the table, eyes hard in the black reflection of the tablet.

23

Benjamin - Elena

Sunday – Hotel Ritz.

'Benjamin?'

'Elena.'

'I saw your messages … sorry, but I could not reply. I had meetings, but then they were cancelled.'

'It's no problem,' Benjamin said from the other end of the line. 'Look –'

'Where are you?' Elena asked.

'I'm at the Ritz –'

'*El Ritz*? You're staying at the Ritz? *Joder, tío, qué bien vives –*'

'What?'

'Joder.'

'Look, I'm just ending a meeting right now, but I could meet up in, say, twenty minutes? I could come to wherever you are, or we could meet around here, near the Ritz.'

'*Que quieres que vaya al Ritz?*'

'What? Yeah, okay – the Ritz. Say, twenty minutes? I'll wait for you here.'

Click.

Elena lowered her phone, staring at it like it had personally insulted her. She was still on the Paseo del Prado, near the police cordon and the growing crowd. *The Ritz?* She could see the hotel from where she was standing. It wasn't where she thought he'd be. He'd said something about an Airbnb. Men who lied about where they slept usually lied about other things, too. Places like the Ritz didn't impress her. They unsettled her. All that hushed money and fake luxury – as if the whole place was simply a pretence, just like the men who walked through it. The type who needed gold trim to feel important. She hadn't pegged Benjamin as that type. Maybe she'd been naive to think otherwise.

She considered sending him a text – *Forget it* – but didn't. Twenty minutes later, she found herself arguing in Spanish with a doorman outside the Ritz.

'*Perdona?* No, *no* – you didn't ask if I was staying here – you asked me if I have an *appointment*. You were questioning if I *belong* here.'

The doorman, suddenly aware that he was no longer in control of the exchange, held his hands up in apology. '*Señorita*, I didn't mean to –'

'*No, claro que no.* You guys never *mean* anything, right? You just always ask the same questions in the same tone. I approach the hotel, and you think – what? I'm lost? I'm a cleaner? A call girl? I'm not rich enough or white enough to walk through your fucking door?'

'I was simply asking if –'

'You weren't simply asking. And I'm not going to pretend this is normal. Not anymore.'

The doorman opened his mouth, then closed it again.

That was when Benjamin appeared behind the glass. He pushed open one of the heavy front doors, blinking in the sudden sunlight, pausing at the scene unfolding two metres in front of him. Elena, half turned towards a flustered doorman, pacing small, furious circles on the pavement. Hands slicing the air. Words machine-gunned in Spanish. He caught maybe three words of it. Something about *cara*, something about *mujer*. Whatever it was, it didn't sound like she was planning to let it go soon.

Ignacio, now standing next to Benjamin, adjusted his tie and murmured, 'You know her?'

'Yep,' Benjamin nodded.

Ignacio watched for a moment longer, then gave a small, diplomatic cough. 'Right. Well, you have the details of where we'll meet this evening, and hopefully with Alfonso, okay? We'll speak again later.'

'Yes – later,' Benjamin said, barely hearing himself.

He shook Ignacio's hand, but with his eyes never quite leaving Elena.

Ignacio walked off briskly; his dark leather folder tucked under one arm.

The plainclothes UDEV agent who'd been observing Ignacio from the lobby, had now also emerged at the front of the hotel, pretending to scroll on his phone. He watched Ignacio disappear, then turned his focus instead on the wild-haired individual he'd met with, and the young, dark woman who was berating the doorman.

Benjamin didn't notice him. What he *did* notice was that Elena was still ranting. The doorman now looked like he was trying to will himself out of existence. Benjamin stepped forward, cautiously.

'Elena —'

She whipped around mid-sentence, eyes sharp. Her expression didn't soften when she saw him. If anything, it tightened — and then she fired off something in Spanish at him.

'De verdad te alojas aquí? En este hotel tan pijo … Vaya sorpresa, Benjamin.'

He didn't catch a single word, apart from 'hotel' and 'Benjamin', and it didn't sound complimentary. He remembered she had a habit of slipping into full-speed Spanish if she wasn't exactly happy about something.

The doorman cleared his throat, but wisely said nothing. Benjamin glanced at him, then back at Elena.

'Can we maybe –' he gestured away from the hotel, '– walk?'

She stared at him a beat longer, muttering something else under her breath.

'Can we walk, please?' he asked again.

'You look like a wreck,' she said. 'But, yeah, okay, let's walk.'

The plainclothes agent raised his phone to his mouth and muttered a voice note, calm and clipped. Then he crossed the street, following them at a safe distance.

24

Borja Falcó

Sunday – Calle de Ayala.

Borja stood opposite his building on Calle de Ayala, the heavy Adidas bag at his feet beneath the green awning of the Jurucha bar – closed at this hour on a Sunday morning. No sign of anyone. No parked bikes, no taxis idling. He'd told himself that it would be safe to come back here for just five minutes. In and out. Grab the passport and maybe a clean, dry shirt. That was it.

The lift groaned on the way up, the old kind with a sliding iron gate and cracked floor tiles. Fourth floor. The flat papá had bought him after the Ibiza years, dressed up like a respectable little pied-à-terre in the *barrio* Salamanca. Papá said it was to help him 'mature'. Instead, it became the place where Borja just learned how to lie better, where he fucked strangers and snorted lines in the dark.

Inside, nothing looked disturbed. The flat still smelt of stale cologne, old weed, spilt beer, and half-emptied delivery cartons. Curtains drawn; bedroom door half-open. He dropped the bag on the designer rug, turned to lock the door behind him – and that's when he heard it.

A sigh. A shift of weight. A creak of floorboard.

From the hallway.

He spun and froze.

A man stood there, already inside the flat. He wore a zip-up jacket and what looked like surgical gloves. He was calm, as if he knew no one was coming to help. No weapon in sight. But his expression said it all: *I've been waiting.*

Borja's mouth opened, but his voice didn't come. He could feel his heart punching through his ribcage.

The man stepped forward. Borja took a step back, his eyes darting towards the door, still unlocked. He thought of the bag, thought of making a grab for it and running – but the man saw through it.

'Don't even try,' he said. Madrid accent but drained of any warmth. 'Let's not make this messy. Yet.'

Borja then heard heavy footsteps on the stairs outside, followed by a knock on the door. Two quick raps.

The man nodded towards it. 'You want to get that? It will be Enzo.'

Borja didn't move. The man opened it himself.

Enzo, his bald, dog-ugly slab of a companion then entered. Shaved head, thick neck, a silver chain glinting like a collar. His face was a battlefield of old acne. In one hand, he carried a nylon zip-up bag – the sort made for car tools or body parts. He was the kind of thug who didn't just hurt people, he liked to take his time doing so. He grinned at Borja.

'Well, well. The boy genius,' he said. This time the accent sounded Italian. He glanced at the Adidas bag on the rug. 'You pack light.'

Borja tried to speak – but the words still wouldn't come.

'You want to sit down?' the pockmarked slab said. 'Or we do this standing?'

They didn't wait for an answer. Borja was dragged backwards by the first thug and then slammed into the wall, hard enough to knock a frame down. A hefty forearm across the throat, not quite choking – just pinning him there. Then came the first punch. Not to the face, but to the ribs. Low. Designed to hurt later. The second, a little higher. The breath left him in a single, gutless moan. Then came a knee to his thigh. Borja collapsed, wheezing.

Enzo, the acne-scarred sadist, crouched. 'I want to show you something,' he said, smiling. From his bag, he pulled out a clear plastic sack. He held it up, let Borja see it, then smoothed it open like a chef preparing ingredients.

Borja tried to lunge, but they had him on his knees

now. The bag then came down over his head. Tightened. His breath hit the plastic and rebounded hot and sharp. He thrashed – hands trying to claw it away – but the first thug was already holding his wrists, while Enzo watched.

'Relax,' he whispered. 'You'll get used to it.'

Ten seconds. Fifteen. Twenty. No air.

Borja's body buckled. They let go.

He wheezed, spit stringing from his mouth. '*What – what do you want?*' he managed to gasp.

'We don't want anything,' Enzo said. 'We're just the warm-up act. Think of it as foreplay.' He pulled a chair into the centre of the room, before taking out some cable wire and pliers from his nylon bag.

The first thug then yanked Borja up into the chair, binding his hands tightly behind it.

'Pliers or bag?' Enzo asked.

Borja was shaking. He'd also pissed himself. '*What do you –?*'

The bag suddenly went over his head again. A hand twisted it shut at the neck. The sound of his breath, frantic against the plastic, filled the room.

25

The Prado

Sunday – Prado Museum.

The second meeting room in the Prado was smaller, starker – bare white walls and harsh fluorescents that buzzed faintly in the initial silence. The air was stifling. No windows, no fan, nothing to breathe. It suited Barroso's mood. He didn't want to be in here with any of them for long. He wanted a whisky, a whisper in his ear telling him this was under control. Instead, he had nothing. No call, no warning, just a butchered corpse in the gallery below.

They'd cut him out. And if they could cut him out, they could cut him down. He'd already made five calls to his contact. No answer. The silence was more than unsettling.

He dropped into the chair at the head of the table, shoulders locked, scanning the faces of the detectives in front of him. Pepe Morales and Lucas Gutiérrez – young, quiet, but both sharp. Ferrer, the chief forensic officer, always looking downcast, his black case perched neatly on the table, a pen clicking restlessly between his fingers. Then there was the hard-faced Pilar Castro. She'd been the first detective on the scene, simply because she was based at the Comisaría de Policia in Calle de las Huertas, directly opposite the Prado.

Barroso had always looked upon her as a tank of a woman, with the kind of frame that could shoulder through a riot without breaking stride. She wore the same shapeless, ugly anorak that she always wore. It should have made her sweat in this morning's heat, but if that bothered her, she didn't show it. Just looking at her bulk made Barroso feel uncomfortable, with sweat already prickling beneath his collar.

She occupied the full width of the opposite end of the table as if she owned the room, taking up more space than seemed possible – spreading and sprawling like a slow landslide. Her eyes were sharp, though, watching him. Always watching him.

'Okay,' he said. 'What have we got?'

Morales cleared his throat.

'The point of entry and exit is confirmed,' he said. 'First-floor window of Room Five, above the Jerónimos courtyard. A steel bar secures the base of the French doors, but one of the full-length windows was smashed. No alarm, no alert – we're looking into why. Whoever did it knew the layout, the camera positions, the system. Inside help, almost certainly. The Jerónimos terrace is where the Café Prado is installed eight months of the year. The public have free access to it, and yesterday it closed at 7.30pm. The courtyard was then locked, with cameras covering the gate and perimeter fence. We're still checking, but so far there's no footage of anyone entering or leaving after closing, and no images of the break-in. We believe the window was smashed soon after midnight. But the first sighting of the intruder inside Room Five is around 3am.'

'Where are we with the catering staff?' Barroso asked. 'The museum would normally be open today. Who arrived, who didn't, and where are they now?'

'The museum's restaurants and cafeterias are run under concession,' Morales said. 'For the last two years, the contract's been with Grupo Dorada – a big, profitable outfit that owns restaurants, cocktail bars and controls the catering at many venues. They've also got delivery and wholesale arms feeding into the hospitality trade. Most of the catering staff here are Dorada employees, a few directly on the Prado's books, but all go through the same security checks, regardless –'

Barroso gave a vague nod. A CCTV grab, six months ago, flickered in his mind. A delivery rider near the Italian Embassy. He'd buried it, but now the image scratched at him again. He shoved it aside. Irrelevant. He couldn't afford distractions.

More importantly: *Dorada*. A name on the table at last. He didn't care about the restaurants or catering – what mattered was that Morales didn't take another step without him. If there was a thread to pull, he'd be the one to hold it. No one else.

'So, we're putting together a list,' Morales continued. 'Management, full-time, part-time, weekend, casual hires, anyone who might have had access to the Jerónimos terrace. Some arrived for work as normal today, only to find the museum sealed off –'

'Wait,' Barroso cut in, his fingers drumming against the table. 'Anyone tied to that terrace, past or present, I see them first. No interviews, no statements, no casual chats – not without me in the room. If they're on shift today, hold them. If they're at home, fine, but they stay put until I say otherwise. Every name, every detail, it comes through me. Understood? Go and organise it.'

Morales nodded. No pushback. He knew better. He left the room briefly while they continued.

'What else do we have?' Barroso asked, turning to the chief forensic officer.

'We're still processing the scene,' Ferrer replied, 'but the weapon is a high-tensile wire, double-looped. Industrial strength, designed to take heavy loads. You sometimes see it in gyms or stage rigging, though it's not exclusive to those uses.' He paused, lifting his gaze to Barroso. 'This isn't something you pick up at a hardware store, and it's lethal as hell.'

The room suddenly seemed hotter. Barroso could feel a cold knot already twisting deep in his gut.

Ferrer glanced at his notes. 'The wire's still embedded, locked into the tissue,' he said. 'We're leaving it in place until the judge signs off to move the body. It's a fixed loop, pulled tight and left there. No sign it was unwound. Which suggests the killer didn't have time, or didn't care. He just kept twisting until the head was nearly severed. Precise, efficient, brutal.'

Barroso kept his face still, but the words clawed at him. *The wire. The style.* He'd seen it before. Different corpse, same cold precision. Something he thought he'd buried. But if Ferrer or anyone else started drawing comparisons, it would all come spilling out. 'Can you trace the wire?' he asked. The question came a little too quickly.

Ferrer hesitated. 'Maybe. Depends on the manufacturer. If it's domestic, we might know in a few days. If it's imported ...' He shrugged. 'Could take weeks.'

'Have you found anything else the killer might have left behind?' Barroso asked.

'Not yet, no, other than the frame of the painting and the cut edges of the canvas. But it's early.' Ferrer gave the inspector a pointed look. 'We'll know more once the body's back at the lab.'

Barroso forced himself to stay still. Morales returned to the room and took his seat next to Gutiérrez. No one said a word until Pilar Castro broke the silence, her voice measured.

'You don't use wire like that by accident,' she said. 'It's professional.'

Barroso's head snapped towards her. 'Or just effective ... or just functional,' he said.

'No,' she said calmly. 'You don't use wire unless you know how to use it.'

'Don't assume.'

'I'm not assuming,' Castro said, leaning forward slightly, her voice still calm yet deliberate. 'I'm looking at the evidence. This wasn't a random killing.'

Barroso snorted. 'The guard was *not* the target. He was simply in the wrong place at the wrong time.'

There was a beat. A glimmer of something crossed Castro's face – quick, but there. He didn't like the way she was looking at him. He needed to shut that down.

'From the images on CCTV,' she said, 'the intruder – the *killer* – clearly paused before leaving the museum. He had time to cut the painting from its frame and just leave, but he was waiting for a guard to arrive – okay, *any* guard – because he must have heard the alarms, and he knew someone would be on their way. While it was random *who* he killed, it would appear he wanted to kill someone, anyone ...'

Barroso stared back at her. For a moment, he saw something beneath the surface. A glimmer of suspicion. Not of the case. Of him.

'*It would appear* ...' he said, in a mocking tone while gathering his thoughts. 'Appear? I don't want things to fucking appear. I want *facts*. Who knows what was going on in the killer's mind? Maybe he hung around to eliminate the guard to ensure he could get away.'

Castro didn't blink. 'Something doesn't fit,' she said. 'Why take just one painting?'

'Maybe that was all he could carry or had time for?' Gutiérrez said.

'Why take a single Caravaggio painting when there are other galleries full of Goya and Velázquez?'

'Too many other cameras, more security, too much risk,' Gutiérrez said. 'They're in other wings of the museum. The painting he targeted was on the wall in the room next to the window he broke through –'

'Why the Caravaggio?' Castro insisted.

'Maybe he had a buyer for it,' Gutiérrez offered.

Castro shook her head. 'Or something else.'

'What – *exactly* – are you trying to say?' Barroso asked.

'The way the guard was killed …' she started, choosing her words carefully. 'It wasn't just efficient. It's almost an echo of the painting itself –'

'For *fuck's sake*,' Barroso snapped, his patience shredded. 'Give us a break.' He'd had enough. He certainly didn't have time for this. He glanced briefly at the forensic officer, who raised his eyebrows back, as if to confirm: *you're the boss.* 'It's a painting, a fucking biblical scene, and we're not in a movie – you get that?'

Castro didn't speak, but she didn't look away, either. Barroso wanted to cut her from the investigation right there, but doing it in front of the others? Too risky. It would only provoke further suspicion and make her dig deeper.

Still, the razor wire gnawed at him. It wasn't random. It had been used before – by men he'd shielded, men who'd promised him a slice of the action once the Italians were squeezed out, men who weren't supposed to move without him. He'd shaken on it.

Every time he'd buried something for them – reports rewritten, evidence 'lost' – he'd told himself it bought him security. And now? Silence. No calls returned. *Had they really shut him out?* Whatever game they were playing, he had to get ahead of it – fast.

'The intruder targeted the painting,' he said finally. 'The guard got in the way.' His words were almost to himself. 'He knew the painting was close to where he entered the museum. As Gutiérrez just said, he probably had a buyer for it. *Who?* That is the question …'

He didn't wait for an answer. He didn't want one – not from anyone in the room, and especially not from Castro. He needed some input from the cultural heritage brigade. He'd lied earlier – to the judge, the museum director, and that little shit from the culture ministry – claiming he'd already spoken to them, simply because he wanted to underline who was in charge. But now he needed to pin them down and keep the pen-pushers where he could see them.

'Where the fuck is Alfonso García?' he said, shifting in his chair. 'Still in Extremadura? Is *anyone* from the BPH even here, or do they plan to handle their part from their armchairs?'

'García should be here soon,' Morales said, checking his watch.

'They're working on it, for sure,' Castro added. 'But these heritage cases –'

'This isn't a heritage case,' Barroso snapped. 'It's a murder case, which also means they report directly to me.' His tone was sharp, final. 'But I don't trust their efficiency. García runs the BPH, so get him here. I want him in front of me.'

'I'll go and find him,' Castro said, her voice quieter but still holding its edge. She gathered her notes, then lifted her large frame from the other end of the table.

Barroso wasn't about to let her wander off and start whispering wild theories to the wrong ears.

'Go with her,' he said, pointing at Gutiérrez. 'Tell García I want a face-to-face. And every piece of information the BPH already has – every call, every lead – comes straight to me. No exceptions.'

'On it,' Gutiérrez said, rising from his chair to join Castro at the door.

Castro's eyes flickered with something – annoyance, maybe – but they stayed fixed on the inspector. She gave a slow, deliberate nod, though her face said she wasn't letting it drop.

Before they left, Barroso turned to Morales.

'Find me a private office here. One with a lock. And get moving on the catering staff. I don't care if it takes all day, I want every single one of them accounted for – and no one talks to them before me. No one.'

Morales gave a curt nod and joined the others by the door, Ferrer trailing after him.

'This meeting's over,' Barroso said, pushing to his feet. He needed space. Room to breathe, to call numbers that still weren't answering.

No one argued. No one dared.

26

Benjamin - Elena

Sunday – Retiro Park.

Elena was still muttering to herself in Spanish as they started walking. She moved with the same smooth yet simmering poise that Benjamin remembered from Barcelona – as if the city owed her something and she wasn't leaving until she got it. Her arms were crossed tightly beneath her chest, her striking eyes focused ahead, with a hold-all slung over her shoulder.

'Do you want me to carry that?' he asked.

'*El Ritz*?' she said, ignoring the offer. 'Seriously?'

'I'm not staying there,' he said. 'I had a meeting.'

'You look like hell,' she said, still walking and without looking at him.

'Yeah, well … it was a bit of a late night.' He glanced at her. She was drop-dead gorgeous. For a while, neither spoke.

They turned up Calle de Antonio Maura, past the private banks, leaving behind the chauffeurs loitering beside their polished limousines outside the Ritz – men in dark suits who looked more like watchmen than drivers. Despite the media scrum at the Prado, life elsewhere was ticking along as if nothing had happened. This was clearly an exclusive slice of Madrid: wide pavements lined with jewellers and high-end estate agencies, restaurant terraces already humming with well-heeled locals.

Benjamin noticed two sharp-dressed female execs vaping outside a grand office façade – celebrating a deal on a Sunday, perhaps. A group of tall young men stood nearby, laughing over a phone, slapping one another on the back, mirror images of each other: wavy, slicked-back hair, long sideburns, slim-fit chinos in beige or white – short enough to show their sockless moccasins – and blue striped business shirts with a single shirt-tail hanging loose. Studied nonchalance. Unmistakably Madrileño.

'*Pijos*,' muttered Elena, as if reading his mind.

Couples strolled past in both directions – young, old, very old – nobody in a hurry. Everyone looked radiant, stylish, beautiful. And Elena most of all.

'So, what are you thinking?' she asked.

'What am I thinking? Honestly? That Madrid is beautiful. And that it's good to be walking here with you.'

'I meant about the Prado,' she said. 'What are you thinking about the Prado?'

Benjamin had temporarily let the Prado slip from his mind. The sun, the chatter of passers-by, Elena beside him – it had lulled him into a sense of ease. Then he suddenly wondered if he'd also missed a call or a message from his daughter, and so he checked his phone as they strolled on. There was nothing.

'*Qué?*' said Elena, watching him. 'Are you expecting something?'

'What? No, nothing – just checking.'

'I was asking you about the Prado.'

'What time did you arrive in Madrid?'

'Why are you changing the subject?'

'Sorry, what –?'

'I had two meetings lined up,' she said, adjusting her hold-all. 'But they were both cancelled.'

'That's a shame –'

'No, it's Madrid,' she said, shrugging. 'I'm working on a report about racism in football, but no one wants to be seen talking.'

Benjamin glanced at her. 'When did they cancel?'

'One didn't show. The other had his agent suddenly remember a prior commitment.'

'Of course.'

They turned right at the top of the street, and then continued a little way along Alfonso XII, the ornate railings of the Retiro park on the opposite side of the road. Benjamin slowed as they reached the Casón del Buen Retiro – a detached annex of the Prado, away from the crowds that always swarmed the main museum, now home to its library, archive and documentation centre.

He'd spent hours in there on previous trips – leafing through catalogues, squinting at provenance records, once even falling asleep at a desk with a pencil still in his hand.

'They used to hang Picasso's *Guernica* in here, you know,' he said, half to himself.

Elena watched him as he stepped closer, peering at the opening hours on the sign outside. She didn't ask permission. Just raised her phone quickly and snapped. He didn't even notice. His gaze was still on the sign, distracted, maybe even nostalgic. The lunchtime sun bounced hard off the stone and glass.

She dropped her phone back into her bag and said, 'So, what's happened?'

Benjamin turned. 'Hmm?'

'The Prado,' she said. 'That's why you're here, isn't it?'

He glanced at her, then over at the gates across the street – the Parterre entrance to Retiro park. It was the one he'd always liked best.

'Let's stroll in the park,' he said.

He stepped into the road, not even waiting for the pedestrian lights to change, and she followed, a beat behind.

'So, that's it?' she said, catching up with him. 'You're just going to pretend you don't know anything?'

'About what?'

'They've just released a statement to say that a

night surveillance guard has lost his life – a homicide – and there are *unverified reports* about a theft.'

Benjamin opened his mouth, but she didn't wait.

'You seem to have a habit of showing up when paintings disappear, and with a false identity. Are you involved?'

Benjamin let out a short, sharp, bark of a laugh. '*Jesus*, Elena –'

'You tell me, Benjamin. I still hardly know you. I mean, do you even have an alibi for last night? Are you involved?'

'*Involved?* No. Not in that way.'

She'd got him.

'*Lo sabía,*' she said, now walking on ahead. 'So, you *do* know something.'

He didn't answer right away. They reached the Retiro park's gates just as a group of noisy schoolchildren swarmed past, herded by weary-looking monitors. Benjamin waited for them to go through, then followed Elena in silence.

The Parterre gardens opened up ahead, calm and composed. There was something about this mini-Versailles that had always impressed him. The order of it. The quiet, clipped geometry and symmetrical design. A reprieve from the noise – both the literal and messier kind that came in the shape of Elena's questions. By the time she'd reached the whimsical shapes of the ancient cypress trees that stood like giant sticks of broccoli, he caught up with her, gazing at her bare shoulders and tattoo, and the slight twist of her wrist as she adjusted her hold-all again.

'Are you sure you don't want me to carry that for you –?' he started.

'*Joder – I* can carry it. I'm fine.'

He didn't reply. Just looked ahead at the cypress trees, their tangled roots having outlived empires.

'Benjamin,' she said, without looking at him. 'You invited me to Madrid –'

'Yes –'

'I've been here before –'

'Yes, you said –'

'You said it would be fun –'

'It will be –'

'But did you *really* think I was going to stay in an Airbnb with you?'

There was a pause.

'There's no WiFi or hot water, but it has two bedrooms,' he said.

'I don't care how many rooms it has. You're ten years older than me. You have a daughter. You're going through a divorce, and right now you look a mess ...' Her voice trailed off. She tried again. 'You invited me to Madrid, and look – I'm here. But I'm also working, okay? Right now, I have no racism report, and just two more meetings that will probably also be no-shows. Just tell me *something* about the Prado – *por favor* – I mean, that's why you came to Madrid, *verdad?*'

'No, I initially came here on another assignment,' said Benjamin.

'Initially?'

'I still am on that assignment.'

'Whatever, Benjamin. You know *something* about the Prado, right?'

He hesitated. Not long, but just enough for her to notice. He smiled despite himself. 'You're persistent.'

She looked at him.

'Come on. Walk with me,' he said.

Sitting on a stone park bench some fifty metres away near the entrance to the Parterre gardens, the agent who'd shadowed them from the Ritz now pretended to end a call on his cell phone. Then he stood up and followed them at a distance.

27

Kai Leroux

Sunday – Glorieta de Embajadores.

Kai sat before the three monitors, the glow carving hard angles across his face. Lines of code blinked where he'd stopped typing. On another screen, news feeds rolled. The guard's death was everywhere – headlines, soundbites, speculation – but still no announcement about the painting. Were they playing a game?

He closed his eyes. For a moment he saw the man's face again, heard the wet gurgling, the wire cutting deeper that it needed to. Too much blood.

A mistake. He could admit that now.

The Principal was right. They knew him too well.

He'd lingered. Waited. And then … enjoyed it.

He should have vanished as soon as he'd cut the canvas from its frame. Had he left anything behind? A trace? A fibre? Would the police find anything that pointed back to him?

He pushed up from the chair, restless, muscles twitching. Then came that old memory again …

A terrace years ago: white light, white furniture, music thudding. He'd followed a friend inside, dressed neat enough, eager in a way he despised now. Some *pijo* toff – slicked hair, careful tan, rich-kid pack around him – had glanced over at him with disdain.

'Kitchen's round the back, shorty,' he'd said, holding out his empty glass. 'If you're serving.'

The laughter that followed had cut deeper than the insult. Kai had fixed that *pijo's* face and his smirking friends in his mind. To them, he'd been a nobody. Too small. Too foreign. A waiter. Not even worth a name.

They'd know different now. If not now, very soon.

His phone buzzed. Not the Principal.

A coded message: *He's started asking questions.*

Good – let him ask. Let them all ask. The ones who mattered weren't the police – it was the syndicates watching the tickers, the feeds, their own ledgers. Respect murmured through encrypted channels.

Then the phone vibrated again. Kai straightened. The Principal's voice was cold iron.

'Barroso is leading the investigation.'

Kai frowned. 'Is he?'

'Is he still ours?'

'He was useful for a while, but we dropped him. Although now …' He caught himself.

'What? Will he talk? Is there any risk? You've already made a mess of things –'

'Are you still angry?'

'Yes, I'm angry. And I'm disappointed – which is worse. We will discuss this when we meet tomorrow.'

'Tomorrow's my birthday.'

'Exactly.'

'They still haven't mentioned the painting,' he said.

'They will. But not yet. They won't announce it until they've contained the scene and the story. Until your mess is cleaned.'

'They should hurry. I want him to know.'

'He will know.'

'And the collateral? You'll use it, right? To get the charges dropped?'

'All in time.' They hung up.

Sometimes, when he closed his eyes, faces swam back at him – throats gripped, lips paling, eyes rolling back. It wasn't sex. It was control. Always control.

He switched off the screens. The loft felt too small, the silence too loud. He didn't want to sit here replaying mistakes. He needed noise. Bodies. One of his clubs – a place where he could remind himself he was feared, not forgotten. He grabbed his jacket and crash helmet, then headed for the door.

28

Benjamin - Elena

Sunday – Retiro Park.

By one o'clock the sun was fierce, carving hard shadows alongside the manicured hedges in the Retiro park. Benjamin and Elena were seated beneath a faded parasol on a café terrace by the boating lake, where a faint breeze carried the splash of oars and the laughter of teenagers rowing badly.

Around them, Sunday had arrived in full colour: a line of Segway tourists glided past behind a guide holding a little orange flag; two kids jostled over a melted ice cream near a kiosk stacked with sweets and sunflower seeds; an accordion wheezed out some kind of tango from a shaded corner, where an old man sat slumped over the keys, half-asleep but still playing. A figure in silver paint stood dead still on the pathway, one arm outstretched, Tin Man style, as if mid-waltz with an invisible partner. Nearby, two men were spreading out counterfeit handbags on white blankets. A small dog barked at a pigeon under a bench, its owner oblivious, scrolling on his phone.

Elena ordered a bottle of cold water. Benjamin asked for a Coke, though what he really wanted was food. His stomach gnawed, but the only options were limp *bocadillos* he'd seen sweating under cling film on the counter before they found a table. He'd sooner stay hungry.

At another table across the half-full terrace, almost within earshot but outside their attention, the plain-clothes UDEV agent stirred his *café con leche* and pretended to read the menu card. His phone rested face-up beside the saucer, ready for the right moment to catch a photo or video.

When the waiter returned with their drinks, Elena leaned forward, eyes sharp and unblinking.

'*Venga*, Benjamin. *Basta* with avoiding my questions. You're in Madrid. There's been a break-in at the Prado. A guard is dead and they're treating it as a homicide. You were meeting with someone in the Ritz just now, next to the museum. What do you know?'

'Less than you, I imagine –'

'*Venga*,' she cut in. 'You know much more.'

He took a swig of his Coke, met her eyes, but said nothing.

'Look, this is off the record, Benjamin,' she said, palms outstretched. 'Between friends, okay? What do you *think* happened?'

'You said you were in Madrid to write about racism in football.'

'I am, but then *you're* here and *this* happens.' She gestured vaguely back in the direction of the Prado. 'How am I supposed to ignore it?'

Silence.

'Come on,' she pushed. 'Off the record. What do you *think* happened?'

'Off the record?'

She nodded, keeping her eyes on him.

'It doesn't really matter what I think,' he said, voice low. 'I'm sure they'll issue another statement later –'

'About what? The stolen painting?'

'I didn't say a painting was stolen. There's no confirmation.'

'It's not *Las Meninas*, is it? Don't tell me it's *Las Meninas* –'

'I'm sure it's not *Las Meninas*.'

He'd meant it as a throwaway – half joke, half deflection – but she dug in further.

'So, you *do* know what painting it is,' she said, eyes lighting up.

'I didn't say that –'

'Is it a Goya or Velázquez?'

He exhaled, looked away. Said nothing.

'It is, isn't it?'

'No. Not a Goya, not a Velázquez ...' He caught himself mid-sentence. Too late.

She didn't blink. Just leaned in closer, eyes even sharper now.

He gave her a flat look. 'Okay. Off the record? Yes. I've been asked to look into something. That's all. It's confidential.' He tapped his fingers lightly on the table. 'So. Where are you staying?'

Elena reached for her water and took a sip.

'Anywhere nice?' he continued. 'I booked the Airbnb as all the hotels were full with last night's football …' He squinted towards the lake where two boys were trying to ram their boat into another one.

'What can you do that the Spanish police can't?' Elena asked, eyes still fixed on him.

He didn't answer at first.

'Benjamin?'

'After what happened in Barcelona,' he said, 'I don't think the police here want my help …'

He let it hang there, fully aware that she knew what he was referring to. His face plastered on the news as a terror suspect, all while he was discreetly trying to authenticate a Dalí.

'Who's asked for your help? The Prado? Insurers? What can you do for them that the police can't?'

Benjamin managed a faint smile. She was still pushing, not letting go – but still looked completely gorgeous while doing so. He knew she was aware about some of his work tracking down stolen and forged art, but not all of it. The rest? Too complicated. Too ugly. Too dangerous to explain. For her sake, and his.

'Let's just say I've had some experience on how things get moved around,' he said, voice low again. 'I know who not to ask and where not to look. Sometimes you ask the right questions in the wrong places. No badge. That opens more doors than you'd think. I have contacts the police can't be seen speaking to.'

'You mean criminals?' she said.

'I don't keep a Rolodex of assassins, if that's what you mean.' He smiled into his Coke. She noticed, and almost smiled back.

There was a silence. A flicker of something unsaid. Birds hopped between tables, pecking at crumbs. She looked down at her bottle of water, then back up.

'There'll be a reward, right?' she said.

'For?'

'For the painting.'

He looked at her, half amused, half wary, and then he shrugged. 'Not sure.'

'You're lying.'

He didn't say anything.

'How much?'

'I have *no* idea, Elena.'

'*Mentira* ...'

Benjamin shifted in his seat. 'You're not getting into this for the money, are you?' he asked, and quickly regretted it.

She leaned forward again, elbows on the table. 'I'm a freelance journalist, Benjamin. I get paid per word. *El País* was going to pay me *something* for the racism report. But if no one wants to talk, and there's a murder and a missing painting ... *bueno*. I'd be stupid not to wonder — *cómo se dice?* — the *going rate* for helping, not just reporting.'

'Off the record … I imagine there will be a fee for information that leads to recovery,' he said.

'Is that how you get paid?'

'Elena —'

'Are you worried that we're competing?'

'No,' he said. 'And that's not what I meant. Any journalist reporting on and resolving a crime — *any* crime — well, I have no idea if a so-called reward would necessarily apply. I mean, it might be ethically questionable —'

'*Ethically … questionable*,' she repeated, rolling the English as if testing the words. She gave him a long look. 'Don't lecture me about the ethics of journalism.'

'I'm not —'

'I think you don't want me to find it before you do.'

'*Elena* —'

'You think I can't find a painting?'

'I think you have to be very careful. There are people out there who —'

'Don't lecture me again,' she said. 'I figured out survival when most kids were learning to ride a bike.'

'I'm not lecturing you, Elena,' he said. 'Please …'

She let out a short, dry laugh — but her smile didn't last.

'I should go, anyway,' she said, checking her phone.

Benjamin looked around for the waiter to pay. 'Maybe we could find somewhere with actual food before you go?'

She shook her head. 'No. I don't have time. I need to check in, make some calls, and then I have an event at six. Some rooftop reception, *Fútbol Sin Fronteras* …'

'For your racism report?' Benjamin said, also checking his phone.

Elena was nodding but distracted. 'Hopefully something for the report, yes,' she muttered.

'You didn't tell me where you're staying,' he said.

'Somewhere that won't let you past the front desk,' she said, standing up and slinging her hold-all over her shoulder again.

He just stared at her and she laughed.

'It's some small hostel, I think – in La Latina area. I haven't seen it yet. Cheap – noisy, too, I imagine – but it will be perfect. It's a city that never sleeps.' She held his gaze, and added: 'You had a late night, yes? Where did you watch the football?'

'In some Irish bar, in the end,' he said. 'But if you'd like to meet up later, we could go to a very good –'

'It was a crazy match, wasn't it?' she cut in. '*Increíble.* Little Monaco beating the gigantic Juventus. *Una historia de David venciendo Goliat.*'

Benjamin blinked.

'Sorry,' she said, waving her hand. '*Cómo se dice en inglés?* – David and Goliath, no?'

She kept talking – something about the referee, red cards, VAR – but Benjamin wasn't listening.

David and Goliath.

Of all the paintings in all the galleries in all of Madrid.

29

Borja Falcó

Sunday – Calle de Ayala.

Borja was on his knees, gasping. They'd released him from the chair, but the plastic bag they'd yanked off his head still hung limply from one ear, fluttering each time he sucked in breath. The flat reeked of piss – his.

'Jesus,' muttered the fat-necked thug, Enzo. 'You stink, you know that?'

Borja twitched. His brain was somewhere underwater. Sweat poured down the back of his neck. Blood mixed with saliva trickled down his chin. They'd split his lip, and his left eye was now closing.

'We're not allowed to kill you,' the pocked-skin sadist said. 'Not just yet.' He grinned. 'The boss wants you breathing. Screaming, maybe. But breathing.'

He walked over to the Adidas bag on the rug, like it was a present waiting to be unwrapped. He glanced at

Borja before kneeling and pulling the zip. He paused a moment, then let out a low whistle.

'Fuck me. Looks like daddy's boy got his bonus.'

The other thug came over. 'Holy shit,' he said.

Both men stared at the stacks of five-hundred-euro notes, rubber-banded, layered deep.

'You don't look like someone who's been saving up, Borjito,' Enzo said. 'This come out of your piggy bank? Or did your new friends fill it for you?'

Borja tried to speak, coughed instead – a raw, wheezing rasp. *'I … I didn't …'*

'No, no. Save it for the big man. Martelli will *love* hearing where it came from. It's proof you were bought. It will make the dismembering more poetic.'

'You think it's counted?' muttered the first thug.

'Doesn't matter. We touch that, we're dead,' pockskin said, low and deliberate.

He turned his attention back to Borja again, crouching next to him, close enough for him to smell his breath. 'You want to tell us where all the money comes from, Borjito? Is this what they gave you for selling us out?'

No reply. Just the wet flutter of Borja's nostrils.

'Time for one more?' said the first thug, as if casually enquiring if he could get another round of drinks in before closing time, and while moving back to his position behind Borja's chair.

Borja shook his head, violently. *'No, no, please –'*

A gloved hand grabbed his hair and forced his chin back. The bag went over.

Borja bucked like a fish on a deck, eyes bulging behind the plastic. It was held tight again — long enough for him to panic and make weird noises no one would hear through the walls. Then the bag was whipped off. Borja gasped, drooled, cried.

Enzo's phone buzzed in his pocket. He checked the screen. One word.

NOW.

'Time to go. Wrap him up. Chop-chop.'

Borja whimpered something, but no one listened. They pulled him to his feet and grabbed the Adidas bag. He could barely walk. He retched and nearly fell sideways. His shoes made little dragging squeaks on the parquet floor as they marched him out the door.

No one stopped them on the landing near the lift. There'd been a man stationed on the stairs, just in case. Another downstairs, dressed like a courier, loitering with a clipboard. The rough wool blanket, the kind used to wrap furniture, concealed most of Borja. From a distance, he was an antique lampstand, a marble bust or a grandfather clock. Nothing unusual for a discreet Sunday job in the Salamanca neighbourhood. Could have been a corpse, too — but no one watching long enough would ask. It was none of their business.

The black SUV was already waiting on the kerb — engine low, the driver a silhouette behind tinted glass.

30

Benjamin - Caravaggio

Sunday – Retiro Park.

As Elena walked off, Benjamin thought he heard her say something about messaging him later, or for him to message her, but he wasn't sure. He stayed where he was for a few minutes, lost in thought, until the sudden splash of paddles on the lake dragged him back.

When he waved for the waiter again, he noticed a man at another table doing the same. Alone. Five metres away. The man caught Benjamin's eye, then quickly looked away.

The man didn't look back a second time. Nor did he wait for the waiter to bring his bill. He just stood, dropped a few coins on the table, and walked.

Is that how people pay here? Benjamin had never noticed it before. Maybe it was what someone did when they didn't want to linger. Or be remembered.

Benjamin kept watching, but if the man knew he was being watched, he didn't show it. Soon he disappeared past the kiosks, swallowed by the shifting array of Segway riders, pushchairs and tourists milling around the boating lake. There was no glance back. But something about his manner stuck – either the bluntness or the practised routine of it.

Paranoia? Forget it. For now, anyway.

He snapped his eyes back to his own table, finally caught the waiter's attention, and paid. Then he stood, checking his phone and wallet were still in his pockets.

Madrid glared in the heat as he left the park, retracing the way he'd come with Elena, down towards the Prado, where most of the access streets to the museum were now sealed off. But he knew the route would somehow lead him back towards his Airbnb.

Alone again, he needed space to think. And something decent to eat.

David and Goliath.

Elena's comment – offhand, innocent enough on the surface – *little Monaco beating the gigantic Juventus … like David and Goliath …*

He hadn't told her what painting had been ripped from its frame. He couldn't. So, she didn't know – *couldn't* know – not until the Prado announced it publicly. But her comment had lodged itself somewhere deep, and now it wouldn't leave him alone.

Who the hell steals a Caravaggio?

As far as Benjamin was aware, there were only sixty known works by the seventeenth-century Baroque painter in existence, with just a few others still in dispute or being debated among art historians.

About fifty of them were held in public collections – with some still in the churches for which they were originally painted, in Rome, Naples and Malta.

The rest – ten, at the most, and mainly smaller works or early pieces – were privately owned. They were so scarce and high-profile that no private collector owned more than one. And as he'd already told Ignacio, no eccentric billionaire would have targeted the Prado's *David and Goliath* out of pure greed. There wasn't a market – nobody *legally* moved a Caravaggio, let alone illicitly. If one went missing, it wasn't just a theft. It meant international headlines and a diplomatic nightmare. Exactly what was happening here in Madrid.

Rome had the most Caravaggios. Six, authenticated. Naples, three. There were only two in Spain, both in Madrid – *if*, and only if, *David and Goliath* was still in the city somewhere. The other Caravaggio – *Saint Catherine of Alexandria* – was over in the Thyssen Museum.

Why not steal that?

A couple of years back a painting surfaced at a minor auction in Madrid, listed as a 'follower of José de

Ribera', with a starting bid of just over a thousand euros. It turned out to be a lost Caravaggio – *The Crowning with Thorns*, or *Ecce Homo*, as it was finally called. They shut the sale down, slapped an export ban on the piece, and then some forty million dollars later it was in private hands.

Why not steal that one?

Up to now, only one Caravaggio had ever been stolen.

Nativity with St. Francis and St. Lawrence – cut from its frame in a church in Palermo, Sicily, in 1969. Rolled up in a carpet that had always sat below it, then removed from the church. Believed to have been stolen by the Sicilian mafia and never recovered. As it couldn't be sold on, stories had since floated around that it was destroyed in a fire, wiped out in a flood, or even fed to pigs. No one knew. A copy now hangs in its place, painted from photographs of the original.

Benjamin knew the drill: every time a mafioso was picked up in Italy – didn't matter how low down the ladder – he'd suddenly have a lead on the *Nativity*. Dangle it for a lighter sentence. Fifty years of the same routine. Thousands of hours wasted chasing shadows.

Surely the mafia weren't behind the Prado break-in …

He was on the street above the Prado now, near the Jerónimos church, looking down over the museum's main entrance – standing among a crowd of others.

He could see the police activity was focused on a court-yard alongside the entrance. There was a forensic tent within a cafeteria area, and tarpaulin half-covering a shattered French window and balcony just a few metres above. He stood and watched.

Why steal David and Goliath?

All crimes, he mulled, were driven by the same urges: love, hate, greed, jealousy, revenge. Or to control. To dominate. Sometimes for a belief. Sometimes a perverse thrill. Sometimes madness. Sometimes just to survive. With most crimes, especially homicides, there was nearly always a *personal* connection – a relative, a friend, a lover, an enemy.

Art crime was different. It interlocked with other pieces of the jigsaw. There was always another layer, another *connection* – a ransom, a payoff, collateral for a deal somewhere else. Insurance scams. Drug routes. Gun runs. Laundered cash. Sometimes even prostitution. Sometimes trafficking.

It was never, *ever* just about the art.

Why steal David and Goliath?

Love or greed? No, not cut from its frame. For its ransom or sell-on value? No, because it couldn't be sold on – and why choose a Caravaggio to ransom back to the Spanish state if you could grab a Goya or a Velázquez? Hatred of the painting? No, not in the dead of night – and why murder a guard? The sheer planning of the crime surely ruled out any illness or psychological issues, and to carry it out for survival or a thrill simply didn't add up.

So, for a belief or an ideology? Possibly. To control and wield power? Also possible, but for and against whom? For revenge? Against the museum? Someone who didn't believe the Prado should own the painting?

Think, Benjamin … *think* …

He was being directed by a police cordon away from the Jerónimos church overlooking the museum now, forcing him to double back to Calle de Antonio Maura again, the other side of the Ritz. From there, he hoped to be able to cross the Paseo del Prado and make his way over towards the area of Huertas. He strolled on, his thoughts churning.

Did the thief and killer have a twisted obsession with Caravaggio?

It wouldn't be far-fetched. Michelangelo Merisi – known by the name of his family's village near Milan, Caravaggio – had lived like his own work, with violent contrasts of light and darkness. *Chiaroscuro*, yes, but in blood and bone, not only in oil on canvas. Most of what was known about him came from the criminal archives of his time. A hothead, a notorious brawler, a man who spent much of his life as a fugitive, wanted for murder. He painted men dying with the same flourish with which he'd once killed one, thrusting a sword through his victim's thigh in a street fight.

Nobody had painted violence and suffering with

such shocking precision, or with such intensity – and only because he'd lived it himself. His masterpieces portrayed spotlit moments of extreme violence, cruelty, agony and human despair.

Was someone trying to imitate them? Turning theft and murder into some kind of twisted homage?

Benjamin remembered what Ignacio had told him at the Ritz – that the museum guard's throat had been slit – but he'd tried his best not to linger on the detail.

After his master's in the restoration and conservation of works of art, he'd gone on to do a PhD in forensic science – but steering well clear of anatomy. Document fraud, pigment analysis, art forgery and counterfeiting – that was his lane. Not blood.

Blood made him light-headed – embarrassingly so – and it often led to him fainting. He knew it was pathetic, but he'd found nothing to completely cure it. If someone so much as described cutting their finger, something shifted in his vision – a thinning of air, a softening of his knees. Autopsy photos? He skimmed, skipped, blocked them out. A severed head? That could undo an entire week.

Not ideal, therefore, to be working on a Caravaggio case.

A painter whose genius specialised in exactly the kind of blood-soaked drama that Benjamin tried to avoid. Throats slashed, blood spurting from severed heads, eyes wide with dying panic, the light always pouring onto the horror – Caravaggio was a man who seemed pathologically obsessed with gore.

As for stealing *David and Goliath,* it felt deliberate. A signature, maybe – not unlike a calling card from a serial killer. You didn't steal *David and Goliath* unless you wanted to send a message, and Benjamin was starting to think the painting *was* the message.

When Caravaggio became a fugitive under a sentence of death, he fled Rome with a price on his head. Anyone finding him on papal territory had the right to execute him on the spot by severing his head in order to present it to the judge.

His later *David and Goliath* wasn't just dramatic, therefore – it was autobiographical. Caravaggio had painted his own face onto Goliath's decapitated head. David holds it aloft, but it's the artist's expression – defeated and hollowed – that haunts the canvas. A self-portrait of guilt. Some saw it as a cry for absolution. *He was offering his own head on a plate.* The artist as the condemned man – a man seeking a pardon.

What if the Prado's thief – the *killer* – had seen it the same way? Someone making a confession and seeking a pardon.

Was that it? Was the killer offering his own head?

Benjamin stopped short, frowning.

Wait – *no.*

That wasn't the Madrid version of *David and*

Goliath. That was the *Rome* version. The one in the Galleria Borghese. The self-portrait as Goliath.

Madrid's *David and Goliath* – the one stolen – was different. Cleaner. Earlier. Less tortured. David still victorious – often even referred to as *David Victorious over Goliath* – but he was tying Goliath's hair with a rope in order to hold up the head triumphantly. No severed self. No Caravaggio-as-victim.

So much for that theory.

He let out a breath, more irritated than relieved. He'd been swept up in the mythology again – as if this whole thing had to be symbolic, dramatic, some coded masterpiece of revenge.

It had to be more straightforward than that.

He thought back yet again to what Elena had said, before leaving him on the café terrace – *little Monaco beating the gigantic Juventus ... like David and Goliath ...*

The Vienna and Rome museums would have been easier to break into than the Prado, if they simply wanted one of Caravaggio's three versions of *David and Goliath*.

But they chose Madrid.

And they chose the Prado.

And they chose last night ...

31

Félix Barroso - Alfonso García

Sunday — Prado Museum.

Inspector Jefe Félix Barroso had sealed himself inside a forgotten restoration lab, tucked in a far corner of the Prado's administrative wing. Door locked; blinds drawn. For now, no one disturbed him.

He paced with his phone in hand, making calls. His contact, the one who'd wired him neat, untraceable sums these past nine months, wasn't picking up.

It wasn't just the money that had his palms sweating. It was the shift he felt in his gut, as if the arrangement had been hurled off a cliff, leaving him standing at the edge. *How long before he fell? Or was pushed?*

What clung to him wasn't the fear of exposure. It was shame. And the bottle — though that, at least, was still a comfort. His marriage had turned to ash in the months after Miguel, their only child, had fallen to his death. His contact had promised him revenge for that – for what he'd swallowed at the time, stupidly, desperately. But life had never returned to him. Not really.

He stared at his phone screen. He was expecting a knock on the door. García from the heritage brigade was supposed to be on his way. Gutiérrez and Castro had been sent to find him, but they hadn't come back. That silence unnerved him as much as the phone.

Then came the vibration, a soft buzz in his palm. A secure notification. No sender name, just a location tag and timestamp. One of his field assets. He tapped it open. Four images appeared.

In the first photo, Ignacio Lázaro – that creep from the culture ministry – sat in the lounge of what looked like a hotel. Across from him was another man. Taller, broader, scruffier. A mop of dishevelled hair. He had a look about him – a face Barroso felt he should know but couldn't place.

The second image showed the other man alone, near the Casón del Buen Retiro. The third showed him walking beside a woman – slim, darkish skin, even darker hair, cut short. In the last one they were both seated at a table near the lake in the Retiro park, appearing to be in deep conversation.

A voice call followed just seconds later.

'Inspector Jefe?' came the clipped, cautious voice of agent Núñez, one of Barroso's surveillance team.

'Tell me,' Barroso said.

'The subject, Ignacio's contact, is a British art detective. Benjamin Blake, flagged by the Guardia Civil as a suspect during the chaos at the G20 summit in Barcelona just three weeks ago. Nothing stuck, but he's known – and he's here in Madrid. Mossos and national police files cross-checked, as well as Interpol notes. Confirmed via facial match. He and a freelance journalist identified as Elena Carmona – also involved in the Barcelona incident – were tailed briefly.'

'And Ignacio?'

'I followed him from your Prado meeting to the Ritz, where the Brit was waiting. The journalist joined as they were leaving. As Ignacio headed off alone, I followed the couple into the park. I didn't stay long as I thought the Brit might have clocked me.'

Barroso didn't speak at first. He just stared – eyes glassy, expression blank. Then there was a twitch at the corner of his mouth. Closer to a tic than a smile.

'Ignacio met with this guy in the fucking *Ritz*?' he said, his knuckles whitening around the phone. 'After the meeting in which it was made *very* fucking clear that the investigation is under a *secreto de sumario*?'

The agent didn't reply.

'And the journalist?' Barroso said, a pulse now throbbing behind one eye

'Not sure about her. But they were talking a long time in the park. She had her phone out. Could have been recording. I couldn't get close enough to confirm.'

Barroso blinked hard. Did they already know something? He had to smother this fast – before the seams split wide open. This wasn't about protocol anymore. This was about survival.

'Pull Ignacio in,' he said. 'Immediately. No heads-up. No pleasantries. Formal order.'

'Inspector Jefe, you really want to –?'

'I just told you what I want you to do – get him into an interview room. For me. Understood?'

'Yes, sir.' The line clicked dead.

Barroso stared at the photos again, pulse hammering. Ignacio from the fucking culture ministry. A bureaucrat playing games behind his back. Bringing in some Brit while the gag order was active. And a journalist already in their orbit. Far too close.

His breath tightened. This wasn't just the painting or the guard's murder. It was everything: the favours, the money, *the things he'd buried* – on paper, if not in flesh. If any of it surfaced, he was finished.

A knock rattled the door.

'About time,' he snapped. He turned the key, then pulled the door open.

Alfonso García from the cultural heritage brigade stepped inside, crash helmet in hand. Neat enough jacket, open shirt, cropped hair, eyes that scanned everything but revealed nothing. Barroso let the door fall back and slammed it shut behind him.

García gave the room a quick inspection – sparse, claustrophobic. He could smell the sweat and something else beneath it. Tension.

'Inspector Jefe,' he said, measured and calm. 'You wanted to see me?'

'I've been waiting for nearly an hour,' Barroso shot back. 'You and your department, only drifting in when it suits you …'

'I came as soon as I was informed you requested it,' García replied, cool but formal. He was a cop, but one who straddled law enforcement and academic expertise. 'We're short-staffed. We're juggling several cases of archaeological looting in Andalusia, Castilla-La Mancha and Extremadura, plus illegal exports and five other active recoveries, one of which –'

Barroso gave a short, sharp snort. 'This isn't an art recovery case anymore. It's a homicide. A guard's throat ripped open. Museum security compromised. *My* investigation.' He paused and stepped forward just enough to close the distance between them.

García placed his crash helmet on a chair, his expression registering little more than professional patience – the kind cultivated over years of working alongside museum bureaucrats and police chiefs who loved to remind him that cultural crime wasn't 'real police work'. He was used to it.

'Let's make this get-together very simple, shall we?' Barroso said. 'Anything – and I mean anything – that your little department knows, suspects, or even *imagines* about who would steal a painting like this … I want it. I want it first. No museums, no ministries, no curators, no diplomats. *Me*. Understood?'

A beat. García noted the flush at Barroso's collar,

the sheen at his brow. This wasn't just pressure. This was *fear*. But of what?

'Understood,' he said, his voice still calm and precise. 'But with respect, we're not in the habit of fantasising. If we'd had intel about an imminent theft like this, you would have known about it beforehand.'

Barroso looked at him with a slow, cutting squint. 'Don't be clever.'

For a moment, neither man spoke. Then García said coolly, 'You seem … tense, Inspector Jefe.'

Barroso flexed his fingers, like a man trying not to punch a wall. 'You're not hearing me,' he said, lowering his voice. 'This is a homicide. You don't run homicide. I do. I don't want anyone confused about that, especially you, or your department, or anyone linked to your department. This case is also under a gag order. Anything your unit touches – intel, tips, contacts – you run it through me.'

García met Barroso's stare evenly. 'Right, but just so we're both clear,' he said. 'If this is about complete jurisdiction over the theft as well as the homicide, then technically –'

'*Technically?*'

'– as it's a cultural crime intersecting with a homicide, your usual toolkit isn't going to cut it.'

Barroso's face hardened.

'With respect,' García continued, 'our unit doesn't function like homicide or narcos. Interdisciplinarity is at the core of how we operate –'

Barroso blinked. 'Inter-what?' His lip curled.

Another woke import, some leftie, gender-neutral bull-shit. He hated that kind of talk.

'Interdisciplinarity. International cooperation is crucial for recovery and restitution. Most of what crosses our desk involves borders – provenance trails, auction houses, offshore entities. We work with archae-ologists, academics, historians, art dealers, even people connected to criminals and traffickers –'

'Save me the lecture –'

'It isn't a lecture, it's the framework,' García pressed, standing his ground.

Barroso snapped forward, palm slamming the table between them. 'I don't give a shit about frameworks, and this isn't a fucking academic conference.'

García's eyes flicked towards the door – just once, a check, a calculation.

'When we walk into the incident room later,' Barroso went on, 'I expect us to be exactly on the same page. You support the homicide lead. You hand over everything your division has. And you make damn sure that anyone sniffing around without clearance will be charged with contempt and gagged – no exceptions. Clear?'

'I know how it works,' García said.

'Good.' Barroso bared his teeth in a joyless grin. His voice dropped, even colder. 'Then explain this. A civil servant from the ministry of culture – Ignacio Lázaro, with close connections to your unit – gets told about the *secreto de sumario* by the judge, and immedi-ately after, he's seen chatting with some foreign art detective at the Ritz. A *Brit*. And guess what? This Brit then spends over an hour in the park with a fucking journalist.'

García blinked, caught slightly off-guard.

'Ignacio, a Brit, and the press. A lovely little menage-à-trois. Care to tell me how that looks?' Barroso pressed.

'You're sure about the journalist?' García asked.

'Positive. Surveillance logged the meeting. Photos. Location. Names. Want to see?'

García shook his head slowly. 'No, I believe you.'

'And we can skip the part where you pretend this is new to you,' Barroso said.

'I'm not disputing your authority to lead this investigation,' García said. 'When Ignacio told me that he planned to meet with a British consultant who was in town, I assumed he'd cleared it with you first.'

'Cleared him to feed information to an outsider?'

'To assist the investigation?' García countered. 'As I said, we're short-staffed –'

'We don't need any fucking assistance,' Barroso barked. He jabbed a finger towards García's chest. 'I don't like outsiders poking around my crime scenes. If I catch anyone from your unit feeding intel to outsiders, or you giving your bottom-feeder pals over at the ministry the green light to drag in some external fucking consultant without my authorisation, then I'll bring charges myself. I'll have every one of you locked down under breach of the judge's gag order.'

'I'll speak to Ignacio,' García said carefully.

'No. You won't. He's being brought in. Until I've finished with him, no one else touches him.'

'You're bringing him in? For what?'

'Just a conversation. For now.' Barroso shot a tight, dry, sinister smile.

The silence stretched. García studied him, longer than he probably should have, the inspector's lips twitching as he started to stare at his phone.

What was Barroso hiding?

This wasn't just procedural turf war. It was paranoia, barely disguised as control. This was personal. He wasn't flexing his authority to protect the case; he was protecting himself. Or someone. Scrambling to contain the chaos before anyone started asking the wrong questions, poking into things that he wanted to keep buried. Something smelled off. He was spooked. He was scared. And scared men were unpredictable – and dangerous.

Maybe, García thought, talking to the Brit wasn't a bad idea at all, with or without Ignacio.

'Fine,' he said, tapping his hands against his hips. 'You've made yourself clear.' Then he picked up his crash helmet, turned and left, quietly closing the door behind him.

32

Elena

Sunday – La Latina district.

She'd left Benjamin in the park without looking back, then taken the metro from Retiro to La Latina, dodging the families, strollers, tourists and backpacks along the way. The hold-all slung over her shoulder had suddenly felt heavier, as if it resented the choice she'd made earlier not to let Benjamin carry it in the park. She'd blinked at her reflection in the window of the carriage. She hadn't managed to grab anything to eat, but now it was adrenaline carrying her, not food.

She emerged from the metro into a slap of early afternoon heat, chaos and street noise – all cracked pavements, fried air, a swirl of smells, shop signs and shouting that somehow made sense in this city.

Terraces were still crammed with families and couples, tables buried under roasts and rice dishes.

Waiters weaved between chairs like jugglers, balancing trays of glasses and bottles. Voices rose, children ducked beneath tables. Hawkers and buskers drifted between the terraces with paper cups, accordion players bleeding out the same tune for the hundredth time, each hoping to snatch a coin or a glance. The air hung thick with grilled meat, garlic, anise and cigar smoke – Madrid's Sunday perfume. The clatter of cutlery and shouted jokes rose like the city's own soundtrack, as if the whole *barrio* refused to let any meal end.

The nearby Rastro flea market had already packed up, but the stragglers never left. A few stalls clung to the kerbsides in the heat, hawking belts, bags and hats as if time itself could be bribed to stay. La Latina didn't care who you were – only that you moved slow enough not to disturb its rhythm.

Elena walked fast, past young couples, groups of shoppers, dodging a kid on a scooter and then a teenager pushing a supermarket trolley full of metal junk. She crossed a plaza faintly smelling of urine and grilled chorizo, as cars honked, dogs barked, and a baby started crying as a waiter dragged a stack of metal chairs across the flagstones.

She passed the Teatro La Latina, grand but faded, then the candy-coloured, graffiti-splashed walls of the Mercado de la Cebada. Further on, the neighbour-hood's usual mash-up of storefronts: *Go Nails & Massage*, *Super Bazar*, a sweet-shop window piled high with lurid sugar spirals, *Zapatillas* which seemed to sell nothing but slippers, a phone-repair shop and a tattoo parlour. Someone smoked a joint in the shade of a shuttered pharmacy. No one looked twice.

She cut down a narrow street lined with iron balconies and laundry swaying from lines, then finally found her *pensión* in Calle de San Isidro Labrador. Small hotel, no questions asked. Just how she wanted it.

'Check-in is at two-thirty,' said the woman behind the counter, without looking up.

'It is two-thirty.'

'Three, then.'

'Fine,' said Elena. 'I'll be back.'

Outside again, sweat pooled at the small of her back. The clock was ticking. If she was going to speak to her editor at *El País* about sending something before the rooftop event, she had to do it now – and from somewhere with a decent signal.

She ducked into a café a few doors down, mostly empty. Locals, not tourists. She asked for a sparkling water and the WiFi code, then opened her laptop and got out her phone at a sticky table in the corner and near the toilet – quiet enough to make a call.

'Tell me you've got something,' Felipe said, picking up quickly but skipping the *hola*. His voice was half-drowned in background newsroom noise.

'I had two meetings lined up. Both cancelled,'

Elena said. 'One ghosted. The other let his agent pull the plug.'

'*Joder.*'

'I've still got meetings tomorrow, and I'll get the report done. I'm also going to an event – I'm doing what I can.'

There was a pause, then Felipe said: 'So, you also sent me a message about this Benjamin guy. He's the Brit you were in Barcelona with, right? Dalí and the kidnapping thing.'

Elena glanced at the clock on the wall. She knew she was crossing a line – but she was doing it anyway. 'He's in Madrid,' she said. 'We walked a bit. Talked. He says he's been asked to help with what's happened at the Prado.'

'He *told* you that?'

'Off the record.'

'Elena –'

'I know, but I thought you might want it. You told me to keep my ears open while I was here. And I've got a photo of him – outside the Prado's archive building this morning. He doesn't know I took it.'

Felipe gave a short exhale that sounded like he was already half-writing the headline. 'He said what, exactly?'

'That he'd been approached to assist. He wouldn't say much more. He said he's been asked to look into something, confidentially. Well, he as good as confirmed that a painting's been stolen, too – not just the guard murdered – but I think we've already guessed that, no? When I pressed him, he said it wasn't a Goya or a Velázquez –'

'Jesus, Elena –'

'I know.'

Another pause, then Felipe's tone turned hungrier. 'Did he say who's asked him to help?'

'No. He dodged that.'

'Still – you said you've got a pic, right?'

'Yes.'

'Then give me a few paragraphs. Quote him. Say he refused to elaborate. That gives us cover. We'll reach out to the police, the museum, the culture ministry. Ask them to confirm or deny if a Brit has been brought in to help. No names. It'll make them twitch.'

'And if they don't respond?'

'Even better. We'll say they declined to comment. Standard stuff. As you have a pic, we'll name him as the same guy involved with the Dalí stuff in Barcelona and who the Guardia Civil got wrong. Throw in the word *controversial*, why not. It's a good line.'

'He's not going to like it. He's a … friend.'

'This isn't about friendship, Elena. If you're sitting on an art recovery specialist showing up *right after* a murder at the Prado, you write. If they've asked for his help, then you use what he told you.'

She didn't reply. She could hear Felipe calling out to other colleagues. There was an urgency and excitement in his tone.

'Look,' he said finally. 'The racism report's still worth doing. But you're here now. And this thing at the

Prado – we're up against the foreign wires. Against everyone. You know what it was like after the Louvre job. If you've got something, we run it. Send me three paras and that photo. We'll post it as part of the rolling update.'

'He didn't say *that* much –'

'Then write what he *did* say. Improvise the rest.'

'You want me to embellish?'

'I want you to *write*. This could lead to something bigger. And if it doesn't, at least we got the first bite.'

'Fine. I'll send you something, but don't run it under my byline. Not for now.'

'Whatever makes you feel better.'

Elena checked the clock again. 'Give me ten minutes.'

'Make it five.' He hung up.

She stared at her phone, then scrolled through to her photos. Benjamin standing outside the Prado's research centre, the Casón del Buen Retiro, his face tilted towards the building's sign. She forwarded the photo via WhatsApp to Felipe, then turned to her laptop and began typing.

33

Benjamin

Sunday – Plaza del Ángel.

At first, Benjamin wondered if it might be a bomb.

Not a very rational thought, but the kind that creeps in when you're slightly sun struck, starving, haven't heard from your daughter in two days, and your head is tangled with Caravaggio's decapitations and divine vengeance. It was the sort of mindset that made a floral suitcase look like an omen.

The case sat like a warning outside the fourth-floor front door of his Airbnb apartment, exactly where no suitcase should be. It hadn't been there last night, and it hadn't been there this morning.

He paused mid-step, then leaned around it carefully, his face pressed close to the wall of the corridor. If it was going to explode, this was probably the angle with the best odds.

Nothing. Silence. He nudged the suitcase gently with the side of his foot. It definitely wasn't ticking. Breathing a sigh of relief, he entered the code for his apartment door to buzz open.

In the end it had been a slow, hot walk back from the Retiro – half an hour of sunlit pavement, the lunchtime sun leaving almost no shadow anywhere. There'd also been a blistering snarl of traffic and noise. He'd forgotten how noisy Madrid and Madrileños could be. Sirens, car horns, police whistles, kids shrieking, adults shouting at each other in the street, albeit in a friendly enough way, but even when they were just a few feet apart. *Why?* Why did they need to shout? Scooters screamed past, dogs barked from balconies, someone slammed a metal shutter, and then some terrace bar was blasting reggaetón over the clatter of beer bottles being stacked for collection.

He'd walked fast, with *David and Goliath* knocking around in his head. The severed head, the stolen painting, the comment about last night's football final that Elena had lobbed at him before leaving.

He'd checked his phone four times en route – still nothing from Sophie. Each silence twisted a little deeper, but he told himself she might have been mid-flight, phone on airplane mode. He knew she was planning to come over. Maybe she'd now arrived, and this was her suitcase. He'd sent her the address of the Airbnb, though not the access code. The timing fit. Just.

It was one way to explain the silence. Maybe a

neighbour had buzzed her in to drop off her case? They hadn't all looked ready for war last night, even if the old dragon with the lawyer husband had threatened to call the police.

He stepped briefly inside the flat. Still empty, still airless. He'd planned to meet Ignacio again this evening, together with the BPH's Alfonso García. He had several calls to make beforehand, ideas to share – loose ones – but the outline of a theory was starting to take shape. Something tying together the symbolism of the painting, the match, the violence.

He needed his MacBook. Needed to change his shirt. And he needed a bite to eat – fast. He was ravenous. But first, he leaned back out into the corridor, one hand on the handle of the floral suitcase.

'Sophie?' he called, not too loud. 'You here?'

Nothing. He stared at the bag again, then checked his phone. Still no message. He typed: *Sophie, is this your bag? Are you here? Where are you? I'm at the flat now.*

Right. Time to quickly thank the neighbours.

He knocked twice on the door of the apartment directly below him – the leathery old bastard from last night. The one who'd shouted at him about illegal Airbnbs, '*fiestas* and *chicas*'.

The door flung open so fast it was as if the man had been waiting right behind it, breathing through his teeth. Same dried-ham face, bald scalp shining under the hallway light, and a lovely mustard-stained vest that looked like it had survived three decades of arguments.

'*Qué coño quieres ahora?*' he snarled.

Benjamin forced a smile, trying for calm. '*Hola.* Sorry. I just wanted to say thanks. I think my daughter must have arrived earlier – I sent her the address. Maybe you let her in? Blonde, about this tall? English?'

The old boy squinted at Benjamin as if he was high. '*Qué coño estás diciendo? Qué has tomado?*'

'I think someone let her in. There's a suitcase outside my door. So, I assumed it was you. Did she say where she was going?'

'*Hija de la gran puta,*' he exploded, jabbing a crooked finger down the hall. '*Hay otras. Inglesas. Ya han entrado. Con música. Con gritos. Una jauría de cabras borrachas.*'

'Goats?' Benjamin said. 'Did you just say goats?'

'*No es un hotel,*' the man shouted. '*Locura.*'

'Brilliant,' Benjamin muttered, backing off a step. 'Thanks for whatever that was.'

The door slammed. The corridor echoed with it. He stared at the wood for a moment, then sighed.

Back on the fourth floor, the floral suitcase was still outside his door. Unmoved. Unexplained. It had to be Sophie's. He dragged it inside, changed his shirt, grabbed his MacBook and shoulder bag, and made a decision. Food. WiFi. Sanity. He'd message Sophie again, warn her there were no towels or hot water, then head off to meet Ignacio and Alfonso later, after he'd made a few calls.

34

Ignacio Lázaro

Sunday – Calle de la Academia.

That morning, Ignacio had parked his car – a grey hybrid with ministry plates – in one of the reserved slots outside the *Fundación Amigos del Prado*, near the museum in Calle de la Academia.

With the police cordons already in place and chaos spilling into the surrounding streets, it had been the nearest viable option when he'd received the early alert. The same alert that had summoned half the cultural ministry's crisis team.

That had been at around 6am. Since then, the day had blurred – an emergency meeting with the judge and some bully of a chief detective in charge, a private chat with Benjamin at the Ritz, several urgent calls and two encounters with his own chain of command, including a meeting with García from the BPH.

They had planned to meet Benjamin again this evening for a longer debrief.

Bringing the Brit in had felt like the right move earlier, but there was something off-kilter about the man. He had the right credentials, but Ignacio had witnessed a streak of chaos in him at the Ritz that he couldn't ignore. There was a volatility there – a looseness. He was now wondering whether a case this delicate could afford that kind of wild card.

As he reached for the key fob in his jacket pocket, there was a voice behind him; calm and neutral.

'Señor Lázaro?'

Ignacio turned. Two men. Short haircuts, unreadable faces. He didn't answer right away. He looked down the street, instinctively. Something wasn't right. He'd felt eyes on him earlier, he was now sure of it.

'Señor Lázaro?' the taller one said again. He held up a badge, quickly, like a dealer flashing a card. National Police. Civilian clothes. No names. 'We'd like you to come with us. Just a few clarifications.'

'What's this about?'

'We've been asked to escort you to a meeting.'

'Escort me?'

One of the men stepped closer, enough to steer him by the elbow. 'If you'd like to come with us.'

Ignacio glanced at his car. He could protest. He could demand an explanation. But the way they were standing told him everything. This wasn't a request. They were taking him, with or without his consent.

35

Benjamin

Sunday – Plaza del Rey.

Benjamin scanned the plaza, its façades a mix of sun-bleached pinks and yellows – old-world charm fraying at the edges. The spot he'd found for a late bite to eat was just off the Gran Via, tucked away from the tourist madness. A modest fountain splashed in the centre, flanked by clusters of ornate lampposts and a statue, worn smooth by time and pigeons. At the top of the plaza, a few stone steps led up to the Ministry of Culture, housed in an old *palacete* with seven tall chimneys standing guard over the scene below.

The bistro had the feel of a hipster joint – rustic, with simple wooden tables and mismatched chairs. It was clearly popular with the locals, though; most of the tables on the terrace were full. He spotted a vacant one and, without hesitation, slid onto a seat before anyone else could stake a claim, hooking his shoulder bag onto the back of it. But then a waiter swooped in, like a hawk.

'For eating?' he asked, through half-lidded eyes, and wagging his finger at Benjamin as if he was a disruptive child – or worse, the type of tourist who'd park himself there all afternoon, getting rat-arsed on pints of sangria.

Benjamin's phone started to ring.

His daughter – *at last.*

He gave the waiter a quick thumbs-up and made an exaggerated eating motion with his hands. The waiter nodded and walked off.

'*Sophie* – hi, darling –'

'Hi, dad –'

'Where are you? Near the apartment? Did you get my last message about there being no hot water or towels? I've just found a place to eat if you want to join me – it's over in the Plaza del Rey. I'll send you the exact location, if you like.'

'*Plaza del Rey?*'

'Yes, it's off Gran Via. You could walk from where the apartment is, but where are you right now?'

'In Norwich, dad.'

'What?'

'I'm in Norwich. At uni. I didn't understand your messages, but I'm fine.'

'You're in *Norwich?*'

'Yes, dad, Norwich.'

Benjamin gazed across the plaza, speechless.

'I'd totally *love* to come and join you in Spain, though – thanks for the invite,' she said. 'Just not sure when I can escape. How long are you even out there for? You said Madrid now, right? The Barcelona thing sounded kind of insane. And has something happened at the Prado? I saw a headline but didn't click.'

'Sophie,' Benjamin managed. 'Sophie … do you own a floral suitcase?'

'No. Why?'

'*Shit,*' he muttered, phone still pinned to his ear, head dropping into the palm of his other hand.

'Are you looking to buy one, dad? I'm sure Amazon can do same-day delivery.'

There was a brief silence.

'Dad, are you okay?'

'No, are *you* okay?' Benjamin said. 'I was worried about you. Claire said you were being followed.'

'She said what?'

'She said that you thought someone was following you, and you thought it was really strange.'

Sophie actually laughed. 'Oh my God, Claire totally misunderstood. I wasn't being followed, like, *followed* followed. I meant *Instagram* followers.'

Benjamin blinked, trying to catch up.

'The band I'm singing with? We did this insane little gig in Shoreditch last week – like, packed out, really cool – and now there's this guy, he's like some kind of top record producer, apparently following me.'

She paused, then added with a grin in her voice: 'I mean, yeah, it's a bit strange, a bit random, but could be nothing. I tried explaining it to Claire, but she obviously wasn't listening.'

A beat.

'Dad … are *you* listening?'

'Yes, yes, I'm listening,' Benjamin said quickly, even half-smiling now. 'That sounds really exciting, Sophie.' He rubbed the back of his neck, already feeling the relief settle – but also the tug of whatever mess he still had to deal with.

'Good. Because I'm fine, I swear. You don't need to freak out over imaginary stalkers.'

'Right. Got it. Imaginary stalkers,' he said. 'That's excellent news.'

'Dad, I have to go,' said Sophie. 'Speak during the week. Let me know what dates might work. Love you lots. Hope you find a floral suitcase.'

The call ended.

'So do I,' Benjamin muttered, staring at the phone like it might answer back.

He unhooked his shoulder bag from the chair and stood up. The waiter reappeared, notepad in hand to scribble the order, eyebrows raised in expectation.

'Sorry – I won't be eating,' Benjamin said, holding up both hands in a vague gesture of surrender.

The waiter blinked, unimpressed. '*Otra vez será*,' he muttered.

. . .

Minutes later, Benjamin stood in the shade of a kiosk, waiting impatiently to cross another road. He was in a hurry to get back to the Airbnb. Sunlight bounced off windscreens; the air wobbled with heat and traffic.

He'd thought he was heading the right way towards Gran Via, but somewhere he'd veered off course. The heat wasn't helping. Nor was the street. The pavements were jammed with herds of tourists, ambling in horizontal formation, like some kind of organised pilgrimage. Why did they have to walk four-abreast? Was it genetic? Why did they move so bloody slowly?

And all the noise again – sirens, car horns, waiters shouting orders through open kitchen windows. A cacophony. The traffic, meanwhile, wasn't even crawling. It was locked in place, despite some poor cop blowing his lungs out with a whistle.

He'd been thinking of grabbing a taxi. Air-conditioned. Civilised. But cars weren't going anywhere. If anything, the pedestrians were making better progress.

Some things were moving, though – bicycles. Electric scooters. Everywhere. Zipping through red lights and gliding past honking cars.

That's when he spotted them – a neat row of light blue BiciMad city bikes, gleaming under the midday sun, silently waiting like a dare. Wiping sweat from his brow, he watched as someone unlocked one, simply scanning a code with their phone.

Nearby, a delivery rider then rolled up on one,

dismounted fast, and disappeared into a restaurant with his thermal box. Benjamin watched him through the open doors, collecting cartons of food from a waiter. He then returned to his bike, scanned the handlebars with his phone, swung a leg over, and was gone. No faffing.

Benjamin looked back at the row of bikes and reached for his phone.

No app. No account. No helmet. No clue.

But suddenly, it seemed like the only sane choice.

He scanned the QR code on the docking post. A link popped up. Download the app. Fine. He did. Keyed in his email address and chose a password to register, then: *enter your phone number.*

He typed his UK number. Next: *validate your phone number.* Okay … he waited for a code. Nothing. He tried again. Still nothing. *Validate your phone number.*

How, Jesus?

An error code then flashed up in nonsensical appspeak, followed by: *verificación externa fallida.* Then another link. Something about first needing a digital *MPass.mobi* – whatever the hell that was.

'*For fuck's sake.* Why make it so complicated?'

He clicked through to register for *MPass.mobi.* The page froze. He reloaded it. Another page then told him he would need to download the EMT app from the *Empresa Municipal de Transportes de Madrid.*

'Bollocks to that.'

He wiped sweat from his neck, then tried the BiciMad app again. Still no code. He kicked the front wheel of a nearby bike in frustration.

'Problem, *guiri?*'

Benjamin turned. A girl in a grey hoodie, cargo pants and battered trainers was straddling a black e-scooter. No helmet, just loitering – but ready to vanish in a blink. She had a short, angular face and a silver nose ring. Maybe eighteen. Maybe younger. Possibly an art student. Or a pickpocket. She radiated *fuck around and find out* energy, but somehow didn't seem threatening.

'I'm fine, thank you very much,' Benjamin said.

She smirked. 'You want hash, MDMA, oxy?'

'No, I do not.'

She squinted as he jabbed away on his screen. 'Won't work,' she said. 'International numbers never get the code. App's dogshit. It hates tourists.'

'I've noticed.'

'I can send you a code from mine. Fifty euros and I'll unlock a bike for you.'

Benjamin snorted. 'Are you kidding?'

She shrugged. 'Your choice.'

He waved her off. 'Thanks, but I'll figure it out.'

He tried logging in again. Failed. Tried *MPass.mobi.* Nothing. Same cycle. Same error. He Googled *BiciMad register international* and found a couple of Reddit threads: 'Worst app in the world' – 'Do not use if you're not Spanish.'

Behind him, the girl lit a cigarette with one hand

and watched him like someone watching a pigeon try to eat tinfoil.

He gave up. Turned around. 'Twenty,' he said.

She took a long drag. '*Venga.*'

He pulled out a twenty-euro-note and held it out. 'You're not going to just grab it and ride off, are you?'

'No,' she said. 'But now I'm tempted.'

She took it, pocketed it, then pulled out her phone. 'You need to give me your number,' she said.

Benjamin hesitated. 'Are you running a scam?'

She shrugged. 'More like providing a public service for *guiris* like you. One bike. One day. No registration. No contract. No bank details. You just go.'

Benjamin sighed, then recited his number. She tapped it in. His phone buzzed.

A six-digit code.

'See?' she said. 'Magic. Enter that.'

He did what she said, then looked at the bikes. 'Which one's free?'

'That one. 10460.'

'Thanks,' he muttered, not sure whether he meant it or not. 'And returning it?'

'You'll figure it out,' she shrugged. 'Or you won't. Either way – enjoy the ride, *guiri*.'

'Lovely,' Benjamin said, climbing onto the bike. The girl had already gone, cutting through traffic with one finger raised to a honking car.

36

Pilar Castro - Pepe Morales

Sunday – Comisaría de Policía, Calle de las Huertas.

An incident room was being set up on the first floor of the Comisaría de Policía in Calle de las Huertas, its proximity to the Prado making it the most practical choice. Detailed maps of the museum's layout were already pinned to corkboards. A city grid hung beside them, dotted with pins marking potential escape routes and points of interest. Tables were filling with case files and open laptops, while a bank of whiteboards stood ready for photos, names, timelines – the groundwork for a full debrief scheduled later that evening.

It wasn't what Inspector Jefe Barroso had wanted. He'd argued for the incident room to be based at headquarters in Canillas, far from the cameras and political nerves in the city centre. But events had outrun his planning, and the higher-ups at the Jefatura Superior de Policía – the kind of desk-bound bureaucrats he couldn't totally control – had moved fast.

Detective Pilar Castro sat at an empty desk two floors above the incident room, her face lit by the cold glow of a flickering overhead tube. She was in a side corridor of the *científica* division, where no one asked questions, and no one looked up. The computers were old, the building's air conditioning stuttering with the heat outside, but she hadn't bothered to remove her anorak. The only sound was the creak of her chair and her heavy fingers tapping at the keyboard.

She logged into Madrid's central database for active and unsolved case files. She had no instruction from Barroso to cross-reference similar deaths – killings by cable-wire or anything that might echo the semi-decapitation at the museum – but she wasn't going to wait for one. He'd been acting strange for weeks. Holding files too close, trying to control every scrap of information as if he could smother things with his own hands.

She filtered her search by weapon type, cause of death and resolved status. Cable wire … garrote … asphyxiation … strangulation … laceration to neck. Homicide, violent deaths, including unnatural, suspicious or suicides with no witnesses. Madrid jurisdiction. Timeframe: past twelve months.

Four cases blinked onto the screen. Four in the last nine months. Two logged as suicides, one as an accidental death, one still 'unresolved'. Each file opened with the same cold rhythm: post-mortem reports, scene photos, officer notes.

Castro clicked through them one by one, cross-referencing keywords, scanning for overlap in the forensic remarks. Her biro scratched across a notepad beside the keyboard – shorthand, initials, times, nothing she'd have to explain later.

All men. The first suicide: *Marco Bernardi*, thirty-five. Found hanging by cable wire from a railway bridge south of Madrid. A freelance physio and fitness coach, contracted on and off to La Liga's youth academy. No family in Spain, no next of kin to push for answers. No suicide note. Still, it had been ruled self-inflicted.

Castro stared at the date: eight months ago. Signed off by Barroso himself.

The accidental death: *Stefano Palonti*, forty-one. Broadcast technician. Chamberí district, four months ago. Found at dawn by a tenant in the penthouse suite, his body crumpled in the inner courtyard below. Injuries consistent with a fall from the roof.

But something didn't sit right. A cable had been wound tightly around his torso and upper arms, as if he'd been carrying or securing equipment at height. The post-mortem noted minor bruising to the forearms and hands – *panic reflex* or *involuntary struggle*, the coroner had written. Health-and-safety inspectors later added a single-line note: *the cable was unusually thin for industrial lifting, closer in gauge to climbing or acrobatic wire than anything used in broadcast work.*

No wife or kids. No one in Madrid asking why an experienced technician had been on a roof alone at night. Signed off by Barroso a day later. Case closed.

The second suicide: *Fabrizio Negrini*, forty-three. Found decapitated in his own vehicle by a jogger in the Casa de Campo, seven months ago. Cable wire fixed to a nearby tree. Anti-depressant tablets found in his pockets. A financial consultant for a Luxembourg-based sports investment fund. The notes described 'extreme mental distress' linked to gambling debts, and the pathologist had signed off quickly. Barroso closed the case the next day.

Something in the file caught her eye. The jogger's statement clearly said the body had been strapped in – seatbelt fastened – yet the photos showed otherwise. The reports also noted that Barroso had personally attended the scene. If the jogger's version was accurate, why would someone planning to decapitate himself first buckle up?

The man's widow told police she'd never known of any depression or medication. No check on his prescription history. Body cremated before further tests. Widow relocated to Milan after 'inheriting a small sum'. Case closed.

Castro underlined the final words in her notes. *Milan. Italian.* She clicked back to the first two files. The railway bridge – *Marco Bernardi*. The rooftop fall – *Stefano Palonti*. Both Italian.

Then she clicked on the last file. *Unresolved.*

Her breath caught. Case #11470 – severed head found. Unidentified. Location: Calle de Lagasca, outside the Italian Embassy.

Forensic observations: *Bruising on the face suggests a struggle prior to decapitation by high-tensile cable, thin and sharp, like a blade forged from wire. No other evidence present.*

She recalled the case, the news reports, the photos carefully cropped, the diplomatic outrage muted by the fact that no one could identify the head or locate the torso. It was six months ago, and still nothing.

The main report was barely two paragraphs long. No follow-up. No updates. She clicked through for attachments – CCTV reports, witness statements, anything from the embassy staff … but there wasn't much. Then she saw it: Barroso had reallocated the primary investigator on the case to another unit.

She whispered into the silence. '*Why?*'

She glanced at the clock in the corner of the screen. She'd been up here too long. Any longer and someone might come looking – or worse, Barroso might suddenly check-in.

She made sure all the case numbers were scrawled in her notebook, then froze.

A sound. A door opening somewhere. Distant, but close enough. Voices. Footsteps.

Shit.

She logged out fast and stood, tugging her anorak into place just as a young officer passed the open doorway and gave a polite nod.

'Detective,' he said, moving on.

She nodded back, heart still thudding.

~

Back over at the Prado Museum, Detective Pepe Morales was in the Jerónimos courtyard alongside the main entrance to the museum, where the outdoor Café Prado was located. The broken French window on the first floor was directly above.

He was standing with two other agents eyeing the Café Prado's ice cream cart that was positioned in the courtyard during the spring and summer months. It was a vintage, hipster-style, Instagram-friendly bicycle cart – white, with a black-and-white parasol – like something from an old summer fair. Tourists loved it, as did foodies with its 'artisanal' picnic-from-a-bike vibe. Morales noted from the retro chalkboard menu that it usually served overpriced ice cream and sorbet – or chilled, gluten-free *gazpacho* in recyclable cups with a QR code to link the ingredients to your favourite Spotify mix … or something equally gastro-hip, vegan, 'sustainable' and infused with cinnamon.

Right now, it was cordoned off with police tape. Officers had examined the cart an hour ago, finding signs that someone had been inside it. Scuff marks. Fibres. Footprints on the top. Morales believed that whoever had been hiding in the cart, waited until the courtyard was locked up, then used it to climb up to the Juliet balcony and break through the window.

'Where's the report on the alarms?' he asked.

'Still waiting,' said one of the agents. 'They're saying it looks like a manual deactivation. System was working yesterday – then dead from around midnight. Same for CCTV covering the courtyard. Someone knew exactly what to disable, and when.'

Another officer approached, waving a printed rota.

'The museum has three eating areas – two inside, and this Café Prado terrace – all outsourced to the hospitality contractor, Grupo Dorada,' he said. 'Here's the list of all staff for the café. Four regular names on the rota for this weekend. Two showed up earlier, one was scheduled for the afternoon shift and made contact with us. The fourth? No news. He's not answering …'

'Name?' Morales asked.

'Jason Zhou. Twenty-nine. Chinese national. Employed by Dorada, not the museum. We're trying to find his address.'

'Push them,' Morales said. 'Find out how he was hired, who checked his documents – and compare any images of him with the intruder on CCTV – anything you can find, send it to me fast.'

'There's something else,' the officer added. He nodded towards the storage area behind the café's kitchen. 'Zhou used to cycle in. Foldable bike. It's still there.'

Morales squinted at the compact bike propped behind the crates. 'Seal it for forensics,' he said.

Another agent called over. 'We've been summoned for the briefing at the incident room.'

37

Elena - Mei Zhang

Sunday – Plaza de España.

Stepping out of the hotel lift onto the rooftop, Elena was momentarily blinded by the blaze of glass and sky. For a second, she thought she'd taken a wrong turn – but then the chatter hit her: champagne flutes clinking, high-end laughter, the low throb of curated house music. A sleek banner overhead: *Fútbol Sin Fronteras.*

So, this was it. The football agent's forwarded invite had worked. No one had even glanced at her ID in the lobby. Just a name on a list and a paper wristband fastened by a bored intern in a black T-shirt, before she was directed towards the lift.

The rooftop unfurled a panoramic sweep of Madrid, a 360-degree view of the skyline. Directly below, the rooftops and spires of the old city – clustered haphazardly – glowed golden-brown in the sinking light. The Cuatro Torres rose like glass needles piercing the sky in the north, while the vast Casa de Campo spread out to the west, a yellowy-green expanse of wildness still clinging to the city's heart. Beyond it, mountains blurred in the shimmering haze, their ridges faint and violet at the edges. In every direction, beyond the cranes and the urban sprawl, you could see where Madrid ended. It was the geographical nucleus of Spain, but then there was nothing other than empty space for kilometres beyond.

The rooftop terrace event stretched out before her. Ruby-red parasols, director chairs and strips of synthetic lawn laid out like some luxury afterthought. A DJ hunched over a minimalist deck; trays of canapés floated past on the arms of beautiful servers. Everyone looked polished and handpicked.

The sudden scent of grilled *gambas* made Elena's stomach tighten with hunger. As she slipped through the cluster of bodies, a waiter passed. She took a skewer of something expensive and unidentifiable and bit down. It was smoky, salty – perfect. From another tray she took a flute of orange juice, ignoring the cava.

The reception was in full swing – a 'grassroots campaign' about empowerment through sport, diversity and women's football. There were banners promoting young women from minority backgrounds, images of girls from across Spain dreaming of the pitch and breaking barriers. These things were always 'diverse' – until they weren't. The reality was that the event felt hollow, like the cause was being used as a backdrop for another corporate showcase. The mood oozed with the self-congratulatory buzz of La Liga middlemen, sponsors and **PR** execs – all gathered around waist-high tables, free booze in hand, leaning in to chat, laugh, back-slap and *ogle*.

It wasn't the noise that hit her. It was the eyes. *Those* eyes. *Those* men. Scanning her legs, her body, her face – like they could strip her bare without a second thought. She could always feel it, and she hated herself for almost becoming used to it. But this time, she saw it clearly: the same eyes were on the young female athletes who'd also been invited. Girls barely out of their teens, faces eager, brimming with hope. To these men, they weren't athletes. They were just fresh meat – something to leer at, to size up – and the men didn't even bother to disguise it. It made her flesh crawl.

She was surprised at how quickly her mind went to Benjamin. His quirky, laid-back vibe would have been a relief among all these lecherous stares. Stubborn, unpredictable – sure. But she'd take that over this.

The moment passed, and she remembered he probably wouldn't want to see her again once he saw *El País*. Her hand went to her phone almost on instinct. She opened the freshly posted article again, eyes running over the paragraphs as if rereading them might somehow change anything. No byline – just as well – but he'd still know it was her, if only from the photo she'd taken. The words blurred a little, the guilt mixing with something else she couldn't quite name.

She turned her attention back to the reception – all

gleam and gloss, and it all felt completely useless. She scanned the crowd for someone official, someone inter-esting – someone *angry*, preferably. Someone who might have a view on racism in sport, and Spain's festering inability to talk about it. A club executive was finishing a speech about 'opening doors for the next generation of girls'. The applause was tepid, polite. She could feel her frustration rising.

'You look like you want to set something on fire.'

The voice was smooth, neutral, but oddly warm. Elena turned and blinked.

The striking woman, perhaps in her mid-forties, stood with a glass of sparkling water in one hand. She was slender, petite, her posture as upright as a ballet dancer's. Her black sleeveless top and linen trousers were simple but crisp, and her minimal makeup and black hair pinned in a sleek knot gave her an air of effortless elegance. Pale skin, high cheekbones and almond-shaped eyes gave her a poised, distinctive beauty. Her gaze carried a slight cool-ness, a touch of distance that made her seem controlled yet disarming. If anything, she looked a little out of place – as if she belonged to another event entirely, perhaps even the organiser or hotel director hosting it.

'I might,' Elena said.

The woman offered a brief smile. 'You're press,' she said, looking at the colour of Elena's purple wristband.

Elena hadn't noticed the difference until she looked at the delicate wrist of the woman. Gold. Sponsor.

'I'm Mei,' the woman said, holding out her hand.

Elena glimpsed a long scar across the back of her hand before she shook it. The grip was light but certain. Mei wore no rings, no jewellery at all.

'Elena,' she said.

'Who are you with?' Mei asked.

'I freelance for *El País*,' Elena said, holding the woman's stare.

'And *El País* cares deeply about diversity and empowerment through women's grassroots football?'

'I'd like to think so, yes,' Elena said, gazing around. 'But I'm really looking for someone who might actually say something *real*.'

'Real? About?'

Elena hesitated. There was something about the way Mei's eyes didn't blink enough. 'Football. Racism. Spain.'

There was a slight tilt of Mei's head. 'Ah. Still?'

Elena froze. 'Still?'

'I mean no offence, but it's a crowded subject, isn't it? A noisy one. You're shouting into a hurricane. The real rot tends to hide beneath the headlines.'

Elena's breath caught, a flicker of déjà vu washing over her – like she'd had this exact conversation with Mei before, on this very same rooftop. The sensation was brief, fading quickly, and she dismissed it as an effect of the glaring sun. 'Rot? What kind of rot?' she asked, her voice steady but curious.

Mei's smile stayed soft. 'Abuse. Not just bullying.

Trafficking. Someone should dig into it. Much harder to prove. But much more interesting.'

They stood in silence for a moment. Elena was intrigued – who was this woman?

'You're a sponsor of this event, is that right?' she said, nodding at Mei's gold paper wristband.

'Let's just say I'm a patron and that I support programmes like this,' came the reply. 'In Thailand, Vietnam, other places. And now here in Europe. In Spain. Grassroots development. Especially for at-risk or disadvantaged young girls. Sport can give them things no one else will: space, strength, dignity.'

Elena felt the words land in her chest harder than she expected. 'So you're the money behind this?'

'Some of it,' she said, without arrogance. 'The things that matter need protection. Especially for those who are most easily discarded.'

There was a quiet edge in her voice – not performance, not brand messaging. Something older. Wounded. *Real.* Elena almost smiled. 'At least you sound like you mean it,' she said. 'That's rare.'

Mei tilted her head again. 'That's because I remember what it's like to be a woman asking questions in spaces reserved exclusively for men.'

The words settled between them.

Elena nodded. 'So do I.'

Mei's eyes stayed on hers. 'Then we understand each other.'

Another speech ended. Applause rose. Neither of

them clapped. Elena caught sight of two men ogling the younger athletes again.

'*Joder*,' she said, unable to hold it back. 'The way they stare. The way they size up the young girls …'

Something hard flashed in Mei's eyes. 'That's just the surface,' she said quietly. 'What you see here? Polite. Public. Safe. After that scandal, no one will ever try kissing a young player during a medal ceremony again – invited or not.' A beat. Her lips pressed tight. 'But behind the scenes … some men treat these girls as if they only exist for their use. Coaches. Sponsors. Managers. The very people meant to protect them.'

Elena felt herself tense. The noise of the rooftop seemed to recede for a moment.

'You get used to it,' Mei added, softer now. 'But you shouldn't have to. None of them should.'

She reached into her clutch bag and handed Elena a cream card with no logo, no company name, just her name – *Mei Zhang* – and a phone number in delicate black print.

'In case you want to write about the things no one here will talk about,' she said. 'The abuse. The trafficking. Underage girls from poor countries lured with promises of contracts or scholarships – futures on the pitch – only to be used for something else entirely. There's a whole network built on it. They say there's a capo at the top who's untouchable. My foundation is trying to protect them, to keep them out of those hands. We can give you leads, if you're serious. That's a story *El País* should care about, don't you think?'

Elena took the card, her pulse quickening. *Trafficking?* A paedophile ring masquerading as sport. It was the kind of story that could swallow careers, maybe even lives. She met Mei's eyes. 'If what you're saying is true … then this isn't just sport anymore.'

'No,' Mei said. 'It never was. But few dare to look beneath the surface.'

Elena slipped the card into her pocket. 'I'll dig into it,' she said, her voice firmer than she expected. 'I don't know how much room they'll give me at *El País* – I'm only freelance – but if there's a real story here, I'll find a way. With them. Or somewhere else.'

Mei studied her for a moment, unreadable. Then she said quietly, 'Others have tried. Not everyone has the courage to keep digging once they see what's underneath.'

Elena felt her throat tighten but forced a nod. 'I only have two meetings lined up tomorrow. One is with the head of the Consejo Superior de Deportes.'

There was a slight narrowing of Mei's eyes. 'The CSD president?' she said. 'Ramón Falcó?'

'Exactly,' Elena said. 'Do you know him?'

Mei set her glass of sparkling water down on a nearby table. 'Who hasn't?' she said, a faint curve touching her mouth – not warmth this time, but a smirk. For the first time, Elena caught a glimpse of cruelty in it. 'Are you sure he'll be available? I mean, if the Falcós haven't already suffered some kind of accident …' Her voice trailed off.

Elena frowned. 'I'm sorry – what do you mean?'

Mei didn't answer. Her gaze drifted across the terrace reception. The sun slipped behind a cloud, casting the rooftop into a brief, silvery shade.

A chill touched the back of Elena's neck. For a moment, she sensed that Mei regretted what she'd just said. 'What do you mean?' she asked again, more firmly this time.

But Mei was already looking away – politely disengaged. The conversation, apparently, was over. A suited man approached and murmured something into her ear. She nodded, then turned back to Elena.

'Be careful who you trust,' she said. 'And don't forget what I told you about the real story. You have my card.' Then she walked away, disappearing into the crowd like a ghost.

From a distance, Mei watched Elena slip into the lift, her figure fading as the doors slid shut.

There was something about her – the way she carried herself. Mei hadn't yet put her finger on it, but her instincts rarely failed her. She took out her phone, found the number, and let it ring. A man picked up.

'You made a good choice,' Mei said, her voice calm. 'But let's see if she follows through, unlike the others.'

She ended the call, the buzz of the reception still swirling around her.

38

Benjamin

Sunday – Plaza del Ángel.

Benjamin's calves were burning, his shirt stuck to his back, and his bag strap had carved a trench into his shoulder. He rattled into a narrow side street off the Plaza del Ángel, the BiciMad bike juddering beneath him. Now padlock it somewhere. That's what people did with bikes, wasn't it?

Except this one didn't have a lock.

He tugged at the handlebars, hoping something would click or bleep. Nothing. He glanced at the wheels, the back wheel hub, hunting for a hidden latch, a release clip, something. There was nothing – no mechanism. The bike just stood there, useless and inert, like it knew it had outwitted him.

Then he spotted a QR code stuck on the frame – laminated, sun-peeled, but official looking. He scanned it, cursing under his breath. A page loaded slowly on his screen, some useless, minimalist BiciMad interface again, pretending to be helpful.

'To end your journey, dock the bike at any official station. Failure to do so may incur penalties.'

Dock it? A map popped up – glowing blue dots scattered across Madrid. The nearest one? About three hundred metres away, and full.

He stared at the bike, and it seemed to stare back. He was stuck with it. Moments later, he tried wheeling it into the ground-floor lobby of his Airbnb building – but just as he was about to jam it inside:

'Oye – bicicletas fuera,' shouted a woman from inside a nearby doorway. Short, furious, holding a mop like a weapon. *'Esto no es un garaje.'*

Benjamin backed out, muttering something about 'just for a minute'. She didn't care. She kept glaring.

He stood outside, sweat rolling into his eyes. Thinking about the floral suitcase. About Caravaggio. About *David and Goliath*. About people he needed to call. He was meant to be chasing answers, not guarding bloody public transport.

From the bar next door – its terrace only half-occupied – a waiter in an apron stepped out to light a cigarette. Benjamin moved fast.

'Excuse me – could you please keep an eye on this bike? Two minutes? It's complicated.'

The man looked at him, baffled.

'Please. I'll be right back. I'm just … upstairs.'

A small shrug. Good enough. Benjamin was

already running inside and up the staircase, two stairs at a time – heart hammering.

He reached the landing and punched the code into the door panel. Wrong. Shit. Tried again. It clicked. He pushed the door open – and then he froze.

The floral suitcase that didn't belong to his daughter was now spread open in the hallway, spilling pink bras, feather boas, plastic tiaras and what looked like a gift box of dildos. His own wheelie bag had been shoved against the wall, half-crushed, as if it had been sat or stamped on. And then there were voices. Several.

'There he is –'

'At last –'

'Are you the towel guy?'

Six women stared at him from the open-plan kitchen. One had glitter across her cheekbones, another was stocking up the fridge. Two others were drinking from plastic cups. A half-inflated penis balloon bobbed against the ceiling.

A beefy blonde with bleached white teeth and a fake orange tan came closer. 'Hi, babes,' she said. 'You got the towels and the WiFi code? Also, hot water ain't working.'

Benjamin opened his mouth, closed it, then opened it again. 'How did you get in?' he managed.

'The kebab fella.'

Mister No Fucking Trouble Right.

'Wait – *I'm* staying here,' Benjamin said.

'No, you ain't, babes,' the fake tan said, folding her arms. 'We are. We rented it.'

'No, look,' Benjamin said. 'I really don't want to cause any inconvenience or anything, but seriously, *I've* already rented this Airbnb.'

'No, seriously, babes. You ain't gonna cause us any inconvenience. But if you don't leave right now, I'll start screaming.'

'No, wait –'

'We're *all* gonna scream, right, girls?' A cheer went up, already a half scream, half shriek.

'Okay, look, wait – *Jesus Christ* – let me just get my stuff and my wheelie bag. It's just over there –'

'Go on then. Be quick. We wanna go out for cava.'

Benjamin scooped up the wheelie, then made a beeline for the bedroom he'd used last night, stuffing the case with anything that looked remotely his – charger, crumpled shirt, a couple of polos, chinos, boxers, socks that didn't sparkle. He snatched his toothbrush and razor from the bathroom, now crowded with spray tan bottles and hair straighteners. He abandoned the rest of his stuff. Whatever was missing, he'd buy again. Or live without.

'Hang on,' said one of the women, as Benjamin reappeared in the kitchen area. 'Do I know you?'

'I don't think so.'

'Yeah, I do. Daily Mail, innit?'

'Daily Mail?'

'Ain't you that art guy?'

'No.'

'Come out with us,' said one of the others. 'A late liquid lunch, babes – you look like you need one.'

'*Yeah, bring a mate,*' shouted one of the others. '*What's your name?*'

A shriek of laughter followed him as he dragged the wheelie bag to the door.

'Babes,' he replied.

He stepped out into the street and squinted in the sunlight, heat slapping him full in the face. He stopped, letting it all settle. This, he imagined, was what it must feel like to be released from a hostage situation. A kind of warped liberation. Frazzled, sweat-drenched, humiliated – but free.

The Airbnb was gone. So was the money he'd paid for it. But weirdly, it didn't feel like the end of the world. He needed a new place anyway – somewhere with WiFi, hot water and towels. Let the shrieking hen party with their blow-up genitalia trash the damned flat. The neighbours will love them.

He rolled his bag along the pavement and spotted the BiciMad bike was still there, upright and untouched, propped up on the terrace of the bar next door – standing like a dog waiting for its owner.

The waiter in an apron nodded towards it. '*Sigue ahí,*' he said. '*Nadie lo ha robado. Todavía.*' He gave Benjamin a sympathetic look that said *rough day?*

'*Gracias,*' Benjamin said, eyeing a free table in the

shade. 'I need to sit down before I commit a crime. Can I have a small *cerveza*, please?'

'*Una caña?*'

'That's it – *una caña.*'

He slumped into a plastic chair and parked his wheelie case and shoulder bag beside him, keeping watch on the bike nearby. There was a menu card and a warm breeze. The cold *caña* appeared quickly, together with a saucer of olives. He was grateful. He took out his phone and scrolled to a London number.

Andy. Bookmaker. Not quite legal.

He dialled. One ring. Two. Then a voice, possibly pub noise in the background.

'Yeah?'

'It's me.'

'Fuck me,' Andy said. 'You still alive?'

'Apparently.' Benjamin leaned forward. 'Listen. I need a favour. Big one.'

'What sort?'

'Football. Last night's final. I need to know if anything funny showed up on the betting exchanges. Especially in Spain, if you can reach your usual degenerates. Anything that smells.'

'Shit. You working or gambling?'

'Just tell me what you can find. Quickly, but quietly.'

He hung up before Andy could say anything smug, then took a swig of beer and ate an olive. It tasted good. He scrolled to a Swiss mobile and made a second call.

'*Benjamin*, what the hell?'

'Hi, Marc. You're not in Madrid by any chance – on another sponsorship jolly?'

'I wish. Geneva.'

'How *is* Geneva?' Benjamin asked. 'I mean, other than outrageously expensive.'

'All cool. It's a Sunday, man. What's up?'

'You Swiss watch guys sponsor everything. Art exhibitions, tennis, polo. Your logo was all over the final last night –'

'Sure, wild match –'

'I'm not a football expert, Marc, but as a co-sponsor … beyond the TV and boards, what do you actually get? Access wise. How far ahead do you plan?'

'I don't do football at all,' Marc said, cheerful. 'But I do hospitality. We co-sponsor the whole tournament, of course. The league phase, the knockout phase, not just the final.'

'Of course. But as far as Madrid is concerned –'

'Big picture: the host city for the final is appointed by UEFA around eighteen months in advance –'

'Eighteen months?'

'From then we start to block-book hotels, flights, venues for side events and build a rolling calendar with UEFA. Guest lists start months out.'

'What access do your guests have?'

'*Benjamin*, what –?'

'I'm curious.'

'The usual. VIP tribune, pre- and post-match receptions, police-escorted coaches, lounge access with a secured route to seats. Some will even have stadium-wide accreditation – but not pitch access, obviously –'

'And who's on your list before anyone knows the teams in the final?'

'*Jesus*, Benjamin ...' Marc said. '*Our clients* – but there are various tiers and a strict protocol. In theory, though, it could be any VIP we want to entertain.'

'Right.' Benjamin rubbed his forehead. 'Last one. How soon in advance do you know the referee?'

Marc laughed. 'Out of my depth, my friend. That's the UEFA referees committee. I think it's usually mid-week of the final. If you want *football* answers, call someone who actually watches the game.'

'I will,' Benjamin said. 'Thanks, Marc.'

'Any time. See you when I'm next in London, I hope. Enjoy your Sunday.'

Benjamin ended the call and stared at his phone. Then he messaged Elena.

What time does your event end? Want to meet later?

The waiter came over again, smiling. '*Quieres algo más? Bocadillo? Otra caña?*'

Benjamin nodded. 'Whatever you recommend.'

As the waiter headed off, he sat back again. Along the pavement, the hen party emerged from the Airbnb building, like a flock of bright, shrieking flamingoes. Three of them already had cans. One wore a sash. Another carried a megaphone. They didn't see him, thank God. For a moment he toyed with the idea of slipping back upstairs and reclaiming the flat. But he knew better. You didn't reason with a hen party in full flight. That way lay trouble.

After another *caña*, a *bocadillo of tortilla*, and a much-needed black coffee, Benjamin felt marginally recharged. Time to move on. Somewhere with a towel, a socket to recharge his phone, and ideally no glitter.

He waved the waiter over again – the only man in Madrid he currently trusted, despite the fact he didn't speak a word of English.

'Hotel?' Benjamin said. 'Anywhere decent nearby? Doesn't have to be fancy.'

The man squinted, tilted his chin at the pale-blue bike propped outside his bar, then thumbed over his shoulder. '*Hotel Elba*,' he said. '*Dos calles más arriba. Limpio. Y hay una estación de bici cerca.*'

From the waiter's arm-waving, Benjamin got the gist: two streets up, bike dock nearby. Perfect – if only he knew how to use one.

He looked at the bike, then his wheelie bag, then the bike again. It would probably have been easier to carry a wounded goat.

Still, he left a generous tip and began the grim procession: dragging the wheelie bag in one hand, steering the bike with the other – shoulder bag hooked over the handlebars – like a Victorian lunatic towing his own guillotine. Two streets on he found a BiciMad docking station: lights blinking, open slots. The end was near.

He wheeled the front tyre in. Nothing. He tried

again, pushing harder. Still nothing. A red light flashed, then died. He pressed buttons. He jiggled handlebars. He cursed. *'Come on, don't be like that.'*

A middle-aged woman smoothly docked her own bike beside him, gave him a condescending smile, and walked away. He hated her a little.

He stood there, sweat re-blooming. It was then he remembered – no official account. The app was crap. No way to finish the ride. He was stuck with the bloody thing. The e-scooter girl hadn't explained how he could dock it. One bike. One day. No contract. *You just go,* she'd said. But now he was an accidental thief.

'Señor?'

A voice beside him – low, patient, vaguely amused.

Benjamin turned to find a hotel porter in a waist-coat and gloves, looking at the bike like it might bite.

'You are staying with us?'

'Yes,' said Benjamin.

'You may leave the bicycle in our parking.'

He reached for the handlebars with such smooth grace, Benjamin nearly wept.

'Gracias, thanks so much,' Benjamin said, handing him a ten-euro note. 'I'll sort out the whatever later.'

The porter nodded, as if people said this sort of thing every day.

Benjamin headed inside the hotel with his bags. He didn't care anymore. He just wanted a decent shower and to get out of the heat and noise.

And some silence to think about *David and Goliath.*

39

The Incident Room

Sunday – Comisaría de Policía, Calle de las Huertas.

The incident room buzzed with a tight, unsettled energy. A forensic team had just come back from the museum courtyard, uploading images into the shared drive. Someone was updating the whiteboard timeline, a red marker squeaking under the strip-lights.

Inspector Jefe Barroso had ordered everyone in – BPH, UDEV, forensics, cyber – a full roll call. He wanted eyes on every lead, every rumour, every scrap of evidence. Anything new was to cross his desk first. No exceptions.

Ferrer, the senior forensic officer, stepped forward with a tablet in one hand and a sheaf of paper in the other. He gestured at photographs pinned on the wall: the smashed French window, the dead guard's half-severed neck, and the frame of the painting from which the canvas had been cut.

'No prints on the balcony, window frames or broken glass,' he said. 'Cable wire used on the guard's neck is consistent with high-tension gear rigging – thin steel filament, common across several outdoor sports. Residue tests are in progress. Lab results to come.'

Barroso grunted but said nothing.

'We've also examined the cafeteria's ice-cream cart in the courtyard. We believe the intruder hid inside that cart after closing hours. Then somehow, he – or she – managed to climb from the bicycle unit onto the balcony to shatter the glass in the French window.'

Detective Morales leaned forward, ready to tell them he had a name for the missing catering employee – but the room was already moving on before he could speak.

'And the timing?' Gutiérrez said. 'CCTV inside the museum picks up the intruder just before 3am – with the guard murdered minutes later.'

'The precise time of break-in is still unclear,' Ferrer said. 'No glass-shatter sensor was triggered. Alarms were disarmed around the courtyard. Either manual sabotage or remote override. CCTV overlooking the courtyard was disconnected before midnight.' He paused. 'It's possible the glass was broken during the football victory celebrations along the *paseo*, spilling down from the Plaza de Cibeles. Noise cover –'

Barroso spat. 'So, while half the city was watching football and waving flags, someone was slicing open a

Prado guard and walking off with a Caravaggio. So much for the museum's fucking security team ...'

'We've still interviewing them,' Morales said, exchanging a look with Gutiérrez. 'And we've been cross-checking the catering rotas – there's –'

'Where are we with locating this Caravaggio?' another agent cut in, louder.

Barroso's eyes snapped past Morales to the back of the room, fixing on Alfonso García. He hadn't tried to push his cultural brigade into the discussion yet, so he seemed to be heeding the threatening message earlier.

'Paintings like this aren't lifted for display,' García said. 'There's no market, no resale. No collector with any brains –'

Barroso cut him off. 'Then give us a list of collectors without brains.'

García shifted from one foot to the other. 'As we discussed earlier,' he said, turning his gaze towards Barroso. 'We're working on it, and we will share whatever we have as soon as we can.'

Pilar Castro caught the look that the head of the BPH had thrown Barroso's way. Not deferential. Not respectful. It was contempt, held in check. It was there and gone in a heartbeat, but she saw it. Clocked it. This time she made a note in her head, not her notebook. If she could catch García alone later, she'd ask – gently – what the hell that was about.

'There's a question of motive,' García continued, turning to face the agent who'd asked the question again. 'If the murder wasn't the initial target, and the theft was the primary goal, then we have to understand why the painting was chosen and who might want it –'

'So? What's your theory?' Barroso cut in again, rolling his eyes.

'We're investigating known trafficking groups. But as you know, this will take time, and many of these networks are international. We rely on –'

'Interdisciplinarity,' said Barroso. There was a sharp silence.

'Okay, so we've got the public outcry over the guard's murder,' Gutiérrez said. 'We've got the press hounding us for a statement about what painting was stolen –'

'Fuck the press,' Barroso said. 'And I don't need to remind anyone that this investigation is under a *secreto de sumario*.'

'Speaking of which,' said another officer, quickly holding up his phone. '*El País* has posted something ... just two minutes ago ...'

He didn't need to finish. One of the agents seated by the laptop connected to the projector – a younger guy, fast on the keys – clicked open the browser, fingers flying. Within seconds the wall-mounted screen changed. The homepage of *El País* snapped into view, then flicked to an *Última Hora* news ticker halfway down the page. A photo loaded: a man standing outside the Prado's Casón del Buen Retiro.

Nobody spoke at first. The agent at the laptop

clicked the link to expand the story. Just four paragraphs – a punchy insert into the live coverage.

Morales read aloud, voice steady but low: '*Source claims the painting stolen is not a Goya or Velázquez.*'

Another voice from the back: '*British art detective asked to help on Prado case.*'

'It's already on social media,' Gutiérrez said.

Morales leaned in, scanning. '*Benjamin Blake, an art recovery expert, is in Madrid to assist in the investigation.*'

The agent at the keyboard scrolled slowly, the projector beam twitching slightly on the wall. '*Recently credited with locating a missing Dalí canvas in Catalonia, Blake made headlines last month when he was erroneously identified by the Guardia Civil in a manhunt during the G20 in Barcelona.*'

Castro looked up, sharply. Barcelona. Dalí. She remembered the noise around that – the manhunt, the confusion. And now this guy was here?

'According to *El País*,' said the agent at the keyboard, 'he's worked with Scotland Yard, Interpol and the FBI. Doesn't name him as the source of the Goya-Velázquez line, but the implication's clear. Someone's brought him in, unofficially or not.'

Morales again: '*El País* says they've contacted the museum, the culture ministry and *us* … for a comment.' He looked up. 'Anyone here been called?'

Silence.

'*Who the fuck authorised this?*' Barroso's words landed hard. Even the low hum of the projector seemed to pause. The image of Benjamin lingered, frozen on the screen on the wall. Several agents turned their heads towards Alfonso García.

He didn't flinch. His expression stayed neutral. Not defensive, not shocked – but not particularly surprised, either. Castro was watching him closely.

'Let's make something crystal clear,' Barroso said, voice low and dangerous. 'Did anyone in this room ask this Brit to assist in my investigation, which is under a *secreto de sumario*?'

No one spoke. Barroso looked around the room, eyes scanning for dissidents. He then turned deliberately towards García.

'Nobody, right, García?'

The head of the cultural brigade nodded calmly. 'Correct,' he said. 'The **BPH** certainly hasn't asked for outside assistance. We're short-staffed, as you know, but I would have personally informed you –'

Barroso barked out a humourless laugh. 'So, it's the little shits at the culture ministry, or that leftie lesbian who shouldn't be running the fucking Prado.'

A few agents exchanged glances. Castro shifted in her seat and cleared her throat to speak.

'If the BPH is short-staffed, and we're stretched on the homicide front, then what's the harm in asking for outside help?' she asked. 'It's a Caravaggio.'

Barroso's head snapped towards her. '*The harm?*' he echoed, mock sweet. 'We're less than eighteen hours into a murder investigation inside Spain's most important cultural institution, with a missing Caravaggio, a butchered guard, and a media circus already sharpening their fucking knives. We're operating under a gag order, signed by the judge. That means no unvetted intelligence comes in, and nothing goes out that hasn't been cleared. No freelancers, no amateurs, no third-party involvement, and no one leaks a fucking thing. Is that understood?'

Castro didn't blink.

'The moment you let an outsider in,' he said, 'you risk contaminating the investigation. Worst of all, you give the press something to tear us apart – *the inept Spanish police have to rely on a fucking foreigner to solve a crime.* You want the judge on my back?' He shook his head, scoffing. 'Unless you'd rather *El País* run the investigation for us, Castro?'

The last comment landed like a slap. Castro's mouth tightened. She almost fired back – *wanted to,* desperately – to ask Barroso, in front of everyone, how many severed heads and Italian 'suicides' he'd left uninvestigated over the past year. To watch him squirm. But she stopped herself. Not here. Not yet.

She then caught García's eye across the room – saw the slightest shake of his head, a quiet warning. Was he suspicious of Barroso, too?

The inspector was now jabbing a finger towards the projected screen displaying the newspaper report, and barking instructions at Morales.

'Get on the phone to *El País* and get them to shut this shit down. Whoever the journalist is, whatever their so-called *source* – issue a warning. Remind them we're under a judicial order and if they pedal rumours, we'll push for sanctions.'

Morales gave a nod, reaching for his phone.

'Also get a message to the judge,' Barroso said. 'She needs to hear about this from us, not social fucking media. And if you find this British prick, tell him to keep his fucking nose out of our investigation.'

A message pinged. Not loud, but sharp enough to break the silence. Moments later, Gutiérrez murmured something low into Barroso's ear.

'Ignacio Lázaro's in interview room two, sir. We've done what you asked with his phone.'

Barroso didn't move at first. His eyes stayed fixed on the photos pinned to the wall. Then he straightened – slow, mechanical – and checked his watch.

'This meeting's over for now,' he said. 'I want updates every half hour. And remember – no one moves without me. Everything comes through my desk first. Is that clear?'

No one answered.

Castro watched him leave – shoulders rigid, jaw set, the pace too deliberate to be calm. The room stayed silent until the door closed.

He wasn't trying to control the investigation anymore, she realised. He was trying to bury it – from them all.

40

Elena

Sunday – La Latina district.

The room was barely bigger than the bed, with a mirror that made it feel lonelier, not larger. The ceiling fan ticked like a metronome while music played too loudly from a second-floor balcony. The tiny bathroom held the tang of lemon cleaner. The WiFi connection was solid. That counted for a lot.

Elena had returned from the rooftop event with a bottle of water, a paper napkin stuffed with a few canapés folded into her bag, and a dizziness from the sun – or from sidestepping too many leering men.

Benjamin had messaged to suggest they meet up later – nothing else. Was it about *El País*? He hadn't said. She hoped he hadn't seen the short piece. Part of her wanted to meet up – another quote, maybe even *on* the record – and it would beat spending Sunday evening alone in a city that had brushed her aside. She caught her reflection in the mirror above the small table. A slight smile, which she immediately erased.

She sat cross-legged on the single bed, back against the wall, laptop balanced on her knees, as her fingers tapped out search terms faster than she could process them.

She started by Googling Ramón Falcó – head of Spain's sports council – the man she was supposed to interview tomorrow about racism in football. At the rooftop event, Mei had suggested he wouldn't be available – *if the Falcós haven't already suffered some kind of accident,* she'd said.

What the hell was that supposed to mean? Was Mei a family friend of the Falcós? Someone close enough to speak cryptically about their private life?

She searched for *Ramón Falcó family*, then tapped through the results: Ramón, his wife Cayetana, their son Borja. One child. No accidents, no illnesses, nothing immediately unusual. Cayetana cropped up in glossy society shots – *Hola!* spreads, charity galas, sometimes with the podgy Ramón beside her.

Borja looked tanned, cocky and smug in every photo she found – arms draped around blonde *pijas*, influencers, champagne in hand, living it large on yachts and at parties. He looked like someone who'd never known a real problem or suffered an accident in his life.

She took a swig of water and dug further. *Ramón Falcó* + *Borja Falcó*. The surname now rang bells. The son ran a sports marketing outfit, negotiating sponsor-ship deals, TV rights – the same murky territory that the football agent Carlos liked to haunt.

She found the headline of an old investigative piece, flagging up the ethics of Borja dabbling in sports marketing while his father ran Spain's sports council. But the link to the full article was a dead tab, a '404 error – page not found'. It had been wiped clean, as if someone high up had stamped it out.

Then she hit something strange. Another old head-line buried a few pages in: *Son of Madrid police inspector dies in Ibiza fall.*

There was a photo – many faces of partygoers, arms raised, plastic cups mid-toast. Mostly *pijos.* Some of them named, including Borja Falcó. He was younger, thinner, paler. Eyes glassy. But it was clearly him, standing off to one side.

She scrolled down and read the article. The name of the police inspector caught her eye. *Inspector Jefe Félix Barroso.* That name triggered something. Another click. Another link wiped clean. Something else that someone didn't want found.

A quick Google of *Inspector Jefe Félix Barroso.* She knew she'd heard the name before; he was the one leading the Prado case.

Her phone pinged. She jolted, checked the screen. Some travel offer from a company she'd never heard of. She rolled her eyes, but the nudge had worked. She opened her email app, flicked through the inbox, then – almost absently – tapped into spam. There it was.

Cristina González / PA to Sr. Ramón Falcó. Time-stamped: 10.15h that morning.

Dear Ms. Carmona, unfortunately Sr. Falcó will be unable to meet you on Monday. We apologise for any inconvenience.

No reason. No reschedule. Just a cold brush-off, a digital middle finger. And sent *hours before* Mei mentioned anything about any possible accident.

Elena sat as if someone had muted the world. She picked up Mei's card and called. Straight to voicemail. No rings, no voice, no leave-a-message – just *click*, gone. She didn't leave one. She stared at her phone, indignant. Mei had said to call if she ever wanted to write about the things no one will talk about.

Abuse. Trafficking. Underage girls from poor countries lured with promises of a future on the pitch – used for something else. A paedophile ring dressed up as sport.

Well, here she was – reaching out. And Mei Zhang – whoever she really was – didn't even pick up the fucking phone.

She went back to Googling.

Mei Zhang.

One hundred million results. Great.

She tried to narrow it down: *Mei Zhang + Madrid.*

Still a mess. A few lifestyle blogs, a restaurant reviewer, but nothing remotely related to football or rooftop events. She added: *Mei Zhang + women's football.* Then + *Ramón Falcó + grassroots + Vietnam + Thailand + charity + Madrid* …

A handful of vague hits. Conference guest lists. Names on charity committees she couldn't trace. She tried Googling the number on the business card. Nothing. No name connected to it. She went to LinkedIn. There were thousands of Mei Zhangs – tour guides, bankers, yoga instructors, B2B sales, multimedia specialists, HR managers in Shanghai …

Back to Google, and it took another fifteen minutes of narrowing the search terms before anything vaguely promising popped up. A cached page from an old sports innovation conference in Lausanne, Switzerland. There was a photo – low-res, cropped, but definitely her – alongside a business card-style bio.

Mei Zhang

Strategic Advisor - Global Partnerships - Women's
Football Philanthropy - Asia-Europe Relations

Former board adviser to multiple cross-border initiatives focused on grassroots sport, female athlete development and social mobility through football. Experience in Asia and Europe. Currently consulting on equity strategy in emerging sports markets.

Elena took a screenshot, then clicked for more, but the link was dead. Still, the fragment had the whiff of legitimacy. She scrolled further down the page that gave more info on the sports innovation conference – skipping past pictures of men in suits shaking hands with other men in suits – until she got to a note about 'Partners & Sponsors'.

With kind support from the Zurich Institute for Global Sport

Equity (ZIGSE), Vitalia Trust, and the Gaming Integrity Foundation (GIF).

Elena took another screenshot, then opened a new Google tab.

Mei Zhang + Zurich Institute for Global Sport Equity.

Mei Zhang + Vitalia Trust.

Mei Zhang + Gaming Integrity Foundation …

The screen on her phone lit up again. She answered the incoming call.

'Elena – how are you?' Mei said from the other end of the line before Elena could speak. 'You called.'

Elena frowned. 'I did. I didn't leave a message –'

'I saw your missed call,' Mei said, warm, precise.

Elena's eyes flashed to Mei's card on the desk. The déjà vu from the rooftop flared. But it wasn't déjà vu – it had been Mei uttering the same words that Elena now realised she'd heard earlier in the day: that racism in Spanish football was a *crowded subject – you're shouting into a hurricane – the real rot tends to hide beneath the headlines.*

It was what Carlos had said, before cancelling her interview with his player and instead forwarding the invite to the rooftop event. *You'll meet people, Elena,* he'd said, with his oily helpfulness.

Meeting Mei now felt like it had been arranged. Had she been set up?

Elena hesitated, then said, 'About earlier – when you mentioned Ramón Falcó and some family accident … what did you mean?'

Mei's voice dropped slightly. 'You're not still on about the Falcós, are you? I would have hoped you'd be looking into the underage trafficking tip I gave you – and the Italians.'

'Italians?'

'It's not difficult to guess who, Elena. You'll have an exclusive on your hands. We can give you the leads, but you'll need to act fast –'

'We?' Elena said. 'Who's we?'

'Not on a call, Elena. We'll need to meet face-to-face again.'

'When? Where?'

'I'll ask my PA to check my calendar for tomorrow,' Mei said. 'We'll message you a time and location.'

'Do that,' Elena said. She paused, then: 'How did you know it was me?'

'I'm sorry?'

'My number. I didn't leave a message. You called back and said *Elena, how are you?* – before I spoke.'

'No, I didn't –'

'Yes, you did.'

'You must have given me your number earlier.'

'I didn't. I just took your own card.'

'Maybe from the event,' Mei said, slightly sharper now. 'They collected the press contacts.'

Something didn't sit right. Elena replayed the moment she'd entered the hotel and made her way up to the rooftop – the ease of it. She'd said her name but hadn't given a card or her number to anyone. No list, just a nod and a smile from the girl with the clipboard, and a wristband.

'I didn't give my number,' Elena said.

'Elena, I like you,' came the reply. 'I think we can work together. We will speak more tomorrow.'

Click.

Elena sat motionless for a while, the phone still at her ear, the room suddenly airless.

Later, she stood, walked to the window, and opened it. Cool air slipped in, carrying the noise of the city – fainter now, but still there, even on a Sunday night.

The slimy Carlos. Two years ago, he'd bragged to her in a club off the Castellana – his *private club*, he'd said – the kind that tolerated dodgy money and loud men. *You'll know where to always find me when you want a real story*. Yeah. Tonight, she'd find him.

She tied her hair back, put on some lipstick and the top that made bouncers pause instead of refuse. Not her preferred look, but it would do the trick.

Her phone pinged again. Another message from Benjamin.

Up for a nightcap somewhere later?

Nothing about *El País*, which was good. He either hadn't seen it or didn't care.

She hesitated, then texted back:

Sí – OK. I'll message you a location later.

41

Benjamin

Sunday – Calle de Diego de León.

'Hello, Benjamin, it's Duncan Carter-James from the embassy again.'

Double-barrelled Duncan, with his galloping, annoyingly jolly voice, the kind that made you want to punch him down the phone. And, of course, his twins screaming in the background, along with his poor wife, who sounded like she was in full meltdown – or maybe wielding a machete and chasing him through the house. You wouldn't blame her.

'It's a really bad line,' Benjamin lied. He could hear Duncan perfectly, but it was unbearable. 'Are you in a war zone, by any chance?'

Duncan's kids were still screeching in the background, while his Spanish wife unleashed a stream of ... what? Insults, orders or just noise?

274

'Er, Duncan, is there something I can actually help you with?' Benjamin asked. 'Or did you just think I was missing the toddler shriekfest?'

'Sorry,' Duncan said, who finally managed to douse the flames at home, at least temporarily. 'Okay, super, well, that's all sorted – I'm just moving to another room – so, anyway, how are you, Benjamin?'

'I'm fine, thanks. I won't ask how you are.'

'No … but yes, *yes*, indeed, you seem to have certainly settled in. Good for you, I say.'

'Settled in?' Benjamin said, glancing around the terrace on a small plaza off Calle de Diego de León, where he was supposed to have dinner with Ignacio from the culture ministry and Alfonso from the BPH, to go over his early thoughts.

'From what I've read, yes, indeed,' Duncan said. There was some more yelling in the background, but then a door slammed on it.

'Sorry, Duncan, but what are you talking about?'

'*El País*. I saw you online in *El País*.'

'*What?*'

'Nice photo, too,' said Duncan.

'What do you mean, *you saw me in El País?*' Benjamin froze, phone pressed to his ear.

'I'll send you the link,' Duncan said. 'Do you therefore know what painting *was* snatched? Give me a clue, I won't tell anyone.'

'What the hell does it say in *El País?*' Benjamin asked, a trace of panic slipping through his voice.

'Not a lot. I'll send you the link. Look, I hope you'll still have time to look at this restitution case with me –'

'Duncan – what does it say?' Benjamin pressed.

'It says you've been asked to help with the Prado investigation. There's a picture of you. The paper quotes a source saying that it wasn't a Goya or a Velázquez that was taken, so I assume that was also you.'

'*For fuck's sake, Elena …*' Benjamin muttered.

'But I'm glad I put you in touch with Ignacio, he's a dear friend and that's why I'm also calling.'

Benjamin had grabbed a table on the restaurant terrace and was trying to open his MacBook with one hand, moving the cutlery, a menu, an ashtray and a small potted cactus out of the way. '*For fuck's sake*,' he muttered again. 'I'm about to meet Ignacio now.'

'Where are you then?' Duncan asked. 'At the police station?'

Benjamin stopped what he was doing and looked around the terrace again. 'No, Duncan, I'm not at a police station. I'm sitting outside a restaurant waiting for Ignacio to arrive. He's late. What's happened?'

'Right,' Duncan said. 'Well, I don't think he'll make it to the restaurant, by the sound of things.'

'What's going on?'

'He's been pulled in,' Duncan said, his tone suddenly flat. No trace of his usual jollity. 'Police questioning. Huertas station.'

'Wait – why? *Arrested?*'

'Not technically. Voluntarily assisting with

enquiries, apparently – but not exactly going home early, either. Or having tapas or dinner with you.'

'He called you?'

'They let him make two calls. One to a lawyer, if he wanted one. The other … he chose to call me.'

Benjamin caught the eye of a waiter and beckoned for a glass of beer.

'He didn't want to call you directly,' Duncan went on. 'He said, and I quote, he *didn't want to complicate things further*. Whatever the hell that means. He sounded like he couldn't talk for long: he was talking low. So, I'm now your glorified go-between.'

Benjamin closed his eyes.

'He said to tell you that he won't be meeting you again after all. And he wants to keep your earlier rendezvous quiet. Strictly between you two.' A beat. 'Bit late for that, isn't it?'

Benjamin's eyes narrowed as he turned the thought over. Ignacio hadn't struck him as reckless. He wasn't loud or showy. If anything, he seemed like one of those quietly efficient civil servants that ministries liked to promote – discreet, reliable, invisible. So why haul him in? Benjamin hadn't told Elena who'd asked him to help. Hadn't even hinted … surely?

'I've just sent you the *El País* link,' Duncan said, amid background screaming again. 'Hang on, I'll call you back.'

A new message popped up on Benjamin's phone, from Duncan C-J. One link, and three words to accompany it in Spanish: *Qué guapo estás!*

He tapped on the link. He scrolled, already half-knowing what was coming. And there it was: a photo. *Him.* Earlier that afternoon, squinting in the sun outside the Casón del Buen Retiro, Einstein hair in full bloom – puffier than he'd realised, too. The kind of shot that made him look important by total accident, arms crossed like some brooding expert they'd just recruited from MI-effing-6. *Jesus Christ.*

It was part of a rolling news story about the Prado that would be regularly updated. He couldn't see any byline on the report about himself, but he knew who'd written it. His eyes skimmed the text, not under-standing it all, but catching the gist – *Prado, asesinato, cuadro robado, británico, Goya, Velázquez, policía, ministerio de cultura* – even the *Guardia Civil, Barcelona* and *Salvador Dalí* got a mention.

For Christ's sake, Elena.

He stared at it for a few seconds longer, then shut the tab. He gazed over his shoulder, not sure what he was expecting – but half-expecting it anyway.

Checking his phone again, he hovered over Elena's number, wanting to call – to rant, to demand an expla-nation. But what was the point? Better to wait until he met up with her later, in person.

His phone buzzed yet again.

'Did you get the link?' Duncan asked. There was a bit of shouting in the background again, but not as bad as earlier.

'I did, thanks – but can you read the report to me. I can't follow all of it.'

Duncan read it aloud, concluding with: '*El País* has contacted the police, the Prado and the culture ministry for comment.'

'So, there's no mention of *who* asked for my help?'

'Correct.'

'And yet the police have dragged Ignacio in for a little chat.'

'That's your conclusion,' Duncan said.

Benjamin didn't respond. But the feeling was already settling in his gut – something didn't sit right. It felt like a warning – not just to Ignacio, but to him. A quiet shove to back off. *To not complicate things further.*

He felt it again. That flicker. He remembered it clearly now – at the terrace in the Retiro park. After Elena had gone, a man catching his eye and beckoning a waiter for his bill, just seconds after he'd done so himself. Had the man been watching him at the Ritz with Ignacio? Had he then followed him with Elena through the park?

Don't complicate things further, was Ignacio's message via Duncan. What things?

He'd expected the police might not want him sniffing around their homicide case – Ignacio had even made that clear at the Ritz. Fair enough. He couldn't stomach blood, and murders gave him the creeps. But a stolen painting? That was familiar ground. It was where he thrived, and how he paid his bills.

He hadn't come to Madrid to get dragged into chaos. It was meant to be a quick trip – low profile, low effort. But now? Now there was a missing masterpiece, an agreed finder's fee, and a culture ministry flunky suddenly too scared to meet. Add to that the financial black hole of the divorce spiralling back in London – well, walking away wasn't really on the menu.

If this was someone's attempt to scare him off, they'd misjudged the target. He didn't mind being warned off – but he hated being underestimated.

He considered his options. He didn't want to make trouble for Ignacio, but he wasn't about to walk away. He could go straight to the Prado's director – they'd crossed paths a few years ago, enough for a polite reminder. Or to Alfonso at the culture brigade, who Ignacio had said would be joining them tonight. He'd liaised with Alfonso's unit before, even helped locate a Goya sketch that had wandered a little too far east.

And now that Elena had kindly plastered his face all over *El País*, anonymity was off the table. No point waiting in the wings.

Nothing sharpened his focus faster than a painting that shouldn't be missing – and a door someone was trying to quietly close.

Suddenly, Duncan's twins shrieked like broken fire alarms in the background again.

'Look,' Duncan was saying, 'as you've been stood up by Ignacio, I'll join you instead. He told me where he'd arranged to meet you.'

'No, wait, Duncan –'

'On my way. Anything to get out of here.'

42

Barroso · Ignacio · Gutiérrez

Sunday — Comisaría de Policía, Calle de las Huertas.

The door of the interview room cracked open hard enough to rattle the hinges. Inspector Jefe Barroso stormed in, face purple, glistening with sweat. He looked like a man on the edge of something irreversible — already yelling before the door swung shut.

'You fucking bureaucrats. You always think you're above us, don't you? Setting up meetings behind our backs. You think we don't see?'

Ignacio kept quiet.

'I want to know what the fuck you were thinking,' he snapped, looming over the table, his spit flecking the table. 'Bringing in an *outsider*? Who the hell is this Brit? What is he to you, to the museum? To *me*?'

Ignacio sat still; hands folded tightly on the table.

'We had you followed. We saw you at the Ritz.

281

Then your *guiri* friend wandered into the park with a fucking reporter.' He stopped abruptly, breathing hard. 'You broke the secrecy order, and you think I wouldn't find out?'

Ignacio hesitated. 'I simply thought —'

'You *simply thought*,' Barroso spat. 'You simply thought we needed help, is that it? The Spanish police, overwhelmed? Poor little overworked BPH? Did the fucking Brit tell you that? Is that what you discussed between cock-measuring contests at the Ritz? You smug little prick.'

Ignacio's jaw tensed. 'I really don't understand what I've —'

'It's very simple,' Barroso cut in. 'We're talking about a breach of judicial secrecy, contempt of court, obstruction of justice, unauthorised disclosure — even improper use of public office during your employment at the ministry of fucking culture.'

'I'm waiting for my lawyer to arrive.'

'Oh, really?' Barroso said, jabbing a finger an inch from Ignacio's eye. 'You think I give a toss about that?'

Ignacio leant away.

'What do you know?' Barroso snapped. 'What does the Brit know? You hiding something from me? Whatever it is, I need it *right now* —'

Ignacio frowned. 'If there was anything —'

Barroso slammed his fist on the table. *Just tell me what you both know.*'

'You're not well,' Ignacio said.

Barroso grabbed the edge of the table, his knuckles

white. '*I'm* not well?' he said. He barked a short, rasping laugh. 'I'm the only one who can see how deep this goes. You have no fucking idea –'

Ignacio tried to stand. Barroso lunged forward, grabbing him by the collar before yanking him halfway across the table. '*Tell me what you know* –'

'*Get your hands off me* –'

'*Tell me what you fucking know.*'

The door burst open. Detective Gutiérrez was there in two strides, grabbing the inspector's shoulders. '*Jefe – let him go – let go* –'

Barroso resisted, breathing like a cornered animal. Then, reluctantly, he let go. Ignacio fell back, his collar creased, his throat red. The inspector adjusted his cuffs as if nothing had happened.

'All I was trying to do was help,' Ignacio rasped. 'I met with the British art expert because I thought Alfonso García could use him. Alfonso was open to it, and said he'd meet him. You don't like it? Ask *him*.'

Barroso went rigid. Then he turned and stormed out, the door slamming hard behind him. He stopped in the hallway, chest heaving, eyes wild, cracking his knuckles.

Halfway down the corridor stood a woman with a laptop tucked under her arm – Lara from cyber. Hair scraped back. No makeup. Fingernails bitten to the quick. She'd heard the shouting.

A moment later, Gutiérrez emerged from the interview room, rubbing his temple, his face tight with the aftershock of what he'd just seen.

'Where's García?' Barroso barked.

'Left the incident room soon after you,' Gutiérrez said.

'And the Brit?'

Lara hesitated, glancing at Gutiérrez before answering.

'We checked the calls made on Lázaro's phone, just before it was returned to him to call his lawyer,' she said carefully. 'There was a UK number – we're assuming that's the Brit. We've put a trace on it. If it's him, he's somewhere in the *barrio* Salamanca. Looks like he's using a BiciMad.'

Barroso's brow twitched. 'A bicycle?'

'Yes, sir. But the account was hijacked,' Lara said. 'The unlock came from his UK mobile, but that number doesn't match any registered user ID in the BiciMad system. No EMT account either. The code request went through a Spanish burner – or a cloned login. He forced access manually. It's … messy.'

Barroso frowned. 'So, he's tech savvy.'

'Or someone helped him,' Lara said.

A dry sound escaped Barroso – half laugh, half snarl. 'Of course. Why not. A fucking bicycle.' He straightened. 'Keep tracking him. I want his location in real time. Every move. And this stays between us. Not a word to García.'

'Yes, sir,' Gutiérrez said.

Barroso turned and strode off down the corridor, the strip lights glaring off his damp collar. His gait was rigid, uneven – a man barely keeping himself upright.

Lara watched him go. 'He's losing it,' she murmured.

Gutiérrez let out a slow breath. 'He already has. We need to stay ahead of him.'

For a moment, neither moved; the corridor still hummed with leftover tension.

He checked the far end – empty – then stepped aside. 'I'll make a call,' he said.

Lara looked up. 'To who?'

'Just keep that feed live,' he said, pulling out his phone.

She nodded and walked off.

Gutiérrez moved a few paces down the corridor and pressed the phone to his ear. 'Pilar,' he muttered. 'Pick up.'

43

Castellana House

Sunday – Paseo de La Habana.

The cab dropped her fifty metres from Castellana House, a cocktail lounge masquerading as a private club. She checked her reflection in a boutique window – hair pinned up, chic-enough top, suitable lipstick to pass the velvet-rope test. The doormen gave her that two-second scan – shoes, legs, tits, lips, eyes – then nodded her through. Professional sleaze in pressed suits and earpieces. Elena was buzzing with anger, and it suited her.

Inside, the club was still very much alive for a Sunday night – music pulsing, the air thick with gin, perfume and money; people leaning in very close, all cocktails and shadows. The main lounge on the first floor glowed.

She spotted him at once – Carlos – spread out at a

corner banquette with two men she didn't know. One broad, smiling, pale. The other, Chinese, early thirties maybe, lean and wiry – his stillness caught her for half a second before she looked away.

Elena crossed before she could lose her nerve.

'Carlos,' she said, voice level but hard. 'You set me up.'

He looked up, that flash of teeth and rehearsed smile freezing halfway. 'Elena. *Qué sorpresa.* We're just having a drink –'

'I said you set me up.'

'Easy, chica.' Carlos gestured for her to sit. 'You want a drink?'

'No, I want answers.' She stayed standing.

'Always the journalist.'

'You set me up. That rooftop bullshit – the invite, the meeting – all of it. You forgot to tell me I was being used. I want to know why.'

The quiet guy with Carlos lifted his eyes from his drink. Not looking *at* her so much as *through* her. The other man – fixed grin, sweating – barely noticed her.

'Lower your voice, *por favor,*' Carlos said, glancing around. 'People here have ears.'

'You mean your friends have ears?' Elena shot back. 'I don't like being played, Carlos. Who was that woman?'

Carlos stood abruptly and touched her elbow. She shook him off.

'Elena, please,' he muttered. 'Not here.'

Elena opened her mouth to speak, then *felt* it – the

stillness beside them, the shift in air. She turned slightly, catching the gaze of the quiet one for half a second. He didn't look away.

Carlos followed her glance. 'Elena, sit down, please, everything's fine, these are –'

'Who?' she cut in

'Friends. Investors. Business colleagues. You like their bars. Maybe you're drinking in one of them now.'

'I don't care who owns this place.'

Carlos looked past her shoulder, then straightened. 'Okay, whatever. Let's drop it. This isn't the place –'

'I like working on an exposé, Carlos. What I don't like is being set up, or someone trying to plant a story. What exactly is she paying you for? She even made a bizarre comment about a man I'm interviewing tomorrow – Ramón Falcó –'

Something jolted across the table – tiny, but visible. The young guy's hand stopped halfway to his glass. A flicker in the jaw. Carlos saw it too.

'Okay, look, listen, that's enough,' Carlos said quickly, catching his companion's eye. 'Go home, Elena. Go back to your hotel, or wherever you're staying.'

'Where *are* you staying?' the young guy asked suddenly. His voice was soft, but the words landed. 'He said *Elena*, right? Where are you staying, Elena?'

Elena stared. 'Excuse me?'

A moment of silence.

'Forget it, Carlos,' he said, still eyeing her. 'She's not interested.'

Elena felt a cold rush behind her ribs – anger or fear, maybe both. 'Interested in what?' she said.

Carlos lifted both hands slightly, placating. 'Elena, please. You're making a scene.'

'I'm asking a question.'

'And I'm telling you it doesn't matter,' Carlos said.

Elena noticed the guy again, still glaring at her.

'There are others,' he said, his lips twisting into a sneer.

Carlos shot him a warning look.

'Others for *what*?' Elena said.

'Drop it,' Carlos said quickly. 'Just go home. Seriously. Take the night off.'

Then, softly, from the young guy: 'Be careful walking back.'

Elena's breath caught. That was enough. She turned and walked. She took the stairs two at a time, strode down the mirrored corridor, past the bar where someone laughed too loud, and out into the street, sweeping past the doormen still eyeing her legs.

Outside, she stopped, pulse kicking hard, the club's glow bleeding across the pavement behind her. For a moment she thought she saw him – the young Chinese guy – step out through the entrance. She crossed the street and kept walking anyway.

The night felt warmer, louder. She'd texted Benjamin earlier, sending him a place for that nightcap – anywhere near Castellana House, Paseo de La Habana. She pulled her phone from her bag, checking if he'd replied, if he was heading this way. If not, she'd call it a night, find a taxi. Her mind was spinning.

In a shop window she caught her reflection – and behind it, on the other side of the road, a shape. The creep had definitely followed her out.

She started walking towards the next block.

Kai watched her under the streetlight, the line of her throat catching the glow. That long neck – the kind he liked to grip.

She'd seen him in the doorway. She knew he was there, knew he was following, but she kept walking as if she didn't care. That irritated him. That refusal to flinch made his palms itch.

When she'd mentioned the Falcós – *of all people* – something in his gut had tightened. Why hadn't he received any news that the Falcós had been cut out of the equation? They should have been butchered by now. Why were things not going totally to plan?

She wasn't just a journalist looking for a headline; she was asking the wrong questions. That made her dangerous. And right now, he relished the idea of making her stop asking anything else – ever.

He fell into step a half-block behind, careful, slow. He stayed on the opposite pavement, waiting for the right moment to cross.

She kept her head high, deliberate, almost daring him. That composure – that performance of calm – he hated it. He wanted to see it break.

He watched her check her phone again, light spilling over her face, thumb flicking. Then a hand half-raised for a taxi that didn't come.

He could see the alley two streets down, the angle of the light, how easy it would be to cross and pull her into darkness – quick, quiet, efficient.

Now.

Do it.

Then some jerk on a BiciMad came around the corner – hair and wheels out of control – his shout splitting the night, splitting the distance between Kai and the girl as horns blared and the bike wobbled without lights. She looked up, called back to him. They waved at one another. Then they were together, and she was talking to him.

They turned and their eyes picked him out together – directly opposite, across the street – like a pair of knives.

Kai froze, the moment gone. Not tonight. He strolled back into the shadows near the club – *his* club – folding himself into the dark and watching them move away.

He would get to her another time. Maybe Carlos had her number.

'Thanks for *El País*, Elena –' Benjamin said, half-falling off his bike. 'What the fuck was –?'

'There's a man following me,' she said quickly.

'What?'

'Across the street.'

'Where?'

'*Ahí.* Look.'

Benjamin ran a hand through his hair as the short figure vanished into the darkness.

'He's going,' he said. 'He's gone. Who the hell was that?'

'*No tengo ni idea.*'

'What?'

'I have *no idea*, Benjamin –'

'Okay, well he's gone. Are you okay?'

'*Sí.*'

'Good,' he said. 'Look, about *El País* – I spoke to you *off the fucking record* –'

'You don't have to swear.'

'I *do* have to fucking swear –'

'It wasn't that bad.'

'Elena, it's dangerous. I've told you this before. After what you published in Barcelona –'

'You never told me the whole story.'

'I don't tell people the whole story. I try to stay discreet. I don't want my photo and name splashed anywhere. I have enemies. From before.'

'You keep saying that –'

'Because it's true. You've no idea what kind of people I've crossed. And *El fucking País* has just told them where I am.'

She didn't reply.

'It's not just me, Elena. My family, my ex – my daughter –' He stopped himself.

'They would have run something anyway. I thought I'd at least make sure it wasn't total bullshit.'

He waited, temper cooling. 'Okay, but you owe me now.'

'*Qué? Qué significa eso … owe you?*'

'You owe me a favour,' Benjamin said.

A beat.

'What kind of favour?'

'You know a bit about football, right?'

'*Joder*, what does that mean?'

'I want to ask you a few questions …'

'Okay,' she said. 'Well, you said you wanted a nightcap, so let's walk and find somewhere – and ask me.'

They started moving along the pavement, Benjamin pushing his BiciMad beside her.

'You going to leave that?' she asked.

'No,' he said. 'Not right now. It's complicated.'

She slipped her arm through his without thinking, matching his stride.

She glanced back once – the pavement empty, but the sense of eyes still there, like heat on her skin.

44

Detective Morales

Sunday – Lavapiés neighbourhood.

Morales had decided not to wait for Barroso's approval. Lara had found Jason Zhou's address an hour ago. He rode in an unmarked car with another agent, no siren, no blue light. No need to tip anyone off. He just wanted to be the first through the door.

The streets closed in as they pushed into Lavapiés – tighter, darker, harder to control. This was different territory. Old tenements stacked over Afro-Caribbean groceries, halal butchers, market stalls and the odd anarchist bar. Madrid's *castizos* were long gone, while many of the new tenants didn't show up on leases, let alone databases. Morales never liked working this *barrio* – too dense, too fast, too many languages yelling at once. And if someone was holed up here, the chances were the neighbours knew and weren't telling.

They pulled up in front of a crumbling apartment block off the Calle del Amparo. Morales got out first, eyes scanning up towards the fifth floor. Pigeons fluttered from a ledge.

'Top floor,' he muttered, checking the number against the buzzer but not pressing it. Then a nod to his companion – no need for words.

Inside the stairwell, the walls were cracked and painted institutional green halfway up. There was a smell of fried onions. On the fifth floor, Morales held up a hand and listened. Voices, a TV, a child crying behind another door – but nothing from 5B.

The metal door was painted brown, its peephole smudged. He didn't have a warrant, but he had no intention of knocking.

Morales met the other agent's eye and flicked his chin – the go-signal. His hand hovered just inside his jacket, fingers resting near the grip of his Glock, hidden but ready. He didn't think he'd need it, but the habit was wired in. His colleague stepped forward with a universal lock-pick gun.

Click. Click. A pause. Breath held. Then a third.

The lock gave, and the door cracked open.

The air inside was stale, the flat neat and clean – but it was also empty. There was a single mattress on the floor, blanket folded. No photos. No clothes. No food in the kitchenette. No sign of Jason Zhou.

'Looks like someone knew we might be coming and decided they wouldn't be here to greet us,' the agent said, scanning the stripped-down bedsit.

Morales didn't answer. He moved slowly through the space, eyes working the corners, around doorframes, under the sparse furniture that there was. By the radiator, something caught his eye – a twisted loop of bright yellow webbing, the Velcro edge curling, one end frayed. A discarded plastic strap. Not much, but out of place. He put it in a ziplock bag.

He glanced towards the open door. He could see some dark scuff marks across the tiles just inside – curved, repeated, tyre-width. A *bike's* tyres.

He frowned. Fifth floor. No lift. No one hauls a bike that far unless they don't trust leaving it downstairs – or aren't allowed to. The space was too small, too bare – no wall hooks, no rack, no balcony, nowhere to store a bike. Maybe it was the folding bike they found at the Café Prado. Easier to carry in and out and easier to vanish with.

Next to the front door, he noticed a stain and shallow dent in the plaster at hip height – like something boxy had bumped the same spot again and again. Then it clicked. A folding bike – and *the strap?* Delivery bag. No question.

Morales gave a nod towards the hallway, then rapped twice on the flat next door. A long pause. Finally, it creaked open on the chain.

'We're looking for the guy next door. Ever see him come or go? Carrying a bike, maybe?'

The neighbour blinked, said nothing, then closed the door again.

Morales didn't bother knocking again.

45

Kai Leroux

Sunday — Chamartín and Gran Vía.

This particular street in Chamartín was dead quiet at night. Shuttered boutiques. Empty cafés with their chairs stacked.

The parlour didn't advertise. It didn't need to. A bronze plaque with bland initials hung by the door, making it look like a dental clinic or cosmetic surgery. Kai pressed a buzzer, and the lock clicked.

A woman with long, black-lacquered nails rose from behind a reception desk as he entered. Her hair was scraped back into a severe knot, pencil skirt tight, blouse crisp enough to cut. She didn't smile. She didn't speak. She turned on a thin heel and started down the corridor. The carpet swallowed the sound of her stilettos, leaving only the faint shift of air as she strutted ahead of him.

Even here, with the silence, the soft light and expectation, he could feel it. That low thrum of anticipation in his gut, a tightening coil just beneath the ribs, a hunger he'd learned to time like a drug.

The woman stopped at a door, her nails clicking once against the frame before she pushed it open.

The room breathed hush and control. Dark wood panels, a padded table fitted with leather straps, shadows in the corners where nothing could be seen clearly. A trace of sweet perfume hung in the air. And, as always, the chair. High-backed, upholstered in soft leather. The voyeur's seat. That was Kai's place. He never lay on the tables. Never submitted, never knelt. It was always about control.

He sat, spreading his knees. Breathing faster now. This was what he paid for: to wait, to watch.

The door opened again. Two entered – sometimes women, sometimes men, tonight one of each. Naked. They didn't acknowledge him.

He watched as they went straight to the table. One lay back, the other moved behind, hands gently skimming skin in a parody of tenderness, slow at first. An arm grazing a shoulder, fingers brushing the collarbone. Then it shifted to the tightening. A hand locked across the throat. Pressure applied.

Kai leaned forward, elbows on his thighs. His lips parted. This wasn't just arousal. It was rehearsal. This was what the Principal wanted of him: choke the competition, choke the enemy, choke Martelli himself until the old bastard had nothing left.

The special moment was approaching – the moment when breath turned to panic, when control narrowed to the span of one hand. Right now, he drank it in – the restraint, the way the victim's eyes flared then dimmed, halfway between fight and surrender. This was the moment he craved.

The thrashing built, legs kicking, muffled sounds tearing at the air. He waited, letting the pressure rise in him as it rose on the table. The image of that reporter girl from earlier – *Elena* – surfaced in his mind. He held it until the brink – until *he* decided. Then he snapped his fingers – the agreed signal.

The hand released. The body collapsed back, sucking at the air, chest rising.

Kai leaned back in the chair, a slow exhale shuddering out of him. Enough. At least for tonight.

Just forty minutes later, he was seated at a console in a basement arcade near Callao. Neon lights throbbed overhead, the place half-empty, boys with headphones hunched in their own battles.

On his screen a figure moved in silence, wire drawn tight around another's throat. A flick of Kai's thumb, the body went slack. Restart. Three minutes later, he did it again. And again. He never tired of it.

The repetition steadied him. The control. Press, hold, release. No blood, no mess, just the quiet ecstasy of watching something choke out under his hand. It was practice, in its own way. Another rehearsal.

The thrill soured as soon as it ended, though. It wasn't enough. He wanted it real. He wanted Martelli in that grip, wanted to feel the panic and silence for himself. The Principal had told him to be patient – *step by fucking step* – but patience was the hardest hold of all.

Outside, the night air cooled his skin. Gran Via still buzzed – cinemas emptying, taxis circling, couples drifting arm in arm. Kai slid onto his bike, rode a few blocks, and pulled up outside a *Supermercado Asiático* – one of a discreet chain they owned, its windows stacked with packs of rice, noodles and tinned lychees, the perfect mask for everything behind it.

The strip lighting glared, humming overhead. A young couple bickered softly in front of a fridge of drinks. At the counter, the staff gave the smallest of nods. No questions. Never any questions.

Kai moved through the aisles towards a back room. Inside, the light softened, but the noise thickened. Screens glowed on the walls, not with La Liga, Serie A or the Bundesliga, but scorelines from Seoul, Manila, Guangzhou. Games long finished, odds frozen, final tallies crawling down the feed.

Note counters rattled as handlers hunched over tables, rubber-banding bricks of cash. The side door cracked open. A delivery rider wheeled in, helmet still on, yellow food-box sagging heavy. He dropped it on the table, pocketed a slim envelope, and pushed his scooter back into the night. Another rider hovered by the wall, helmet dangling from one hand, box in the other. In ten minutes, he'd be weaving through traffic, not with a take-out, but with cash – logged on paper as *wholesale invoices* for rice, beer, kitchen stock. By Monday morning it would be washed clean, cycled back through Grupo Dorada's books as if it had never sweated under strip lights.

The flow never stopped – bags in, bundles out. Kai liked to watch the rhythm of it – the pulse of control.

His phone buzzed and he answered.

'The play went through clean,' a man said. 'No noise, no loose ends. The market saw it. Rivals saw it.'

Heat slid through him – not from the room, but from the words. They were watching. Not just the punters glued to screens in Manila or Guangzhou, but the syndicate men in Milan, Tangier, London. Men who had once deferred to Martelli.

'They'll come to us now,' the man said. 'But gently. The summer is long. We keep the referees warm; you keep the pipeline open. Autumn is when it matters. You understand?'

Kai did. He hung up without replying. Around him, bills kept piling. But in his mind, he saw Martelli gasping, losing air, losing face.

A tightness bloomed in his chest – like the moment before a chokehold slackened. Proof. Recognition.

The syndicates were shifting towards them, but impatience still gnawed at him.

Still no announcement about the painting – absurd, almost insulting. As if the police were teasing

him, holding the moment hostage. And the Falcós …
nothing. No bloodletting, no panic, no public humiliation. There should have been carnage; they should
have been screaming by now. Instead: silence. A silence
that felt wrong.

It dragged him back to the Prado – the guard's
throat, the wet choke, the wire biting deeper than it
needed to. Too much blood. Had he left something?
Was there any trace, a print, some microscopic smear
that could crawl back to him?

And now journalists were sniffing in places they
had no right to; Carlos letting the wrong questions drift
to the wrong ears. Sloppy. Reckless. Things needed
tightening, tidying: conversations shut down, curiosity
redirected.

Maybe he should reach out to Barroso again –
smooth him, steady him, pay him again. Find out what
the police really had. Control the flow before someone
else tried to.

Tomorrow had to go right. Tomorrow had to be
the moment everything turned.

And tomorrow, the Principal would have to
congratulate him. On his thirtieth birthday, they would
finally crown him as the successor he was meant to be.

46

Lorenzo Martelli - Borja Falcó

Sunday – southeast Madrid.

Borja's wrists were cable-tied behind his back, a bloodied plastic bag still looped around his neck like a scarf. The three men in the SUV hadn't spoken since crossing the city's outskirts.

They'd driven southeast, through quieter streets, past warehouses, shuttered shops, roads where even the stray dogs kept out of sight. Their destination was an old abattoir. Closed for a decade – officially, anyway – but it still had the hooks, the drains and the stench. Plastic curtains hung like ghosts.

They'd hauled him out of the vehicle and dumped him onto a low stool inside. Fluorescent lights hummed overhead, broken in places. Two men flanked him – one holding the plastic bag, the other the pliers. The Adidas bag was on the floor nearby. The bundles of euros were now neatly stacked on a stainless-steel worktop like butchered loins.

Borja coughed up blood, his chest heaving. His clothes were torn and damp with sweat. His lips were split, one eye was swollen shut. The other blinked towards a phone camera, which had been set up on a tripod facing him.

Lorenzo Martelli stepped in. He was immaculate. Tailored suit, pale linen shirt, a thick gold watch gleaming on his wrist. Slicked-back silver hair. Those ice-cold eyes. He didn't speak at first. Just circled Borja once, twice, like he was admiring a piece of livestock.

'*Beh,*' he started in Italian, '*fai proprio schifo a vederti.*' You look like shit.

Borja coughed up blood again, eyes flickering. 'Señor Martelli – *please* – I beg you – I didn't –'

Martelli held up a hand. 'Save your breath. You'll need it.'

Borja slumped, sobbing.

Martelli glanced over at the blocks of cash stacked on the worktop. 'Two hundred and fifty thousand euros,' he said. 'That's what your life is worth to someone else. Or was.' He crouched a little, eye level with Borja now. 'I want to know who gave it to you. Who asked you to betray me? I want names.'

Borja's voice was a rasp. 'I don't know names.'

Martelli nodded to Enzo, the silver-chained thug with the crater face holding the plastic bag. In a flash, it was pulled over Borja's head again. This time it was held in place much longer. Martelli smiled as he watched the seconds ticking by on his watch. Just as Borja appeared to give up struggling – just as the convulsing slowed – he nodded at Enzo again. *Air.*

Borja was gasping, his face smudged with sweat, snot and blood.

'I'll ask you once more,' Martelli said. 'Who asked you to betray me?'

Borja could hardly speak. *'Asians ... Chinese ...'*

'A *name*,' Martelli snapped. 'I want a name.'

'I swear ... I have no names ...'

Martelli nodded to Enzo, who then went to the phone on the tripod and started a video call. Ramón Falcó's face appeared on the screen – grey, glassy-eyed – watching from wherever he'd been told to wait.

'Ramón, good evening,' Martelli said. 'Don't hang up.' He paused, as the thug adjusted the angle of the phone. Then: 'Say hello to your son.'

'Please, no ...' Ramón's voice squealed on the loud-speaker. 'He didn't ... he couldn't ... I didn't know ...'

Martelli raised a finger. 'Of course you didn't. You've been distracted, haven't you?' He turned his gaze to Borja, then back to the phone. 'But what should we do with distractions, Ramón?'

'Please, no ...'

'I'm giving you a front-row seat. Family privilege. Because it's not just your son who's betrayed me. It's both of you. And the Falcó family will pay. In full.'

'No –'

'Don't interrupt me. You let a cockroach into our business arrangement. Your own idiotic son. You bred a traitor, Ramón. And this is what happens when families fail me. First the son. Then the wife. Then you.'

He moved closer to the phone. 'Say one word to anyone about what's about to happen, and I'll peel back your life like an old scab. Every bribe, every kickback, every offshore wire – I'll make sure it becomes public. You'll burn, Ramón. Not just your career – *you*.'

He paused, smiling.

'But that's not what I want. I want you solvent – bleeding slowly. Repaying me for your son's betrayal, not just in money, but in dread. You'll say nothing. You'll do nothing. You'll go to your son's funeral, hold your wife's hand and play the grieving father. And you'll look over your shoulder every day, knowing I'll come for you. When I do, it will be personal.'

Ramón was silent. Borja was sobbing.

Martelli gave a flick of his hand. The camera stayed fixed on Borja as the bag went back over his head. Minutes passed. He thrashed. There was a kick, a final flailing moment, then stillness – almost.

Borja continued to briefly twitch, his mouth making small, defeated shapes beneath the plastic. The phone captured it all, before the screen went black.

'You know what to do,' Martelli said to Enzo, wiping a speck of bloody mucus from the sleeve of his suit. 'Take him to the viaduct. String him up. Wait until the early hours. Make it look like it always used to up there.'

Part Four
Monday

47

Benjamin - Elena - Castro - García

Monday 9 June – La Latina district.

Benjamin jolted awake, the air-con rattling. He was on the floor of Elena's hotel room, a cushion wedged between his head and the wall. Like Madrid, he'd barely slept.

Fragments of last night crept back: an early supper with Duncan he couldn't politely refuse; wine, more wine; Duncan moaning about his wife and twins, demanding a nightcap; bumping into the hen party – the same lot who'd colonised his illegal Airbnb. Duncan had hurled himself at them like a rabid dog in a butcher's; Benjamin had slipped away, thank God.

Then he'd met up with Elena, which was … fun.

He hadn't planned to wake up here. He hadn't planned to nod off here, either. He hadn't planned anything here. Two or three loud bars, four hours of talk; too much booze. She'd laughed – *properly*, which was magical – at his Airbnb saga and his BiciMad fiasco. Then up here to 'show him something on the laptop, nothing else'. She'd said it; she meant it; it stayed that way.

She didn't grill him about the Prado or the painting again – she barely seemed to care. She didn't apologise for the *El País* piece, either, but he let it go; the silence felt like a tacit admission. He didn't pursue it. The less she pressed him on what was snatched, the better.

Instead, she talked about the rooftop event: an Asian lady, empowerment in women's grassroots football. He latched onto the football bit, tried to ask about UEFA refs and the Champions League; she kept talking – a row with her editor over a sex-trafficking lead with an Italian thread, whispers in Spain's sports council, an 'exclusive' dangled and refused, a rival paper already sniffing around – and that creep he'd seen stalking her near Castellana House, a friend of some slimy sports agent she knew. She had a talent for attracting lechers. And for making enemies – something they had in common.

He rubbed his eyes and pushed himself up. The room was half-dark. A smell of hotel soap and Elena's perfume – citrus with trouble – but no sign of Elena. He felt surprisingly fine: not hungover, just short on sleep, par for the course after a night out in Madrid.

Where was she?

The bed was empty; a dent in the pillow where her head had been. No blue glow from the laptop on the table she'd been talking over when he finally zoned out. No shower noise. He checked his watch. Six o'clock. Not even daybreak. Where the hell was she?

'Elena?' he called. Nothing.

He clocked the bathroom – dry towels, a glass by the basin – and her things: hold-all by the chair, clothes draped over it. The cardkey wasn't in the light socket, though. She'd taken it. If he left, and pulled the door to behind him, the latch would catch. Probably fine. Possibly not.

His phone bleeped.

Not WhatsApp, just a bare SMS: *Benjamin? We must meet to compare notes. Where are you staying?*

He stared at it, thumb hovering. No name, no emoji, no digital footprint. Someone keeping it clean. He typed back: *Who is this?*

The reply came quick: *Alfonso García, BPH.*

Benjamin reread the message.

Of course.

Alfonso García wanted to meet because Ignacio was in custody, as the ever-jolly Duncan had already told him last night. That in itself had been a warning: *to back off.* Someone running the police investigation didn't want any outside help, and especially not from Benjamin. Which made Benjamin even more determined not to walk away.

Yet Alfonso wanted to meet, simply *to compare notes?*

Like two overworked scholars leafing through parchment in a dusty archive. *What the fuck.*

Benjamin wasn't in this for camaraderie. He wanted answers, evidence – and then a fat finder's fee. He stared at the message yet again. No mention of what Ignacio had promised him – no acknowledgement of any deal. Ignacio was culture ministry, sure, but Alfonso would have known.

Could he trust Alfonso? He'd tangled with him before – over that missing Goya sketch. He'd played the overburdened Spanish culture cop, all deference and bureaucracy, but Benjamin had done all the work and Alfonso had taken the credit.

He'd decide if he could trust him once he saw the whites of his eyes again. He texted back:

I'll come to you. When and where?

Calle de Bailén.

Elena hadn't really slept. She'd been hunched over the laptop until a couple of hours ago – Googling, making notes, scrolling and scribbling until her eyes burned. Benjamin had stopped answering and slid into a doze on the floor. It had been good to laugh with him. At some point she nodded off in the chair, woke, then drifted onto the bed.

At five, she gave up. Checked the news alerts — always her reflex: agency wires, the overnight churn of social media. A headline flashed up: Body found hanging from the viaduct on the Calle de Bailén. Just a few blocks from her hotel. She felt something in her gut — a pull she couldn't name. By six, she was there.

In the growing grey of dawn, blue lights strobed against the viaduct's stone arches. The bridge was half-cordoned off, police tape flapping in the breeze. A body was being hauled from the rail and onto a stretcher. A second ambulance pulled away empty, no siren, no hurry. Uniforms moved in clusters. Elena stood back, watching.

Another journalist lingered, and just a few metres away a pap lensman was shoved back by a police officer for zooming in on the victim's face. Not before he'd fired off a few frames. He spoke to his colleague as he slung his kit over his shoulder, and Elena caught one word before they turned for their scooter: *Falcó*.

The engine coughed, the back wheel skidded on the damp tarmac, and then they were gone, weaving past the tape before anyone could stop them.

Detective Pilar Castro had been at the Prado since three-thirty the morning before, worked straight through, helped set up the incident room, and had even started digging into Barroso's neat stack of 'suicides'. Now here she was at the viaduct, bulky brown anorak zipped to her neck, snug against the weight of her chin – one of the first on the scene, as always. This was her life. No partner, no one waiting at home, nothing to pull her away. Better a crime scene than a vending machine.

She scanned the edge of the cordon, eyes moving over the usual crowd – gawkers with phones out, an old man in slippers, a pair of students whispering like they'd stumbled onto a film set. And then one who didn't fit.

A woman. Standing back, notebook in hand but not scribbling. Watching too closely, not looking away when the stretcher lurched past.

Castro moved across. 'Were you here when it happened? Did you witness anything?'

The woman turned. Younger than she first thought. Dark hair, tired eyes. She shook her head. 'No.'

Castro let her gaze flick to the notebook. 'Press?'

A hesitation. 'Yes. But not for this.'

The detective gave a dry snort. 'There's no such thing as *not for this*. If you saw something, better to tell me now and not later.'

The woman said nothing. Just held the notebook tighter, as if squeezing words back inside. Castro studied her a moment longer, then turned towards the bridge. 'Then stand back. Take your notes.'

Out of the corner of her eye, she saw her still rooted to the spot, as if she did have something to say. But nothing came.

'*Pilar.*' A forensic tech called her over. Stocky man, latex gloves tugged on tight, snapping at the wrist.

She ducked under the tape and stepped closer.

The body lay flat, sheet folded back. Youngish, mid-thirties maybe. Expensive jacket, shoes scuffed raw. Ligature marks at the throat, deep and ragged. And more: bruising on the face, swelling at the jaw. Not just hanging. A beating first.

'As you suspected, this isn't suicide,' the tech said, matter of fact. 'Not here. Not anymore.'

Castro knew the viaduct had been the place for jumpers once. Until the city sealed it behind a perspex barrier. No one was leaping now.

Another officer came over with a tablet, breath fogging in the crisp air. 'Pulled CCTV from two hours ago,' he said. 'Jeep stops midway across the bridge. Two men on the back. They don't even get down. They hurl a rope round the lamppost, then drag a body up from the back – looks dead already, no movement. They heave it over the barrier and let it hang. Thirty seconds, maybe less.'

Castro squinted at the grainy footage: figures silhouetted against headlights, the rope snaking taut before the body toppled out of frame. 'Registration?' she said.

'Partial. We'll push it to cyber, but even if we trace it, odds are we'll find the jeep burned out in some field outside Madrid.'

Castro nodded once, curt. 'Then get me what you can before that happens.' Her eyes returned to the body. Murder dressed as suicide. She'd seen plenty of both, but rarely the two stitched together this crudely.

A younger forensic tech crouched by the body, lifting the jacket with gloved hands. She pulled something from a pocket – a key on a leather fob, and a small twist of clingfilm with white residue inside. She dropped both into separate evidence bags.

'No wallet, no phone, nothing with a name,' she said. 'But I swear I've seen him before. Falcó, isn't it? Ramón Falcó's son? Used to be in all the magazines. Though he looked prettier back then.'

The name meant nothing to Castro. A body was a body – and she had no time for Spain's *prensa del corazón*. That world of pretty, preening faces and celebrity gossip could rot for all she cared. 'Who's that?' she asked anyway.

'I think his dad now runs the CSD.'

Castro kept her tone flat. 'Then run facial recognition, check prints. We're not guessing on a homicide. Whoever it is, we'll need a formal ID from the family. This won't be a pleasant morning. And next time, don't let a paparazzo close enough to grab his face. Keep things tight.'

The tech nodded.

Glancing back towards the tape, Castro could see the press girl was still there, notebook clutched to her chest, not reaching for her phone, not snapping pictures like the rest. Just staring. Odd.

'Pilar,' another agent called, pulling her back to the work. She turned away, pondering the next steps.

. . .

Elena kept watching the police work. The bulky detective who'd asked if she'd witnessed anything had glanced her way more than once. She knew she should say something. But not yet. Not here. *Pilar* — that was the name the other cops had called her.

~

Monday — Cuesta de Moyano.

By 8am, after a quick shower and change at his hotel off Calle de Moratín, Benjamin coasted down Huertas on his BiciMad, rattled over the cobblestones on the Paseo del Prado and into the Cuesta de Moyano.

Going downhill was fine, but he still couldn't end the trip. No app, no account — and the smart lock might as well have been a bank vault. Late last night the assist had finally died; he'd been pedalling dead weight ever since, swearing at every rise. Each BiciMad rack he passed blinked its little green lights at him like a taunt. He'd seen faster and more reliable yellow bikes around the city — better than the municipal ones. He'd chosen the wrong brand.

The pedestrian slope beside the Botánico gardens was waking up: grey wooden stalls creaking open, boxes of secondhand books, postcards and maps dragged onto the pavement, the air already damp with paper dust. A few browsers loitered, keeping an eye on their dogs.

He climbed off the bike with his shoulder-bag, fought with the bike's kickstand, swore at it, then gave up and propped it against a railing. Alfonso García was easy to spot at the far end, leaning on a motorbike, crash helmet in one hand, sleeves rolled up. Not at the Prado, not at the police station – here, in this sleepy row of bookstalls. Already Benjamin didn't like it.

'*Guiri* wheels?' García called, smirking at the bicycle.

Benjamin ignored it, closed the distance fast. No handshake. 'Why here, Alfonso?'

'Safer than email. Safer than voicemail.'

'Am I in, or not?'

García's mouth twitched, not quite a smile. 'You're in, if you don't get us burned. But it's complicated. Homicide has the case. Barroso – heavyweight, erratic, too close to the judge. The *secreto de sumario* means no leaks, no outsiders. Ignacio was detained overnight – he crossed the line, and too soon.'

Benjamin shook his head. 'Too soon? It's probably already too late. The painting could be halfway round the world by now. And what line did he cross? He asked me to help. How does that break a gag order? Unless someone doesn't want me anywhere near the painting.'

'You might be reading too much into it.'

'I don't think so,' Benjamin said. 'Ignacio promised me a fee. Finder's commission, too, if I get close. But now he's in … what, custody? I've got nothing in writing, and you've dragged me out to a secondhand bookstall instead of your incident room, where people actually brief each other.'

Alfonso lifted both hands. 'I can't vouch for what Ignacio promised. That's ministry business. But I'll have a word – with him, if I can. He was allowed home early this morning, but I haven't spoken to him yet. He's with lawyers, bosses, maybe the minister. For now, he's lying low.'

Benjamin watched him. The same act as a few years ago with the Goya job – overworked, burdened, careful with every word. 'I want to know what's going on – and I want to know I'll be paid for it.'

'You'll be paid.'

Benjamin let it go. A shutter rattled on one of the stalls, a box of books thumped onto the pavement. 'How was Extremadura?' he asked. 'Ignacio mentioned a looting. Archaeological site?'

'Another mess. Farmers digging, artefacts flogged online. We'll recover most of it.' He shrugged it away.

Silence settled. Browsers thumbed through boxes of yellowed paperbacks while stallholders dragged out more boxes.

'Look,' García said, 'one name has come up. Grupo Dorada. Catering contract at the Prado. A worker's gone missing. Don't get excited – it's housekeeping. We're pulling the employment records, that's all I know.'

'Who's the worker?'

'Jason something. I'll get details in the briefing.' He checked his watch.

'And the guard? How was he killed?'

'That's confidential.'

'For Christ's sake, Alfonso. If I'm supposed to help, I need to know. Ignacio said his throat was slit – true or not?'

García hesitated. 'Wire cable. Half-severed. And no one must know I told you.'

Benjamin felt his stomach turn. He didn't ask the obvious. They'd already be checking if guards were shifted, or rotas juggled during last night's football chaos.

'You're going through the guard schedules, I assume,' he said instead.

'Of course,' García nodded.

Benjamin studied him, searching his eyes. Nothing. No flicker that he saw any bigger picture, no hint of connecting a stolen Caravaggio to the result on the pitch. Was Benjamin reading too much into it himself?

No. He knew he wasn't. But he wasn't about to share it yet. 'Any other leads?' he asked. 'Other staff? Alarms, CCTV … inside help, obviously.'

García checked his watch again. 'We'll know more in the briefing. Homicide's running it. You're not meant to hear any of this.'

Benjamin leaned in. 'Then give me something else. Timing. What time did it happen?'

'What do you mean?'

'The guard. Last night. What time was he killed?

What time was the break-in? Start to finish, when did it happen?'

'Just before midnight until three in the morning. That's all we know.'

Benjamin nodded once. 'So Dorada hasn't even been approached yet?'

'I imagine not until Barroso says so.' He put on his crash helmet. 'I've already said too much.'

Benjamin stepped closer. 'And the fee, Alfonso? Ignacio promised me –'

'I said I'll have a word. That's all I can promise. I'm telling you about Dorada first. Do what you can with it. But for now, pretend we haven't talked.' He kicked his bike stand up, then added: 'Mind how you go on your … wheels.'

The engine barked to life, drowning out the rustle of paperbacks.

Benjamin watched him go, then looked at his own transport, the BiciMad slumped against a railing like an abandoned shopping trolley.

Dorada. A crumb tossed his way like he should be grateful. Crumbs didn't pay bills.

48

The Incident Room

Monday – Comisaría de Policía, Calle de las Huertas.

The incident room was already stifling, despite the fans rattling in opposite corners. A dozen agents filled the tight space, laptops open, whiteboards half-scribbled, walls plastered with floorplans and time-stamped CCTV stills. A city grid marked with pinheads and yellow stickers filled one wall, above a table littered with printouts, labelled bags of trace material, plus empty takeaway cups.

Morales stood near the centre, a USB stick in one hand, a sheet of paper printed with a headshot in the other – Gutiérrez nearby. Alfonso García stood at the back, shirt sleeves rolled up, arms folded, saying nothing. His crash helmet sat on top of a filing cabinet beside him, a damp streak of sweat still marking his collar. He shifted his weight, watching, eyes unreadable.

Inspector Jefe Barroso rubbed his thumb against the ridge of scar tissue on his palm again. He hadn't expected them to move anything forward overnight. Hadn't expected them to move at all without him.

What the hell had he even done himself last night? After interrogating the Ignacio creep from the culture ministry, he remembered a bottle, another glass, the dull ache in his chest. After that it blurred – calls unreturned, silence on the line. And now Morales was here, fresh and precise, pinning things to the wall as if he'd been working the whole night instead of drowning in whisky. Barroso felt the heat in his throat, a crawling sense he'd let his grip slip for just a few hours and the case had started running without him.

Morales made space on one of the boards and pinned up an image of a young Asian male – short hair, pale skin, tired eyes – taken from an ID badge.

'This is Jason Zhou and he's missing,' he said, letting it hang in the room. 'He didn't show up for work yesterday. No sick note. No call. No messages. Job title: barista-slash-server at the Café Prado. He wasn't hired by the Prado, but subcontracted through the catering provider.'

Barroso blinked once, masking the jolt. 'Missing how? Are we sure? He could be lying low, hungover, avoiding a shift.' His words came out too quickly.

Before Morales could reply, the door opened. Detective Pilar Castro slipped in, still wrapped in her huge anorak despite the rising June heat. Her face was drawn, eyes heavy.

'Viaduct,' she said to Gutíerrez as she passed. 'Body's on the system. We're seeking a family ID. Not quite a jumper but not relevant to this. Sorry – carry on. I'll catch up.' She filled a chair without another word, flipping open her notebook, pen poised but idle.

Barroso's eyes lingered on her for a moment. *Another body at dawn. 'Not relevant,' she said. Always so quick to box things off.* He forced his gaze back to Morales, fingers drumming against the table.

'Jason Zhou is twenty-six,' Morales continued. 'Chinese national, born in Fujian province – has been in Spain just over four years. First on a student visa, now under a converted residency permit – *arraigo social*, via the hospitality employer. Everything checks out for now, assuming the ID is real.'

'The hospitality employer being Grupo Dorada,' Gutiérrez added. 'They hold the café and catering contract for the museum. Same for several other venues across Madrid.' He nodded at his colleague to carry on.

'HR records show Jason Zhou was hired twelve months ago by Grupo Dorada,' Morales said, sliding a printout onto the table. 'Standard contract. Nothing flagged, no disciplinary issues. But – when we spoke to them last night, no one could remember actually interviewing him.'

Barroso's head came up hard, his voice cutting across the room. 'You *spoke* to them? Last night? I gave clear orders – no contact without me. Who did you speak to? At that hour?'

Morales didn't flinch. 'A duty manager. He said front-line hiring is handled through an agency – Madrid Flexi Jobs, based in Usera.'

A ripple went around the room. Castro's pen still paused above her notebook; she flicked a glance at García. He'd raised his eyebrows but stayed silent, arms folded.

Barroso felt the heat rise in his chest. *They'd gone behind him. While he was in a bar, waiting on calls that never came, they were pushing on Dorada without him. The last thing he needed was anyone trampling in there ahead of him.*

'And?' he snapped.

'And that's where it stops. Number's dead. Website offline. Social media abandoned a year ago. No office address we can trace. Could be they folded. Could be they were a shell.'

'You're saying he ghosted in through a ghost agency?' Barroso said. *Who the fuck was this Jason Zhou?* The image pinned to the wall sparked nothing. Just another face. But if he was missing, it was already a problem. If someone else got to him first, the wrong questions would start being asked. No – he had to find him before anyone else did. Shut it down.

'As far as immigration goes, Jason Zhou appears to be legal,' Morales said. 'Original student visa, four years ago, listed a private language school here in Madrid. We're verifying that school's records. A previous employer before Grupo Dorada – a noodle bar in Tetúan – no longer exists. On paper it all checks out. But it's all paper. No in-person vetting. No fingerprints logged since the residency permit.'

'You think that's his real name?' asked one of the agents.

Morales shrugged. 'Hard to tell. The documentation's clean, but it could all be alias-based. He'd learnt enough Spanish to take orders, serve coffee, scoop out ice cream from the retro bike cart and even work the counter solo. It sounds as if he kept his head down. No police record, no traffic violations, no tax anomalies. Too clean, almost.'

'He's lived here a while, too,' Gutiérrez added.

'Long enough to know all there is to know about the Prado's courtyard cafeteria,' Morales said, nodding. 'Where the camera blind spots are, when the catering deliveries arrive, and long enough to know how to vanish.'

With that, he inserted his USB stick into a laptop. Images from a small, poorly lit bedsit filled the projector screen: a kitchenette, two chairs, mattress on the floor. 'This is his empty den in Calle del Amparo, Lavapiés,' he said.

Barroso's chair scraped back. 'You went there? Already?' His voice was now sharp enough to still the room. 'Without clearance or a warrant? Without me?'

'We secured the flat, *jefe*,' Morales said calmly. 'Door was locked, but we got in clean. No force, no damage, no neighbours complained. We logged what we found – nothing more. It's been standard procedure before, right?'

No one answered. Castro wrote something without looking up.

'Anyway, the flat was empty,' Morales continued. 'No note, no cash, no passport, nothing even in the fridge. No Jason Zhou – but the rental contract is in his name. We don't know exactly how long he'd been living there, but he sure as hell knew we'd be turning up. Or someone did.'

Barroso felt the jolt hit – anger and dread knotted as one. Morales had gone further than he'd imagined: calling Dorada, breaking into the kid's flat, parading it all here in front of him. And the case – *his* case – was slipping, inch by inch, out of his hands. He stared at the projected images. Not just an empty bedsit; a hole in his control. Zhou might have bolted or been taken, but that wasn't the point. The point was Morales had got there first, while he'd been drowning himself. *Enough.* It stopped here. Morales wouldn't take another step without him. *No one would.*

Gutiérrez was clicking on the laptop and then other images appeared: some close-ups of the bedsit's floor and dirty white walls.

'These are bike marks – plus tyre and chain oil residue,' Morales said. 'One neighbour confirmed that he brought a collapsible bike in and out of the flat every day. He also cycled to the Café Prado when it was his rota, and they let him keep the bike within the courtyard, folded up in the storage area. The one that forensics are still checking.'

Gutiérrez clicked through to yet another image: a yellow plastic strap.

'This was found in the flat,' Morales said. 'Looks like it comes from a delivery crate. Possibly a food service box. He could have been moonlighting as a delivery rider, but we're running checks.'

Barroso's fist tightened on the edge of the table, then released, then tightened again, knuckles whitening each time.

Castro stiffened as she squinted at the screen. That strap. Something was itching at her memory. She jotted in her notebook without speaking.

'Are we saying this is our suspect? The killer?' asked one of the agents.

'No, we don't believe he was the intruder or the killer,' Gutiérrez said. He pointed to the CCTV images from inside the museum that were pinned to the wall. 'From what we have ascertained, Jason Zhou is taller and heavier. The intruder was very small, wiry, possibly even younger. He moved distinctively.'

A few murmurs ran through the room.

'We believe Jason Zhou was the facilitator – at least one of them,' Gutiérrez continued. 'Maybe even responsible for deactivating the courtyard's cameras and alarm system. If he helped someone in, he's either hiding now, or he could have been silenced … eliminated, possibly dead.'

'What else do we know about the employer?' Castro asked.

Barroso shot her a glance but said nothing. His eyes then moved slowly around the room, silent, watchful, fist tightening and loosening. Anyone else might have mistaken his silence and stillness for approval. Only García, arms folded at the back, caught the strain in his shoulders.

'Grupo Dorada,' Castro pushed. 'If the hiring agency – Madrid Flexi Jobs – has folded, then we need to go back to Dorada, right? Who's talking to them? We need Jason Zhou's full employment file, managers, rota records. Somebody from their side will have to answer questions.'

Another agent, a soft-voiced forensic accountant, leaned forward. Rimless glasses, thinning grey hair combed with bureaucratic precision.

'Grupo Dorada's part of a larger group,' he said. 'They have an events arm, hospitality delivery, their own restaurants and bars. Public filings list a company registered in Málaga, but it's tied to a holding company in Luxembourg. Minimal executive presence in Spain, but we're trying to trace the key players. Majority stake sits with a Singapore-based trust.'

That made Barroso shift. 'Singapore?' He scratched his neck, tried not to betray the flicker in his face. But García caught it.

'So, what are we saying here?' another agent asked. 'Do you mean it's some kind of Asian network?'

Barroso rolled his shoulders back, neck stiff, like a

fighter loosening before a swing. Then he was on his feet.

'*You've got nothing,*' he spat. 'Other than a fucking Chinese disappearing act with a folding fucking bike, you've got nothing.'

A couple of agents chuckled, uncertain. The sound wilted fast. The mood was brittle as Barroso's glare swept the room.

'*No one* sets foot at Dorada without me,' he said. 'No one lifts a phone to them. No calls, no visits, no exceptions. Understood? Not unless I'm there in person.'

A couple of nods, no one eager to meet his eyes. Morales gave the faintest shake of his head towards Gutiérrez, who sat rigid. Castro had seen Barroso's face turn crimson, his fists clench. He wasn't just furious about losing control of the investigation — something else had rattled him. Her eyes met García's across the room, then also Gutiérrez's. Something was off. And now they all knew it.

'You think Dorada will hand over staff files because you ask nicely?' Barroso pressed. He didn't wait for a reply. 'They'll have lawyers lined up. They'll clam up. So we do this by the book. We'll need a warrant and I'll speak to the judge this morning. Until then, it waits.'

He could feeel the weight of the room. They wanted to move, and he'd just chained them to the table. *Good.* They didn't like it, but they'd obey. They had to. A warrant bought him time — time to dig further, to find out what Dorada might know, to get there first if he had to.

'You've got plenty else to do in the meantime,' he said. 'Witness lists, CCTV trawls, other catering and security staff to interview. Get on with it.'

A few agents shifted in their chairs, exchanging quick looks.

Barroso stood still, his gaze lingering on Zhou's photo pinned to the wall.

'Inspector,' Castro said. 'Can we talk about two suicides that were signed off earlier this year? I have a file here, but things aren't very clear.'

He swung round and glared at her, twitching, before he finally turned for the door.

The room stayed still until his footsteps had gone. Only then did the first whispers start.

Barroso was halfway out the building when his phone rang. He didn't recognise the number but answered anyway. 'Barroso.'

'Inspector,' she said, clipped, formal. 'Judge Varela.'

He stopped walking. 'Yes?'

'I've made a decision regarding the stolen painting. After consultations this morning, including with the culture minister, I see no further legal justification for withholding its identity.'

Barroso frowned. 'But there are operational risks –'

'I've taken those into account,' she cut in, 'and I'm satisfied that the benefits of transparency now outweigh the risks.' Her tone left no room. 'It's not a question of leaks anymore, not since *El País* spat out its little scoop about it not being a Goya or Velázquez. The museum and the culture ministry are being hounded by every other media outlet, national and international. The minister himself was accosted by reporters at two separate events last night –'

'Oh, *poor him* –'

'It's no longer sustainable.'

'So, we give them a headline instead?' Barroso said.

'We give them *clarity*,' came the reply. 'There's public interest. Or would you prefer they all keep guessing until someone leaks it properly?'

'And this all comes from the preening little culture minister? Was he pissed off because we detained one of his faggot sidekicks for questioning?'

'Inspector, mind your words,' she said, voice tightening. 'The minister made his views known. I make my own, and independently.'

Barroso said nothing. All he could think of was the diversity darling himself, Matías-cocksucker-Ramos, Spain's patron saint of pillow-biters – another prancing little leftie and the country's first openly-gay cabinet minister, as if that were a credential. The only thing that slimy cocksleeve had ever led was a Pride float. And now he was whispering in the judge's ear? Jesus wept.

Ramos had taken *paternity leave*, for Christ's sake –

when he and his soft-palmed husband adopted some sickly African twins. The media lapped it up: 'Modern Spain' – 'progressive family values'. Barroso had nearly puked in a squad car. The left-wing press called Ramos charismatic, elegant, articulate. Barroso preferred *maricón*. Señor *suck-a-dick-for-the-arts*.

The ultras and anonymous trolls online had torn into Ramos like a wolf pack over the paternity leave. The memes, the nicknames, the doctored images – Barroso had scrolled through them all one night with a bottle of scotch and a wide grin. Wonderful.

Say what you like about the old guard, but back in those days Spain's ministries had real men in them. Hard men. Men who didn't weep on TV or hold hands with other men, let alone outside a maternity clinic. Now it was all minorities and woke bollocks. Even the Prado used to be sacred. Now the tour guides probably weren't even allowed to mention Columbus in case it upset someone. The whole culture sector was infected – and Ramos was the smiling tumour at the centre of it.

'Inspector?' Varela's voice snapped him back. 'Did you hear me?'

'Yes. I heard.'

'The statement is being issued now,' the judge said. 'Not by you – through the ministry and the museum. There's also a hotline for information, but nothing more. No talk of rewards.'

'Understood.' His voice was flat.

'And Inspector – I wasn't pleased with *El País*

quoting anonymous sources, or *any* sources. Neither the ministry nor museum have officially engaged any outside help, I'm certain of it. The secrecy order applies to the entire investigation, and so I expect full discipline from your team, too. If I see one more leak, I'll assume it's deliberate. Is that clear?'

'Crystal.'

She hung up.

Barroso was burning. Another order from above. Another decision made without him. Another crack in the façade.

Part of him wanted to kill someone.

The other part knew he'd already lost control.

And he hadn't breathed a word about Dorada. Hadn't asked for a warrant. He never intended to – not until he'd stripped it of anything that could implicate him.

49

Lorenzo Martelli

Monday – Hotel Ritz.

Martelli had enjoyed it more than he expected. Borja's face sealed in the plastic, the twitching panic, the frantic clawing, the scuffed shoes hammering the floor – it had pleased him in ways no confession ever could. The boy had given him nothing of substance, no names, just those pathetic words: *Asians. Chinese.* But watching him suffocate had been enough. Almost.

He'd made Ramón watch, front-row on the phone, his son gasping in close-up, eyes bulging as the bag crackled and tightened under his men's hands. The father sobbed, begged, but had offered nothing.

Afterwards, Martelli had rewarded himself with dinner because appetite always returned. A table to himself, the meat rare and bleeding, the red wine smooth, the lemon tart chilled to perfection, sharp against the tongue. He'd eaten with the satisfaction of a man who had settled a debt. The Falcós punished; Ramón broken; Borja erased. Balance restored – at least on the surface.

But the words still gnawed at him. *Asians. Chinese.*

They pulled at shadows he kept carefully locked away. Nights when he had demanded the youngest, the slightest, the wide-eyed girls brought to his tables, his yachts, his island. Fragile little things, chosen precisely because they broke so easily. He liked the way their wrists lay tiny in his crushing hands. He liked the jolt when the air stopped, the freeze in their bodies, the panic sparking their eyes.

He had upset fathers, brothers, whole families – of course he had. That was half the pleasure. To take what they prized, reduce it to nothing, then send it back ruined or not at all.

When anyone asked questions, he had silenced them. The young journalist from Singapore, too clever for her own good, had been guillotined by falling glass – written off as an accident. Another lesson. Another warning.

Yes, he'd left scars in places he barely remembered. But those people had no reach. No weight. No one in the alleys of Manila or the slums of Guangzhou could get close to him. Last night, he hadn't imagined it could be any of his partners or clients, either – the syndicate men in Macau or Singapore trying to tighten the terms. They knew better than to play games with him. They needed him.

And yet Borja, choking in the plastic, had said it anyway. *Asians. Chinese.*

Martelli had slept well enough in his Ritz suite afterwards, belly full of meat and wine, but those final words clung to him through the night, turning over with the sheets. They were still there now.

Last night's match was never supposed to reach extra time, let alone penalties. Juventus against Monaco – a certainty. But he'd still ordered Ramón Falcó to buy the officials as a safeguard, a guarantee. Nothing left to chance. Then came the penalty in the shoot-out: disallowed by VAR, ruled a double-touch, as if the striker had struck the ball twice in one motion. An obscenity. The feed itself looked tampered with, the frame frozen unnaturally. Someone had stolen his fix and peddled it elsewhere.

If Martelli had had his way, the VAR technician would have been dragged from the booth by the lanyard round his neck, choking on his own accreditation until his face turned purple. He'd ordered his men to pin down all the match officials, to get names, to make inquiries. But there'd been a secure cordon, tight and impenetrable. By dawn they were gone, spirited out under guard. Whoever had bought the match had also bought the exits.

Millions had been lost last night, not just in prize money but in bets – his bets, his cuts, all siphoned away. But Juventus's loss wasn't just financial. It was personal. A message aimed straight at him.

He realised it after the calls began.

The first came from Warsaw, before the sun had properly climbed. A relegation battle he had bought weeks ago – referee, assistants, even the VAR officials. It was supposed to finish one-one, with an own goal in the second half and two red cards to pad the odds. That didn't happen. Worse, the markets in Manila had collapsed hours before his people even placed a cent. The Asians had got there first, bribing the same officials he thought he owned. His guarantee – sold twice. The second time sold without him.

The next call came from Paris. One of his fixers on the ground had the update: a referee Martelli had groomed for years – softened with gifts, blondes, a Maserati and weekends in the Riviera – was due to oversee an international friendly next weekend. The script was already written: one penalty each, yet an easy win for the home side. Reliable, lucrative, his kind of fix. But the fixer reported the man was already out of reach, sequestered with his national federation, guarded like a state asset. Someone else had got to him first. Martelli pictured the whistle rammed back between his teeth, choking him with every useless breath.

And then more messages. Berlin: a linesman he thought he owned, now suddenly 'unavailable'. Copenhagen: a midfielder refusing to take his runner's calls. Dublin: a UEFA delegate he'd bribed for years, suddenly speaking to Martelli's Irish fixer in clipped, careful tones. Glasgow: a casino licence meant to be renewed, now stalling in committee. It spread like rot, city to city, man to man. Everywhere, little betrayals. A Borja in every country.

This was the truth he couldn't spit out. They weren't just stealing matches; they were stealing him. For twenty years he'd been the broker of certainty, playing God with the game, the *capo* who made Europe's football feed Asia's gambling hunger. But now the arteries were being cut. Fixes hijacked. Cash rerouted. The tap of gambling profits turned off.

His empire was vast – property, construction, shipping routes, casinos, football, Formula One. Visible wealth, visible power. But much of it drew from a hidden feed. The games. The fixes. And the gambling cash they spawned – his share of Asia's billions washing back through Europe. A subterranean engine, a bloodstream that kept the rest alive, laundering shadow money into palaces, vineyards, yachts.

That was the danger. It wasn't one lost game. It was the unravelling of a position he had kept sacred. For years he had skimmed both sides – the fat fees for fixing matches and a share of the gambling profits those fixes unleashed. If Asia could buy European referees, runners, even VAR itself without him, the fees disappeared, the profit-stream dried up. His leverage bled away.

The old families who had protected him in the first place – the Neapolitans, the Sicilians, the investors who expected their slice – had stayed loyal because he delivered. If those families began to doubt, protection would turn into pressure. Debts would be called. His empire wouldn't rot slowly. It would be torn down with precision.

Then the screen caught his eye.

The television on the suite wall, muted but spilling live news. A crawl across the bottom: the Prado had just confirmed the identity of the stolen painting. Caravaggio's *David and Goliath*. They were showing an image of the painting itself.

He'd seen that image before.

His gaze slid across the suite, to the table strewn with baskets and gift-wrapped boxes that had been waiting for him when he arrived yesterday. He strode over, ripped through ribbon and cellophane until he found it among the envelopes and embossed invitations: a glossy postcard. He held it up to the screen. The same painting. *David and Goliath.*

In his hand, the detail bit deeper.

David tying the hair of Goliath's severed head with rope in order to lift it in triumph, straddling the giant's torso, one knee pressed onto its back. Light caught the boy's flank, his thigh, the slope of a shoulder – but his face was swallowed by shadow. A wound on Goliath's forehead showed where he'd been felled by the stone from David's sling. Nearly everything else was darkness. No soldiers, no battlefield, no crowd. Just the boy and the dead giant. A killing made private. Personal.

For a moment Martelli just stared, postcard and screen together, his thumb pressed into the gloss until it bent. Then, slowly, he turned it over. Five words, written in neat block letters:

NOW WE'RE COMING FOR YOU.

He read them once. Twice.

The card snapped in his fist.

'Who the fuck sent this?' His voice split the suite, hard enough to make the glass vibrate.

Matteo, hulking in the suite's second lounge, was on his feet before the echo died. He loomed forward, thick hands balled, waiting for orders. Another guard, Enzo, filled the doorway in an instant.

'Every basket, every ribbon, every gift box,' Martelli hissed, flinging the crumpled postcard onto the table. 'Concierge, deliveries, florist, vintner or cigar merchant. Find the hand that touched this card. Bring it to me.'

Matteo went for the gifts, his hands ripping through wrappings. Enzo barked into his radio, ordering the foyer to sweep deliveries. Martelli stayed very still. Eyes fixed on the screen, the shadowed face of Caravaggio's David watching him from the dark.

Nearly an hour later, Martelli was on one of the sofas, the gifts gutted across the table, the postcard sitting like a stain beside the fruit and flowers. Matteo and Enzo had come back with nothing. Concierge records blurred, delivery slips unsigned, CCTV useless. Too many deliveries, too many hands. Lost in the noise.

He didn't trust asking himself. The concierge would smile, bow and feed the answer straight to whoever had planted the postcard in the first place. No. Better to wait, to watch.

So, he had been watching. News loops of the Prado theft, scrolling feeds, reports stacked on his phone and tablet. Always the same image: the boy tying the head, the shadows swallowing his face. *David and Goliath.*

It had to be the same hand. The painting, the match, the postcard – one operation. The canvas screamed his name without saying it. This was an attempt to break him. They weren't merely humiliating Lorenzo Martelli. Three of his men in Madrid had been erased in the past six months, two of them decapitated, each killing a message carved in blood; now they were after his own head. They were coming for *him – il capo*. The postcard had spelt it out.

He wasn't afraid of violence or death. He had lived beside both for too long to flinch. But he would not watch his network be looted. He would get to them first – and God help them when he did.

'You're coming for me?' he said aloud, quiet as a threat. The laugh that followed was slow and dangerous. 'Try it. Try me.'

But how to find them? Not the Spanish police. They hadn't investigated the beheadings of his men in depth; they were useless to him. And if he opened that door, they would dig too deep, find too much and never stop. Nor could he lean on any politicians or judges – that world was closing in Spain until he found a loyal replacement for the Falcós.

He stood and paced. The suite swallowed his steps

– carpet soft, curtains cut heavy against the morning light. The television had been a background wash; he hadn't been looking. Now the screen snagged him. Another banner was running underneath new footage: *International art detective in Madrid, helping with Prado investigation.* A face flashed up – ragged hair, shabby attire, not the tweed-jacket professor you might expect. This one looked like he belonged on the street. Martelli almost half-smiled.

He sat back on the sofa, one eye on the screen as the caption slid past under the scruff's face: Benjamin Blake.

The phone was in his hand before he'd thought about it. *El País* came up first – stories multiplying, the theft and the dead museum guard already a national drama. Professors gave sober warnings about cultural heritage. Then, halfway down the page: 'Sources say British art expert Benjamin Blake, currently in Madrid, is helping the investigation'. No quote. No flourish. Simply there, named, unavoidable. And 'controversial', the paper called him.

Controversial.

Martelli let the word roll once in his head. It intrigued him. He switched to *Corriere della Sera*. Same pattern. Paragraphs of Caravaggio experts weighing in from afar, their faces neat, their hair neat. And then the oddball. Blake. 'Known in some circles for his proximity to both museums and the underworld' – odd phrasing, careful but pointed. Another page had dredged up the Guardia Civil's error from weeks before – 'briefly wanted in connection with an unrelated case, later dropped'. Yet another: '*A man as comfortable with crooks as with museum curators.*'

Martelli let the line sit. That was no insult. It was a credential. It meant the man might walk in both worlds. Someone who might know where the painting had gone, and who'd taken it. That made him useful.

He scrolled further – *Repubblica, La Stampa* – both quoting the same chorus of polished academics. And threaded through, like grit in the marble, the misfit Brit currently in Madrid. Misfits were dangerous, but they could also be bought.

Martelli stared at the photo again, thumb smudging the screen, then let the phone sag in his hand. An outsider in Madrid with the Prado's ear. If the thieves wanted to keep track of the investigation, they might have planted him. If this Benjamin Blake was already in his enemies' pocket, he was bait. If not, he was leverage. Either way, he was a possible route to the bastards who'd fixed the match, stolen the painting, and now thought they could take Martelli's own head. Martelli needed him – alive, willing or made to talk, then bent to his use.

'Enzo,' he said, without raising his voice.

The guard appeared in the doorway.

Martelli turned the phone, the grainy shot of the misfit glowing in his palm. 'You know him?' he asked.

Enzo shook his head.

'Find him,' Martelli said. 'Bring him here. I want a chat.'

50

Benjamin - Elena - Pilar Castro

Monday — near Atocha.

Earlier, Benjamin had watched Alfonso roar off, the motorbike's growl thinning past the row of bookstalls. He'd then given his BiciMad a shove and left it. Someone else could deal with it.

The Prado was a hundred metres away, police vans parked nose-to-tail along the *paseo*. He'd turned the other way, towards Atocha.

Coffee. WiFi. Somewhere to think.

What had Alfonso really given him? Not much. No promise on the fee Ignacio had dangled. No pendrive with rotas, names, CCTV stills. In fact, no pendrive at all. Just the caterer's name – Grupo Dorada. A missing employee, Jason-something. A guard with his throat half-severed; the painting cut from its frame. The time-line: between midnight and three.

But nothing about the choice of painting being like the underdog beating the giant in last night's final.

Picture them, Benjamin.

The underdog. The giant.

Monaco and Juventus.

David and Goliath.

Who steals *that* painting and why? Not a fence — there's no resale. Not a collector. Not protest — not at that hour. Ransom? Possibly. More likely belief — an ideology — or a message. And they chose last night to send it, as the final tilted from giant to underdog.

Coincidence? No, he didn't believe in those. They chose last night for a reason: a city distracted; police at the stadium; cameras glued to goals. They stole a picture that is the beheading of a giant. Whoever did it understood how to send a message — not a broadcast, but targeted. That was the underworld's handwriting.

He read a crime scene like a work of art — and art had its own logic. But here, no one was letting him into the Prado to study it firsthand; maybe just as well — the blood would still be there.

What had he actually seen? Yesterday morning, walking the perimeter, he'd stopped near the Jerónimos church and looked down over the main entrance. Crowds. Police clustered in the side courtyard. A forensic tent in the cafeteria area. Blue tarpaulin sagging over a narrow balcony.

So — cafeteria, catering. Grupo Dorada. Start there.

He'd found a quiet café with cracked wicker chairs and no tourists. Blue tiles, a chalkboard menu, the

WiFi was sufficient. He took a table half in the shade, half in the street's glare. His MacBook woke up and he searched for Grupo Dorada. Dozens of hits; he went straight to the corporate site.

We've grown from a single hospitality venture into one of Spain's most dynamic private conglomerates in urban living and logistics. Headquartered in Madrid, with operations across the Iberian Peninsula and Southeast Asia, Grupo Dorada brings together innovation, sustainability and service excellence under one trusted name.

It looked like a limb of some larger conglomerate – glossy, over-designed, but all very above-board. There were four 'corporate divisions', each presented with gleaming imagery.

Restaurants & Catering – crystal glassware, wine poured mid-arc, conference buffets, cocktails; links to restaurants, bars, event venues. He thought he recognised a couple of the restaurant names, but clicked on.

Wholesale to Hospitality – warehouses, aisles of cling-film and glassware, delivery vans, a B2B sign-up; someone in hi-vis smiling at a loading bay.

Dorada Mobility – 'sustainable city solutions' with *Dorada e-Bikes* – *we believe in a future where cities are pollution-free* – pictures of those fast, golden-yellow bikes he'd seen overtaking his useless BiciMad. Clean streets, smart travel, shared future.

Dorada Delivery – polished, smiling riders, e-bikes, couriers, clean yellow thermal boxes: *calm, reliable deliveries, citywide coverage, speed and efficiency.* 'Moving Madrid, one meal at a time.' A big 'Work With Us' button underneath.

He hovered.

He'd always half-fancied being a rider: wind in your face, fresh air, paid to learn a city by its shortcuts. Then he remembered he didn't know Madrid well enough, didn't know Spanish, had just abandoned his BiciMad. Maybe they'd supply him with one of their golden-yellow D-e-Bikes, though – and then he'd be dispatched with an oversized yellow box into streets he couldn't pronounce.

He clicked 'Work With Us' anyway, out of curiosity. A cheerful page in Spanish and English invited him to an open-day induction, Wednesdays and Fridays from 9.30am: *Bring DNI/NIE, smartphone (data plan), reflective vest (supplied if needed), helmet, bank details*. He had no intention of going, but he read on. A 'typical day', 'your starter kit', shift times, bonuses, affiliate programmes, own transport or rent-from-us? – it went on and on.

He smiled, then let the smile go. He read again, slower. Micro-hubs. Shifts. Loading bays. Access badges. *Dorada Delivery. Dorada Mobility.* Combine that with a group handling hospitality at venues – the Prado included – through its *Restaurants & Catering* arm, and a *Wholesale* division pushing a supermarket-style supply line 'dedicated to the hospitality customer', plus 'non-food products for the catering industry' ... someone in this ecosystem had excuses and clearance to be near the wrong door at the right time.

He leant back. Digging into Dorada would be police work: delivery rotas, loading-dock CCTV, and a search for the missing employee – Jason whoever.

He needed the *why*. Who sat behind Dorada? Why would Dorada have any interest in *David and Goliath* – if they even did?

The website didn't have a *Who We Are* page. No names or executive headshots. He scrolled to the bottom: *Aviso Legal y Política de Privacidad.*

Operado por Dorada Mobility Pte. Ltd. (Singapore).

Singapore.

He took a screenshot, then briefly checked his emails. News alerts – the Prado had finally named the stolen painting: Caravaggio's *David and Goliath*. That ought to flush a few informers out of hiding.

He closed the MacBook a finger's width, and let the café sounds back in: the espresso machine, a spoon on china, the door chime that rang for nobody, a radio dissolving into static.

His phone lit up on the table. An unknown Madrid number. He put his thumb to the screen.

Ciudad Universitario.

Elena took the metro's Linea 6 out to Ciudad Universitaria. The carriage was full of students – either half-asleep, wired on coffee, or chattering in bursts of slang she barely followed. On the escalator they shuffled shoulder to shoulder, backpacks brushing, all shapes and styles: piercings, sweatpants, ripped jeans, one girl in a flamenco dress over Doc Martens.

When she surfaced, the air felt different. Wider. Greener. The city's noise slackened into open space: broad avenues, neat pines lining the pathways. A purple canopy stood by the metro exit, offering leaflets on gender violence; two young women in T-shirts were arranging stacks of flyers. Elena caught the smell of resin from the trees, and then – harsher – the drone of traffic from a motorway underpass. Police sirens wailed somewhere closer to Moncloa, the prime minister's residence.

She'd checked her phone automatically, the way she always did after coming up from the metro. A cluster of alerts waited. One headline: the Prado had named the painting – Caravaggio's *David and Goliath*.

For a second, something tugged at her memory. A conversation with Benjamin, maybe. Something he'd said, or hinted at. But the thought slipped away almost at once. He was the one chasing the painting now, not her. She had enough on her plate.

And one thing *wouldn't* leave her. What Mei had said on the rooftop yesterday evening about a Falcó family 'accident'. She'd told Benjamin all about it until the early hours, but she wasn't sure he'd been listening. Then before dawn – just hours ago – she'd stood at the viaduct and watched Borja Falcó's body hauled away.

She'd planned to tell Benjamin more about it, but he wasn't at the hotel when she returned.

And now, at ten-thirty this Monday morning, she was supposed to be sitting across from Falcó senior himself – the president of the Consejo Superior de Deportes – politely discussing how much money the CSD had spent 'combating racism in football', and where, *exactly*, it had gone. An appointment booked days ago, cancelled by his PA during yesterday, long before Borja was found dangling in the early light. Cleared diary. No explanation.

Officially, nothing was out yet. No confirmation of the body. No headlines. She'd argued with her editor about it – her pulse thudding with the knowledge she already carried. That strange cocktail of dread and adrenaline – being one step ahead of a news cycle – prickled under her skin.

She was hungry, restless. Mei had fed her just enough to whet her appetite, and now she couldn't let it go. Abuse, trafficking, power games wrapped up in the gloss of sport – and now the son of Spain's top sports official dead. Where was the father? A journalist couldn't walk away from that. She needed to dig. And she would.

She crossed towards the low, functional bulk of the CSD building. Students swerved past on scooters; a group kicked a football along the pavement, the ball thumping off a parked car. Outside the entrance, two men with cameras loitered, the same tabloid hacks she'd seen at the viaduct. One of them lit a cigarette, watching the doors with a bored patience.

Inside the entrance, two security guards stopped her. No, Ramón Falcó was not available. She said she had an appointment. They didn't care or believe her. He was 'on leave', anyway. No further comment. She flashed her press card; half-hoping persistence might get her waved through. No chance.

She turned back, scanning the lobby – and froze. The lift doors slid open. Out stepped the bulky detective from dawn, anorak zipped to her chin. Pilar. She exchanged a few words with a woman holding a clipboard, then was steered towards the exit.

Their eyes met across the lobby glass. Recognition. Pilar paused, the same assessing look she'd given her at the viaduct, before pushing through the doors into the glare outside.

They fell into step along the pavement, the sun ricocheting off the mirrored façade behind them. Elena planning to walk towards the metro; Castro heading for the staff car park. For a while, neither spoke. Then Castro broke the silence.

'You were at the viaduct earlier.'

Elena glanced at her. 'It was Borja Falcó's body, wasn't it?'

'I can't possibly comment on that,' Castro said.

'I was told that the Falcó family might suffer an accident before the body was even found.'

That stopped Castro cold. Her head turned sharply. 'Who told you that?'

Elena felt a small tug of satisfaction. 'I can't comment on my sources, either.'

Castro studied her, then started walking again, slower now, testing her tone. 'What's your name?'

'Elena Carmona. I was supposed to interview his father this morning. Ten-thirty. He cancelled yesterday. No reason.'

'Convenient,' Castro said.

Elena didn't miss the edge in her voice. 'The Falcós have always been convenient. Rumours of kickbacks, dodgy sponsorship deals, corruption probes that never stuck – at least from my research. You think his death ties into that?'

Castro didn't reply. She kept walking.

Elena pressed. 'I've also heard whispers about young girls – promises of contracts or scholarships, futures in football that never existed. Instead: abuse, trafficking. You think the Falcós ever dipped that low?'

The detective's eyes stayed ahead.

'Borja wasn't just some spoiled playboy,' Elena went on. 'He was in Ibiza a few years ago – at the same party where a kid went off a roof. Some called it suicide. Some said pushed.'

Castro's stride faltered – Elena caught it.

'The kid who died was the son of a police inspector,' Elena said. 'Félix Barroso. Did you know that?'

Castro stopped walking. They were in the shade of the car park now. She turned slowly; the silence heavy.

'You know him?' Elena said softly. 'Do you work with him – Barroso?'

Castro's eyes had shifted – not in surprise, but calculation. She remembered the whispers: the Ibiza scandal, the boy who fell. Everyone in the department had pitied Barroso then, even those who despised him. The drinking, the temper, the bullying – maybe that was the grief bleeding through. But pity had its limits.

'Did he ever get over it?' Elena asked.

'The judge ruled it an accident. Open and shut.'

'But not for your boss?'

A pause. 'No, not really,' Castro said. 'It's what changed him, I think. Not the job. Not the blood or the corpses. The silence afterwards. No justice. Just silence. Some say he was paid for that silence.'

They walked on a little. Castro's mind was racing. Borja dead. The father vanished – *on leave*, his PA had said. Neither he nor his wife were at their house in La Moraleja. Hiding? Scared? Why wouldn't a man demand answers if his son had been strung up from a bridge? No complaint. No call. Nothing. And now this journalist was tying the Falcós straight back to Barroso. Surely he hadn't gone that far. Surely not.

They were beside her car now. Castro stopped, turned, appraising Elena again. Then: 'Get in. I want to show you something.'

Inside the car, the air was cool. Castro pulled a clear plastic sleeve from her folder. Two men in a hotel corridor, slightly blurred by a security camera: one unmistakably Borja Falcó, head down; another man beside him, shorter, half-turned, caught mid-gesture.

'Taken last night,' Castro said. 'Hotel near the stadium, a few hours before kick-off. We tracked Borja's movements. He never made it to the VIP box with his father later on.' She tapped the plastic. 'Do you know the man on the right?'

Elena shook her head too quickly. Her mouth opened, then closed again. But the stillness in that blurred profile was unmistakable. The cheekbones. The cropped hair.

The young Chinese man from Castellana House last night – the guy sitting with Carlos, the agent. The creep who'd followed her out into the street.

'Elena?' Castro said.

No answer.

'Elena?'

Elena hesitated, the photo still burning behind her eyes. 'I was supposed to be doing a story on racism in football,' she said. 'But there's a bigger story here.'

'Good,' Castro said. 'Then maybe we can help each other. But you don't print a word. Not yet. You tell me what you know first – and if it checks out, I'll give you access when this breaks.'

Elena held her gaze. 'And if I don't?'

'Then I'll find out the hard way what you're holding back. And you won't like how I do it.'

A beat.

Elena let out a long breath. 'Deal.'

51

Félix Barroso - Kai Leroux

Monday – Plaza de España and Pintor Rosales.

It had been a year ago now, but it still felt like yesterday. The light dim, the club thick with stale smoke. He'd sat at the back, nursing a whisky he didn't need. The young man who slid into the seat across from him moved with a practised calm – not hesitant but choreographed.

Late twenties, maybe early thirties. Short build. Asian. Jeans, black T-shirt, eyes sharp, hair cropped tight and neat. Everything about him said control.

His accent, when he spoke, was precise yet unplaceable, each word carefully measured, an unfamiliar rhythm beneath the polished Spanish.

'Inspector Barroso,' he'd said, with the hint of a smile. 'I've heard you're a man who can make ... complicated problems disappear.'

Barroso had looked him over. No handshake. No introduction. Just that half-smile – and a thick envelope placed between them on the table. 'I'm not in the business of solving problems for strangers,' he'd replied.

The smile stayed. 'You'll know me soon enough.'

Barroso hadn't touched the envelope, but he could already feel the weight of its contents – cash. Six months' salary, maybe more.

Whoever had set this up had done their research. They knew he was an Inspector Jefe, but they also knew the other side of him – about Miguel, or at least the ghost of that tragedy, how his son's death had torn through his life and left it rotting, especially after his wife walked out a year later. They knew about the bottles, the girls, the lines that kept the nights from ending. He was still good at his job, but the cracks were showing. Debts stacking up. And now here it was – an easy fix, delivered in a fat brown envelope.

The young man had leaned forward. 'We're moving in on a market that isn't yours to worry about – Italians mostly. Men who made the wrong enemies. Men you don't want in Madrid. We'll help you clean the city of them. All you need to do is make a camera stop working here and there, reassign a couple of detectives, certify one or two sad accidents as suicides, and flag a cash pick-up to the right traffic cops so Italian money vans get stopped.'

There was a long silence.

'We know you've accepted gifts to assist others before, Inspector,' the young Asian finally added.

'Are you blackmailing me?' Barroso asked, a laugh like a cough.

'Of course you might think that. But no. We want to work with you.'

Barroso's pulse had quickened. 'What's in it for me?'

'Money. A lot. A cut when the market is ours. Protection. And – if you want it – closure. We will avenge your son's untimely death.'

A tremor had passed under Barroso's ribs, so fast it could have been fury or grief or shame. 'What has my son's death got to do with this?'

The young man smiled. 'It still keeps you awake, doesn't it? The Falcó boy and his *pijo* friends who walked free from Ibiza. Your son fell – or was he pushed? Either way, that family struck a deal with you to cover up the drugs. They bought your silence – they paid off your son's gambling debts, too – money that would have brought men to your door to break kneecaps. They promised to speak to a senior politician in their pocket to get you promotion. It never happened. They paid you to make it all clean. But it wasn't clean, was it, Inspector? It never is. Help us to now rearrange the balance. Get your revenge. The Falcós feed the Italians; the Italians depend on them, at least in Spain. We take the market; you get your cut – and you get to watch them lose everything.'

Barroso should have walked away. He'd known that even then. But he'd opened the envelope.

· · ·

Monday morning. Same bar, same table at the back as a year ago – the same cracked red leather seat sticking to his crotch. The light was different now: curtains half-drawn, clock edging past 11am. Two whiskies down, another on the way. Two girls were still there from the night before – it was where he'd ended up. One scrolling through her phone, the other pretending not to be bored. He didn't know their names.

He'd stormed out of the incident room an hour earlier, fully intending to march over to Grupo Dorada's offices himself. But what had unsettled him – what had *really* thrown him – was that lump of a detective, Castro, asking about the wire cable and those 'uninvestigated' deaths from the past six months. The bitch.

Control of the investigation might have slipped from his hands, but those smug bastards could dig all they liked. They'd never get close to who really pulled the strings.

The Asians.

Silent now for weeks. No calls. No cash. No instructions. Like he'd been cut loose the moment they got what they wanted. He'd risked everything – the files, the favours, the small shifts of paperwork that only he could make disappear – and for what?

They still owed him a serious cut. He'd been promised. The silence itched and he didn't like it. You don't just vanish on a man like him. Not when he still had things he could say.

A waitress in a short, tight skirt appeared beside

him, set the third whisky on the table and gave him a lazy pat on the shoulder. He didn't look up.

His phone vibrated beside the glass. Unknown number, foreign prefix. He frowned, thumb hovering before opening it.

Lorenzo Martelli is responsible for the Prado hit.
Detain him while he's still on Spanish soil.
His jet leaves tonight.

His throat tightened. No signature. But he knew.

The screen lit again – the same number, now calling. He answered.

'Inspector Barroso,' the voice said.

He straightened in his seat. 'Who the fuck is this?'

'You know who this is.'

'No. I don't. And I don't appreciate –'

'We met in the same club you're sitting in now.'

Barroso jumped up, half-sending the whisky over the table, one hand going automatically to his inside-jacket holster. He glared around; the two girls from last night made no move, the barmaid in her miniskirt was chatting with regulars. No one was looking. He scanned the walls and ceiling for cameras. Then it hit him – a delivery rider with a thermal box had come in about twenty minutes earlier, dropped something off at the bar, then left. Amazon? Glovo? What the fuck.

'Relax, Inspector,' the caller said. 'I have good news. You will be pleased. You wanted the Falcós punished. Consider it done. It took longer than expected, but Borja, at least, has been lynched.'

The silence hung heavy, sharp with the smell of spilt scotch.

'What are you saying?' Barroso managed, lowering himself back into the chair.

'They found him at dawn, hanging from the viaduct.' The voice was polite, almost courteous. 'One of your detectives was at the scene early. Did she not tell you?'

Barroso felt a cold, ugly satisfaction twist through him. Castro had mentioned something about a body on a bridge, but he'd brushed it aside. 'You did this?'

'We helped to orchestrate it. It's what you wanted,' the caller said. 'I hope Falcó senior will join his precious little boy very soon – which is what I want to talk to you about.'

Barroso's fingers groped blindly for the whisky glass. 'You've taken the market you wanted. What about my cut? You vanish for weeks and then call with this. Where's my money?'

'You'll receive what you were promised,' the caller said. 'But we require a little extra cooperation. First, Lorenzo Martelli must be detained and questioned while he is still on Spanish soil. His jet leaves tonight.'

Barroso barked a short, ugly laugh. 'You want me to detain the billionaire Martelli? You've gone mad.'

'Do it, and you secure your position. Refuse, and someone in your own team will be made to see to it.'

'Listen to me,' Barroso hissed, leaning forward,

voice dropping. 'My unit's been poking around a bedsit belonging to a Jason Zhou. They're checking out Grupo Dorada. They're analysing every speck of blood at the Prado because *someone* left something. They're re-examining past fatalities. I can't cover you anymore unless I'm paid. Forget any Italian billionaires – pay up. Cash. Or you'll find the investigation takes an unpleasant turn. I'm not your fucking errand boy.'

For the first time the caller went quiet – a silence that felt like a held breath. When the voice returned, it was slow and flat. 'That wasn't very polite, Inspector. I was about to ask you how the investigation was progressing, and whether everything was … under control. Is it? I need information. Any evidence found at the museum? What do the police have? Anything?'

Barroso hesitated. 'No one will move on things unless I direct it,' he lied. This little Asian brat wouldn't know the truth. 'But there's a cost to keep that status quo. As I said: cash.'

The caller held for a beat. 'If you want cash, we must meet.'

Barroso stiffened. 'Now? Where?'

'Pintor Rosales. The old Teleférico. Not far from where you are.'

Barroso had downed two more whiskies before setting off on foot from the club tucked behind Plaza de España, heading west towards Pintor Rosales. He could handle his drink – or so he liked to think – but the warmth in his gut had turned sluggish, and the sun was already punishing. He kept to the shade, walking not as steadily as he might have liked.

Every few steps his hand went to his inside-jacket holster – a quick pat, a silent reassurance. His good friend. His insurance. Just in case.

The call had given him a perverse lift – gratification at the Falcós getting their comeuppance. He'd also reasserted himself, put the little bastard in his place over the Martelli nonsense. Worst case, he thought, he could bump the Asian off; men who tried to blackmail him didn't tend to last long.

The old Teleférico – a strange place to meet strange people, perhaps, but it made sense. Close by. Quiet. Out of circulation. The cable cars that once ferried tourists from the Parque del Oeste to the Casa de Campo had been dead for years, the city still pretending they were *under renovation*. Everyone in Madrid remembered them; no one expected them to move again. Another civic ghost. He'd read the council had put out another tender – probably a scam, another trough for the same pigs.

Now the site was a carcass: overgrown shrubs, graffiti, ticket windows smashed. Eerie at night, harmless in daylight. A safe enough place to collect a load of cash.

Pigeons flapped off the rusted girders as he trudged up the slope, sweat crawling down his neck. He wished he'd taken a piss before leaving the club. He stopped, wiped his forehead, and scanned the empty terrace.

Nothing moved – just the hum of traffic and the faint, sour smell of oil and birdshit.

Then he saw them – three delivery riders, astride their idling bikes at the far end of the terrace. Yellow boxes, helmets, black clothes. Just chatting, comparing phones, scrolling their apps.

They looked up. All three. Then began moving his way. They all looked the same – same build, same helmets, same boxes. He could have passed any one of them a hundred times that week and never noticed. *You didn't, did you?* They were everywhere – faceless, nameless, anonymous, part of the city's hum. And now that made him uneasy.

His hand went to his jacket.

One of the riders called out – slim build, wiry. 'You came alone, Inspector?'

Barroso nodded. He watched as they spoke quietly among themselves, then two of the riders peeled away, yellow boxes swaying as they pedalled off across the park, vanishing between the trees.

The one who'd called out approached, pushing his bike, the box still strapped to his back. When he reached the railing opposite Barroso, he unclipped it, set it down, and leaned the bike against the metal.

The face was the same he'd seen in the club a year ago – the same sharp eyes, cropped hair, that quiet geometry of a man who never moved in panic. He hadn't remembered him being quite so small, and something about that prickled him.

'Inspector,' he said, nodding. 'We meet again.'

A distant horn sounded. A dog barked half a block away. A couple of joggers passed in the mid-distance.

'The Prado's a fucking mess,' Barroso said.

'We've told you who's responsible for that –'

'An Italian billionaire?' Barroso cut in, snorting.

'Someone else can uncover it, then,' came the reply, calm and flat. 'You'd receive far more than what's in this box – but it's your choice, Inspector.' He nudged the yellow box closer with his foot. 'Take it,' he said. 'We're still grateful for what you've already done.'

Barroso took a step forward, eyes on the box, then up at the delivery rider, then down again – a quick glance left, right – the bark of a dog somewhere distant again – another look at the young Asian, unsmiling, still watching, still waiting for him to bend down and open the box, to take the cash, *to play his role* – and he would, *yes*, of course he would – but something itched under his skin, the *childlike size* of the guy – *of course* – this had to be the killer himself, the figure on the Prado CCTV half-severing the guard's neck – the same rider caught on the embassy footage, too – that *kid* racing off on a bike after hooking a plastic bag with a severed head onto the railing – and Barroso knew he was dealing with fire with these Asians – he knew they were dangerous, *they were killers* – but it had never really hit him that his point of contact was *the* killer himself.

He looked up again.

The rider wasn't there.

He'd moved – *fast*, impossibly fast – like a bullet, like shadow – he was *behind* Barroso now – and then the wire was there, the pressure sudden and absolute, cold against his throat, a burning line tightening each time he gasped – his hands went for it instead of his pistol – useless – fingers slipping, clawing at nothing – and then the air was going, his own breath turning against him – he tried to shout but what came out was only a broken rasp, a choke, a hiss – and then he felt it, the warmth spreading down his chest, the splash of it against the unopened box on the ground, his own blood bright against the yellow – *absurdly bright* – red and yellow – and he thought stupidly about the glorious colours of flags, the Spanish flag, back in the good old days when it meant something – and about his son Miguel falling, about the Falcó boy hanging from the viaduct – *was this what it felt like?* – how strange to lose your balance, your weight, the ground tipping, knees buckling – the cable-car girders above him catching the sun as if the whole city was turning red for him now – and then he was down, his eyes fixed on the yellow and red-streaked box … unsure whether his head was still fully attached to his body or not.

Kai let the body slide to the concrete, the head twisted to one side. Far too much blood again – but he'd enjoyed every second of it.

Someone was shouting now. Screaming.

He picked up the box, wiped it as best as he could, then calmly attached it to the back of his bike. By the time anyone reached the terrace, he was gone.

52

Benjamin - Lorenzo Martelli

Monday – Hotel Ritz.

The request for a meeting had really been a summons. Quick, polite, but edged with intimidation – Benjamin hadn't been given a choice. When a man with a thick Italian accent called to say that his *signore* in Madrid wanted a word about the Caravaggio – that he might have 'information' to offer – it wasn't something Benjamin could turn down. Following every lead was part of the job. Even when it led to the darkest alleys. Like this one.

He'd had calls like this before. Those who wanted to meet usually did have something to offer or trade; they were rarely the problem. The ones who didn't – who preferred silence first, violence later – were the ones to worry about. Even so, the call had thrown him.

'How did you get my number?' Benjamin asked.

'That was not … how you say … difficult, Mister Ben. Madrid, she small.'

'It's actually Benjamin.'

'Mister Benjamin.'

'Well, actually, it's Benjamin Blake. So it would be Mister Blake. What's your name?'

'My name is Enzo, Mister Blake. Is now a good time?'

'For what, exactly, Mister Enzo?'

'For a meeting. With my *signore*.'

Benjamin let the silence stretch. 'Why me?'

'You have been invited by a man who respects your expertise. I suggest you do not keep him waiting.'

'Your *signore* has a name?'

'I am not … authorised … to say on this call.'

'Then why don't you call again when you are?'

'You do not understand, Mister Blake. This is not a choice. The *signore* will speak to you in comfort. At his Ritz suite.'

Benjamin blinked. The Ritz again. He'd been there yesterday with Ignacio – and somehow still had to cough up for the coffee himself. 'And if I say no?'

'You will not say no.'

Twenty minutes later Benjamin was back in the lobby of the Ritz, all marble calm and muted piano, where the staff seemed to glide and float instead of walk. Which made the man waiting for him stand out like a bruise.

Mister Enzo. Up close, the acne scars looked almost geological, as if someone had tried to mine his face for minerals and given up halfway. A silver chain clung to his bloated neck, glinting each time he breathed.

'Mister Blake,' he said, that same thick accent rolling through what was left of yellow, broken teeth.

Benjamin hated moments like this. As feared, a slab of meat was thrust forward to shake, and it didn't feel like a handshake at all – more like a juice extractor.

'This way, please.'

Benjamin nursed what was left of his hand, then nodded and half-smiled – the kind of politeness usually reserved for customs officers and men holding guns.

Two other slabs in suits detached from the marble pillars as they crossed the lobby, each giving Benjamin a courteous nod that somehow still felt like a threat. The lift arrived with a soft chime. Enzo gestured him in, then followed – far too close.

Benjamin kept his eyes on the numbers climbing. The mirrored walls caught their reflections: his own frayed self beside a mountain of flesh.

When the lift reached the top floor, they stepped into a hushed corridor, the air cool and still. Enzo moved ahead, stopping at some double doors. A curt nod to the guard outside, a swipe of a keycard, and the doors opened onto a suite that could have belonged to a head of state.

Gold light spilled across the room. A view of Madrid like a private kingdom – the Prado adjacent, the fountains of the *paseo*, the parliament building beyond. Chandeliers, deep sofas, a dining table, a study, a lounge, adjoining rooms. Champagne in ice buckets, wine bottles in rows on the sideboard. Pale drapes softened the sunlight. The air smelled faintly of lilies and money. And in the centre of it all, like a monarch awaiting news from his court, sat the man who'd summoned him.

He stood to greet Benjamin – tall, broad, slicked-back hair, polished within an inch of his life. An immaculate shirt, cuffs open, a watch that could fund a small village. His eyes were heavy with calculation, his smile thin and rehearsed – a lizard easing into warmth.

'Benjamin Blake,' he said – voice smooth but weighted, the kind that expected to be listened to. Then: 'Lorenzo Martelli. The pleasure's all mine.'

He'd said it automatically, replying to something Benjamin hadn't said – *a pleasure to meet you.*

He looked like a man who heard the phrase every hour and believed it each time. That people, *sycophants*, were pleased to see him, to meet him. But, no – the pleasure was always *his*, probably in every sense. The words slid from his mouth like something already well-used. Hedonism disguised as charm. Benjamin didn't reply. He already disliked the man – and, a heartbeat later, realised who he was facing.

Lorenzo Martelli – a man who almost needed no introduction – Benjamin had heard of him, of course he had, the name had floated through the years like a rumour that refused to die, impossible to avoid, the sort of name that appeared in headlines without explanation, a shorthand for money and reach and danger – *Martelli*, Lorenzo Martelli – wealth that seemed to leak through half of Italy, the kind of fortune that built itself on something harder and dirtier than business-school optimism – construction empires, maybe media, maybe property, shipping routes, casinos, even a Formula One team somewhere in the mix – because wherever the money flowed this man had already been there first, buying, selling, greasing palms, leaving a trail of speculation and fear – was it all legitimate, hardly, there'd been investigations, tax scandals, prosecutors who retired early or vanished, the usual pattern – too powerful to charge, too well connected to fall – maybe politics once, or maybe he just had every politician in his pocket – but yes, *art*, that was it, there'd been something about art, the man was known to have *unusual* tastes, a collector of the grand and grotesque, someone had written that he bought beauty to possess it, not to look at it – and Benjamin remembered a story from years ago, a rumour that Martelli owned a disputed second version of Caravaggio's *Cardsharps*, hidden in some vault or villa, never authenticated, experts sneering, the press laughing, yet it fit – the obsession with control, illusion, cheating, betrayal – maybe that was why Benjamin had been summoned here, to talk Caravaggio, to talk about *David and Goliath*, to hear a boast about another hidden version or a promise to return the stolen one, some obscene gesture of cultural philanthropy from a billionaire buying redemption with publicity – but then his eyes shifted – a glint of light on a chair, a framed photograph, a white envelope stamped in black, the Juventus crest, the faint smell of leather and champagne and power – and suddenly it clicked. *Of course.* Juventus. Something else he as good as owned. His club. Last night's match.

The one he wasn't supposed to lose.

'Welcome. *Per favore* – come. Sit.' Martelli gestured to the sofa opposite, a single motion that managed to be both an invitation and a command.

Benjamin hesitated, then crossed the expanse of carpet and lowered himself carefully, wary not to sink too deeply into the cushions. The low table between them gleamed like still water.

'Can I offer you something?' Martelli asked. 'Coffee? Wine? Champagne?' His smile was thin as a blade.

'Water's fine,' Benjamin said, though he doubted any would appear. From the corner of his eye he could see Enzo hovering with another thug near the entrance to the suite, blocking any escape route.

'So,' Martelli said. 'Madrid suits you? *Ti piace?*'

The man radiated control. Tailored, tanned, faintly terrifying. His voice carried the weight of someone unused to repeating himself – but Benjamin stayed silent.

'I asked you a question,' Martelli said, smile unmoving. 'Do you like Madrid?'

Benjamin held his gaze. 'What is it you actually want from me?'

'You help people find things they've lost,' Martelli said smoothly.

'What have *you* lost?'

Martelli's face darkened just a shade. 'Do you have any enemies?'

'Enemies?'

'Yes, enemies. I think you do.' Martelli leaned back slightly, as if enjoying a moment of private amusement. 'I've discovered things about you. There are people you've upset. In Berlin, Amsterdam … Paris, certainly. The Joussets – Cécile and Claude. Correct?'

Benjamin said nothing.

'We know the Joussets,' Martelli went on. 'And we know they're looking for you.' He let that hang, then added, almost lightly, 'But we can fix that for you.' A nod towards Enzo and the other bulk near the door. 'We have ways of making little problems like that disappear.'

'Señor Martelli, with all respect –'

'Lorenzo,' he interrupted softly. 'Call me Lorenzo.'

'I'm not looking for any protection. Lorenzo.'

Martelli chuckled. 'Everyone needs a little protection, Benjamin … even if only from me.'

For Christ's sake, Benjamin thought. He briefly considered shoving the low table against the Italian's legs, trapping him there while he made a dash for it. Futile, obviously – but the thought helped.

As if reading his mind, Martelli clicked his fingers. Enzo's mammoth frame began to move. He crossed to an Adidas bag near the dining table and started rummaging inside. The rustle of plastic bags carried across the room.

So, this was it. A claw hammer? Secateurs? He'd been threatened with just about everything before. What body part would they require he leave behind this time – a finger, a kneecap?

But then Enzo approached the low table and placed something down between them: a brick of neatly stacked euro notes, bound tight with rubber bands. He then stepped back to the door without a word. The money sat there between them like a hostage.

'I read about you in *El País*,' Martelli said, as if the act of Enzo placing a brick of cash on the table hadn't really happened.

'I wouldn't trust everything you read in *El País*,' Benjamin replied.

'I read that you're helping the *spagnoli* recover their lost painting.'

Spagnoli, Benjamin thought. *Spaniards*. Not the Prado. Not the police. Not the culture ministry. Spaniards. And he'd said it with a hint of a sneer.

Had he misread the man? Italian art made up the third-largest school in the Prado – most of it drawn from centuries of Spanish rule across Italy. The Habsburgs had controlled Milan; Philip II had ruled from El Escorial, dispatching ambassadors northeast with blank cheques and royal seals. Madrid's great collectors had followed suit, their tastes borrowed from Florence and Rome. Some of Caravaggio's paintings, too, had travelled west through those channels – gifts, tributes, dowries, pleas for mercy, papal pardons – all blurred into 'provenance'.

Was that what this was all about? Was Martelli going to demand the return to his homeland of *David and Goliath* – if and when it was ever recovered – a nationalist fantasy about Italian heritage, with Benjamin as the middleman? Or was his interest to compensate for his own ridiculed version of *The Cardsharps* ... the one *not* painted by Caravaggio.

'You're interested in the Prado's missing painting,' Benjamin said, matter of fact.

'No, I'm not interested in the painting,' Martelli replied. 'I'm interested in who took the painting.'

'I think everyone's interested in that.'

'Who's paying you to help?' Martelli asked. 'The museum or *la polizia spagnola*?'

There it was again, Benjamin noted – that sneer when he mentioned the Spanish police.

'Neither,' he said – which was the truth.

It had been Ignacio, the culture ministry bureaucrat, who'd since been detained for doing so. He was still waiting for Alfonso García to confirm that the arrangement was still on. His gaze flicked, just for a second, to the brick of cash on the table. He looked away, but not quickly enough. Martelli had noticed.

'*That*,' the Italian said, lifting his chin towards the notes, 'is only to cover your initial expenses.'

'Expenses?' Benajmin said. 'For what exactly?'

'For something I want you to do.'

Benjamin drew a slow breath, his eyes drifting around the suite. 'Lorenzo,' he began. 'I'm afraid I already have too many things that I'm –'

'I think someone inside my network has crossed me,' Martelli cut in. His tone hardened, the little warmth now gone. 'And this painting was their way of showing it. I want to know who.'

Benjamin held his gaze. He was intrigued, but that was all.

Inside, his mind kept circling. *Someone in your network crossed you and used a painting to show it?* In Martelli's world, crossing the boss wasn't a long-term career move. Anyone inside his network who'd tried would already be gone – and not quietly. Men like the thugs by the door made sure of that.

So maybe it wasn't inside. Maybe it was outside – someone trying to get under his skin by stealing a painting. A painting he'd once hoped to own, or planned to steal himself? *Was that it?*

He couldn't yet tell whether he'd been summoned as an investigator, a pawn, or the next exhibit. He liked puzzles; he liked art; he liked *recovering* art from crooks, mobsters and murderers – but he didn't enjoy sitting across from men who looked as if they ate people for breakfast.

'Look, if anyone's crossed you, Lorenzo,' he said evenly, 'you mentioned earlier that you already have the means to make little problems like that disappear.'

Martelli didn't move, but something in his eyes tightened. 'Once I know who and where they are,' he said, 'yes.'

Benjamin stood up.

'Where are you going?' Martelli asked.

'It's been interesting to meet you, but I really need to get going,' Benjamin said. He could feel Enzo's gaze tracking him from across the suite.

'I don't think you understand,' the Italian said, still seated, one leg crossed, the picture of ease. 'I need a name. And where I can place my hands on that name.'

'I don't have a name –'

'*Yet*,' Martelli cut in. 'You might not have a name yet. But you will. And I want to be the first person to know it.'

Benjamin hesitated. 'Why me?'

'I've done my homework. You know how these things move. You have … a scent.'

'Why not ask the Spanish police to keep you informed. They're the ones running the investigation.'

Martelli's jaw twitched, something colder showing through. 'Don't insult me. You think I'd trust *la polizia spagnola* with anything? They've never helped me. They exist to protect themselves, not the truth.' He leaned forward and pushed the stack of euros across the low table. It stopped just short of Benjamin's shin. 'Take it. Just a gesture of faith for now. There will be more later.'

Benjamin looked at the cash but didn't touch it. 'No, thanks. If I take it, I work for you.'

Martelli offered his lizard smile again. 'You already do,' he said. 'Those who work for me are protected. Work against me …' He let the silence do the rest. 'Consider it insurance. For your continued good health.'

Benjamin's eyes flicked to Enzo. He left the money where it was.

Martelli inclined his head. 'As you wish. We'll hold on to it for you.' He added the threat like a casual fact: 'Enzo will be watching you. If you share any names with anyone else before I hear them, he might take that personally.'

Benjamin remained silent.

'Midnight,' Martelli added. 'That's when I fly to Milan. But Enzo and his *amici* will remain. Waiting. Listening. We'll expect your call.'

The Italian stood up and extended a hand. Another large hand, firm and confident rather than crushing. The grip closed around Benjamin's already bruised fingers, not so much shaking as *claiming*.

'Thank you for coming,' Martelli said. 'The pleasure was all mine.'

53

Judge Varela

Monday – central Madrid.

Detective Castro was driving back from the Ciudad Universitaria area to central Madrid, Elena beside her, when the police radio crackled to life.

'*Inspector Jefe Barroso, deceased. Pintor Rosales. Homicide. Same garrote method as the Prado guard.*'

'*Joder,*' Castro said. She glanced sideways at Elena. 'You didn't hear those details. Understood?'

Elena shrugged, then nodded.

The dispatcher's next words came through static: '*All senior officers summoned by Judge Varela, immediate.*'

Castro looked at Elena again. 'Our chat will have to wait. You call me later – about the Falcó thing, what you know. You've got my number now, right?'

'Yes.'

Castro pulled over near a metro stop. 'Good. Then

go. Call me from somewhere quiet. And keep your head down.'

Detective Morales was being driven by another agent towards Grupo Dorada's offices when his phone lit up.

Barroso is dead. Drop everything. Judge wants us all now.

He swore under his breath.

'Turn around,' he told the driver.

The car swung hard by the Plaza de Castilla towers and shot south again.

Gutiérrez was still at the incident room in Huertas, going through the notes on Barroso that Castro had shared with him – the so-called suicide cases with severed heads, the closed files, the wire, the loose ends she hadn't dared bring up in front of the others – when a duty officer appeared in the doorway, calling out.

'They've found the *jefe* – dead. Pintor Rosales. Same way as the Prado guard. Judge Varela's called an emergency meeting. All senior personnel right now.'

Gutiérrez looked at the clock, then down at the photos across his desk. *Christ.*

He picked up the file, grabbed his jacket and stepped into the corridor. Lara was there – the tech officer who'd tapped into the culture ministry bureaucrat's phone and tracked the Brit's movements through BiciMad. Barroso had told her to keep feeding him updates. She stood frozen halfway down the hall, a hand pressed to her mouth, eyes wide. She'd already heard.

'Send me everything you sent him,' Gutiérrez said.

Then he was gone.

At **BPH** headquarters, Alfonso García was staring at the muted news feed looping on his screen, the morning's press statement with the *David and Goliath* title still scrolling along the bottom – when his phone rung.

He recognised the forensic officer's number and answered.

'You'd better sit down,' Ferrer said.

'I am. Why?'

'Barroso. Murdered. Identical to the museum. Judge wants everyone at her office – immediately.'

A pulse of silence filled the line. Ferrer hung up.

Alfonso lowered the phone. He felt the air shift – the weight of it settling in. He hadn't liked Barroso; no one had. But there was something obscene about it – a cop executed in the style of his own case.

Were any of them safe now?

The blinds had been half-shut against the midday glare. Files and photographs were spread across the table. Coffee cups, cold. Nobody sat easily.

Judge Varela had opened the meeting in a fury. 'Thirty-two hours,' she'd snapped. 'Thirty-two hours between the Prado murder and this. My lead investigator throttled in broad daylight. Can someone tell me what the hell is going on?'

Chief forensic officer Ferrer had led off, outlining what little his team had so far pieced together, as he gestured towards the photos spread across the table – a brutal, bloody scene.

The body had been found beneath the old Teleférico station – a location, he'd said, likely chosen for its lack of security cameras. Discreet. Empty. No witnesses. Two joggers had come across it, probably only minutes after the killer had left.

Estimated time of death: noon. Same type of garrote implement, same wire – still embedded in Barroso's neck when they found him. Blood everywhere. Whoever did it would have been spattered, too. Trails on the ground, possible footprints leading away. Even some tyre marks from a scooter, bicycle or motorbike through the smear.

'Here,' Ferrer had said, tapping a rectangular gap among the stains. 'Something was on the ground when the blood hit – a box, suitcase, maybe a briefcase. Whatever it was, it's gone. Maybe Barroso had gone there to hand something over. Or to collect something.'

Castro and Gutiérrez exchanged a glance.

'What are we looking at here?' Varela said, her voice tight. 'A serial killer? Or had Barroso stumbled too close to the truth?' There was a pause. 'Why was he at the Teleférico? Someone's been checking his phone, right? Calls, messages – come on, speak up.'

'His phone's being analysed,' Gutiérrez said. 'What we know is that the last message came in less than an hour before death. Encrypted number, followed by a two minute call. This is what the message said …'

He handed around a printout.

Varela read aloud, voice flat.

'Lorenzo Martelli is responsible for the Prado hit. Detain him while he's still on Spanish soil. His jet leaves tonight.'

A silence fell over the room.

'Lorenzo Martelli?' Varela said at last, incredulous. 'Am I missing something? Has information been kept from me? Has the Prado investigation thrown up *anything* to suggest any connection to Lorenzo Martelli?'

She looked from face to face – detectives, agents, the judicial secretary – each shaking their head or shrugging.

Varela's tone hardened. 'And you're telling me that Barroso went to meet whoever sent him that message?'

'It looks that way, your honour,' Gutiérrez said. 'Call came right after. He left a bar near Plaza de España and headed on foot towards Pintor Rosales. No further activity after that.'

'So he walks into an ambush,' the judge said. 'A message naming an Italian billionaire and a corpse within the hour. Marvellous.'

For a moment, no one spoke.

'Where *is* Martelli?' Varela asked, scribbling a note to herself after murmuring something to the judicial secretary.

'He's been staying at the Hotel Ritz since Saturday,

your honour,' Morales said. 'His jet's on standby at Barajas.' He hesitated, then added: 'We've contacted the airport police and Guardia Civil to flag anything unusual to us, just in case.'

'Okay,' the judge said, nodding. 'If anything, we could request a courtesy interview at the hotel. But let me speak first with the Attorney General and the Interior Minister – it might even go higher. We make no approach whatsoever to Señor Martelli until I have written clearance. Understood?'

There was a murmur of assent around the table. The room was heavy with the sound of pens scratching, paper rustling, the low hiss of the air-conditioning.

'What else does his phone show?' the judge asked. 'Other calls made or received – messages?'

'He's made multiple unanswered calls to two specific numbers since the Prado murder,' Morales said. 'We're trying to identify the recipients –'

'And he insisted on keeping a check on the whereabouts of the Brit mentioned in *El País*,' Gutiérrez cut in.

Varela frowned. 'Remind me,' she said. 'What Brit mentioned in *El País*?'

'Benjamin Blake, your honour,' Alfonso García replied. 'We had a bit of a fallout with the culture ministry over them seeking outside help –'

'Right,' nodded Varela. 'And? Did Barroso meet this Brit? If so, when and where?'

'We don't know if they met, your honour,' Gutiérrez said. 'All we know is that he wanted to be kept informed of the Brit's whereabouts. The Brit was using a BiciMad, which was initially easy enough to track –'

An agent at the far end of the table gave a short chuckle.

'*This is a serious matter*,' Varela snapped, glaring at him. Then she turned to García. 'Are you in touch with this … Brit?'

García hesitated. 'Yes and no, your honour.'

'Yes *or* no, García. Which is it?'

'Yes. I had a very brief conversation with him early this morning. But I really don't think we need to worry about –'

'I'll decide what we need to worry about, García,' Varela cut in. 'Tyre marks in the blood at the Teleférico. Barroso wanted the Brit tracked – he'd been using a bike. I want the Brit's movements and whether he met Barroso. We have a murdered chief inspector. We leave no stone unturned. Find this Brit now and ask him – or order someone to do it. But not alone. I can't risk anyone else being put in danger.'

Morales, García and Gutiérrez exchanged looks, all nodding. Gutiérrez rose slightly from his chair, turning away as he made a quick call on his mobile – short, clipped phrases, a tone that carried across the room. Then he sat back down.

'Lara's on it,' he said. 'She'll be accompanied if she makes any approach.'

'Good,' Varela replied.

'And we're also trying to track down Jason Zhou,

the missing Café Prado employee,' Morales added. 'Also used a bike.'

'Yes – I've seen that in these reports,' Varela nodded, flicking through the files. 'Where are we with Grupo Dorada and that temp agency, Madrid Flexi Jobs?'

'I was on the way there,' Morales muttered.

Varela was distracted by the judicial secretary for a moment; she scribbled another note, murmured something back, then looked up.

'We don't know what Barroso had uncovered,' she said. 'We don't know why he went to the Teleférico – it was clearly a trap. The crime scene is no longer just the museum. As for Dorada or Flexi jobs: we need warrants, and we must move with extreme caution.'

There was a silence. Then Castro spoke up – edged on by Gutiérrez, who'd caught her eye again as he tapped the file she'd shared with him.

'Your honour, if I may.'

Varela looked over. 'Go on.'

'Over the past eight months we've had three suspicious deaths involving cable wire around the neck or torso,' Castro said. 'All ruled suicides. Barroso closed every file himself. There's also another pattern. The three victims were all Italian nationals. Six months ago we also had a severed head outside the Italian Embassy, unidentified – but Barroso assigned that case to another department.'

The room froze.

'All Italians?' Varela said slowly.

Gutiérrez slid the file across. 'We're re-opening each case,' he said. 'Today.'

Chairs shifted. Someone swore under their breath.

'Why didn't you say this earlier?' Varela asked, staring at Castro.

'I only pieced it together overnight,' Castro said. 'I shared it with Gutiérrez before coming here.'

Varela looked at her for a long moment, expression unreadable. Then she turned to the judicial secretary. 'Get me full forensic accounting on Barroso,' she said – just loud enough for those nearby to hear. 'Bank statements, transfers, anything that doesn't fit an inspector jefe's pay grade. Quietly.'

The secretary nodded and began typing a message on her phone.

'There's something else,' Castro added quietly. 'This morning's hanging – Borja Falcó. Son of the CSD president; he ran a sports marketing firm. There's a link to Barroso's own son, who fell from a rooftop in Ibiza a few years ago – you may recall. Falcó senior has vanished. No distress call, no statement regarding his son. One theory: if Barroso wanted revenge on the Falcós for that Ibiza mess, someone may have wanted revenge on him. The timing's very close.'

She slid another printout across the table. 'And this – thirty-six hours before the hanging, Borja Falcó was seen at the Arena Hotel, near the stadium. CCTV confirms it. He should have attended the match in the evening but his seat in the VIP box was empty. This is a still from the hotel camera, showing Borja with another man.'

Judge Varela leaned forward. The photo was blurred; Borja's head was half-turned towards a smaller man beside him, Asian features, compact build.

'Name?' she asked.

'We're working on it,' Castro said.

'Looks familiar,' Morales said, staring at the photo, 'but I can't place it right now. The Falcós were investigated a few years ago. Nothing ever stuck. The son's marketing firm had sponsorship ties with –'

'Italians,' Gutiérrez said.

The room went still again – colder this time.

Varela glanced at the judicial secretary, busy taking notes, then drew a breath. 'And this morning Barroso gets a message blaming an Italian billionaire for the Prado hit …' She paused, tapping her pen on the table. 'If what we're sitting on is linked to organised crime – possibly international – then we need UDYCO looped in.'

She stood, gathering her notes. 'I need to make a call to the ministry. No one moves until I'm back.'

The door closed behind her.

For a moment, no one spoke. Then the chairs began to creak. Morales poured more water into his glass, his hand shaking slightly. García leaned in and muttered something to Gutiérrez. Across the table, Castro scrolled through her phone, checking for any further updates from the incident room. An agent at the far end stretched, moaning about the heat. The low hum of voices slowly filled the room again – exhaustion, adrenaline, disbelief.

Five minutes later, the door opened. Varela re-entered and sat at the table again, expression harder than before.

'A representative from UDYCO is on his way,' she said. 'Organised crime unit. I've briefed the ministry. We're not handing anything over yet – but we're on their radar now. So let's make sure we look like we know what we're doing.'

The room went quiet again. Only the air-con broke the silence.

54

Benjamin - Elena - Carlos - Kai

Monday – central Madrid.

The first thing that hit Benjamin after leaving Martelli's air-conditioned suite at the Ritz was the lunchtime heat. Heavy, baked – and the instant, intense noise of the city again: horns blaring, sirens wailing, scooters screaming, and open-top double-deckers crammed with tourists simply getting in the way.

He finally took one of the taxis in line outside the hotel and asked the driver to take him back to his own. He hadn't slept there last night, but he had no regrets about waking up on Elena's floor. He hadn't heard from her yet, despite sending a couple of messages.

Once there, in the calm and cleanliness of his own hotel room – bed still made, curtains half drawn – he did what he'd been longing to do: wash the Ritz off him. Martelli's cologne, Enzo's stare, the stink of cash and menace. He stood under the shower, letting the water run hot at first, then cold enough to feel alive again, before wrapping himself in a towel and ordering a roll and coffee from room service.

Fifteen minutes later he was at the desk, MacBook open. He had no intention of helping Martelli, but the man's words kept spinning in his head:

Someone inside my network has crossed me.

This painting was their way of showing it.

I want to know who.

Benjamin had challenged him. If it had been someone inside his network, Martelli would already have sniffed them out – or erased them. It had to be someone outside. But his empire was sprawling, the kind that bred enemies faster than it made money. Where did you even start with a man like that?

The Italian's suite had been full of quiet tells: the Juventus crest embossed on notepads; the black-and-white scarf flung across a chair. He hadn't mentioned Saturday night's fiasco on the pitch once, which in itself said everything.

Monaco beating Juventus – David beating Goliath.

Elena's phrase from yesterday floated back again, half teasing, half prophetic.

Martelli and his team had been humiliated in public, the world watching. Maybe that's why he hadn't spoken of it; the wound was still raw. Italians didn't talk about losing football matches.

But was it only pride? Caravaggio's *David and*

Goliath stolen the same night – coincidence? No. It had to be deliberate.

He could see it now – Saturday night, the Irish bar near Plaza de Cibeles, not far from the Prado. The game roaring from every screen. Firecrackers going off outside as it went into extra-time, another volley before the penalties. A dog had barked inside the bar, startled by the noise. The same across Madrid – the city on its feet, spilling into the streets, police braced for riots. Security stretched thin; the perfect window to disappear in plain sight, if you timed it right. If you *knew*.

Alfonso had said the Prado timeline was between midnight and three in the morning. Midnight to slip in while the city was distracted; three to slip out again, when it lay dead quiet.

Whoever planned the break-in knew the match would go to extra-time and penalties. Had they fixed it that way – to make Martelli's beloved team lose?

It was symbolism: toppling the giant, removing its head. Martelli had been humiliated on the pitch – publicly – but also privately, professionally.

But by whom?

Juventus was a Goliath, sure.

But who saw Martelli as Goliath, too?

Martelli – Goliath – had been sent a message. The man had said so himself: *Someone's crossed me. This painting was their way of showing it.*

But no one broke into the Prado to steal a

Caravaggio just to send a message. There had to be another motive – another game in play. A message to others, maybe.

He thought again of the football – Juventus the favourites, Monaco a long shot. He thought of the betting margins, the odds, the timing – and felt a spark.

Match-fixing on the pitch, art theft and murder off it. All on the same night. David toppling Goliath.

He grabbed his phone to call his contact in London again.

'Andy?'

'Yeah – I was going to call you.'

'And?'

'It's an odd one, mate.'

'In what way?'

'It's not just what happened on Saturday night, it's what's happened since. People are placing bets through some new AI platform – decentralised, blockchain-based, runs off a predictive model that hides the transaction trail. I think it uses AI to bundle bets through fake accounts, too – so the trail just vanishes. We used to be able to follow the chatter, spot the spikes, cluster the IPs – but this thing strips it all out. It's like the whole market's gone dark.'

'Andy, I have absolutely no idea what you're talking about.'

'No?'

'No.'

'Put simply, we used to be able to track the timing of bets — red cards, penalties, own goals, you name it. It helped us monitor the spikes, spot anything dodgy during possible match-fixing. But there's a new player now — a big syndicate that's swept the market.'

'Italian?' Benjamin asked.

'What?'

'An Italian syndicate?'

'No, mate — nothing that small. This is Asian money. Half the planet. Hong Kong, Singapore, Macau — even Shanghai. Crawling all over Europe now.'

'You're saying Saturday's match was fixed?'

'Hard to say. The odds on Monaco spiked a few minutes before kick-off, then levelled out again. We thought it was an algorithm glitch, but maybe not. If someone knew the AI model inside out, they could ride the odds like a wave — cash out before anyone noticed. And if they already knew it was going to extra-time and penalties … well, they'd have cleaned up.'

Elena was back in her small hotel room — no sign of Benjamin — and had just put the phone down on her editor at *El País*. He'd told her to slow down, to speak slower, but that wasn't easy for Elena, especially today, with everything churning through her head.

They'd talked about a rival paper running head-lines about 'sinister Italian links' and sex-trafficking rings. Elena had said, yes, she'd been offered that same 'press release', but she hadn't bought into it – *yet*. The editor had sounded confused. She'd tried to explain there was a bigger story out there – Borja Falcó dead, murdered – yes, he'd heard; no comment yet from the family – and now the chief inspector on the Prado case also found with his throat slit. The same pattern. The same circle.

She hadn't bothered to mention the woman who'd predicted the Falcós' 'accident', or the photo that Detective Castro had shown her – Borja at a UEFA hotel hours before Saturday's match, beside the creep who'd stalked her last night, hanging around with that slimy football agent Carlos. She hadn't told him she'd been in Castro's car either, or that she'd overheard how the inspector had been killed the same way as the Prado guard.

The editor would have tried to pull her off the story, hand it to someone else – and she wasn't about to let that happen. As it was, he'd still tried to push a photographer her way: *'A burly, handsome guy, you'll like him – he can protect you.'*

She hated that. She'd told him there was no need; she could protect herself, and she didn't want a photographer slowing her down. And with that, the call had ended – somewhat abruptly.

She was determined to still write her racism report. But she could feel it now – racism was only one part of a wider rot running through the sport she loved: bribes, laundering, sponsorship corruption, match-fixing, even whispers of trafficking. Whatever it was, she was going to get to the bottom of it.

And she was going to start by calling Carlos again.

'Elena – chica –'

'Don't *chica* me –'

'*Joder*, Elena. Why the hell did you turn up at the club last night, mouthing off in front of Kai?'

'Kai?'

'Yes, Kai.'

'Who is he?'

'He owns the club … and he's an associate.'

'An associate?'

'Listen, chica, you stick to your job, and I'll stick to mine.'

'That's exactly what I'm doing, Carlos. My job. And I want to know why this so-called associate of yours, Kai, was seen with Borja Falcó at a UEFA hotel on Saturday – and then Borja was found hanging from the viaduct this morning.'

There was a silence. Elena could hear him breathing, the faint sound of traffic in the background.

'Where did you see that?' he said finally, voice low.

'A police contact showed me the photo. I was also supposed to interview Ramón Falcó this morning. Guess what? He cancelled.'

Another pause. Longer this time.

'Elena,' he said. 'You need to stop asking questions.'

'Why?'

'I'm saying this isn't your story.'

'Then whose is it?'

'Drop it.'

'I'm not dropping anything.'

'Then you're going to get yourself in trouble. Or worse.'

She didn't answer at once.

'Were you there too, Carlos? At the hotel?'

He gave a dry, nervous laugh. 'Football brings together all kinds of people – players, agents, sponsors, hospitality – you know how it works.'

'Sure. And referees,' she said. 'Nothing to do with talking to the UEFA lot, I imagine?'

'You're playing in a dangerous league, Elena. You don't know these people.'

'That sounds like a threat, Carlos.'

'A final warning. Friendly. You think you know how this world works, chica, but you don't.'

'Try me.'

'No. You've already said too much'

The line went dead.

Carlos paced the balcony outside his office, the phone pressed to his ear, cigarette half-burnt. Traffic noise below, Madrid heat above.

Kai answered quickly. 'What is it now?'

'We've got a problem,' Carlos said. 'That journalist – Elena. She's still sniffing around. Asking weird stuff.'

A pause. Background hum – maybe an extractor fan. 'What kind of stuff?'

'The dangerous kind. She just called me again. Says she knows you were with Borja Falcó at the UEFA hotel on Saturday.'

Kai didn't reply.

'She claims a police contact showed her a photo,' Carlos went on. 'She's too close, *hombre*. I should have just stuck with the tabloid lot. My fault …'

A still silence. Then, cold: 'Yes. Your fault. What exactly did you tell her?'

'That she had to stop asking questions. That it wasn't her story. She's asking too much. Connecting things she shouldn't even know about. I'm telling you, she's trouble.'

'We've resolved trouble before,' Kai said. 'She's just another reporter. How do you know her?'

'From an innocent assignment she was working on over a year ago – and this time it was racism. I added her name to the journalists on our list. Sent her along with others to that rooftop event yesterday. But this one's stubborn.'

Kai said nothing.

'She said she'd been planning to interview Ramón Falcó this morning,' Carlos added. 'Any word on his fate yet?'

'Not yet,' Kai muttered. 'Which is also a concern. As for pulling in Martelli, the cop who was helping us refused to go any further. He also threatened to talk, so I removed that little problem.'

'*The cop?* What the fuck have you done now, Kai? You've already gone too far. I helped you get access to players, officials – even Borja, and then the key UEFA lot when we had him down in Marbella. But Madrid's crawling now. You think the Principal's going to protect you from all this? They've summoned you, right?'

'They want to talk, yes,' Kai said. 'It's my birthday. They'll be appointing me.'

'Right,' Carlos said – half a laugh, half a cough. 'Yeah. Happy Birthday, mate.'

'I told you – I'll fix this. But it was your fault.'

'I hope you can.'

'You said she was at the rooftop event, right?'

'Sure – talking to everyone, no doubt.'

'Then you have her number, yes? Send it to me.'

'Okay.'

'Good,' Kai said. His voice changed – steady again, controlled. 'I have a plan. A small one.'

Carlos exhaled smoke through his teeth. 'Like what?'

'I can check through the guest logs on the admin portal … and then tie up this loose end.'

'How?'

But Kai had already hung up.

Carlos stood for a long time, the phone still warm in his hand, watching the slow crawl of cars down the Gran Via. Then he stubbed out his cigarette.

'*Joder.*'

55

Benjamin - Elena

Monday – Plaza Mayor.

Benjamin had left his hotel room for a walk – if only to remind himself he still could. He wasn't about to let some Italian mafioso's veiled threats turn him into a troglodyte, surviving on minibar rations like some hairy hermit in Madrid. The city was for walking, not hiding. Mad dogs and Englishmen, he thought – or idiots with death wishes.

The heat hit like a hair dryer to the face. He stuck to the shade as much as possible, drifting with the flow of tourists down towards the Plaza Mayor, doing his best impression of a man with nothing to hide: hands loose, phone out, slow pace. Safety in numbers, he told himself. No one got whacked next to a family from Osaka taking selfies.

He resisted the urge to check every shopfront

reflection for Enzo or one of his *amici* on his tail. He passed no end of souvenir shops – Real Madrid shirts, castanets, flamenco dresses, fans, plastic bulls – and between them the inevitable *Museo del Jamón* bars beckoning tourists inside. He kept moving, sweat creeping down his spine.

When the square finally opened up before him, he chose the shadiest table he could find, ordered a beer and a plate of his own overpriced *jamón*, and watched the pigeons harass tourists for crumbs. If he was going to get bumped off, at least it would be with a cold beer in hand.

He called Andy again.

'Yeah?'

'Andy, give me something I can use.'

'Christ, you don't stop, do you? I don't know what else I can tell you.'

'You said something about Asian money and a new AI platform –'

'Yeah, the new AI log code. The algorithm bundles bets so the usual IP-cluster methods don't pick them up.'

'Whatever that means,' Benjamin said.

'It means the syndicates are telling their betting platforms to reverse the log-in code – to flip the pattern – so the tracking tools can't trace where the money starts. And there's another thread. Payments. A fintech front that keeps popping up whenever you follow the payouts. Across Asia it's GoldenPay. Not sure what it's called in Spain or Latin America … hang on … yeah.

It's been set up as DoradaPay. Same thing, different badge, I'd say.'

Benjamin let the words land, ended the call and stared at the screen for a beat.

Dorada. Golden.

He fished a pen from his pocket, pulled the napkin from beneath his plate of *jamón*, and wrote: *Dorada – Golden*. Then, because habit had him double-checking everything, he thumbed the translate icon on his phone: *golden – dorada*. He added another note – *Asians + AI log-in* – and stuffed the napkin into his pocket, the ink already sweating from the beer.

Back in the shade of the arcade, Benjamin took out his phone again and scrolled to the Grupo Dorada home-page he'd skimmed earlier that morning. The glossy front page was the same – corporate yellow-gold, words like *micro-mobility*, *sustainability*, *urban living* and *reducing our carbon footprint along the entire value chain.*

He'd half-laughed at it before; now he was reading it differently. The four neat divisions he remembered – catering, hospitality, mobility, delivery – weren't just corporate arms; they were loops in a system. Food fed logistics, logistics fed bikes, bikes fed data.

He scrolled to the bottom. A small link he hadn't noticed before: *DoradaPay.*

He tapped it. The subpage opened in English and Mandarin. *Empowering transactions for a mobile world. A secure digital platform connecting hospitality, delivery and mobil-*

ity. The same buzzwords, polished to a shine. And at the very bottom, two addresses: Singapore and Madrid.

He slipped the phone into his pocket and stepped back into the sunshine. Whether today was a recruitment day for delivery riders or not, he was going to pay them a visit – and he was going to turn up on one of their own D-e-Bikes while he was at it. If Dorada ran the whole chain – Pay, Ride, Deliver, Eat, Bet, repeat – he wanted to see how it worked from the ground up.

Just fifty metres on, he stopped dead. Something tugged at him.

He took out his phone, reopened the Dorada website and clicked through to the *Restaurants & Hospitality* division.

There – among the sleek logos of bars and event venues – was one he recognised from last night.

Castellana House.

The sun had dropped a notch, but the heat still clung to the city like a fever. He'd finally managed to reach Elena; they'd agreed to meet at a small corner terrace off Recoletos. She was alone at a table, a coffee half-gone, notebook open, pen tapping against her lip.

'New *bici?*' she said, glancing up and grinning as he approached.

'Yeah,' he said, setting the yellow e-bike on its

stand. 'Less fascist with the docking bays and an easier app than the BiciMad shambles.'

'Shambles?' she said. *'Qué significa esa palabra?'*

'A dog's dinner.'

'A dog's dinner?'

'Yeah – total clusterfuck.' He leaned in. 'Why Castellana House last night? Why did we meet near that place?'

Her brow tightened. 'You checking up on me?'

'Call it curiosity. Castellana House belongs to Grupo Dorada.'

'Never heard of them.'

'Same people who run these bikes.'

She gave a short, mocking laugh. *'Joder.* Didn't realise you'd become so brand-loyal overnight. Castellana House is just some *pijo* club.'

'So why go there?'

'Do you remember anything I told you last night before you passed out?'

Benjamin didn't answer.

'Because it's where the slimy football agent Carlos hangs out,' Elena went on. 'I wanted to question him for setting me up to meet people – and now about the Falcós.'

'The who?'

'You really don't read Spanish news, do you?' She leaned forward. 'Borja Falcó – the one hanging from the viaduct this morning. And his father, Ramón – head of the sports council – vanished. Both mixed up in football marketing which, in this country, usually means something else. Carlos knows them. Or used to. Now he's got a new … associate.'

He watched her carefully, the sound of passing traffic filling the pause. She took a sip of her coffee, then looked past him, scanning the street as if replaying everything.

'Who were you set up to meet?' he asked.

'Well … in the end, I actually met a very interesting lady. Mei – Mei Zhang. She runs some charity about empowering girls through football – at least, that's what it says on paper. Supposedly a philanthropist. Looked like she could buy half the hotel if she wanted to. But she knew things no one should. Said the Falcós would be hit by an accident before their son was found swinging from the viaduct. You tell me.'

Benjamin frowned. 'You think Carlos was involved in that?'

'I called him again this morning. He told me to stop asking questions and hung up. But I think an associate of Carlos might be involved – Kai, he called him – the same guy who was following me last night, right before you showed up. Apparently, he also runs that club.'

'What makes you think he was involved?'

'Okay, wait,' Elena said, lowering her voice. 'This is strictly between us. A detective showed me a photo of him. That same creep, standing beside Borja Falcó at a UEFA hotel on Saturday, hours before the match.' She checked her watch. 'I'm supposed to meet her later, trade notes.'

'Jesus, Elena – you've been busy,' Benjamin said quietly. He sat back, thinking – about his earlier call with Andy in London, about the shifting odds, the talk of Asian syndicates, and the way Saturday's match had stretched into extra-time just as the Prado was hit. Football, art, money – all fixed to the same clock. Then he asked, 'Why was Carlos trying to set you up with people?'

She sighed, shrugged. 'Carlos is trying to feed me stories – and even Mei was trying to plant the same narrative – something *El País* won't yet touch, and I don't blame them. All about *Italianos* and sex-trafficking in women's football. Someone's been anonymously posting on social media about it, even tagging Lorenzo Martelli. The post was deleted, but you know how it goes – someone grabs a screenshot, and boom, it's everywhere. More rumours, more gossip, more *abogados* sharpening their knives.' She paused, searching for the right words: 'If there's no real evidence, God knows why they're – *como se dice?* – obsessed with it all. Instead, I think *they* might be the story. And definitely this Kai-and-Borja thing ...'

Benjamin had gone still. His expression shifted – not shock, but recognition, the quiet tightening of someone connecting dots.

'Lorenzo Martelli?' he said, almost to himself.

Elena looked up. 'You've heard of him, right?'

He met her gaze, his voice flat. 'You could say that.'

56

Mei Zhang - Kai Leroux

Monday – Chamartín district.

Mei sat in the temporary duplex apartment high above Chamartín, the one the corporation often used for visiting execs to avoid any hotel history. Air-con humming. Afternoon light hitting the glass like metal. A sleek desk, a laptop, two phones, a large wall safe.

He'd called her from Soto del Real. They never allowed him long – ten minutes, sometimes less – but the prison guards knew whose time they were cutting, and they took care to cut it neatly.

'You have the minister?' he asked. His voice sounded distant, thinned by the line.

'I have his conduit,' Mei said. 'It will be enough.'

'And the boy?'

'Being dealt with.'

A pause. The click of a cigarette lighter.

'Good. The blood must stop now, Mei. One thing is a dead museum guard. A cop is another matter. Spain will never forgive it.'

'He understands nothing about forgiveness.'

'Make him understand necessity. Singapore needs calm. Madrid needs our money. They're courting each other again – investing in telecoms and renewables. No one wants a scandal that smells Asian and bloody to get in the way. Spain will want their painting back, but they'll still want our sovereign wealth. Keep it clean. If everything goes to plan, I'll walk out of here within a month.'

'If,' she said.

'*When*,' he corrected. Then, after a pause: 'And a Happy Birthday to the boy. Thirty, isn't it?'

'Yes.'

'A good age to learn humility.'

She could sense him smiling down the phone.

The call ticked out – one minute left – then the familiar click. Silence pressed against her ear.

For a moment she imagined the weight of his hand – a man who understood her body. They had both built things out of compromise, out of leverage and quiet blackmail. Not clean but ordered.

She'd built her empire's foundation through hospitality and delivery – the perfect front for other activities: gambling, phantom invoices, washed cash. On the surface she was a poised philanthropist, running a foundation for girls, grants for education, offering partnerships with international aid programmes. Behind that compassion lay calculation – cold and precise.

Singapore turned things global. The man currently locked in Soto del Real wasn't just a sentimental partner; his money and diplomatic reach made their now joint empire untouchable. His capital moved like mercury – through hospitality firms, logistics companies, gaming platforms, AI and fintech. Grupo Dorada was only the Spanish cog in a machine that now stretched from Macau to Marseille, and soon, if the new partnerships held, into Latin America as well.

She'd never expected to have a child, let alone Kai – and that, in its own way, meant she had never really treated him as a son.

Not in the ordinary sense.

More a potential protégé.

He had grown up thinking of her not as a mother but as his *Principal* – the person who set the rules, drew the boundaries, defined the world. The one he looked up to, not out of any affection, but because she was the only point of reference he'd ever been given. The architect of his life.

She had schooled him the way other people trained assets: languages before friendships, coding before toys, business modelling before sleep. When he leaned into combat sports she didn't stop him. She observed. Curious to see what sort of creature discipline and violence might carve out when praise was rationed, and affection omitted entirely.

She'd raised him alone, but never with warmth. Only with purpose.

And yet she should have anticipated this moment.

She'd chosen the painting herself. Symbolic, poetic justice – a year's planning – and the perfect asset to ransom back.

Her protégé had handled the logistics and tech side of things. She'd let him run with it, proud of his ingenuity. But she should have seen this coming.

The heist was never meant to be chaos, let alone bloody. Somewhere along the line, the message turned feral. The guard's blood, the spectacle – and now the murdered cop – none of that had been part of her plan. It was supposed to be surgical: a demonstration of reach – *revenge*, yes – but not a declaration of war.

At least the painting was still her leverage – the one clean piece left in a game now covered in blood.

She heard the low hum of the private lift stopping on her floor, the brief pause, then the quiet slide of metal on metal. The air in the room seemed to change temperature. His reflection appeared first in the glass wall, face half-shadowed by the skyline. Then he stepped in, helmet in hand, jacket slung, posture all insolence and entitlement.

'You've cut me out, Principal,' he said.

Not a question. An accusation.

She didn't flinch. 'Happy Birthday,' she replied. 'I've given you the best gift I can offer. Safety. You're not an executive, Kai. You're a liability – to the corporation, to our partners, to yourself.'

Kai's jaw flexed, a small tic she recognised from childhood – something she had hoped he'd outgrow.

'After everything I've built for you,' he said.

'You built nothing. You executed instructions. Badly, in the end.'

A beat. *There* – the flicker of rage in his eyes, quick and bright as a blade catching the light.

He stepped closer. 'You trained me for precision, Principal. Precision requires control. And control requires information. Which you often withheld.'

'Because you weren't ready,' she said, calm as ice. 'You never were.'

Something shifted in him – humiliation, fury and something else beneath it: a cold, settling stillness. The kind of quiet that preceded catastrophic decisions.

Kai lowered the crash helmet to the floor with care, as though setting down a ceremonial object.

'Is this why you called me here?' he asked. 'To tell me I've failed your syllabus – and on my birthday –'

'We've never really celebrated your birthday –'

'You think you can retire me?'

'I called you here,' she said, 'to tell you you are no longer part of the organisation. You'll be funded, monitored, protected – discreetly – but you will do nothing. You will instruct no one. You will not engage with any operations in Europe again.'

'This isn't over, Principal,' he said. 'I have someone at the airport with access to Martelli's jet. I'm asking the police to board it and inspect. Same way we doctored the VAR frames, we've got videos, photos, deepfakes –'

Mei sighed, cutting in. 'You think they'll care?'

'If they find what we're putting on that plane, he's finished for good,' Kai said.

'If they find what's on that plane,' she said, her voice losing the small human inflection it sometimes kept for him, 'they will come for those who planted it. They will trace it to you. Sources even tell me there's an image of you with the Falcó kid before the match. You promised me there would be no trace of your meetings. Then we have the blood at the Prado. A murdered chief inspector. Yes, we've won over the syndicates, but you have failed me on everything else.'

'You don't understand,' Kai said, taking a step closer. 'It's not over.'

'It is over.' Her fingers folded around the edge of the desk. She pushed a folder towards him – paper, for once. Tickets. Authorisations. Account numbers written by hand. 'Macau first. Then Singapore. Keep your name off the customs form. Live clean for six months. There is money. There is quiet.'

'If you do this, I will finish it without you.'

'You won't,' she said. 'It's already finished.'

Kai's breath hitched. He came around the desk

slowly and stopped directly in front of her chair. His hands rose and fell lightly to her throat – not to squeeze, only to measure. His eyes, bright and empty, met hers. She did not look away. His hands fell as if he'd tested and found nothing.

He picked up the folder. 'Whatever you demand, Principal. But I first need to tie up a few things.'

She nodded. 'Afterwards, just go. Get on that plane tonight. Live where the cameras are not looking. You will have money, new papers, a route.' She stood, smoothed her blouse. 'If you don't draw attention to yourself, you'll live well.'

'And if I do?'

'Then you won't.'

When he left, she waited until the lift hum had vanished. She went to the window, then to the safe. She pressed her palm flat against it.

The damage couldn't be undone. But it could still be negotiated.

She sat again. Tapped another command into the device. A Hong Kong account blinked empty. Another cleaned out. She'd prepared for this – always the worst-case scenario. She then returned to the draft email that she'd started earlier. Soon, she would prepare for her own departure. Just one more letter to write …

57

Benjamin

Monday – Chamberí district.

Benjamin had spent half an hour trawling the Grupo Dorada corporate website, napkin from the Plaza Mayor spread beside him. Only then did the scale of it really hit him. Dorada wasn't a company so much as a machine, a *system* – sprawling, relentless, everywhere.

Yes, two headquarters were listed on the main site – Madrid and Singapore – but working out where the individual divisions actually operated was another story.

He traced them one by one on his phone map. *Restaurants & Catering* – same address as the corporate HQ, up on the Castellana. *Wholesale to Hospitality* – industrial estate somewhere beyond the M-40; no chance of reaching that on a D-e-Bike. *Dorada Mobility*

– depots scattered across Madrid, the main 'sustainable city solutions' hub somewhere out by Legazpi.

And finally, *Dorada Delivery* – the tricky one.

Dozens of micro-depots across the city, each serving its own postcode, but none that looked like a head office. It took him several searches and a buried contact link before he found it: the *Dorada Delivery Recruitment & Training Hub.*

It was a few streets north of Alonso Martínez, wedged between a Zara store and a small business hotel – a quiet, semi-gentrified corner of Chamberí, where Pilates studios and old hardware shops still shared the same pavement.

He arrived on his own D-e-Bike – a small gesture of camouflage. He docked it outside, easing it into a row of identical yellow frames. The charger clicked, the dashboard light blinked green. If anyone inside was watching, he'd look like one of their own – a courier clocking off, not a man about to start snooping.

He took the long way round the block first, keeping to the shade. He wanted to see the back.

Down one ramp, rows of yellow e-bikes stood hooked to chargers, each with a thermal box balanced behind the saddle, all stamped with the same D-e logo. A couple of helmets lay abandoned on a bench. Further along, a side window looked into a low-ceilinged room lined with plastic chairs and whiteboards – training sessions and induction briefings for the gig economy, or whatever passed for initiation in Dorada's army on wheels.

No one was around. He raised his phone and took a few quick shots – the rows of bikes, an information board covered in half-erased scribbles he couldn't quite read. He was about to move closer when he heard it: a soft, mechanical whirr above him. The slow swivel of a CCTV camera resetting its angle.

Benjamin froze.

A bead of sweat rolled down his temple. He glanced up. The black dome tilted; a red light pulsed once. He pocketed his phone and walked off fast, rounding the corner towards the front office, forcing his breath to steady. Maybe he'd already been seen. Fine. He'd play dumb.

He'd rehearsed his cover story: out-of-work Brit, new to Madrid, decent cyclist, looking for something temporary. It wasn't far from the truth – just missing a few critical details. He told himself it was reconnaissance. Undercover fieldwork.

Glass doors led into the main entrance, a polished floor, a whiff of detergent. The reception area was almost empty – a narrow counter, a few plastic chairs, a vending machine humming in the corner. To his left, a taped-up notice in Spanish and English on another glass door read:

Cerrado – solicitudes online únicamente.

Closed – applications online only.

He hesitated, then pushed through anyway.

The corridor beyond was long, sterile, lined with

Dorada posters – *Ride Smart, Earn Fast, Join the Future.* A flickering light buzzed overhead. Somewhere deeper in the building, he could hear the faint echo of a lift door closing.

At the far end, behind another desk, sat a young woman in a pale-yellow Dorada polo shirt, earbuds in, half-watching something on her phone. There was a stack of folders and paperwork beside her monitor.

Benjamin ran a hand through his hair, fixed what he hoped was a friendly smile, and walked towards her – trying to look like a man who'd simply turned up to apply for a job.

'*Hola,*' he said. 'Delivery? *Trabajo?*'

She looked momentarily shocked to see him standing in front of her, pulled out her earbuds and looked up. '*Cerrado,* closed, *señor.*' She pointed back towards the sign on the glass door that he'd just ignored.

'*Sí,* I saw,' Benjamin said. 'But as I'm already using one of your brilliant bikes, I thought that maybe I could … fast-track things a little.'

Her brow creased. '*Solo online.*'

'Today's not an open day?'

'*Solo online, señor.*'

'Right. Of course.' He nodded, pretending to look for something in his pocket. 'And this is the main office for … DoradaPay, too?'

'*No lo sé.*' She frowned, the slightest edge of suspicion entering her face. '*Creo que no.*'

'Or Mobility,' he said quickly. 'Someone told me to come here.'

'*No, señor.* Delivery only. You need *cita.*'

'Appointment?'

She nodded. '*Sí. Pero solo online.*'

He took out his phone, pretending to scroll for the online form.

'*Aquí no, señor, por favor.*'

Benjamin gave an apologetic shrug. 'Could I maybe just use the bathroom while I'm here?'

She hesitated, glancing down the corridor as if to check. '*Al fondo,*' she said finally.

He smiled again. '*Gracias.*'

He started down the corridor – slower this time – the sound of his shoes on the polished floor echoing back as he passed a wall of internal posters: *Ride Smarter – DoradaPay – DoradaWallet – Staff Only.*

He raised the phone, took some quick shots of the small print on each poster and the corridor beyond. He was lining up another photo when the voice came behind him.

'*Oye! Qué estás haciendo?*'

Benjamin turned. Security. Stocky, shaved head, eyes like stone.

'Looking for the gents,' Benjamin said. 'End of the corridor, right?'

The guard pointed at the phone. 'No *fotos*. Why you take *fotos*?'

'I'm not taking photos.'

'*Sí* – you took *fotos* earlier, too. We have you on CCTV.'

There was a short silence. Benjamin noticed another camera on the ceiling of the corridor, pointing straight at him.

'You know how these things work then, right?' he said, nodding up. 'How to switch them off. Before a break-in, say.'

The security guard stared at him. '*De qué estás hablando?* Give me your phone.'

Benjamin tucked his phone deep into his pocket, then half-raised his hands. 'Easy,' he said. 'I was just curious about the company. Big operation you've got. All part of Grupo Dorada, right?'

The guard didn't answer. Just stared – jaw tight, the shaved head gleaming under the strip light.

Benjamin's mind was running: what Andy had told him about DoradaPay – a fintech front for payments through an Asian gambling syndicate *'crawling all over Europe'*. He thought about the name Elena had mentioned earlier – *Ken, Kyle, Kai?* – the Chinese guy who'd stalked her. She'd said he ran that Castellana club, part of Grupo Dorada – yeah, *Kai*, that was it – the one linked to a football agent, the one she said was at a UEFA hotel before Saturday's match, with that kid who ended up hanging from a bridge. That *suggested* match-fixing, taking down the Goliath Juventus on the pitch at least – although whether it had anything to do with taking down the Goliath Martelli was anyone's guess. Still, if Dorada held the catering contract at the

Prado, then the Caravaggio could have been snatched and moved on through any corner of their sprawling delivery-and-mobility network, just another package in transit …

'I'm just looking for work, you know,' Benjamin said. 'Kai sent me.'

The word landed like a spark in dry grass.

'*Quién?*' said the security guard.

'Kai. He's —' He didn't finish.

'Give me your phone now,' the guard cut in.

'Can't do that.'

'Then come with me.'

'*Or*,' said Benjamin, stepping forward, eyes fixed on the exit behind the man, 'you just let me walk past and leave the building.'

For a second the guard didn't move. Just the hum of the lights and the faint buzz from somewhere down the corridor. Then he shifted his weight, blocking the way. 'No one leaves until I see what's on your phone.'

Benjamin kept walking towards him. 'That's not going to happen,' he said.

He didn't see the backhand coming, only felt it after his nose exploded — blood hitting the cream wall in a fine spray. He didn't know what was worse — the crunch of bone as his nose met the guard's knuckles, or the instant sight of the blood. His vision flared with stars, the floor tilted, his breath escaped in a high, shocked rasp — and there was a metallic taste in his mouth. But he still managed to shout, '*You utter fucking bastard,*' as he straightened and came back hard, shoving himself against the guard – a measured, animal shove that caught the man off-balance – and then he drove his shoulder into his chest, forcing him back just long enough to barge past.

Benjamin's hand went to his nose but he didn't dare look at the blood seeping through his fingers. A curse followed him, boots scuffing, but he was already through the glass doors – half-running, half-stumbling into the glare of the street.

The concierge behind the front desk of the small hotel next door gave Benjamin the look sensible people reserve for men with bleeding noses and a hand pressed to their face. He asked if he was okay, pushed a half-pack of tissues his way, then pointed towards a corridor and a bathroom. Benjamin nodded, mumbled thanks, staggered further inside. The man then reached for a mop and began checking the floor in front of the desk.

Inside the bathroom, Benjamin eased his hand away and dared to look. His nose was bent and already twice the size of what he remembered it to be.

Focus on that, not the blood, Benjamin, he told himself – but he still felt queasy.

There was a hand dryer, no paper towels. He turned on the tap, splashed cold water over his face. The tissues from the concierge lasted seconds, disintegrating into pink pulp. He checked the cubicle for a loo roll – only thin strands from a dispenser drum – then patted his pockets and pulled out the paper napkin from the Plaza Mayor.

The bleeding had slowed, but his face was a wreck. He dabbed at his nostrils with the napkin. It had writing on it – notes he'd scribbled while talking to Andy earlier: *AI log in – Dorada – Golden.* In the mirror it was gibberish – upside down, reversed – but something made him turn it round a few times as he dabbed at his nose. Nothing golden about it. Just red, purple, raw. The upside-down *in* from *log in* was smeared with blood, the ink dissolving before his eyes – leaving just *AI log*, reversed, upside down, also smudged.

What had Andy said? Something tech, something incomprehensible. Or was it?

Asian money and a new AI platform.

A new AI log code.

The syndicates are telling their betting platforms to reverse the log-in code – to flip the pattern – so the tracking tools can't trace where the money starts.

Reverse the log-in code. What log-in code? Andy had called it a chatter thing – people placing bets through a new AI platform, reversing and taking down any previous AI log.

Benjamin blinked hard. He tilted the napkin, squinted at the mirrored letters, then looked at the napkin in his hand.

A I L O G.

Reverse it, Benjamin – just like Andy had said.

G O L I A.

Reverse it and take it down.

Take down G O L I A.
Golia.
Goliath, in Italian.
Caravaggio's *David e Golia.*

He pulled out his phone and set it on the edge of the basin. He hit loudspeaker, dabbing his nose in the mirror.

'You again?' Andy groaned.

'Andy – *the AI log.* Reversing it. Taking it down. Remember?'

'What's up with your voice, mate?'

'Andy, *listen. Golia* – does it mean anything to you?'

'Golia?'

'G-O-L-I-A,' Benjamin said slowly

'G-O-L …' Andy repeated. '*Gol,* yeah?'

'Gol?'

'Yeah. *Gol* is goal, mate.'

'Goal … I-A–?'

'IA – could be international *apuestas,* if you're still in Spain – international betting. Could be anything. I think the Italian syndicates use a deep-web protocol or algorithm to mask the betting flows. People called it Gol-IA or something … because, you know – everything starts with a *gol.*'

The hotel bathroom suddenly felt too small. The throbbing pain in his nose sharpened into a bright, terrible clarity. Everything – the match, the painting, Martelli's humiliation, Andy's half-garbled tech talk, DoradaPay – snapped into alignment.

Gol-IA. Reversing it. Taking it down.

The Italians' betting protocol – compromised, hijacked, flipped.

The Asians had been telling syndicates to trust in them – not Martelli's network. Take down the Goliath – on the pitch *and* online. Martelli humiliated – personally, professionally.

The painting was a symbol – proof they could do it. A message to the gambling world, timed to land at exactly the same moment as the result they'd fixed on the pitch. But why target Martelli *personally*? Why the obsession with him? What was behind it? And where was the painting now? More importantly – now they'd toppled Goliath in the flesh, what might they want in return for giving the oil on canvas back?

He stared at his reflection and his busted, bent nose for a final moment, then stuffed the blood-streaked napkin into his pocket.

Time to find Elena.

As he re-emerged from the hotel, a black Alfa eased away from the kerb across the street. Dark windows – no view in, only the city reflected back.

He couldn't see the driver, but he could feel the stare – long, appraising, familiar. Then the car slid off into the traffic.

He told himself it was nothing.

. . .

In the street, he called his contact in Geneva again.

'Marc?'

'Are you okay, Benjamin? You sound weird.'

'I'm fine. I just need one more thing, Marc. How soon in advance would you know what VIPs would be attending the final again?'

'Benjamin —'

'No, look, Marc, *this is important.* I'm talking, say, the Juventus VIPs —'

'Juventus? They were in the final, Benjamin —'

'I know that, Marc —'

'But, okay, look — as they won the trophy last year, the top brass would have automatically been invited this year … whether they'd reached the final or not … I mean, as title holders …'

Kai returned to an office he kept at Dorada Mobility in Legazpi, helmet under his arm. He wasn't finished yet, despite the Principal's final instructions. He pulled out his phone and checked the last message:

Foreign man asking about you and DoradaPay over at Delivery. Taking photos. We're sending you the CCTV.

58

The Incident Room

Monday — Comisaría de Policía, Huertas.

An hour after leaving Judge Varela's chambers, the investigative unit was back at the incident room in Huertas — tempers still sharp.

Someone had switched off the air-con again. The air felt heavy, thick with heat and frustration. The whiteboards were already being rewritten: new arrows, fresh boxes, photos of Barroso's body pinned beside those of the Prado guard, the blood-spattered ground near the Teleférico, and a printed screenshot of Barroso's last received message — the one naming Martelli.

Gutiérrez dropped his folder on the table as agents moved in and out, trading fragments of news — forensic updates, phone records, lab requests.

'All right,' he said. 'Let's keep this clean. The judge

and UDYCO were clear: we've got no grounds to move on Martelli just because Barroso got a text with his name in it. The Guardia Civil will be monitoring his private jet at Barajas. No warrants without evidence. And we ignore the social-media circus, even the sex-trafficking rumours. If it's gossip, it's just noise – a distraction. We also can't move on Dorada's HQ until we get a watertight warrant.'

'And Barroso himself?' Castro asked.

'Still dead,' Morales said dryly. 'So for once we can do this by the book.'

'The judge has ordered fiscal forensics to dig through his accounts,' Gutiérrez said. 'If there was any financial incentive for him to not investigate dead Italians, we'll find it. Until then, we keep digging where he didn't. Go back through the cold files – the head on the railings at the embassy, any of the suicides he closed in the last year.'

Castro nodded.

'In the meantime,' Gutiérrez added, gazing at the photos on the boards, 'we focus on the pattern linking his murder to the Prado guard – the wire, the garrote, the blood, the choice of location: the Teleférico. Witnesses, CCTV in the area, the tyre marks, our search for Jason Zhou, and the Brit's whereabouts. Everything else feeds into those lines.'

'And this?' Castro asked, pinning to the board the same photo she'd shown the judge earlier: Borja Falcó at a hotel with a shorter man beside him – thirty-six hours before he was found hanging from the viaduct.

Gutiérrez leaned in. 'Do we think it's relevant?'

Morales, still by the whiteboard, turned from his notes. His frown deepened. 'Hold on,' he said. 'That face. I said earlier it looked familiar ...'

Across the room, another agent was already opening an old investigation thread on screen. 'One of the *Prado by Night* events, sir,' he said. 'We'd been cross-checking the guest list against patrons, sponsors, suppliers and the *Amigos del Museo* group, remember? Here, look ...'

Silence followed. Even the hum of the computers seemed to fade.

'So,' Gutiérrez said at last, 'the man seen with Falcó thirty-six hours before his death was also inside the Prado a year ago – as a representative of Grupo Dorada. Is that what this is?'

Castro nodded again.

Morales squinted at the photo. 'He's small,' he said. 'What – maybe a metre sixty? Less? That's about what forensics estimated for the intruder on the museum footage. Same build, too. Could be nothing, but ...' He let the thought trail off.

A new silence fell. The air-con rattled weakly, then stopped again.

A thought tugged at Castro – she still needed to get back to that journalist, Elena. The woman had gone pale when shown the photo earlier, as if she'd seen the same face somewhere else, but had chosen not to say so.

Morales's phone buzzed. He read through the long message before speaking.

'Forensics just sent the summary on the foldable bike from the Café Prado,' he said. 'The one we lifted from the courtyard. Same one we believe Jason Zhou used to haul up and down the stairs at his bedsit. We know he cycled it to work most days.'

Gutiérrez looked up. 'Go on.'

'The lab's dismantled it. Sections of the frame had been forced open and resealed – definitely not factory work. Inside, they found light glass residue and abrasion marks along the tubing, suggesting it once carried tools – possibly a glass cutter or a compact hammer. But whatever was hidden inside has been removed. The brake cable's also missing – cut cleanly, likely repurposed as a wire tool. Then the frame was folded back up and left in the courtyard, like nothing had been touched.'

Castro frowned. 'Meaning it was used to carry in the tools.'

'Exactly.' Morales checked his phone again. 'We tried tracing where the bike was bought, but no luck – no serial hits, no retail record. However –' he turned his screen so the others could see – 'forensics have found a maintenance QR hidden under the hinge near the crankshaft. Serviced six months ago by Dorada Mobility – a division of Grupo Dorada.'

The room went still.

If that alone hadn't been enough to justify calling Judge Varela back for the warrant they'd been waiting on, the sudden entrance of Lara from tech made it inevitable.

'You told me to notify you the moment we located the Brit,' Lara said – laptop wedged under her arm. 'New bike ID. Not BiciMad anymore. He's switched to a D-e-Bike. Belongs to Grupo Dorada.'

That got everyone's attention.

'Tell me he's not heading there,' Gutiérrez said.

'According to GPS,' Lara replied, 'he's already been to the Dorada Delivery offices in Chamberí – and now he's in Legazpi. That's where Dorada Mobility is based.'

'Then that's enough,' Gutiérrez said. 'I'll get over there with a team.' He swept the files together. 'Morales, call Varela's clerk — we need the warrants for every division of Dorada right now.'

The room shifted gear – chairs scraping, phones ringing, jackets snatched from chair-backs. A new pulse of movement, sudden and purposeful.

Outside, another siren wailed down the Paseo del Prado.

Just minutes later, Castro was halfway through her sixth coffee of the day when the duty sergeant called out.

'Señora downstairs asking for a private interview. Says it's urgent.'

'They all do,' Castro said.

'Name's Cayetana de Arellano – married to some Falcó. Came with a lawyer.'

She held still for a beat. Then she pushed back her chair, zipped up her anorak, and went down.

Two people were waiting in the glass vestibule. The woman stood very straight, dark glasses, silk scarf drawn high across her cheekbones. Even half-hidden she radiated money – the kind that didn't have to prove itself. The man beside her looked like a lawyer out of central casting: slim attaché case, pinstripe arrogance, already looking impatient.

The sergeant buzzed them through.

Castro gestured to the inner door. 'This way,' she said, leading them into an interview room.

The woman lowered her scarf but kept her sunglasses on.

The lawyer frowned as he followed. 'We were hoping the Inspector Jefe might be available.'

Castro stopped herself from saying *you'll find him in the morgue*. Instead, she dropped into the chair opposite and nodded at them to sit. 'He's not,' she said. 'You've got me.'

The lawyer's eyebrows lifted. 'And you are –?'

'Detective Pilar Castro,' she said, eyes fixed on the woman, not the lawyer.

The woman removed her sunglasses and sat. Up close, her eyes were rimmed red, but the rest of her face looked carved. Castro studied her for a moment: the Chanel jacket, the perfect nails, the composure built like armour.

'My name is Cayetana de Arellano Falcó,' she said, as if it should mean something. 'My husband Ramón is president of the Consejo Superior de Deportes.'

'I know,' Castro said. 'I was on the scene where your son was found. We've been trying to reach you and Señor Falcó.'

The lawyer also sat.

'You will be unable to reach Ramón,' Cayetana said. 'He's had a breakdown. Close friends have flown him to a clinic in Switzerland.' She paused. 'I have come here in confidence. For protection. For myself and for Ramón.'

Castro nodded. 'Then start at the beginning. Who's threatening you?'

The lawyer cleared his throat. 'Before we continue, my client needs assurances regarding witness protection. Preferably relocation.'

Castro sighed. 'You're not there yet, counsel. First, I need to know what this is all about.'

The woman leaned forward. Her voice was calm. 'Lorenzo Martelli. And at least one of his men – someone called Enzo. You must know the names.'

Castro's hand froze over her notebook. 'What about them?'

'They murdered Borja,' she said, eyes filling. 'They made Ramón watch – through a video call.'

The lawyer placed a phone on the table, half-wrapped in a clean white handkerchief.

'This is my husband's,' Cayetana said. 'He left it for me. There are calls and messages from Italian numbers from Saturday night through to late Sunday. Enzo, mostly. And one long video call. Nothing recorded, but you'll find the call details in the log – and you have my husband's word.'

Castro rose, opened the door, and called down the corridor to the duty sergeant: 'Get me Lara. *Now.*' Then she came back to the table and sat again.

The lawyer cleared his throat once more. 'I believe my client has now –'

'While we wait,' Castro cut in, 'you can help me understand something. Why would Lorenzo Martelli or this Enzo want to kill your son? And why make your husband watch?'

Cayetana's chin lifted. 'Because Borja failed them. Possibly because he tried to take their money and thought he could disappear with it.'

Castro turned towards the lawyer. 'Disappear?'

'My client understands that such disclosures could affect her husband's standing – possibly his career,' the lawyer said. 'She is not privy to the details of the business arrangements between the Italians and her son's company. Something soured. She's here because she wants to prevent any further deaths.'

Castro nodded slowly. 'You understand,' she said, 'that you're implicating an international businessman in a homicide under Spanish jurisdiction.'

'I understand,' Cayetana said. 'I'm giving you what you need to detain him – hopefully.'

Castro glanced towards the corridor where foot-steps were approaching. 'Then I'll need you to repeat everything on record. We'll start a formal statement as soon as my colleague arrives.' She took out a plastic evidence bag and carefully slid the phone and handker-chief inside.

A young officer appeared at the door. 'Lara's on her way.'

'Good,' Castro said. 'When she arrives, get us connected to Judge Varela – and tell forensics I want this phone examined.'

59

Dorada Mobility

Monday – Legazpi.

The message from Mei Zhang had come through two hours before.

Elena, I can meet later on. Dorada Mobility, Legazpi (near Matadero). I'll be there for sports sponsorship meetings. 17.15h if that works for you. I'll have my phone off during the meetings but will expect you then.

Elena had read it twice, wondering why a mobility company instead of a hotel or café, then Googled it. Dorada Mobility co-sponsored the Madrid and Barcelona marathons, padel tournaments, even part-nered with the Women's Basketball Federation. It looked authentic enough.

It also fitted with what Mei had said at the rooftop event yesterday evening – philanthropy, grassroots, female-athlete development, social mobility through sport. So what the hell.

All Elena wanted was more on the Borja Falcó connection for her editor. Detective Castro hadn't called her back. She'd shown Elena that photo – the Chinese guy with Borja at the UEFA hotel – and promised to be in touch, but nothing since. If Elena could get more from Mei in the meantime, she'd have something concrete to trade when the detective finally resurfaced. The more she had, the more Castro might share – and the more she'd have for *El País*. You did what you had to do.

So, yeah, meeting Mei again made sense. The right step. Or so she thought.

Ninety minutes later, she texted Benjamin while on her way over there. *'Meet up later? Will be over at Matadero area, Legazpi, after meeting at Dorada Mobility.'*

He called her immediately. 'Dorada Mobility?'

'Estás bien?' Elena said. 'You sound … nasal.'

'Had a problem with my nose.'

'Right. See you later?'

'Why are you going to Dorada Mobility?'

'To meet this Mei woman again.'

'Don't – it could be dangerous –'

But she'd already cut him off.

Now, standing at the edge of the Matadero complex, she felt the heat of the pavement through her shoes. The red-brick pavilions across the road – once the city's slaughterhouse, now a sprawl of galleries and performance halls – glimmered in the late afternoon sun. She'd always meant to visit. Today, of all days, she was finally here.

Away from the cultural centre's arches, a mesh fence marked off something less inspiring: the Dorada Mobility depot. Large yellow words stencilled on corrugated metal read: *Cleaner Streets. Smarter Travel. Shared Future.*

Heading closer, she could see a row of banners through the gates:

Sustainable City Solutions.

Reducing our carbon footprint.

Empowering communities.

Another poster showed glossy faces of young athletes under the slogan: *Social Mobility through Sport.*

She smiled faintly as she approached the gate, the heat shimmering. In the forecourt, several vans stood half-loaded with D-e-Bikes, serviced and ready to be redistributed to docking stations across the city. To the left of the depot stood the offices. She went straight in. Beyond the first glass door was a small reception space: one of those modular lobbies with a coffee machine, a touchscreen sign-in tablet and motivational posters about *driving tomorrow's movement.*

The office beyond was deserted. A few lights still burned behind tinted glass – empty desks, headsets, swivel chairs slightly askew, a screen saver looping the Dorada logo. She leaned towards the open doorway.

'Perdón –? Señora Zhang?'

A woman's voice answered from somewhere deeper inside, muffled.

'They've all gone now. If anyone's still here, they'll be in the depot.'

Elena thanked her, though she couldn't see who had spoken.

She followed a corridor; the floor changed from carpet tiles to concrete, the air turning metallic. A half-rolled shutter at the end of the passage opened onto a cavernous hall – racks of yellow e-bikes, stripped scooters, even two compact ride-share cars with Dorada Mobility logos on the doors. Another van waited, stacked with e-bikes due for servicing.

No voices. Just the far-off echo of traffic outside, and a low electrical hum that seemed to come from everywhere and nowhere.

To one side, a wider shutter stood half-open – high enough for a van to pass through.

She checked her phone. 17.15h.

Right time. Right place. No one waiting.

'Mei?' she called out.

No answer.

A scrape of something behind her. She turned.

He was standing there, jacket unzipped, hands restless.

She took a step back. The same creep – the one who was at Castellana House with Carlos, the one who'd followed her out, the one in the photo that Detective Castro had shown her.

He was shorter than she remembered from the dim

light in the club last night: taut, every muscle straining to look taller than he was.

Something jolted in her. The yellow e-bikes, the boxes, the hum of charging docks – it all twisted into a memory. Yesterday morning. Hotel Eurobuilding. Waiting for that federation executive who never turned up. The lift doors opening and that delivery rider stepping out: scarf, dark glasses, cap pulled low, a yellow box hooked over one arm. She remembered his build exactly – slight, spectral, avoiding her gaze. Not this man in front of her now, no. But close. One of his? One of these ghostlike riders slipping in and out of hotels and stadiums with envelopes, packages, pay-offs? Invisible because no one ever looked at them. Was that how this whole thing moved?

'You came,' he said.

'What do you want?' she said. 'Who are you?'

'You don't recognise me?'

'Where's Mei?'

'You don't recognise me? From last night?'

He was holding a length of cable, twisting it lazily between his fingers – a gesture so casual it chilled her.

Up close, she realised she was taller. Even in flat pumps. He wore thick-soled trainers – almost platform height – and still had to look up at her.

She kept her voice steady. 'You think I remember every little man who tries to talk to me in a bar?'

His expression didn't change, but the temperature seemed to.

'Was I that insignificant?' he asked, eyes raking her.

She ignored him, took out her phone, tried to call.

'You won't get a signal,' he said, glancing at the walls. 'You won't be located, either.'

Elena didn't speak. He was right about the signal. Her thumb slid across her screen, opening her recorder app instead.

He scoffed, catching it. 'Still recording other people's stories?' he said. 'You should start worrying about your own.'

'What do you want?'

'Many things,' he said, stepping closer. 'But mostly to tie up a few loose ends.'

He drew the cable tight between his hands; the faint, high twang cut through the low industrial hum of the depot.

Elena swallowed. 'What is this? Where's Mei?'

He smiled – small, reptilian. 'Mei …' he echoed, almost amused. 'You mean the Principal. Someone like you would call her a mother. She said she has better things to do.'

She blinked. 'Your *mother*? So … you set this up. You sent the message.'

'Let's say they tried to block me out,' Kai replied. 'But I'm always a step ahead.' He tilted his head slightly, tightening the cable between his palms as if testing its pitch. 'I have a cloned admin control. I got your details from the Principal's call list … the one that *I* control.'

Elena didn't speak. Didn't move.

'You shouldn't have called Carlos again,' he said. 'You made him nervous … asking too many questions.'

'I'm a journalist,' she said. 'That's what we do.'

He laughed – a short, ugly sound. He took a step closer. She could smell the mix of sweat, chain oil and cologne. His eyes were unblinking.

'You killed Borja Falcó,' she said quietly.

'Not true. I simply set Borja up to *be* killed. Big difference. He just had to do the stupid things he was very happy to do.'

Elena's grip tightened on her phone. 'What things? What did he have to do? Help you to bribe UEFA officials, for example?'

'Still more questions? Don't you ever stop?'

A shutter clanged somewhere deeper in the depot. His eye flicked to the wall clock. A small thing – a second – but she saw it. He was running out of time.

She moved, he moved – animal-fast – looping the cable tighter between his hands as he slid to her side, trying to come round behind, to duck under her arm already reaching for a long screwdriver on the nearest bench. She swung; the metal rasped air. He staggered – missing the point by a fraction – then came up behind her, the cable whipping. He aimed for her throat, but it never hit flesh – the phone she was holding up took the brunt of it, the wire trapping the glass and plastic case against her chin and neck. It meant she could still breathe as she hit back with both fists. He hauled her towards the wall like a dog on a lead, her feet skidding on the concrete. She hammered at his ribs, knees, anything. She kicked backwards – a move she'd practised years ago in a gym – and thought she'd caught him in the *cojones*. But he didn't fold. He only tightened his hold as she screamed – her phone case still wedged between wire and neck.

Outside, noise rose – a clatter at first, metal on asphalt – then a yellow flash through the half-open shutter: a D-e-Bike, not graceful but fast, a man on a machine with momentum, crashing into the depot and blotting out most of the daylight between them.

For a moment both Elena and Kai stopped struggling and turned, speechless, to look at the rider – Benjamin – astride the bike, wild-haired, his bent nose bloodied, shirt streaked with dried blood.

Kai's expression flickered from confusion to disbelief. Then he spoke. 'Give me a fucking break. Not the fucking cavalry. A knight in shining armour – *not*. Who the hell are you? Bike repairs are closed. *Adiós*.'

'*Let her go*,' Benjamin shouted. It came out nasally, but it came out.

Kai tilted his head, eyes narrowing, still holding Elena tight with the cable, her phone wedged between the wire and her throat. 'It's you,' he said. 'The idiot from Delivery. They sent me the CCTV. Still looking for a job or a funeral? Because you just rode into the wrong one.'

Benjamin wiped his crooked nose with the back of his hand. 'Let her go.'

'No. Fuck off.'

Benjamin caught Elena's eye – *bear with me, remain calm, don't do anything stupid* – then said, 'AI log.'

Kai frowned. 'What?'

Benjamin took the blood-spotted napkin from his pocket, holding it up like a piece of evidence. 'AI log. That's what you called it, right? Your clever little reversal trick – the code, the perfect timing, the match fixing, the theft, the odds, the bets. A message to take down a Goliath in every possibly way.'

Kai didn't say anything.

Benjamin swung a leg off the bike and took just one step forward, palms out. 'You know,' he said, 'it was Elena here who first described the match on Saturday night as being like *David and Goliath* … so really, she deserves the credit.'

Elena just stared at him.

'Don't come closer,' Kai said, tightening his grip on her.

'Where's the painting?' Benjamin asked.

Silence.

'Where's the painting, Kai?'

Elena started to wriggle. Benjamin caught her eye again – *wait. We can do this.*

'This is what's going to happen, Kai,' he said, taking another slow step forward. 'You're going to let her go. You're going to tell me where the painting is. And you're going to tell me this: why Martelli?'

Kai's face seemed to squirm – rage, panic, something older and more poisonous.

'Why Martelli?' Benjamin said again, his voice

rising. 'Why is he your Goliath? What did he do to you?'

Silence.

'You can make this go away, Kai. Just tell me where the painting is – what drove you against Martelli? You can do this. What did he do to you? *What did he do to you?*'

Kai's jaw twitched. His voice dropped to a low mumble. 'He doesn't know me.'

'What?'

'He doesn't know I exist.'

Benjamin frowned, stepping closer. 'Who doesn't?'

Kai's eyes glistened. '*Martelli.*'

For a beat, nothing – just the hum of chargers and the faint buzz of fluorescent light.

Then – *click.*

A pistol being cocked. Behind Benjamin. He froze.

Elena saw it first – a broad, heavy figure in the half-light by the shutter, the outline of a gun raised against his shoulder.

'You still following me?' Benjamin asked, without turning.

A voice, low, Italian: 'Is this the man?'

'I don't know,' Benjamin said, keeping his eyes on Kai. 'He won't tell me. You can ask him yourself.'

Kai stiffened, the cable still looped around Elena's throat and phone.

Enzo – the silver-chained thug with the crater face – stepped into the light, gun steady in his hand. 'Are you the man who crossed the *signore*?' he asked, level-ling the barrel at Kai's head.

Elena jerked, trying to pull free.

'*Let her go,*' Benjamin shouted. '*Enzo, no – wait –*'

'*You don't understand –*' Kai blurted.

'Enough,' Enzo said. 'Let the girl go. You're coming with me.'

He didn't wait for an answer. He crossed the space in two strides, seized Kai by the collar and slammed him towards the centre of the floor. The cable slipped from Kai's grip, the wire uncoiling like a dead snake. He hit the concrete hard, one knee down, twisting to face the gun.

'You don't know what you're doing,' Kai spat. 'Tell Martelli –'

Enzo kicked him in the chest. 'You'll tell him your-self. Get up. *Move. Go.*'

Outside, sirens began to rise – faint at first, then swelling, echoing off the red-brick pavilions of the old Matadero.

Enzo yanked Kai to his knees and started to drag him by the collar across the ground. '*Get up – move –*'

But the sirens were already on them – a flash of blue light through the shutter gaps, tyres screeching, shouts.

Kai twisted, feral-eyed, driving his head into Enzo's gut – the impact dull, useless, barely making the big man flinch. Enzo just stepped back, raised the pistol and fired once. Clean and close.

Kai dropped where he stood – the back of his skull

thudding against the concrete, blood pooling, eyes still open, the coil of wire trailing from his wrist like an afterthought.

The shutter burst open as the police poured in.

'Policía! Quieto! Manos arriba!'

Enzo half-turned, raised his gun again and aimed, but was hit by a volley before he could fire. He staggered forward, one leg folding, then dropped onto the floor beside Kai.

For a moment there was only silence, smoke drifting in the blue light.

Detective Gutiérrez was one of the first through.

Benjamin stood near the bikes; hands raised. The sight of the blood around Kai and Enzo made him feel queasy again.

Elena was against the wall, trembling, her phone cracked but still recording.

Outside, sirens wailed against the warm Madrid evening. The fading sunlight clung to the brick façades of the Matadero, where the first café lights were flickering on and Madrileños slowly started their night out.

60

Morales · Jason Zhou · Martelli

Monday – from Huertas to Barajas Airport.

The call came through just as Morales was finalising
the paperwork for Judge Varela – a warrant to hit every
Dorada division at once, even as Gutiérrez was already
en route to the Mobility depot in Legazpi. The incident room was still a mess, the whiteboards a constella-
tion of photos, forensic tags and red string.

'We've got Barajas airport on the line,' said an
agent at the next desk, one palm over the receiver.
'Guardia Civil, executive zone. Says it's urgent.'

Morales nodded and the call was put on speaker.
Around him, agents began to move closer, screens
flicking to flight data and security feeds, the room tightening around the sound of the line connecting.

'Guardia Civil, airport command.' The voice was
clipped, Madrid accent flattened by fatigue. 'We have

an active security alert, flagged to us by a private-jet management company – *Premium Aviation Services* – possible identity fraud, linked to one of your missing suspects.'

Morales motioned to Lara, their tech specialist, to pull up Premium Aviation Services – anything she could find. 'Go on,' he said into the speaker. 'Any name?'

'Negative. No confirmed ID. The individual came in claiming to represent *Grupo Dorada* – said he was delivering documents on behalf of one of their share-holders. Staff recognised the logo on the package he was carrying and let him through to the office side. But a few minutes later he was seen leaving with airside credentials belonging to another employee. The badge is missing, and the employee's been located inside, unharmed but unaware. We're locking down the exec-utive terminal.'

'You've got CCTV?' Morales asked.

'We're pulling it now. Descriptions from witnesses: Asian male, mid-thirties, slim build, dark clothing. Similar to the alert you shared with us – Jason Zhou, correct?'

Morales straightened, every muscle waking again. He nodded at a couple of agents across the room, already reaching for his jacket. 'Correct,' he said. 'We're on our way.'

The call ended. Lara's fingers were still hammering at her keyboard. '*Premium Aviation Services* – private-jet management outfit. They offer aircraft maintenance, ground handling, hangarage, trip support, concierge services, catering – the whole works. Dorada Capital took a minority stake last year through a holding in *Dorada Infrastructure*, based in Singapore –'

'Get it over to the judge with these other documents,' Morales said, grabbing his phone and pushing a file across to her. Then he was out the door with two agents, calling over his shoulder to an admin clerk as he left: 'Tell Judge Varela the Dorada warrant just grew wings.'

The drive from Huertas to Barajas took less than twenty minutes, sirens clawing a path through the traffic, blue lights bouncing off windscreens and mirrored glass. Morales sat forward in the passenger seat, phone in one hand, radio in the other, voices bleeding through the channels – a wall of chaos, fragments of mayhem layered over each other:

'… *Mobility depot secure, two confirmed dead* …'

'… *female journalist on scene, name Carmona, Elena* …'

'… *Italian national Enzo Gallo, confirmed bodyguard to Martelli* …'

'… *Kai Leroux, senior at Grupo Dorada … both deceased.*'

He turned the volume up.

'Repeat that,' Morales said.

A burst of static, then Gutiérrez's voice, sharp, breathless: 'Leroux was shot by Gallo, Gallo shot by police – self-defence, witnesses will confirm. Scene secured, forensics en route. Carmona recorded the entire thing – she's safe, being questioned. Leroux also shouted something about Martelli being in possession of the painting, possibly on his jet. But this Blake art guy's here, too, giving a different version. Either way, you need to stop that jet. Judge Varela's fully updated. UDYCO's preparing an approach to the Ritz – they've tracked Martelli's location. Guardia Civil will coordinate with your unit at Barajas.'

Morales gazed at the heat-hazed skyline ahead. The sun was sinking, flooding the motorway in a burnt-orange glow. A plane lifted off, its silver belly flashing once before vanishing into the haze. 'Understood,' he said. 'We're two minutes out.'

'Pepe,' Gutiérrez added, his voice lower now, calm but tight. 'We've got Dorada and Martelli covered – but there's someone we still need to locate: Mei Zhang.'

The first Guardia Civil patrol cars came into view as Morales's vehicle swung off the service road into the executive zone. Barriers were already down, more blue lights pulsing in the heat. He was out of the car before it stopped, the rising thrum of jet turbines rolling in from somewhere beyond the hangars.

A sergeant in a bulletproof vest hurried over, radio pressed to his shoulder. 'Detective Morales? We've got the suspect pinned down behind the second hangar, east side. Staff said he was trying to get to that jet over there.' He pointed to a white Gulfstream parked in the orange glare. 'It's registered to Martelli Holdings.'

Morales stared at the jet. The tail number gleamed: I-MART.

'We've locked down all departures,' the sergeant went on. 'Suspect had a package in his hands when we subdued him. Dogs have been over it – no trace of explosives. Package remains unopened and clear of the suspect. TEDAX are en route, just out of protocol. Come on, I'll take you over.'

Morales followed at a jog, boots slapping over the tarmac. The air smelled of jet fuel and scorched rubber.

Behind the second hangar, Guardia Civil officers stood guard near a man kneeling on the ground, wrists locked behind him, head lowered. The package lay roughly fifty metres away, surrounded by two uneasy bomb-techs and a pair of bored dogs. Morales glanced at it – not a bomb, but not the shape of a painting either. Not even a rolled canvas.

He crouched beside the suspect, studying him: sweat streaking down his face, mouth half-open, eyes glassy but defiant. Younger than the ID photo, thinner, adrenaline still burning through him.

'What's in the parcel?' Morales asked quietly. 'What were you trying to get onto Martelli's jet?'

The man swallowed, voice barely a rasp. 'No idea. I'm just the delivery guy.'

'Try again, Jason,' Morales said. 'You're just a delivery guy, who also knows a thing or two about concealing tools and weapons in a foldable bike, and about disabling alarms and CCTV at the museum café where you worked. That's a very specific skill set for a delivery rider. Start talking.'

Hotel Ritz.

The first sense that things had gone wrong came when Lorenzo Martelli received a call from Enzo's sidekick – the other thug who'd been tailing the British art expert with him. The voice was ragged, shaking. Enzo had been shot dead in Legazpi after following the Brit to some warehouse. *Had the Brit led them into a trap?* The line died before Martelli could ask again.

He stood by a window in his Ritz suite, phone heavy in his hand. Then another call: Barajas. His ground crew. Guardia Civil officers were preparing to search his jet. The aircraft had been grounded.

What the fuck was going on?

He started dialling – the Italian Ambassador in Madrid, unavailable; a number in Milan, another in Rome. He even tried his old acquaintance, the Italian Prime Minister's private line. Voicemail. Again. The silence between rings began to feel obscene. His phone had stopped ringing back. No one – not even his lawyer – was taking his calls.

He was still shouting orders to no one in particular

when the knock came – a deep, deliberate thud that made the chandelier tremble. His bodyguard moved first, hand to his weapon, but the door burst open before he reached it. Four men entered: two plain-clothes, two Guardia Civil in uniform. The first plain-clothes officer lifted a folder.

'Sorry for the intrusion, Señor Martelli,' he said, voice clipped, almost polite. 'We have a warrant to search this suite and require your cooperation.'

Martelli's fury detonated. *You know who I am?*' he bellowed. 'I have friends in Rome, in Brussels – you touch anything in here and I'll –'

The second plainclothes officer cut him off, step-ping closer. 'We know exactly who you are, señor. That's why we're here. And you're not in Rome now.'

Martelli's bodyguard lunged but was slammed against the wall, the crack of bone on plaster echoing through the suite. A tray of champagne bottles went over, glass and foam flooding the carpet. Martelli kept shouting – reeling off names: lawyers, ambassadors, presidents, monarchs – but his voice was hoarse now, breaking at the edges.

Two more agents entered to assist, another took position by the door. The search team moved through the suite with surgical precision: unzipping luggage, peeling open drawers, cataloguing wads of cash, watches, and a pistol still warm from its cleaning kit. One lifted a laptop from the desk, closing it with a soft click before tucking it away. Another took Martelli's phone straight from his hand as he tried to redial yet another number, sliding it into a bag without a word.

'You'll be able to contact your lawyer through official channels once we're done here, señor,' the man said, ignoring his shouts of protest. 'For now, no calls.'

The bruised bodyguard, still slumped against the wall, reached for his own device, but a uniformed officer was already there, plucking it from his pocket. 'Same rule applies,' he muttered, sealing it into a pouch.

One of the officers paused by an open suitcase on the bed. Among the folded shirts and silk ties lay one rolled-up suit jacket, its sleeve streaked with something dark – a dried, rust-coloured smear. He didn't comment, just signalled for a bag.

For the first time in his life, Lorenzo Martelli realised he wasn't giving the orders anymore.

Part Five
From Tuesday

61

The Connections

Tuesday 10 June – Calle de las Huertas.

By Tuesday, Madrid was pretending it hadn't happened.

Most of the Prado Museum had reopened to the public; the front entrance looked ordinary again under the early June sun. Only the shuttered Italian Baroque galleries – and police vans still idling on nearby corners – betrayed the truth: one painting was still missing.

In the Calle de las Huertas, the investigation had finally been moved upstairs. The air-con worked in this new meeting room, and the blinds filtered the light instead of magnifying it. Someone had even thought to bring bottled water. It was the first sign of order after seventy-two hours of chaos.

Judge Varela sat at the head of the long table. To her right were Detectives Gutiérrez, Morales and

Castro; opposite them, Ferrer from forensics, Lara from cyber and Alfonso García of the BPH. Several other agents lined the walls, notebooks open.

Lara's laptop was already wired to the projector, the opening slide frozen on the image of a cardboard package.

'Let's begin,' Varela said.

The room stilled. Lara clicked once. The first grainy image appeared on screen – a hotel corridor, timestamped with Lorenzo Martelli in frame, arm around a girl who looked far too young to be there.

'These images were recovered from drives and memory sticks in the parcel seized at Barajas,' Lara said. 'No encryption, no attempt to hide them. Whoever planted them wanted them seen – and wanted *us* to see them first.'

She clicked again. A jet cabin this time, champagne bottles visible in the seat pockets, two more young girls, *very* young, smiling awkwardly for the camera.

'Private flight recordings,' Lara said. 'Interiors of Martelli's jet, yachts, hotel suites. Passenger manifests correspond. We're checking for any deepfakes, but these –' she pointed – 'these are real.'

No one spoke.

She advanced a few more slides: blurred shots, hotel beds, then sordid, explicit images. The same man again and again – Martelli, in his element. One young girl was clearly in tears.

'*Joder*,' Gutiérrez muttered. 'Bastard.'

Alfonso García shifted uncomfortably in his seat, eyes on the table.

'Whoever tried to plant this on Martelli's jet,' Lara said, 'wanted us to see it. They knew we'd take it seriously. It's a message – not to extort, but to expose. They wanted us to see what he was.' She clicked to another image, and someone at the back turned away.

'Another *Lolita Express*,' Castro said.

'I think we've seen enough,' the judge said, her voice level. 'The man's depravity is now officially documented. Proceed. What's next?'

Morales exchanged a look with Ferrer, who slid an evidence wallet and a brief report across the table.

'Blood traces recovered from the sleeve of Martelli's jacket taken from his Ritz suite,' Morales said. 'Forensics confirm a DNA match with Borja Falcó. He was present during, or immediately after, the beating that half-killed him.'

'Cayetana Falcó's testimony aligns with that,' Castro added, 'based on what her husband said he was forced to watch via a video call.'

Gutiérrez opened another file. 'Messages in Italian sent from Martelli to his thug, Enzo. Instructions to find the son first, make the father watch. To notify him when Falcó was at the location.'

Varela gave a small nod. 'Continue.'

Lara clicked to another slide – two bank transfers side by side – and nodded to Castro.

'Inspector Jefe Barroso received transfers from an offshore account held in the name of Kai Leroux,'

Castro said. 'The timeline matches the string of Italian *suicides* over the past nine months. We believe Kai first targeted Martelli's network by taking out one or two of his key players. Barroso was drawn in by those payments and later lured to the Teleférico meeting on the promise of more. When he refused to keep working for them, he became disposable.'

Lara advanced again, another slide: two DNA profiles, crisp white on black. 'Okay, firstly – Kai Leroux,' she said. 'His DNA was found at the Teleférico, in the Café Prado courtyard, on the frame of the smashed French window, and on the cable wire used to kill the museum guard.'

'*Brake* wire taken from Dorada Mobility bikes,' Morales added. 'Same type of wire used on Barroso as on the guard. Also, Jason Zhou has now given a full statement. He admits tampering with CCTV and alarms at the Café Prado, admits bringing in tools hidden inside a foldable bike. He let Kai into the courtyard just as the café was closing. Kai broke into the museum during the football fireworks, went off script, overstayed and killed the guard. His size fits the images of the intruder on CCTV inside the museum. Jason claims he thought it was just a *job*, with no blood.'

'And the other DNA?' Varela asked, nodding at the projected slide.

'Martelli's sample from the Ritz,' Lara said. 'Cross-matched with Kai Leroux, previously known as Kai Zhang. Ninety-nine percent relation.'

The silence in the room was absolute.

'Father and son,' Ferrer said.

Lara nodded once.

'Martelli denies knowing him,' Morales said. 'Claims he never met the mother – Mei Zhang.'

Varela's tone cooled another degree. 'Of course.'

She paused, glancing around the table. 'So – we have enough on Martelli for homicide complicity, child sex abuse, trafficking, you name it. On Kai as the author of the Prado theft and two murders. We still don't have the painting.' Before anyone could add anything further, she went on. 'If they were father and son, why was Kai even targeting Martelli's network? What do we have on Grupo Dorada – anything?'

Castro finally spoke. 'Your honour, at the moment our investigation points towards rival organised crime groups – Asian targeting Italian – with football corruption at the core. Possible match-fixing linked to illicit gambling. That also connects to the Falcó murder: we know that the fiscal crime unit had previously investigated the Falcó family for kickbacks from sports sponsorship and TV rights, and the journalist, Elena, was chasing that story. We've added a note on this meeting's agenda to further question the Brit who was with her at the time of yesterday's shooting.'

Varela looked down at her file. 'Okay. Then bring in this señor Blake.'

The judge was still sifting through her notes when the door opened and a guard showed in a tall, dishevelled man with shaggy hair, a bruised, twisted nose – and a face that said he hadn't slept. For a moment no one spoke. Lara stifled a grin.

'Are you feeling okay, Mr Blake?' Varela asked, in perfect English.

Benjamin gave a nod. Still standing, he glanced around the table and caught Alfonso's eye. '*Hola* again, Alfonso,' he said, giving a little wave.

'Please, take a seat,' the judge said. 'This is just an informal consultation, but we do have a few questions. I hope you understand.'

Benjamin nodded again and sat.

Elena was having coffee with her editor from *El País* in a hotel on Calle Lope de Vega, parallel to Huertas, when a text message from Mei arrived on her phone.

An apology – and a request. This is really me. Before, my protégé cloned my number. He acted without my consent. I owe you an apology for what he did, and what he almost did.

I cannot undo that. But I can return what was taken.

You will soon hear from the authorities. We are negotiating for the painting's return. We will not hand it to them. They would only turn it into a performance. I will hand it to you.

Bring your art companion – the Englishman. He will know what he is looking at. He will verify it. From what I have been told, you both stood in the fire and didn't lie. That is enough for me. When they ask, say yes.

Elena read through it twice, quickly – then showed it to her editor.

~

'We appreciate your time, Mr Blake –' Varela started.

'Benjamin, please.'

'*Benjamin,*' the judge repeated. 'We appreciate your time. We'll try to keep this as simple as possible.'

Benjamin nodded, glancing over at Alfonso again.

'We understand that the late Inspector Jefe Félix Barroso was keen to know your whereabouts in Madrid over the past forty-eight hours, Benjamin,' Varela said, checking her notes. 'Did you meet with him?'

'I have no idea who that is,' Benjamin said.

There was a pause.

'Right,' Varela said.

'My contacts here in Madrid have been Ignacio Lazáro from your culture ministry, and, er – Alfonso here,' he said, nodding across the table.

Varela glanced at Alfonso, then continued. 'We're going to put aside the confusion over whether it was the ministry or the BPH who requested outside help, Benjamin, and focus on the events of yesterday evening in Legazpi.' She nodded to Morales.

Morales leaned forward, elbows on the table. 'At

approximately seventeen-forty you were present at Dorada Mobility's depot in Legazpi, correct?'

'That sounds about right,' Benjamin said. 'Not the sort of place you forget easily.'

'You arrived how?'

'On a D-e-Bike,' Benjamin said. 'They're quite good, actually – better than those bloody BiciMads, if and when you can get them to work –'

Lara's mouth twitched.

Morales ignored it. 'Why were you there?'

'Why was I there?' Benjamin echoed, looking at Alfonso again, who was busy scribbling notes. 'I'd been checking out the Dorada group, following a couple of leads that might have led me to the stolen painting. I'd been to the Dorada Delivery division earlier, which didn't go at all well – hence this nose – and then –'

'So, it wasn't a coincidence,' Castro cut in.

'No,' Benjamin said. 'My friend – Elena – told me she was heading to the Mobility division to meet someone called Mei. I thought it might be dangerous.'

'Mei Zhang?' Varela asked, looking up from her notes.

'Yes, probably,' Benjamin said. 'It turns out she's Kai's mother – Elena told me that – but you must know all this already.'

The detectives nodded and exchanged glances. Then Morales continued.

'You were heard shouting … *Enzo, wait* … during the shoot-out in Legazpi. Why?'

'Because Enzo was about to shoot someone,' Benjamin said.

Lara coughed into her sleeve to hide a smile.

'Yes, of course,' Morales replied. 'But did you know this man before? Enzo Gallo?'

Benjamin nodded to himself, realising what they were driving at. 'Okay, wait,' he said. 'The answer is *no* – I didn't know him. Only as one of Martelli's thugs.'

'You know Martelli?'

'Like everyone else who's heard of Martelli …' He paused, hoping that would be enough. It wasn't. 'Okay,' he said. 'I'd been summoned by Martelli – at the Ritz. I had no say in the matter. He wanted to know who'd taken the painting, and he wanted me to help him find that person. He said someone had betrayed him and that the theft was part of a message – an attack on him personally, professionally, and against his business interests. He ordered Enzo to keep track of me, but I thought I'd shaken him off.'

The room was silent.

'Look,' Benjamin said. 'I refused his money. And he offered a lot. I wouldn't work for a scumbag like Martelli.'

'*Scumbag*?' Varela repeated.

One of the agents leaned in and murmured a translation.

'I was working for myself,' Benjamin went on. 'And, technically, still for Ignacio at the Culture Ministry – and for Alfonso here – seeing as they'd promised me a fee if I helped locate the painting.' He waited. 'I have nothing in writing yet, however … and the painting's still missing, right?'

His eyes met Alfonso's again. There was an awkward silence. Then Gutiérrez spoke.

'From Elena's recording of yesterday's events, Benjamin,' he said, 'you're heard shouting at Kai Leroux – asking him things – just before he was shot by Enzo.'

'Yes,' Benjamin said. 'I asked him where the painting was –'

'You also asked him why Martelli was his *Goliath*,' Gutiérrez cut in. 'And what Martelli had done to him.'

'Yes, I probably did.'

'Why?'

'Why what?'

'Why did you ask him that? What did you mean by it?'

Benjamin gazed around the table. All eyes were on him. Everyone was waiting for a reply. He gently rubbed the bridge of his buckled, swollen nose. 'You don't have all the pieces, do you?' he said finally. 'I had assumed you did.'

There was a beat.

'Benjamin,' Judge Varela said. 'We can share one piece we do have with you, in the hope it fits with whatever pieces you might have yourself.'

'Please,' Benjamin said. 'Go ahead.'

'Kai Leroux,' Varela said, 'was Martelli's son.'

Benjamin blinked, slow, then started patting the

tabletop in front of him. '*Of course*,' he said. 'Yeah, that figures –'

'Benjamin –' started the judge.

'But Martelli didn't know, did he?' Benjamin went on, voice quickening. 'Because one of the last things Kai said was, *he doesn't know I exist*. And I presume Martelli denies knowing his mother, too – am I right?'

'You are,' Varela said. She studied him for a moment – the bruised face, the restless energy sparking off him, the mind running at full voltage. He looked half-deranged yet was utterly lucid.

'So that's why Kai was targeting Martelli, too,' Benjamin said. 'Out of personal revenge. For denying that he and his mother ever existed. *That's it*.' He slapped the tabletop again, harder this time, the sound sharp in the still air.

Lara and Castro exchanged a glance; Lara biting her lip, Castro suppressing the flicker of a smile.

Varela noticed. For a second, she caught herself watching him the same way – this wired, manic Englishman lighting up the room without any notes or hesitation, but with something very rare: clarity.

Benjamin was already gathering speed.

'You see, they all connect,' he said. 'All Kai's motives – I count four so far, how many do you make it?' He didn't wait for a reply. 'Motive number one – taking advantage of the *timing*, of course. This took a year to plan, engineered down to the minute, because they *knew* Martelli would be in Madrid – Juventus being the title holders from last year. The football final was the distraction – perfect cover. Crowds, fireworks, extra-time, penalties – and Kai knew that because he'd *fixed* it that way. He'd turned the UEFA officials who Martelli normally had in his pocket. Monaco defeating Martelli's beloved Juventus. David overcoming Goliath on the pitch.'

Castro's pen hovered above her notepad, frozen mid-word. Varela had leaned back slightly, eyes never leaving him.

'What did that achieve?' Benjamin went on. 'Motive number two. Money – and a message. My sources pointed me to the truth: Martelli's visible empire was underwritten by something far darker – football corruption and match-fixing across Europe. *Not* Juventus. Other teams, other leagues, every division in every country.'

He was tapping the table again, words gathering speed.

'When the Asians fixed Saturday's match, it wasn't just about the scoreline – or the millions it made overnight. They were showing they could steal the Italian billionaire's fixers, his referees, his runners, even his VAR officials. They bribed the same people in other cities that he thought he owned. They even used a code to spread the message across the syndicates: reverse and take down the old AI log.'

He held for a moment, smiling briefly.

'It took me a while to get it, too. Reversed, it spells *Golia*. Not only is that Italian for Goliath, but Gol-IA is, or *was*, an algorithm used by the Italian syndicates to mask betting flows. So, reversing and then replacing the AI log was a message to every bookie from Turin to Singapore that the old European giants were finished, and that the Asian networks were in charge. David had taken down Goliath again – but this time digitally, in betting form.'

The room remained silent. Even Morales and Gutiérrez now looked impressed.

'Motive number three,' Benjamin said. 'Symbolic, maybe, but a deep, personal revenge. To ram the point home to the father who'd never acknowledged him – a Goliath, a *monster* in his eyes – the man who probably built an empire out of other people's pain.'

He rested his arms on the table, his voice gathering traction again.

'And not just any revenge. It had to sting. A few years ago, Martelli paraded a fake Caravaggio around his friends, swore it was real, and got laughed out of half the collectors' circuit. So, Kai steals a *real one*. And he times it perfectly – the same night Martelli's Goliath loses on the pitch, the same hour the syndicates reverse the AI log chatter. Every screen, every bookmaker, every phone in that underworld was flashing the same message: the giant has fallen. Martelli was watching the match from his VIP box, unaware he was being taken down in real time.'

He paused, fingers drumming softly on the table.

'That's not coincidence. That's design. He wanted his father to feel it on every front – football, fortune, pride, ego. To make him relive his own humiliation.

And maybe, somewhere in that twisted head, he wanted to prove something to his mother, too – that he could take over and finish what she started. Motive number four.'

Benjamin reached across the table to pour himself a plastic cup of water. Lara offered to help. Meanwhile, Gutiérrez leaned towards Morales; a low exchange in Spanish followed.

'It explains Kai's message to Barroso, trying to implicate Martelli,' Morales said.

'And the package at Barajas with images they wanted us to see,' muttered his colleague.

Judge Varela's phone buzzed. She checked the screen, eyes narrowing slightly, then looked up.

'Just four motives, Benjamin? You seem remarkably certain.'

He smiled. 'It's what I do,' he said. 'Investigate the connection between art crime and real crime. Because no one steals art just for the art.'

No one spoke for a moment.

'Well, we now have a fifth motive,' Varela said, lifting her phone. 'Kai's mother is offering the painting back – in exchange for getting someone out of jail.'

62

David and Goliath

Tuesday – Chamartín district.

The sound of a police helicopter's rotor blades thudded somewhere above Chamartín.

Benjamin and Elena took the lift to the top floor of the building, following the instructions they'd been given. Security cameras blinked overhead, verifying it was only the two of them – to whoever was watching.

The glass-walled duplex stood at the end of a short corridor; the door already unlocked. The windows were shut; the air-conditioning off; the place was warm, airless, stripped of life.

'Looks temporary,' Elena said.

Benjamin nodded. 'Corporate housing. At least not an Airbnb – legal or otherwise.'

Outside, the helicopter tilted away, leaving a momentary silence that felt like pressure.

. . .

The arrangements had taken a while to confirm. Mei Zhang's message had reached Spain's Ministries of Culture, Interior and Justice almost simultaneously – and, somehow, the Prado Museum itself.

For over twelve hours, the system dithered. Lawyers were summoned, judges consulted, statements drafted and redrafted. Somewhere along the chain, the Prime Minister's office at Moncloa was also briefed.

After the Policía Nacional and the Guardia Civil had carried out exhaustive but rapid checks with Interpol and the FBI, the conclusion was straightforward: David Sim, the Singapore businessman who Mei Zhang wanted released from a Spanish prison, posed no terrorist threat.

He had been held in pre-trial custody for just over a year, arrested in Marbella on suspicion of crypto-linked money laundering, then transferred to Madrid when investigators tied his Spanish shell companies to offshore accounts. His lawyers had been appealing the *prisión preventiva* order for months.

His alleged scheme – funnelling betting revenue through logistics subsidiaries – had collapsed under its own weight, but nothing connected him to weapons, drugs or human trafficking. Nothing connected him to Grupo Dorada either.

A final report from CITCO – Spain's Intelligence Centre for Counter-Terrorism and Organised Crime –

endorsed the Interior Ministry's view: David Sim posed no threat to national or international security.

'It's financial crime, but not violent or political,' one Interior adviser wrote. 'Releasing and deporting him doesn't put anything at risk.'

'One expendable crook financier for one priceless painting,' a Spanish prosecutor added. 'We can live with that.'

From there, the decision moved quickly. The exchange was agreed – discreetly, no headlines, no ceremony. All on Mei Zhang's terms. Her David released in exchange for Caravaggio's Goliath.

Benjamin, meanwhile, refused to move until his own paperwork was in order. He'd reminded the culture ministry – twice – that they'd promised him a fee and a substantial finder's commission if he helped locate the missing Caravaggio.

'I'll go wherever you want,' he told them, 'but not until I've got that figure in writing.'

An hour later, the confirmation came through – emailed, stamped, approved. He'd already decided he would share it with Elena.

In the end, it was not a 'handover' of the painting, but a collection.

By the time David Sim's release order had been signed – pending the painting's return – Mei Zhang, if that was still her name, had already vanished. No digital footprint. It was as if she had dissolved.

She had clearly decided not to hang around and risk detention. Her name had been quietly removed from all Grupo Dorada subsidiaries; her resignation back-dated, notarised, filed through a Singapore holding office.

Police units sent to known addresses in Madrid, Barcelona and Seville found nothing. Private-jet manifests showed no trace of her departure, though one flight plan from Madrid to Dubai was later amended with a false passenger code.

Grupo Dorada itself had also moved fast. The corporation announced it was relinquishing its Prado catering concession 'to allow for a full internal review'. New directors – Spanish, appointed through Singapore – promised transparency and 'a renewed commitment to invest millions and create further jobs in Spain'.

The company statement expressed 'shock and disappointment' at the misuse of its mobility network by 'temporary subcontractors', blaming 'rogue recruitment agencies exploiting the gig-economy' and 'a breakdown of supervision'. There was no mention of Mei Zhang or Kai Leroux.

As for Dorada's accounts, Spain's fiscal crime units and independent auditors found nothing overtly illegal – at least nothing that survived on paper. Everything was in order; the Asian subsidiaries were beyond jurisdiction. There was no paper trail linking any Spanish operations to gambling, match-fixing or illicit financing.

The press, meanwhile, found easier targets.

El País, *La Vanguardia*, *La Repubblica* and the British media turned their lenses on Martelli's downfall – the sex-trafficking allegations, sports corruption linked to UEFA, and the end of the Falcó dynasty at the CSD.

Few reporters, other than Elena – and even she, discreetly guided by her editor – were talking about the Asians moving in to fill the vacuum.

Earlier, they'd been waiting in a cafeteria area at the Interior Ministry, two agents hovering nearby. Benjamin was wrestling with the coffee machine when Elena's phone lit up with a single message: an address in Chamartín. She nodded to the agents; they radioed their superiors.

Moments later, they were on their way.

Now, at the top of the glass tower, the apartment was silent – empty except for a chair, a glass table, an open safe near the wall, and a cardboard delivery tube resting beside it.

Elena instinctively lifted her phone and began taking shots.

Benjamin stepped forward, put on some gloves, crouched beside the tube and unfastened the seal. He gently unrolled the canvas across the marble floor. The edges were frayed; the paint cracked in places but otherwise intact. It was unmistakable – the boy, the darkness, the fallen giant. Light from the apartment's window caught the severed head of Goliath and the human terror of defeat in his dead, half-closed eyes.

Elena, now filming, watched Benjamin's face more than the painting. 'Well?'

'It's the Caravaggio,' he said quietly.

'Are you sure?'

'Completely.'

Elena made the call.

Down on the street, an unmarked car idled. Another circled the block. Somewhere, a line connected.

'They've confirmed it,' an agent said from the control room.

'Good,' came the reply. 'Let him go.'

At Barajas, David Sim stepped through the jetway with his passport. Border guards looked the other way.

Only as Benjamin and Elena were leaving the apartment did she notice the lone envelope on the glass table, her name written neatly across it. She opened it and began to read, sharing it with Benjamin as she did:

Elena, If you are reading this it is because you have collected the painting as I requested. I imagine that you neither like or admire me, but I want you to know that in the brief time that we met — I admired you. I imagine you are angry about being 'set up' by the agent to meet me. However, it is still important to me that you, and your newspaper, know something of my story. So here it is …

My name was Lin-Mei when I arrived in Naples as an au pair — aged just sixteen. The agency had arranged my airfare and a week of lessons on table manners and politeness.

The villa overlooked a bay. His wife was elegant yet bitter, and was mostly away. The children were at boarding schools. The housekeeper spoke Neapolitan to me, but too fast to follow. I had to wear a uniform that itched. I learned not to speak unless spoken to.

He was already rich, already powerful. The first time he called me into his study, he poured a small glass of limoncello and told me to drink it — 'to calm my nerves'. I had no choice but to obey. What followed stayed with me not just as a memory but as structure: the burn in my throat, his fingers pressing on my neck. Later, I would not remember how I ended up on some cush-ions on the floor. Only the weight and smell of him. The way he said 'good girl' to me as if I was a dog.

No one in the house looked at me differently. No one asked about my tears or the marks on my neck.

I bled for two days after the third time. I tried to leave. The agency told me I would be deported. That I owed them fees. That I had brought dishonour.

So, I stayed — working, listening, learning. I discovered how men moved money, how favours were traded across dinner tables, how fear travelled through families faster than gossip. I wrote everything down in a small notebook in Chinese. One evening, I crossed out Lin and kept only Mei.

Six weeks later I was 'released from my contract' and given an envelope of cash. I'm sure the family found another young girl.

I was already pregnant.

I told no one who the father was. Kai arrived six months later – silent, tiny, yet healthy. Eyes like mine.

I raised him on nothing, across borders, through cities, jobs, industries. I worked bars, moved product, learned fast. It wasn't easy. I had never planned to be a mother – and never felt like one.

When he was still a teenager, I told him the truth: who his father was, how he'd been conceived, how a journalist friend who tried to name that man had been silenced – decapitated – a warning to anyone who tried to cross him.

Eventually, he took a new surname, something to fit in with what he hoped Europe would bring for him. He chose Leroux.

Years later, in a Singapore hotel lobby, we were together when I saw the monster's photo again. He was older but had the same cold eyes. The caption read:

'Lorenzo Martelli, the kind billionaire – a family man.'

That was when my protégé vowed to plot the revenge. It became an obsession – the child of violence, reborn to erase the man who made him. There was nothing I could do to stop him.

Elena – I give you permission to share this letter with your editors and to use it for any legal reasons they deem necessary. Someone must finally expose this man for what he really is. I give you my word that everything I have written is the truth.

Sincerely, Mei Zhang.

63

Benjamin - Elena - Duncan

Wednesday 11 June evening – Salamanca neighbourhood.

'*El País* has offered me a full-time role,' Elena said, glass of wine in hand.

'So they should,' Benjamin said, touching his glass to hers.

She smiled. 'I'm not sure I'll take it yet. There's still so much we're uncovering with this investigation …'

She checked no one could overhear. 'Between you and me – my police source has been feeding me a few things. Detective Castro, yes? She's my new *amiga*.' She took a sip. 'Apparently they found Borja Falcó's wallet and phone in the glovebox of that Italian thug Enzo's jeep.'

'Charming.'

'Calls, messages, the whole chain … it shows the Asians used Borja to get to UEFA's VAR officials –

bribing them with money and very young girls, then blackmailing them with videos that would brand them as paedophiles. Vile stuff. But here's the thing: Carlos was the one who introduced Borja to Kai. Carlos has been working both sides for years – first the Falcós with the Italians, then happily switching to the Asians when the money got better. A complete *cabrón*. He's fled to Andorra, but the police are on to him.'

'Is *everyone* in football corrupt?' Benjamin asked.

'A minority,' she said. 'But a few can do a lot of damage. My editor thinks the Falcós were helping the Italians fix matches long before this – laundering money through Borja's sports marketing set-up. Then the Asians cut them out entirely. Now the police can't trace the Asians anywhere in Spain. They're running it all from Singapore, offshore and untouchable. But we'll be digging into that … hence the full-time job offer.'

Benjamin lifted his glass to congratulate her again.

'And you know,' she added, 'everyone keeps pointing to that Barça referee scandal a few years ago like it was the big one – a few million paid over the years for technical reports. But compared to this shit? That was *nada*.'

'You think the Asians are controlling football across Europe?'

'I think they're trying to,' Elena said, nodding. 'And the rumour is that UEFA either can't get out of their arrangement with them … or doesn't want to.'

'And what about Mei?' he asked. 'Any sign of her?'

'None. She's vanished completely. We've shared the

letter with the police. We'll use it, but we have to follow legal advice and let the Martelli case run its course. He's not getting out for years. If ever.'

'Fingers crossed,' Benjamin muttered.

'And Ramón Falcó's wife, Cayetana … she went to the police in the end,' Elena said. She took another sip of wine. 'It's ironic, no? Borja and Kai both dead. Two sons – *cómo se dice?* – dysfunctional? And now Cayetana's under witness protection and Mei's disappeared. Two mothers, strangers to each other, bringing down the man who killed one of their sons and fathered the other …'

Benjamin nodded, refilling their glasses.

'Anyway,' Elena said, waving a hand. 'I don't want you to share your fee or your reward with me. I mean it.'

'We're not doing that argument again.'

They fell quiet. The evening was warm, the light soft. The noise from the bar and the terraces around them had settled back into something reassuringly ordinary.

'What are you going to do about your nose?' she asked.

He laughed, touching it warily. 'Try to get it fixed. Or at least pointing vaguely in the right direction.'

His phone started to ring. He looked at the screen and sighed. It was the double-barrelled, relentlessly jolly Duncan – no doubt chasing him about the restitution case that had brought Benjamin to Madrid in the first place.

'Talking of dysfunctional,' he said. 'I'm sorry, but I need to take this.' He took a gulp of wine. 'Duncan,' he then said, bracing himself for the usual madness of screaming twins in the background. But all was calm.

'My wife's left me, Benjamin.'

'Oh, no – I'm sorry to hear that, Duncan.'

'It was after the night out with you on Sunday – the hen party, remember?'

'I do. I left you with them. Did you get home okay?' He took another sip of wine.

'Not exactly. Ended up at their Airbnb. They kept calling me Babes.'

Benjamin almost spat out his wine. Elena tilted her head: *Qué pasa? Todo bien?* He regained his composure and raised his glass to her.

'What's worse,' Duncan continued, 'is that it was an *illegal* tourist flat. Neighbours went absolutely berserk, and the police arrived. They accused me of running a scam from a nearby kebab shop. It all got very messy.'

'Illegal?' Benjamin said, dabbing his eye with a paper napkin. 'That's awful, Duncan.'

'Yes, it was ghastly. The embassy's not thrilled, either. There's talk of disciplinary action.'

'Right. Well, I'm really sorry to hear that, Duncan Babes –'

'Don't.'

'Sorry. Shall we speak in the morning?'

'Yes, but just one thing. The restitution case – the family's insisting that the painting is still theirs. They've moved it out of Madrid. Heard you were here, and don't want you sniffing around. The Gómez de Longoria family. Old fascist money. Franco-era aristocrats. Ring any bells?'

'Any relation to Beltrán Gómez de Longoria?'

'He's one of the grandsons. Know him?'

'He's the one who put a manhunt on me in Barcelona, Duncan. Where have they taken the painting?'

'Malaga.'

'Malaga?'

Elena looked up from her drink again. *Malaga?'* she said, half-smiling. Her eyes were sparkling. 'Ever been?'

The sound of distant traffic drifted in through the warm evening.

Epilogue

Four days later – Nyon, Switzerland.

Low mist veiled Lake Geneva, the Alps pale beyond it. The road into Nyon ran quiet except for a few early commuters heading towards UEFA's glass headquarters above the lake.

Ramón Falcó walked briskly along the pavement, coat collar raised against the light drizzle. He looked healthy again – the clinic had done its job – though his eyes still carried the hollow shine of someone who'd stared too long into the abyss.

He was on the phone with his wife, Cayetana.

'Yes, I'm fine,' he said. 'No, not Geneva anymore – Nyon. They want to talk. Maybe even collaborate again. It's all politics, *cariño*. You'll see.' He smiled to himself, quickening his step. 'I'll call again later. Maybe we'll have something to celebrate.'

The lane beside him narrowed near a roundabout. A cyclist appeared from behind – delivery jacket, black helmet, mirrored visor, yellow thermal box attached to the back of the bike. The drizzle softened the sound of tyres on tarmac.

A single *phut* broke the morning hush.

Ramón fell, his phone clattering against the kerb, still glowing with Cayetana's name.

The cyclist didn't look back.

Acknowledgments

When I lived opposite the Prado Museum in Madrid during the late eighties, I used to plan how to rob it – for *fictional* reasons, of course. So, I think my research for this book started back then – 37 years ago.

Over the last two years, I lost count of how many times I 'cased the joint', specifically Rooms 2 through to 8A, as well as the outdoor Café Prado in the courtyard. A number of guards and other staff at the Prado always eyed me suspiciously, and they would have caught me staring up at their CCTV cameras and making detailed notes of their positions. As would the Italian Embassy in Madrid, as I often strolled around the perimeter of that building, pinpointing their own cameras. Readers of my Substack blog will know I take my research very seriously.

A very kind officer at the Comisaría de Policía in Calle de las Huertas provided some invaluable insight into how my police investigation might unfold at the Prado Museum nearby – once I'd assured him it was for fiction. As for BiciMad, I never got the app or my own bike to work.

I'd like to think that Madrid is a character itself in this book, as was Barcelona in the 'prequel'. I've experienced every district, neighbourhood, hotel, park, plaza, restaurant and bar mentioned. Every real location, except – *so far* – Soto del Real prison.

As well as viewing as much of his art as possible, I've also read many books and research documents on Caravaggio, and I specifically recommend Andrew Graham-Dixon's excellent *Caravaggio - A Life Sacred and Profane*. As for corruption in football, Declan Hill's fascinating *The Fix - Soccer and Organised Crime* proved invaluable for my research. I also recommend Graham Johnson's *Football and Gangsters*, and Andrew Jennings' *The Dirty Game: Uncovering the Scandal at FIFA*.

I thank Roxanne Rowles, my editor and 'partner in crime', for her patience, advice and suggestions throughout the early draft versions of the book, as well as all her brilliant ideas and help with fine-tuning during the rewrites.

With many thanks again to Llorenç Perello for his superb cover design.

And thank *you* for reading it.

Last, but most importantly, with so much love and thanks to Juliane for all her support and for putting up with me again while researching and writing this book, 'without whom' …

Look out for *The Malaga Connection*.

Tim Parfitt - October 2025.

About the Author

Tim Parfitt has worked in the media in London, Madrid and Barcelona, predominantly for Condé Nast, where he ran the Spanish company, helping to launch *Vogue España* and eventually launching *GQ* in Spain, among other titles. He later also worked for the Press Association, *La Vanguardia* and Grupo Planeta, editing, publishing, launching and re-launching titles as diverse as *Lonely Planet* and *Playboy*.

A Load of Bull – An Englishman's Adventures in Madrid was first published by Pan Macmillan in the UK. It was published in Spain by Almuzara under the title, *Mucho toro – las tribulaciones de un inglés en la movida*.

The Barcelona Connection was published in April 2023. It is the first book in *The Connections* series of books based around the art detective, Benjamin Blake. It is currently in development for the screen.

Tim lives near Barcelona. He can be found at www.timothyparfitt.com and also writes on Substack at timparfitt.substack.com

www.ingramcontent.com/pod-product-compliance
Lightning Source LLC
Chambersburg PA
CBHW061609210726
48287CB00001B/53